IMMIGRANTS AND PATRIOTS

GEOFF BAGGETT

Cocked Hat
Publishing

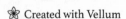

Patriots of the American Revolution Series

BOOK FIVE

ALSO BY GEOFF BAGGETT

Patriots of the American Revolution Series

1 - Brothers and Warriors **

2 - Partisans and Refugees

3 - Frenchmen and Long Knives

4 - Soldiers and Martyrs

5 - Immigrants and Patriots

Patriot Kids of the American Revolution Series

1 - Little Hornet

2 - Little Warrior

3 - Little Spy of Vincennes

4 - Little Brother

5 - Little Camp Follower *(Coming in 2019)*

Kentucky Frontier Adventures

1 - A Bucket Full of Courage

My Colonial Journal for Girls

My Colonial Journal for Boys

**Title available on audible

For the most part, the characters in this story spoke some dialect of German as their primary language. Please remember this fact as you read. Though my personal knowledge of German is quite limited, I have endeavored to "color" the dialog with an occasional word or phrase in common use. This is just a simple device to remind you of the true language and heritage of these Colonial Pennsylvanians.

Geoff Baggett

PART I

IMMIGRANTS

1

NEW BEGINNINGS

Somewhere in the North Atlantic - August 11, 1750

Julianna relished the momentary reprieve from the searing pain in her back and hips. The contractions were almost constant, and less than a minute apart. It would not be long. This child ... her first child ... was coming. It was a force of God and nature that she could not hinder, even if she wanted to. Soon, she would stare into the eyes of this fruit of her husband's love, and the hope of her own future.

She could scarcely believe that her own body had constructed and nourished another human being. And now, that newly-created person was attempting to emerge into the world from between her stretched, aching legs. She was ready to meet him ... or her. She cared not whether it was a boy or girl. It had been so many hours since her pains began. She simply wanted it to be over. She could bear the agony of labor no longer.

Julianna rested silently, eyes closed, on the almost-comfortable bunk. She tried to imagine being someplace else. Anywhere else. Her mind searched its corners for a peaceful thought. Her memories transported her back to her father's small vineyard outside Landau.

She imagined herself as a little girl, playing in the cool shade of the almond trees that surrounded the vineyard. She remembered the fresh, rain-kissed air and the sweet smell of her father's grapevines in bloom in the spring.

A shrill, almost annoying, voice extracted her from her peaceful memory. She returned mentally to the place where she lay ... on board a ship that was bound for America. Far from the peaceful and clean tranquility of her father's vineyard, this tiny room reeked of fish, tobacco smoke, grease, and human bodies.

"Look at that hair! This little one is as furry as a bear!" exclaimed Emma Krause, the enthusiastic, sparsely-toothed midwife, in her distinctive dialect of Palatine German.

Julianna did not care about the presence or absence of hair. She wanted the baby out of her ... all of it ... not just the crown of its head. She asked tersely, "What time of day is it?"

There was no response from the silent midwife. She lifted her head slightly and looked for the customarily chatty woman. She could feel Emma, but she could not see her. Her own elevated knees, covered by a stained sheet, filled the lower portion of her view. Above the sheet, on the wall beyond, she spied a smoke-stained painting of a seaport. The old painting shifted gently along the darkened wood of the wall with the rocking of the ocean's waves. Timbers creaked and popped in the walls of the ship. Glass and tin eating utensils and implements clicked and chirped on various tables and shelves as they rubbed and impacted against one another from the movements of the ship.

Julianna was becoming irritated by the woman's failure to respond to her query. "Emma! Did you not hear me? What time of day is it?"

Suddenly, a round, red, sweaty face popped up over the top of the sheet just as the next contraction made its way from the center of her back inward toward the birth canal.

"It is morning, child. The sun will be up soon. Do not worry. It will not be long now," the woman promised.

Julianna began to moan. The pain was returning to her back and groin. The muscles began to tighten their grip as they endeavored to expel the child from her womb. This was going to be the worst contraction yet. She could sense it.

"The child will not come with this groaning, but almost certainly with the one that will follow. The head is about out. Persevere, child. Your labor is almost done. I shall deliver you of the burden of this baby."

The young woman gripped the coarse wood of the headboard. The tightening muscles caused her back to arch upward. She uttered a scream, not only of pain, but also of defiance.

"*Mein Gott!*" she wailed. "Will this torture never end?"

The spasms tore through her body. She felt as if she were being ripped apart. She could almost hear the bones straining and cracking in her hips. As the contraction subsided, her scream trailed off into a whimper.

"The hardest part is done, my dear," Emma assured her. "The head is out, and the shoulders, as well. One more push, and we shall have us a baby!"

NICKLAUS YEISLEY STOOD STOICALLY on the quarterdeck of the merchantman *Phoenix*, the vessel that was carrying him and his wife to the British Colonies in America. They were a mere two souls among three hundred and thirty-eight Palatine German passengers and three dozen crewmen. This was a relatively light load, according to the captain. On the previous trip, he had set sail with almost six hundred souls on board. Nicklaus wondered where the captain and his crew had kept them all.

The *Phoenix* had departed Rotterdam in the Netherlands on the twenty-third day of June. The vessel had been at sea for a total of six weeks, following a one-week stoppage at the British seaport of Cowes. The voyage had been surprisingly quiet and without incident. They had suffered no ill weather, and only two of the passengers had died thus far. Both were quite elderly, and likely should not have even attempted the journey. It was, indeed, a most fortuitous trip for the *Phoenix*. The captain was accustomed to losing as much as one-fifth of the passengers to starvation and disease.

The sun had only recently risen, yet Nicklaus could barely keep his eyes open. He had been sleepless throughout the stress-filled, agonizing night. His wife was in labor, and soon to be delivered of his child. He desperately wanted a son. But, more than anything, he wanted his precious Julianna to survive the childbirth. He could scarcely imagine life without her.

Nicklaus had never planned to marry. Indeed, he had no deep desire to do so. There were no women in his home village that suited him. His mother often teased him that he was married to his loom, and that there was no room for a woman to fit between him and his beloved warps and heddles. But all that had changed on a business excursion to Landau, a quaint, charming village near the French border. He had departed home to relieve himself of a wagonload of coverlets, tapestries, and sundry textiles. One month later, at thirty-five years of age, he returned home with an empty wagon, a pouch full of money, and a wife.

He would never forget the day when he had first spied the damsel walking along the village highway. She was guiding an enormous horse that was pulling a wagon filled with wine barrels. He loved the young maiden from the moment that he first saw her. Two weeks later, after a whirlwind and secret courtship, she was thoroughly in love with him, despite being almost twenty years younger than he.

The girl's father had forbidden her courtship with such an older man, especially since he was an unknown stranger from another district. But she was not to be denied this first and only great love of her life. So, in her first-ever act of defiance and disobedience toward her father, and at the tender age of seventeen, she eloped with Nicklaus. They were married just over the border in France by a Roman Catholic priest who cared little about their backgrounds, nationalities, or parental permission. He seemed interested only in receiving a generous fee for his services.

That was eleven months ago. But, to Nicklaus Yeisley, it seemed like a lifetime had transpired since the young couple had departed Zweibrücken and sailed down the Rhine toward Rotterdam. Now, four months later, they were only days away from the port of Philadelphia and a new life in America.

Nicklaus took a deep, cleansing breath. He faced aft, toward the sunrise in the east, and allowed the cool, stiff westerly wind to refresh him. He watched, mesmerized, as the newly-risen sun touched the top of the sea and painted its surface with a glimmer of pink and gray. He jumped when another agonized scream emanated from the captain's quarters beneath his feet.

From below, he heard the muffled but unmistakable voice of his young wife exclaim, "*Mein Gott! Will this torture never end?*"

Her shrieks of pain continued for several seconds before subsiding. Nicklaus stared anxiously at the floorboards of the deck. It grieved him that his beloved was in so much pain.

Captain John Mason appeared at his side and offered him a small silver flask. "This will help, *Herr* Yeisley. Surely, it cannot be much longer." He nodded reassuringly. "Your little Julianna will be fine. You shall see. She is a young, strong girl and in the prime years for birthing." He patted Nicklaus on the shoulder.

The anxious father-to-be nodded and took the flask. He tilted his head backward and took a deep drink. It was the rum that sailors enjoyed liberally and often. The alcohol scorched his throat and landed in his empty belly with an explosion of fire.

Nicklaus handed the flask back to Mr. Mason. "*Danke,* Captain. You have been most generous to allow us the use of your private quarters for the birthing. Words cannot convey my gratitude."

Captain Mason waved his hand dismissively. "It is the least I could do for such a distinguished passenger, *Herr* Yeisley."

"Please, Captain ... call me Nicklaus ... for I am not, as you say, 'distinguished.' I am but a humble weaver from the even more humble village of Zweibrücken."

"And yet, you paid for your passage in advance, *Herr* Yeisley. That makes you distinguished enough for me. It is a rarity these days. And, besides, you are anything but a humble weaver. Your work is exquisite. I shall forever cherish the magnificent bed coverlet that you gifted unto me. That sizable bedcover, alone, is more than worth the price of your voyage."

"It is an honor to know that you will sleep warmly for many years beneath a bed cloth that was woven by my very own hands, Captain." Nicklaus smiled. He turned and looked toward the west. "How long do you think it will be until we reach Philadelphia?"

The captain grunted. "Two weeks, maybe less. We have had many days of very poor winds. But, lately we have been making up for some of our lost time. The winds these past three days have been vigorous, indeed."

Both men leapt with surprise at the next scream that came from below. It was far louder and longer than any of the previous ones. It finally ended with a loud groan. Moments later, another shriek followed, but this one bore the sound of joy rather than pain. Soon came a sharp, ringing sound of flesh against flesh. The midwife had slapped the newborn baby's bottom. Immediately, there was a piercing scream. The baby wailed shrilly. The voice was loud and strong. Nicklaus experienced an overwhelming sense of pride ... and relief.

The latch soon clicked on the doorway to the captain's quarters. Both Nicklaus and Captain Mason darted toward the railing overlooking the main deck. Mrs. Krause squeezed her large frame through the narrow door beneath their feet and emerged sporting a huge smile. She casually wiped blood and bodily fluids from her hands with a stained linen towel.

"Well?" demanded Nicklaus. "What news?"

"Mother and child are just fine," Mrs. Krause responded pridefully. "It took *Frau* Yeisley a little longer than I expected, but in the end, we still delivered a baby." She smiled teasingly.

"And?" Nicklaus questioned. The drama of it all was torturing him. "Is it a boy, or is it a girl?"

Emma grinned broadly. "You have a son, *Herr* Yeisley."

Nicklaus thought that his heart might explode. It was the happiest moment of his life. He raised his fists victoriously in the air and yelled with all his might, "*Ich habe einen Sohn!*" The German travelers scattered about the decks joined him in a cheer of victory.

He looked back down toward Emma. "When can I see them?"

"Soon. I am still awaiting the afterbirth. I must also clean up the captain's cabin. *Frau* Yeisley has made quite the mess down there."

Almost instantly, groups of men began to sing. Soon, various instruments joined in. Men and women danced. It was a joyful celebration in the midst of a very trying time.

"Congratulations, Nicklaus," declared the captain. He shook the proud father's hand and nodded toward the people celebrating on the deck. "It is good that these people have something to celebrate. Perhaps it will take their minds off of the travails that await us still."

Nicklaus nodded and grinned. "I am sorry about the mess in your cabin, Captain."

"Worry not. Mrs. Krause will take care of everything. You son is not the first to be born in my bed, and I am certain he will not be the last." He paused. "By the way ... what will you name your boy?"

Nicklaus stared resolutely at the captain. "Michael ... like the archangel. His name is Michael Yeisley."

The captain nodded approvingly. "I shall enter his birth in my log. That will bring us to three hundred and thirty-nine passengers. I may have to charge you an extra fare." He winked and grinned.

August 28, 1750 – The Delaware River

THE MUSIC and celebrations began the moment that the ship passed through the mouth of the enormous Delaware Bay. That was well over an hour ago, and the festivities had not decreased by any noticeable amount. While the other German immigrants danced and sang to celebrate their successful arrival, Nicklaus and Julianna stared over the port taffrail toward the banks of the slowly narrowing river. Julianna leaned gently against her husband's strong, muscular chest. She cradled their sleeping baby, Michael, comfortably in her arms.

"It almost looks like home," declared Julianna over the din of jubilant celebration that filled their ship.

Nicklaus nodded and thought, "*Julianna is right! It does look like home!*"

The sprawling vista revealed a scenery that was not unlike their native lands. The color of the water matched the hue of the familiar Rhine River. The banks were lined with a thick growth of dazzlingly green trees and tangled thickets. Farms, houses, pastures, and small docks appeared at regular intervals within breaks in the thick vegetation. The appearance of it all was hauntingly like home, except for the absence of older stone buildings and castles. There were no such ancient dwellings here in the "New World."

The river, itself, was crowded. Other vessels, some large and some small, made their way upstream and downstream. The *Phoenix* had already passed three large vessels headed back out to sea. It was a very busy river, indeed ... a veritable highway made of water that snaked its way through the beautiful, green wilderness between New Jersey and Pennsylvania.

Julianna was confused. "I do not understand. I thought that Philadelphia was a big city."

Nicklaus pulled his wife closer to him. "We have not yet arrived at Philadelphia. This is the river that leads upstream to its port and docks. The captain called it the 'Delaware River.' But, we are very close. We shall not be much longer."

"Will we live here, along this river?" she inquired innocently.

Nicklaus chuckled. "*Nein, mein Lieber.* These lands were claimed long ago, and are no longer available. Besides, we are not people of the ocean. I can still smell the salt and the stench of fish in the air." He pointed toward the west. "We shall go inland in search of fresh, unclaimed farmlands. I will find us a perfect home. I promise."

Julianna smiled broadly and snuggled the top of her head against her husband's smoothly-shaven chin.

The river had taken a distinctly eastward turn. The ship was slowing down. Several small boats approached the *Phoenix* from the northern bank, each with a single occupant manning the oars.

The fellow in the nearest boat waved warmly and shouted, "*Guten Tag! Willkommen in Amerika!*"

Julianna stared, surprised, at Nicklaus. They were fellow Germans, and had come to greet the newly arriving pilgrims.

Nicklaus shouted back, "*Guten tag! Danke!*"

The man guided his boat close to the huge ship. He inquired, "How are the people on board? Is there much sickness?"

"Not really," responded Nicklaus. "The captain believes this to be his best journey ever. Our food supplies are quite low, but there is no sickness."

The man in the rowboat smiled. "Good! I have something for you all. Lower a rope."

A crowd began to gather along the port rail, curious about Nicklaus' conversations with the man from shore. Nicklaus and another fellow standing close by quickly grabbed a rope from the top of a nearby barrel. They tied their end secure to the taffrail and dropped the line to the fellow in the rowboat. He skillfully tied three large cloth bags to the end of the rope.

"What is in the bags?" Julianna inquired.

The man below grinned. "Fresh apples! The harvest is plentiful this year. My wife insisted that we share with you newcomers."

"We are grateful," Nicklaus responded, tipping his hat. "We have not tasted food fresh from the earth in many weeks."

The man waved in response. "You are most welcome. Good luck with the inspections. I hope that you come ashore soon. May God bless you all."

He turned and began to paddle back toward a small dock on the northern shore. A woman and four children stood at the end of the dock, waving to the people on the *Phoenix.* The passengers waved enthusiastically in response.

"America is going to be wonderful!" Julianna declared. "The people are so kind and hospitable."

Just at that moment, they rounded a small island in the river channel and spied a large building on the northern shore. It seemed a bit out of place. There were no other structures nearby.

A voice from behind them interrupted their thoughts. "You will not think Philadelphia to be so hospitable after we visit *that* place."

It was Captain Mason. He joined the Yeisleys at their position on the port rail. He nodded toward the building. "That is the new hospital on Providence Island. They were building it the last time that I arrived. I am certain that it must be complete by now."

"Why would they construct a hospital out here?" asked Nicklaus. "I do not see any other buildings or houses. Are we close to Philadelphia?"

The captain pointed forward. "The port is another eight or ten miles upstream. The city leaders built this hospital for you folks. It is where they hold the medical inspections. Anyone who is sick must be removed from the ship and placed under quarantine. All passengers must be given clearance by a physician before continuing on to the port."

Julianna stared, silent and thoughtful, at the seaman. "You concern me, Captain."

Mason chuckled. "Worry not, *Frau* Yeisley. You people are the picture of health. We have only a handful of sick folk who may have to remain at the hospital for a few days. The physicians will come on board and give everyone a quick look. But, I am quite confident that Nicklaus will swear his oath and your family will disembark before darkness falls this day."

"I hope so. No offense, Captain, but I am weary of your ship," Nicklaus mumbled.

❧

"SUCH A STRANGE PLACE!" exclaimed the gentleman walking behind Nicklaus.

He had to agree. It was, indeed, the queerest town that Nicklaus had ever seen.

Philadelphia was large, loud, and crowded. Everything looked brand new. Nicklaus had never seen anything quite like it. All of the cities and villages in Europe were filled with buildings and homes that were hundreds of years old. The structures that lined the streets of Philadelphia looked freshly-built. Indeed, there was new construction ongoing on almost every city block.

It was also a large city ... larger, even, than Rotterdam. The town center was laid out in wide blocks. There were rows upon rows of buildings and houses. Interspersed throughout were open areas, livestock yards, small gardens, and open markets. The entire place was a beehive of activity and commerce, even in the late afternoon.

Nicklaus marched at the head of a single-file line westward along Chestnut Street, leading the other one hundred and forty adult male immigrants from the *Phoenix*. The men were headed to the Pennsylvania State House, where they would swear their oaths to England and King George II. A squad of British soldiers led the group toward their destination, and ensured that none of them attempted to disappear into the crowds of the city without paying for their passage.

Like the captain had claimed, most of the passengers easily passed the health inspection. They removed only four frail souls for housing in the hospital on Providence Island. The families of the stricken moaned and wailed their objections, but the authorities were not swayed. The health of the populace of Philadelphia was too important. The sick would remain under quarantine for at least two weeks. But, the other passengers were free to make their arrangements to disembark.

The next step, after the medical inspection, was for all of the men age sixteen and older to swear their oaths to King George II. Then, they had to make arrangements to pay for their passage. A handful of the German pilgrims, like Nicklaus, had already paid for the voyage to America. Several others claimed that they had friends or relatives awaiting them in Philadelphia who would pay their passage and other fees. Most, however, were destined for years of indentured servitude.

Captain Mason had explained the entire process to Nicklaus in painful detail. Beginning the morning after administration of the oaths, wealthy citizens of Pennsylvania would begin descending upon the newly-arrived ship to examine the "human cargo." These were the people who had come to America on "credit." The only collateral that they had to offer was their future personal labor.

The wealthy visitors would select their desired servants, then make offers and negotiate a term of servitude in exchange for payment of passage. Depending upon their age and state of health, most adults could count upon four to six years of indenture. Any unaccompanied children were usually indentured until age twenty-one. Occasionally, in the most tragic situations, entire families were decimated as husband, wife, and children were purchased by different individuals.

It was a hard, wicked way to go in search of opportunity in the Colonies. But, the immigrants knew what was waiting for them before they departed. In the end, most deemed the indignity of the process to be worth the resulting freedom, albeit delayed freedom.

Nicklaus turned and looked back down the line of familiar faces and wondered how many of these men would suffer the indignity of servitude, or even worse, lose their wives and children. He shuddered at the thought of it as his mind wandered back to his beautiful bride and infant son.

The Pennsylvania State House suddenly came into view. The appearance of the newly-constructed, stately building purged the overwhelming, depressing thoughts from Nicklaus' mind. The beauty of the brick building was breathtaking. The center was comprised of a large, high-ceilinged, two-story brick structure. Nicklaus counted seventeen long windows that surrounded a central entrance on the northern side. Two closed arcades extended from each side of the building toward smaller two-story outbuildings. It was an impressive government house, indeed.

Nicklaus continued to admire the architecture of the building as the soldiers led them through the gate and up the steps through the front door. He glanced to his right and saw what appeared to be a courtroom. A row of beautiful chairs sat high upon a large judge's bench. There were testimony booths on either side of the room. The entire chamber was painted a curiously subdued tan-orange hue. It was a bright, cheerful color.

Once inside the central hallway, the guards quickly ushered Nicklaus through a large, decorative doorway into the empty legislature's assembly room. It was an open, airy room, painted in dull gray. Several small tables, covered with green cloths, and dozens of chairs were pushed against the walls on both sides of the room. There were three large windows facing Walnut Street and three identical windows that opened into the back gardens. Nicklaus was impressed with the woodwork and the attention to detail.

An overweight, red-faced gentleman sat behind an expansive desk that filled an elevated platform on the eastern side of the room. The platform was flanked by two dormant fireplaces and two exterior doors in the corners that led outside into the arcades. Two guards stood in the room, one by each of the corner doors. The fellow leaned forward in a lovely Chippendale arm chair, and was busy studying a document that lay on his desk. A pair of spectacles clung loosely to the end of his nose. His right hand toyed with a goose-feather quill that rested on its stand beside a silver inkwell.

The gentleman glanced over the top of his spectacles as the group filed into the room. He rose to his feet.

"Excellent! Excellent, Captain Philpot! The day grows late, and my suppertime draweth nigh. We must work quickly. Bring them all in, and line them up in an orderly fashion. These are the men of the *Phoenix*?"

"Yes, Mr. Daughtry," responded the captain. "Three hundred thirty-nine souls total on board, with one hundred forty men ready to make their oaths."

"Well done, Captain. We shall begin as soon as the men are made ready."

It took only a few minutes to usher all of the men inside the room. They stood, shoulder to shoulder, in eight lines facing the desk. The Germans were completely silent. No one uttered a single sound, much less a word. They were confused and afraid.

The gentleman behind the desk cleared his throat and declared loudly, "Welcome to Pennsylvania. I am Thaddeus Daughtry, His Majesty's representative in his Department of Immigration to the

Colonies. King George the Second extends his greetings, and welcomes you all as citizens of these British Colonies, with entry through port of Philadelphia. Kingdom law requires that, before you are released to pursue your lives and fortunes here, you must pledge your allegiance to the Crown, and renounce all allegiance and ties to the Pope and the Roman Catholic Church. Do you understand?"

For the most part, the one hundred and forty men stood stoic and unresponsive. A handful of them, businessmen and tradesmen like Nicklaus, understood some measure of English. They nodded their understanding. However, most of the peasants did not speak a single word. They had no idea what the man was saying, or why they were gathered in the room.

Mr. Daughtry appeared to be a bit flustered. He waved his hands, frustrated, at the captain of the guards. "How can we administer oaths to men who know or care not about the language and senti-ment of the oaths? Did you not engage an interpreter?"

"No, sir," responded Captain Philpot, stepping forward. "I am new to my post here, and have neither the means nor the authority. This is my first time to have charge over a ship-load of immigrants. I quite assumed that your office would handle its own engagement of inter-preters. I do not believe it to be within the military's mandate."

Mr. Daughtry stomped his foot and began to unleash a string of curses and threats at the impetuous young officer.

Nicklaus glanced about at the confused faces around him, and then bravely took one step forward. He interrupted the official's tirade. "Sir ... Mr. Daughtry, if you will allow it, I will interpret. I can explain what you have said to these men."

The British official stopped mid-curse and glowered at him, quite surprised by his speech. "Indeed, you may, sir. What is your name?"

"Nicklaus Yeisley, sir."

"Very well, Mr. Yeisley. Please explain the circumstances to these men. I shall count upon you to translate for me throughout the remainder of our time together today. You shall be reimbursed adequately for your labors."

"It will be an honor, sir," Nicklaus responded.

He turned to face the men and explained the oath, allegiance to the King, and the repudiation of the Pope. The men all smiled and nodded enthusiastically. They had absolutely no problems with the requirements of the oath, especially the part regarding the Catholic Church. The German Palatinate was prime Martin Luther country, and all of the men hailed from Reformed congregations.

Nicklaus turned around and faced Mr. Daughtry. "The men understand, sir. They are ready."

Mr. Daughtry was most pleased. He smiled broadly. "Very well, then. I shall read the oath in the King's English, you shall repeat in your local flavor of the German language, and the men shall repeat after you. Understood?"

"Yes, sir. We are ready and eager, sir," Nicklaus affirmed.

"Then let us begin. Please raise your right hand."

Nicklaus did as commanded, and encouraged the other men to follow suit.

Mr. Daughtry cleared his throat, and then began the three-part process of administering and translating the oath. He read the words, one phrase at a time. Nicklaus translated, and the men of the group repeated his words. It was an awkward, slow, time-consuming process.

"I do solemnly and sincerely promise and declare that I will be true and faithful to King George the Second. I do solemnly, sincerely and truly profess, testify, and declare that I do from my heart abhor, detest, and renounce as impious and heretical that wicked doctrine and position, that princes excommunicated or deprived by the Pope or any authority of the See of Rome may be deposed or murthered by their subjects or any other whatsoever. And I do declare that no foreign prince, person, prelate, state, or potentate hath or ought to have any power, jurisdiction, superiority, preeminence, or authority, ecclesiastical or spiritual, within the realm of Great Britain or the dominions thereunto belonging. I do solemnly, sincerely, and truly acknowledge, profess, testify, and declare that King George the Second is lawful and rightful King of the Realm of Great

Britain, and of all others his Dominions and Countries thereunto belonging."

Mr. Daughtry removed his glasses. "That is all, gentlemen. You are now citizens of Great Britain and loyal subjects of King George the Second. You will now come forward in an orderly fashion and make your signature, or make your mark, on this document. Mr. Yeisley, I shall require your assistance for this, as well."

Nicklaus nodded and bowed slightly. The Englishman seemed pleased at the gesture.

While Nicklaus explained the process to the immigrants, Mr. Daughtry issued orders to the soldiers. "Captain Philpot, once all of the men have signed, you will return them to the charge of the master of the *Phoenix* to dispose of as is his prerogative."

The captain snapped to attention. "Yes, sir." He pointed to the soldiers in his squad. "Arrange the men in two lines. Let us make quick work of this. Evening approaches."

THE FINAL, waning gleam of dusk glowed dimly in the west when the soldiers herded the group of tired, excited men back up the plank and onto the deck of the *Phoenix*. Julianna was waiting for Nicklaus near the starboard railing. She held the infant, Michael, against her breast.

"Is it done?" she asked excitedly.

Nicklaus grinned and nodded. "We are British subjects now." He reached into his weskit pocket and pulled out two silver British coins. He displayed them proudly in the palm of his hand.

Julianna's eyes widened. "Where did you get those?"

"I earned them," he replied matter-of-factly. "I translated for the British magistrate. He reimbursed me for my troubles. He called them, 'sixpence.'"

"What are they worth?" she wondered aloud as she stared at the strange coins.

"I do not know. But, they are silver, so they must be worth something." He carefully tucked the coins back into his pocket.

"So, we are not even on shore, yet, and you are already making your fortune?" she teased.

The broad smile on his face morphed into a look of loving earnestness. He gently touched his bride's face. "It is a good omen, *meine Liebe.* A sign of things to come." He wrapped his arm around her shoulder and pulled her close. They turned and faced the twinkling lights of Philadelphia. "Tomorrow, we begin our brand-new life in America."

Julianna sighed and closed her eyes as she leaned in toward his broad, strong chest. "I pray that it will be a prosperous and peaceful one."

2

INDENTURED SERVANTS

Eighteen Years Later - October 14, 1768
Upper Milford Township - Northampton County, Pennsylvania

Michael Yeisley, age eighteen, was squatting in front of a tall stack of crates. The devilishly handsome young man was clad in typical business wear. He sported a new pair of dark green coarse linen breeches and a light brown fine linen shirt. A mustard-yellow wool weskit complemented his shirt perfectly. He wore a gray linen workman's apron to protect his clothing from the dust and dyes behind the counter. His finest brown silk stockings and shiny, black buckled shoes decorated his feet. The young man hummed a familiar tune as he searched through the huge stack of wooden crates.

Michael was the master of the store on this fine day. As usual, he was in charge of the customer service portion of the family's business in his father's absence. Michael was laboring diligently to satisfy Mrs. Maria Entler, one of Nicklaus Yeisley's most demanding and, on most days, most frustrating customers. Thus far, Michael had been unsuccessful in fulfilling her strange request for a pound of orange annatto seed dye.

It was mid-morning on Friday, and Michael's father had just departed on his quarterly five-day journey into Philadelphia to procure supplies and, perhaps, some skilled labor from amongst the newly-arriving German immigrants. The Yeisley family's textile business was booming. Nicklaus produced high-quality cloths and colors at a fraction of the price that comparable imported English products demanded on the everyday market. The people of Bucks and Northampton Counties no long bothered with shopping for cloth in Philadelphia. They could purchase almost anything they needed from Yeisley's Shop in Upper Milford.

The constant problem that Nicklaus faced was a shortage of skilled, experienced labor. Though he was not particularly fond of the practice of indentured servitude, the system had resulted in his locating several acceptable workers and apprentices for his shop. He currently had two families indentured, providing six women and girls for wool washing and spinning, and two men and one teen-aged boy to operate the looms. He hoped that this latest trip might secure him at least two more spinners and one more man or woman to master the large loom.

Unlike many of his contemporaries, Nicklaus was most fair in his arrangements with potential servants. He never separated husbands from their wives or parents from their children. When Nicklaus offered an indenture in exchange for passage to America, it was always for an entire family. He put the skilled weavers and spinners to work in his weaving shop and helped the other working-age family members find jobs in local businesses or on nearby farms. Indentured servitude was, without doubt, a harsh and imperfect system. Still, Nicklaus Yeisley determined that he would introduce as much fairness and compassion into the system as he was able.

Though a weaver by birth and training, Nicklaus' eldest son, Michael, much preferred managing the storefront and interacting with customers over laboring in the manufactory. He even favored dealing with Mrs. Entler's often bizarre requests as opposed to the agonizing process of threading intricate patterns on his father's loom. Making sales, searching through inventory, and loading wagons and carts made the day pass quickly. Twelve hours of pulling thread and weaving raw cloth seemed like endless torture to the socially-inclined, affable young man.

Michael growled silently as he unstacked the heavy boxes of raw dye. As usual, the hue that Mrs. Entler requested was at the bottom of the stack. It almost seemed as if the woman lay awake at night plotting to make Michael's work as difficult as possible. Though his back was to her and he could not see her face, Michael was convinced that the horrid old woman was smiling. He could almost feel the wicked grin on her face.

"Here it is!" he proclaimed, feigning surprise. "At the bottom of the stack!"

The woman grunted. "At last! It took you long enough. I was beginning to think that I might have to take my business elsewhere."

He surreptitiously rolled his eyes. The closest 'elsewhere' that the woman could possibly go was Philadelphia. He could not imagine her trekking over fifty miles for a single pound of dye.

He exclaimed, "By no means, *Frau* Entler! The Yeisley Shop is quite capable of meeting all of your textile and clothing needs." He smiled his best businessman's smile.

Mrs. Eltler grunted again as she placed an empty tin box on the counter. Michael despised her haughty mannerisms. However, he chose to ignore them. He carefully and skillfully weighed a pound of the fine, expensive, dark orange powder on his father's German-made scale and then transferred it to her tin.

"That will be four pence, *Frau* Entler."

She groaned in protest and wailed, "Such a high price!"

Michael shook his head as respectfully as he could manage. "This is our most expensive dye, *Frau* Entler. The seeds come all the way from South America. And it has been that same price for as long as I can remember." He grinned mischievously. "Besides, it is the best price you will find in the county." He knew, full-well, that no one else in Northampton County offered cloth dye for sale.

"Do not be disrespectful to me, young man!" the prudish woman barked.

"I meant no disrespect, *Frau* Entler." He remained resolute. "Still, your fee is four pence."

The woman shook her head, seemingly displeased, as she opened the cloth purse that dangled from her wrist. She began counting copper coins. She slapped three smooth, well-worn copper pennies and two newer half-pennies on the counter.

"There you go, boy. If I should suffer the indignity of being robbed on the way home, it will not be the first time today!" She picked up her tin, spun smartly, and marched through the open doorway into the dusty street.

Michael called after her, "Have a pleasant day, *Frau* Entler!"

The woman did not respond. She turned toward her right and disappeared in the direction of the dry goods store.

Michael chuckled and mumbled to himself mockingly, *"And a pleasant day to you, Michael Yeisley."*

The only solace that he took in the woman's unpleasant visit to the store was the knowledge that the most difficult customer in town had already come and gone. The rest of his day was sure to be a joy in comparison.

He strode to the far end of the counter and began to re-stack the crates of dye. He had just returned the final crate to its proper place when he heard a voice that sounded of distress. He stood still and listened intently. With all of the din of activity that filled the Yeisley Weaving Shop, it was sometimes difficult to hear people speaking. Dozens of sheep bleated in the pen just beyond the western wall of the building. Four women and girls just inside the door of the back room were busy spinning thread on identical, large walking wheels. In the back of the building, two small looms clicked busily, expertly manned by two of Nicklaus Yeisley's young German apprentices. The large, four-post box loom popped loudly as the wood boards and various moving parts slapped against one another.

He listened intently, and then heard the voice once more.

"Michael! *Komm her, bitte!* I need your help with this pot!"

It was his mother, Julianna Yeisley. She was out back of the shop dyeing wool and linen thread. No doubt, she had filled one of her iron pots with water until it was too heavy for her to move without assistance.

Michael glanced to make sure that no customers were out front, and then headed toward the back door. He called out, "*Ja, Mutter! Ich comma!*"

He emerged into the open back lawn to find his mother stooped over a large pot that was suspended beneath an iron three-legged stand over an open fire. She was stirring the steaming liquid in the pot with a large paddle. The hem of her petticoat was dangerously close to the flames.

"*Sei vorsichtig, Mutter*! You must be more careful around these fires!"

She tapped the paddle on the side of the pot and then hung it on one of the legs of the fire stand. She placed both hands on her wide hips.

"This is not my first pot of dye or my first fire, Michael Yeisley. I need neither your advice nor your supervision. However, I do need your strong back. This pot of walnut dye is ready. I need you to move it over to the work table."

Michael was a bit annoyed. As shopkeeper for the day, he should not have to be lugging pots of dye around the back yard. He was, after all, wearing some of his finest clothes.

"Where is George? I thought he was supposed to be helping you."

"I sent George to *Herr* Keller's dairy for some milk. I need it for the baking that I am planning for this afternoon. I assume that you would like to enjoy some of my *Streuselkuchen*, would you not?"

Michael nodded and grinned. "*Ja, Mutter.*"

He grabbed an iron hook from a nearby table and approached the fire. He steadily and carefully lifted the pot from its hook on the iron fire stand, being careful not to spill any of the dark brown dye or get any on his clothing. He placed it on a large iron rack next to the work table.

"*Danke, mein Sohn.* I can do the remainder of the work myself. You need to get back to the shop."

Michael glanced at the crib that rested against the trunk of a nearby oak tree. His two-week-old brother, Henry, slept soundly in a soft bed of linen cloths. Michael smiled. The infant was a much-unexpected addition to the Yeisley clan. Julianna had been childless since the birth of her only daughter, Elizabeth, almost five years ago. She had assumed that her child bearing days were done. Little Henry managed to convince her otherwise. Still, his birth had been a long and agonizing task for Julianna. It was a particularly difficult labor. To be honest, Michael was amazed that his mother had survived the event. He prayed that Henry was, indeed, her last child.

"You need to do less and relax more, *Mutter*. We have ample thread in stock. Why are you making more today? You should be resting."

"I grow weary of resting, Michael. You have all been doting over me long enough. I feel just fine, and I want to contribute." She grinned. "Even mothers must earn their keep."

A bell tinkled inside the store. Michael had a customer.

"Get back to work, Son. I shall get this batch of thread in the pot and then I will get started on dinner."

Michael turned and trotted back toward the building. He called over his shoulder, "What are we having?"

"Farina soup and fresh bread."

"But, I want some meat!" he protested.

"I will slice some of the venison sausage and cheese for you to enjoy with your soup."

He paused at the back door and grinned. "I cannot wait!" The bell rang again. He turned and stepped inside.

On Board the Schooner, Minerva
Philadelphia Docks - October 15, 1768

IT WAS late in the afternoon. A thick fog had settled upon the ships that were docked in the Philadelphia harbor. The temperature was dropping rapidly. Nicklaus Yeisley exhaled a heavy white vapor into the cold, wet air. He shivered and pulled his wool coat tightly around his neck.

Nicklaus was waiting for the master of the *Minerva*. He stood barely one step off of the boarding plank, clinging tightly to the port railing. Though the ship bobbed only slightly in the relatively still water, the movement of the deck was disconcerting to him. Nicklaus recalled his weeks on board the *Phoenix*, and the trials of his days at sea. He experienced sensations and emotions that he had long-since buried deep in his memories. He did not like it. Every fiber and sinew of his being wanted to turn and run back down that plank to the comfort of solid ground.

Though his voyage to America had been relatively painless, Nicklaus despised stepping on board these more modern immigrant ships. The last two times he had done so, his eyes and nose had come under assault by the stench of human body odor, urine, feces, death, and decay. It seemed that conditions on board these ships had deteriorated dramatically over the past eighteen years. More than ever before, his fellow German migrants were being treated like disposable human cargo.

The *Minerva* displayed, perhaps, the worst conditions that he had ever witnessed. The decks were stained with human waste and blood. He doubted that any amount of cleansing and mopping could ever remove the stench. The poor souls on board were hallow, gaunt creatures. There were hundreds of them, and they had obviously suffered from lack of food. Disease abounded. Nicklaus was beginning to wonder if he had made a mistake even coming here. He was just about to turn and descend back down the boarding plank when a distinctly English voice interrupted his intentions.

"*Herr* Yeisley, I presume?"

Nicklaus turned and faced a smartly-dressed ship's captain, wearing the decorative regalia of a former officer of the British Navy.

"*A military man*," thought Nicklaus. "*One would think he might run a tighter, cleaner ship.*"

He forced himself to respond. "Yes. I am Nicklaus Yeisley. Are you the master of this ship?"

The man bowed slightly. "Indeed, I am. Captain Thomas Arnott, at your service, sir."

Nicklaus glanced, his heart filled with pity, toward the expectant men, women, and children who lined the railings on both sides of the ship.

"How long have you been here, Mr. Arnott? There remains quite a mob on board. Surely, not many of your passengers have disembarked."

The captain chuckled. "You arrived at the perfect time, *Herr* Yeisley. You are only our second customer. We arrived five days ago, on October 10, and only cleared the medical inspection this morning. We have been tied off to this dock less than one hour." He puckered his lips slightly. "As you can tell, we had a bit of illness on board. I lost forty-nine passengers during the journey." He sniffed and displayed a look of dissatisfaction.

Nicklaus snarled his nose. "Of that I have no doubt. This ship wreaks of death and filth. I can scarcely believe that a man trained in His Majesty's Navy would let his vessel descend into such a state."

The captain stood a bit taller and bristled in offense. "Sir ... a ship's captain cannot stem the tide of illness that strikes passengers on the high seas."

"Indeed. But surely a ship's captain could order someone to mop up the excrement and vomit from his own decks," Nicklaus retorted.

The ship master's cheeks and ears flushed red. He clearly had no desire to receive criticism for the way he ran his ship from an uppity German businessman.

He barked, "Did you, or did you not come here to do business, *Herr* Yeisley? If you came only to judge and complain, then you are welcome to leave at once. I shall, no doubt, have plenty of other paying customers in the coming hours and days."

Nicklaus nodded. "I did, indeed, come for business, Captain."

"What is it that you seek, then? Let us conclude our transaction swiftly." The master of the ship was curt.

"I am in textiles, Mr. Arnott. I need a weaver and spinners ... workers in linen, wool, dyes, and thread. Experience in hands-on work with sheep would be most ideal. I do not need to fill an entire factory, mind you. One family will do nicely."

"So ... you are willing to take on an entire family?" The captain appeared surprised. "You, of course, have the option of taking the experienced workers only. There will be plenty of farmers who will come and claim the boy children." He winked. "And there will be plenty of other business folk here in Philadelphia who find some use for the young girls."

Nicklaus growled with disgust. "I can only imagine." He inhaled a deep and rather unpleasant breath. "No, Captain, it is my practice to hire out families. I will not count myself amongst those so-called men who are so heartless as to rip little boys and girls from the arms of their mothers." He spat on the deck. "If you have a family on board that might meet my needs, I should like to confer with them."

The captain nodded and rolled his eyes slightly. "As you wish. We may be able to help you. I believe there is, indeed, a suitable family on board." He turned and shouted to one of his officers, "Levtenant Scott! Bring the manifest!"

A voice from the quarterdeck responded with a smart, "Aye, sir!" A young man, no older that his own son, Michael, quickly descended the steps. He approached the captain, clutching a small stack of weathered papers.

The captain declared, "Mr. Scott, this is Mr. Nicklaus Yeisley. He owns a textile business. He is in search of weavers and thread makers. Do we have any suitable candidates?"

"One moment, sirs."

The young fellow scanned his list. His lips moved slightly as he read the names and associated comments. After several seconds, he declared, "Here it is!" He tapped his finger victoriously against his papers.

"Your report, Levtenant," demanded the captain, who was growing impatient.

"There is one man, Heinrich Muller, who is listed as a weaver. He hails from the Palatinate. Passage is due for husband, wife, and three children. Forty Pounds Sterling."

The captain turned to Nicklaus. "Would you like to speak to this man?"

"I would, indeed. Where might we meet?" Nicklaus inquired.

The captain's face betrayed his amusement. "We are fresh out of meeting rooms and private spaces, *Herr* Yeisley. You shall have to meet the fellow here, on the main deck." He nodded to Lieutenant Scott. "Fetch Mueller and his family."

The young fellow clicked his heels smartly. "Aye, sir!" He walked swiftly toward the stern of the boat. Moments later, he returned, followed by a tall, thin man and three girls.

The lieutenant made the introduction. "Mr. Yeisley, this is Mr. Mueller and his family."

Mueller bowed respectfully and mumbled, *"Guten Tag, Herr Yeisley."*

Nicklaus stared, speechless, at the four of them. The man's clothing was threadbare. He wore neither stockings nor shoes. His feet were stained black. Above the ankles, his flesh displayed a sickly, gray tone. His dark gray breeches hung loosely and in tatters. He had neither coat nor weskit. He wore only a heavy brown shirt, which was ripped open on his left side. Nicklaus could actually see the man's skin stretched across his ribs. The pitiful fellow appeared to be freezing.

The girls appeared only slightly better in comparison to their father. The two older ones were in their teens. Indeed, the tallest one was nearing adulthood. The smallest of the three appeared no older than age seven or eight. All three wore linen wraps that covered their entire bodies. A rope around the waist secured the humble coverings. Instead of bonnets or mob caps, they wore simple linen scarves which were tied beneath their chins. All three of the girls were trembling and cold. Their teeth chattered.

The captain declared, "We shall leave you to your negotiations. Levtenant ..." Both of the officers turned and ambled toward the steps that led to the quarterdeck.

It was a most uncomfortable moment. Nicklaus had only done this twice before. He hated the negotiations of an indenture even more than he hated stepping on board the ship. He knew, full well, how unscrupulous businessmen preyed upon the helpless, poverty-stricken passengers and entangled them in a system that was little more than a form of glorified slavery. He could scarcely believe that so many of his fellow German-American businessmen could treat their own countrymen thusly.

He nodded respectfully to the man. "*Herr* Mueller. Are you a weaver by trade?"

The man nodded excitedly. "*Ja, Herr* Yeisley. I trained in my father's shop. It was his father's shop before him."

"And where are you from in the Palatinate?"

"Berkoth. It is a small village. I doubt that you have heard of it."

"Is it near the Eifel Mountains?" Nicklaus asked.

The fellow's sad eyes suddenly brightened. "It is, indeed! You are familiar with my village?"

"I remember the mention of it, though I have never been there." He paused. "I barely remember my own village sometimes, *Herr* Mueller. I came here eighteen years ago."

The man nodded his understanding. There was an uncomfortable moment of silence.

"Did you sail from Rotterdam?" Nicklaus asked.

"*Ja.*"

"And these are your daughters?"

The man's face brightened somewhat. "*Ja*. The oldest is Maria Magdalena. She is seventeen years old. The middle one is Anna Emelia, age eleven. The youngest is Emma Andrea. She is six." He nodded proudly. "Magdalena and Anna are both experienced spinners. Magdalena has also worked for about a year on a small loom. Emma is learning, but she is very young. Still, she helped out with small tasks around our shop. I am confident she will one day be an excellent worker."

Nicklaus nodded. He asked bluntly, "Why did you leave your home?"

Mueller inhaled deeply and considered his answer carefully. "We suffered three seasons of crop failures and famine, *Herr* Yeisley. The people in our region were starving. There was no currency to speak of. Poverty abounded. It did not help that the *Katholiks* constantly reached across the border from France to rob us of what little we have left. I could tolerate the suffering and injustice no longer, so I joined a group of pilgrims bound for America."

"Then, you are of the Reformed Church?"

Mueller nodded. Nicklaus was pleased by his response.

Nicklaus glanced behind the man and his daughters. "And where is your wife? Is she ill?"

Mueller's countenance fell. He shook his head slightly. "*Nein, Herr* Yeisley. She perished during the journey." A tear crawled down his dirt-stained cheek. "She caught a fever three days out of Portsmouth. She never recovered." He wiped his face with his filth-encrusted sleeve. "They tossed her overboard, as if she were refuse."

Nicklaus placed a comforting hand on the man's shoulder. "How long did your dear wife suffer?"

"Three days. Four, perhaps. The memory is so very confusing. She died during a horrible gale. It seemed like we were all barely clinging to life during those days."

"So, she lived only one week out of England?"

"*Ja.* One week. We have been without her for over two months."

"It took you nine weeks to travel from England?" Nicklaus asked in disbelief.

"Ten and a half, *Herr* Yeisley." He gulped. "And we ran out of rations three weeks ago."

Nicklaus gasped. "You have not eaten in three weeks?"

"Only rats. I managed to capture four during that period." He grinned timidly. "It is all right, *Herr* Yeisley. We fared better than most."

Nicklaus stared disbelievingly at the man. He trembled in his soul. He scanned the people who occupied the decks of the ship. He looked into the eyes of over three hundred fellow Germans. They were starving ... and hopeless. He inhaled another deep and exceedingly unpleasant breath.

"I should like for you to come and work for me in my manufactory, *Herr* Mueller ... you and all of your girls. I shall pay your passage in full. In exchange, I will offer a contract for five years of service from each of you. You will help operate my looms. The girls will work sheep and make thread. You will receive housing, food, and ample clothing. I will also pay you a modest wage so that you may save for your future or purchase luxury items. You may pay any remaining debt on your contract whenever you are able, and whenever you should choose. Are these terms fair and acceptable to you?"

"Five years?" Mueller echoed in disbelief. "I expected far more."

Nicklaus shook his head. "Five years is fair for a skilled workman such as yourself. At the end of that time, if your work is satisfactory and you wish to stay, I may offer you a permanent position. If, however, you wish to move on and make your own fortune in America, you shall do so with my blessing." He paused. "Do we have a deal?"

Heinrich Mueller did not speak. He simply extended his thin, filthy hand toward Nicklaus. They shook.

Nicklaus smiled. "Good. Now, let me speak to the captain. It seems that he has inflated the price of your family's passage. He is attempting to charge a fare for your wife, even though she did not make the mid-way point in crossing the sea. I shall put him in his place." He grinned. "Gather your things. We shall go straightway to the inn where I am lodged and secure baths for all of you. I have already arranged for a room for your family. I also brought fresh clothing for each of you in my wagon. My wife prepared a sack filled with many garments of various sizes. There is also a tin of dried fruit and a sack of dried, smoked beef."

Mr. Mueller did not speak. He stared at Nicklaus with eyes of gratitude and disbelief.

Nicklaus cautioned, "Do not let the girls eat too much. Since they have not eaten in so long, I do not wish for them to become ill." He grinned and gently slapped Mr. Mueller on the back. "Tonight, we shall sup together. I have a tavern in mind that serves an excellent roast chicken and a tantalizing cabbage soup. We shall attend services, rest, and otherwise enjoy the Sabbath tomorrow. After I conclude my other business on Monday morning, we shall depart for home. We should arrive in the evening on Tuesday."

"Home?" repeated the youngest girl, Emma. It was the first time that Nicklaus had heard any of the girls speak.

Nicklaus leaned forward and gently pinched the little girl's nose. "*Ja*, Emma. Home. I have a wonderful little cottage that is waiting for you. It has a bed that will be all your own! Shall we go?" He smiled broadly.

Little Emma nodded excitedly.

NICKLAUS GUIDED his team northwest along the King's Highway through Upper Milford. It had been a long but uneventful day. The weather was perfect for mid-October. The fellowship during the journey had been pleasant, as well. Nicklaus quite enjoyed his endless conversations with Heinrich Mueller. The two of them hit it off quite nicely. Heinrich was not only going to be a fine, experienced worker. Nicklaus could foresee that he was also going to be a good and loyal friend.

He pointed ahead and to the left. "There it is, near that cluster of trees. That is our shop. My home is in the back. The worker's cottages are just beyond the trees." He glanced at Heinrich. "Your girls will sleep in their own beds tonight."

Heinrich turned in the wagon seat and looked at his daughters. The three girls were dozing comfortably on a bed of raw wool in the back of the wagon. Magdalena lay in the middle. The younger girls each nestled under her arms. Heinrich smiled.

"I never thought this day would come, *Herr* Yeisley."

"Heinrich, I shall not say it to you again. You *must* call me Nicklaus. Every time you say, '*Herr* Yeisley,' I look to see if my father is standing behind me."

Mueller chuckled happily. "*Ja*, Nicklaus ... though I am not quite comfortable referring to my master by his given name."

Nicklaus cooed at his horses and pulled back on the reins. The team eased to a stop one hundred yards short of his weaving shop. He turned and faced his new friend.

"Heinrich, I am not your master, and you are not my slave. I am merely your contracted employer for the next five years. Our families will labor together, side-by-side. Outside of work, you are free to live out your life as you please. You will pursue whatever brings happiness to you and your girls. Do you understand?"

Heinrich smiled warmly. "*Ja*, Nicklaus."

"Good. I should hope that we will never have this particular conversation again. Now, let us complete our journey and see what my lovely bride has prepared for supper. I quite imagine that she will be thrilled to see your girls. We have but one daughter, and she is very young. Our house is filled with boys. Therefore, you must prepare yourself for her motherly ways. She is certain to spoil your girls."

Heinrich laughed joyfully.

THE YEISLEY KITCHEN was filled with family, warmth, activity, and tantalizing aromas. Four loaves of fresh bread were cooling on the table, filling the room with their yeasty sweetness. The distinctive, spicy smell of Julianna's stewed venison and onions perfectly complemented the smell of the bread and indicated that suppertime was drawing nigh.

Julianna was leaning toward the fireplace. She nudged her large stew pot, which dangled on the end of a fireplace crane, one inch closer to the dancing flames. Michael was seated near the dining table, skillfully cleaning the beautiful long rifle that he had used to fell the venison that was simmering in his mother's pot. Fifteen-year-old George was seated on the other side of the table and reading a German novel. Little Nicklaus, whom the family affectionately called Nikki, was beside the warm hearth, fighting a pretend battle with painted lead toy soldiers. Four-year-old Elizabeth was happily playing with a doll in the corner. The newborn, Henry, slept soundly in his cradle, despite the din of house life that surrounded him.

Nicklaus burst loudly through the kitchen door, tossing the heavy oak portal open and banging it against a nearby ladder-back chair. He proclaimed, "The man of the house has returned from Philadelphia! Woman, what shall you feed him?"

Nikki instantly exclaimed, "Papa!" He jumped up from the floor and ran, quick as a flash, toward his father. He locked his arms around Nicklaus' leg and squeezed him with a huge hug. Elizabeth and George followed immediately.

Julianna spun on her heels and then quickly approached her husband in as dignified a manner as she could muster. She peeled the children off of their father, then wrapped her arms around his neck. He planted an exaggerated, wet kiss on her cheek. She slapped him playfully with the cloth that she was holding in her left hand.

"Behave yourself, Nicklaus Yeisley! You have arrived just in time. I thought that we were going to have to start without you." She smiled and kissed him soundly on the lips. "Did you have a successful trip?"

"I did, indeed. And I hope that you have prepared enough stew for guests, *meine Liebe*."

She clapped her hands and exclaimed, "Did you find some helpers for the shop?"

"An entire family of weavers and spinners. Allow me to introduce you." He stepped to the door and motioned to his unseen guests. "Heinrich! Girls! Come! Come inside! There is no need to linger out there in the cold."

The timid Heinrich Mueller stepped into the warmth and light of the family kitchen. His daughters followed close behind. The youngest entered first. The last was the young woman, Magdalena. When she stepped through the door, Julianna almost gasped.

Heinrich Mueller's oldest daughter was stunningly beautiful. A wisp of her shiny, light blonde hair peeked from beneath the brim of her mob cap. She had dazzling, bright blue eyes. Her face was perfectly proportioned, with high cheekbones and a diminutive nose. The girl smiled meekly. The curve of her lips magnified her beauty.

Magdalena was wearing one of Julianna's old petticoats. It was made of dark, chocolatey brown linen, and was a bit short for her tall frame. Still, when combined with the dark green short gown that elegantly hugged her torso, it revealed a perfectly proportioned and voluptuous body.

The sudden, sharp scrape of chair legs grinding across the oak floor echoed from across the room. Nicklaus turned and spied Michael rising to his feet and staring, mouth agape. He and Magdalena were peering at one another. Neither of them blinked. Magdalena's mouth curled into an almost indiscernible, embarrassed grin.

The rifle that Michael was holding unexpectedly slipped from his fingers and fell with a loud crash to the floor. Nikki and Elizabeth giggled. Michael's face turned beet-red as he bent over to retrieve the weapon. Nicklaus chuckled beneath his breath at his ordinarily socially adept son's sudden descent into awkward clumsiness.

"Julianna, this is Heinrich Mueller and his lovely daughters, Magdalena, Anna, and little Emma. They have agreed to work with us for the next five years."

Julianna beamed with pleasure. She shook each of their hands. "Welcome! Welcome to you all! Please, come inside and make yourselves at home. Supper will be ready shortly. There is water in the jug and soap on the basin to wash your hands. If you need the necessary house, it is just out back. George will be more than happy to show you the way. Now, if you will excuse me, I will set the table." She turned her attention back toward the hearth.

Anna quietly whispered something to her father. He declared, "Anna needs for George to show her the way." He grinned.

George, ever the enthusiastic lad, declared, "Follow me!" He sprinted toward the back door of the kitchen. Anna sheepishly followed.

The Yeisley children returned to their activities. Heinrich escorted Emma to the basin to assist her in washing her hands. Magdalena hovered, alone, near the front door. She and Michael stood motionless, staring at one another. After several awkward seconds, Michael placed his rifle in the corner and then slowly and reverently stepped around the dining table and approached her.

"*Guten Tag, Fräulein Mueller.*"

"*Bitte, Herr Yeisley* ... but you must call me Magdalena."

Michael smiled warmly and nodded. He reached for her hand, gently lifted it to his lips, and declared, "Very well, then, Magdalena. And you must call me Michael."

She bowed slightly and responded softly. "It will be my pleasure ... Michael." She smiled.

The sound of his name coming from her smooth, cherry-red lips melted Michael Yeisley's heart. He knew in that instant that Magdalena Mueller would be his bride.

3

DEATH SHIP

The Schooner Betsey – Crossing the Atlantic
October 20, 1768

The bow of the *Betsey* raised high into the air and hovered precariously at a steep pitch. The helpless passengers, each of them huddled in the various chambers and holds throughout the battered ship, clung desperately to ropes, timbers, bunks, nails … and to one another. Then, violently, their bodies lifted into the air in a semi-weightless state as the ship plunged over the crest of yet another towering wave.

Far to the aft, in the rearmost cargo hold, Dr. Nicklaus Schell's head slammed against the bulkhead above him. He felt a warm trickle on his forehead and a sudden burning in his left eye. He was bleeding from a scalp wound, and the blood was flowing directly into the eye. It quickly began to cloud his vision.

He cursed in his native German, *"Verdammt!"* He attempted to wipe the blinding flow away with his soiled, blood-soaked sleeve. He was having little success.

A shrill voice barked, "I will get it, son. Tend to your patient."

Katharina Schell wiped her son's face with a damp towel. She

quickly and skillfully ripped a piece of linen from a discarded petticoat and fashioned a makeshift bandage. She placed it on his head
and applied pressure to stem the flow of blood that was oozing from
his scalp. Nicklaus smiled in admiration at his mother, then shuddered when he recognized the cloth of the bandage. The colorful
material reminded him of the now-deceased owner of the petticoat.

She was a beautiful *Fräulein* from Anderach on the Rhine. The
poor maiden had perished no more than four hours prior. Katharina
managed to salvage her cloak and petticoats for bandages moments
before the ship's crew tossed her body overboard. Nicklaus could not
remember her name. He hated himself for not being able to do so. He
shook his head and endeavored to dismiss the heart-breaking image
of the stricken girl from his mind. He had to focus on the still-living
woman who lay suffering before him.

"Is it bad, *Mutter*?" he inquired of his wound. "Will it require
stitches?"

She lifted the bandage and examined his scalp, then declared her
prognosis. "*Nein*, Nicklaus. It is only a small crack in the skin. You will
be fine." She patted him reassuringly on the shoulder. "Back to work,
mein Bärchen!"

"*Danke, Mutter*." He cut a quick, smiling glance at his mother.

Katharina Schell looked exhausted. Despite the filthy state of her
gray petticoat and faded blue short gown, she remained a beautiful
woman. Her blonde hair, touched by just a hint of gray above the
ears, dangled loosely from beneath her stained, threadbare bonnet.
Tiny, branching wrinkles decorated the corners of her sunken, dark,
tired eyes. And she was gaunt, having lost almost twenty pounds from
her already-tiny frame during the arduous journey. But still, she
persevered and labored on beside her diligent son. Even without
food, water, or sleep, she continued to minister to the other hopeless,
helpless souls on board the *Betsey*.

Yes, Katharina Schell was a wonder, indeed. Nicklaus could
scarcely believe it when his mother declared her intention to depart
her ancestral home in Ibersheim and accompany him on his journey
to America. He had discouraged her at first, but eventually realized

that she, too, needed a fresh start in life. She was barely fifty years old, and recently widowed when her beloved husband, Johann, perished in a hunting accident. She was all alone, except for Nicklaus, her only son. It made sense that she would desire to go with him to the New World.

Nicklaus thanked God every day that his mother was by his side. He doubted that he would have survived the journey, along with its unexpected demands, without her assistance. Dr. Schell was the only remaining physician on board the ailing ship ... and he was just a passenger. The "official" ship's surgeon had perished on the third week of the voyage. Nicklaus, along with his most capable mother, toiled valiantly in his stead in their makeshift infirmary. However, they were fighting a losing battle against an onslaught of injury and death. Indeed, Nicklaus was beginning to doubt whether any of the passengers would reach Philadelphia.

The *Betsey* was under the assault of yet another horrific storm. It was their fourth gale in three weeks. The relentless series of storms had claimed roughly two dozen lives, either from drowning or washing people overboard. Tragically, the ship was only one week from the docks of Philadelphia. The frightened, helpless pilgrims were almost to their destination. But, their proximity to America meant nothing to the powerful, thundering, roiling sea. More people were going to die. If the ocean tempests did not kill them, incessant illnesses and diseases would.

The living conditions on board the *Betsey* were, in a word, unbearable. There was no place on board the ship that remained undefiled by disease, filth, or rot. In addition to the deaths due to storms, common maladies had claimed another one hundred lives since departing England. Various fevers were rampant, afflicting over half of the passengers. The bloody flux killed one passenger, on average, each day. Most of the people on board were infested with an incurable itch. And, just when Dr. Schell thought it could get no worse, three older men had presented with the symptoms of smallpox over the past two days. Nicklaus had, of course, placed those men in isolation and under quarantine in the forward hold.

Ultimately, dehydration was their most pressing issue. The ship's fresh water supply had been contaminated by seawater during the first storm. Since that horrible night, the crew had been unable to replenish the fresh water because of the lack of measurable rain. Each successive storm, accompanied by huge waves crashing and washing over the decks of the ship, added more and more salty contamination to the drinking water supply.

The people continued to drink the filthy, brackish concoction, yet they could not quench their scorching thirst. Their bodies ached for water. Unbeknownst to the passengers, that salty, unsatisfying water had also been contaminated by their own disease-infested feces. Thus, came the outbreak of the most dreaded fever of all ... "ship's fever" ... cholera. When the diarrhea caused by that horrible infection ravaged already-dehydrated bodily systems, death was inevitable.

Furthermore, the passengers' bellies ached for food. Tragically, there was none left. The ship's ill-prepared stores had been depleted for almost a week. Even before the supplies were gone, what had been available for consumption was food in name only. It had been neither appetizing nor nutritious since the day the ship departed England.

No matter how diligently Dr. Schell labored against the onslaught of disease and death, he could not reverse the combined ravages of malnutrition and dehydration. He felt helpless. He felt hopeless. He felt desperate.

The dire straits facing the handful of remaining children on board burdened Nicklaus the most. Of the forty-seven youths that had boarded the vessel in Rotterdam, only fourteen remained alive. Measles infected the ship while docked in England. The horrid childhood disease was deadly enough when conditions were favorable. But, when accompanied by starvation and exposure on board a frigid, damp, filthy, disease-ridden ship, it was nothing short of a death sentence.

Time and again, Dr. Schell had watched helplessly as the ship's crew tossed the dead little ones over the rails. The oldest had been thirteen. The youngest had been a mere four months old. Unimaginably, one couple had witnessed all five of their children discarded thusly over a period of three days.

Then, to further challenge his medical skills, there were the expectant mothers. Nicklaus had absolutely no idea why a pregnant woman would attempt such a voyage. But, three women, each on the verge of giving birth, had boarded at Rotterdam. Two had already delivered during the voyage. Both babies succumbed to the conditions. Only one of the two who delivered, the wretchedly pitiful Inga Mahler, survived the childbirth. That was two days ago. Her husband was washed overboard into the sea less than an hour after the death of her newborn baby. Her entire world and future were claimed by the cold, merciless Atlantic in a single day. Like so many other surviving passengers on board the cursed ship, she was completely alone.

There remained only one pregnant woman on board, and, as fate would have it, her womb elected to expel its fruit in the midst of this raging gale. She was Dr. Schell's current patient. As far as he was concerned, she was his only patient. He ignored the plights and pleas of all others save her. She, alone, had been the object of his attentions throughout this long, frightening night.

The girl shrieked from her torturing pain. Her body writhed in concert with the swaying of the storm-tossed ship.

"Hold her still, *Mutter!*" Nicklaus demanded. "I cannot do this if you cannot keep her still!"

"How can I keep anything or anyone still in the midst of these waves?" she screeched angrily at her son. "I am doing the best that I can!" She stared indignantly at him.

"*Es tut mir Leid, Mutter.*" Nicklaus glanced sheepishly at Katharina. "Please forgive me. I am simply frustrated. Still, I should not take out my frustrations upon you."

Katharina nodded forgiveness to her son. She turned her attention to the tortured young woman. "There, there, child," she cooed. She leaned across the girl's chest and dabbed a towel against her forehead. "I know it hurts, my darling. But, you must be very still so that the doctor can do his work. Do you understand?"

The girl nodded slightly. She turned her eyes to Katharina. Her heart responded to the kindness imparted unto her by the older woman. Though her lips did not move, Katharina was able to discern the faintest of smiles in her otherwise empty eyes. But, as she stared searchingly into the young woman's beautiful green eyes, Katharina could also see her life ebbing away. Death was drawing near.

No one knew very much about Adrianna Etelwein. But, what they did know was that she was not married, she was traveling alone, and she was great with child. It had been the subject of much gossip amongst the women who had, thus far, survived the Atlantic voyage. Nicklaus shook his head in disgust as the visions of those self-right-eous, judgmental women filled his thoughts. He remained dismayed that women whose husbands and children were starving to death could still make time for gossip and slander.

Dr. Schell, personally, cared neither about the unmarried woman's sins, nor her spiritual transgressions. To him, such petty things were irrelevant in the current situation. He only knew that this young lady was in horrible pain, on the very verge of death, and that he absolutely had to attempt to do something ... anything ... to try and save her.

It was not as if she were the only soul in need of his care. Two dozen sick, helpless passengers lined the walls of the room. The life-less bodies of one dead woman and two dead men tumbled awkwardly in the sludge of seawater, vomit, urine, and feces that sloshed shin-deep in the squalid chamber that served as Dr. Schell's infirmary. The room reeked of death, yet it also still held fast to the faintest hope of new life in the baby that was struggling to find its way out of the womb. But, that hope was fading quickly.

It would have been a difficult delivery even in the best of circum-stances. The woman had been in labor for almost fourteen hours. She lay on top of a large crate that served as her birthing table. The crate was lashed to the starboard side of the boat, and she was, in turn, tied to the crate to keep her from tumbling into the flooded floor.

Another monstrous wave slammed the bow of the ship, this one pressing the nose of the vessel downward. The room swayed. The people seeking refuge there screamed and wailed in fear. Candles flickered. Some of them were extinguished, drowned in the sloshing of their own molten wax. It took several seconds for the bow to rise and for the ship to right itself. The timbers of the vessel groaned helplessly against the overwhelming onslaught of the water.

Nicklaus braced his shoulder against the wall to maintain his balance. He was up to his elbows in blood. He re-inserted his right hand deep into Adrianna's birth canal. With his left hand, he attempted to massage the baby and turn it to point the head downward. Thus far, he was having little success. Though he strove valiantly to save the woman and her unborn child, deep in his heart Nicklaus was becoming convinced that death awaited them both.

Fraulein Etelwein's baby was breech, and Nicklaus had tried every method he knew to turn the infant for a normal delivery. But, something had ruptured inside of her. She was bleeding profusely from between her legs. Nicklaus knew that he had to get this baby out immediately. Time was of the essence.

Another contraction tensed the frustrated muscles of her womb. Blood poured forth out of her vagina. The hollow wail of her painful cry pierced the cacophony of thunder, screaming winds, and pounding rain. Her wail increased in intensity and then slowly diminished into a weak moan.

Captain Samuel Hawk, master of the vessel, stood near the doorway. The man grunted sadistically. It was an unmistakable, '*See, I told you so,*' kind of grunt. Nicklaus' heart pounded in anger. He wished that the man would depart his infirmary. The unwanted, invasive seaman had been hovering about for hours, uselessly, inside Nicklaus' improvised aid station. He remained there, no doubt, because it was the driest room on board the ailing ship. Nicklaus attempted to ignore the man's obnoxious noises.

"'Tis time, Doctor," the captain urged. "You have made a valiant effort, son. No one can find any fault in your labors to save this girl. I will attest to that."

Nicklaus pretended that the captain was not there.

Captain Hawk cleared his throat. "Please stand aside, Doctor."

"Do you not have someplace else to be?" retorted Nicklaus. "Surely, the captain of a vessel should be up on deck and be in command of his boat."

"I am in command, and this boat remains in good hands, Dr. Schell," the man growled. "Now, stand aside and let us take the girl."

"You need to leave this room immediately, Captain. Your presence is neither required nor wanted here."

A strong wave smacked the port side of the ship, rolling it several degrees to starboard.

The captain sighed loudly as he grabbed a bulkhead for support. He was growing frustrated with this condescending German physician. "Doctor, enough of this misery! You must allow Mr. Clark and meself to bury the lass."

"*Du Hurensohn! Fraulein* Etelwein is not dead!" Katharina Schell shrieked.

"She's just as good as so!" retorted the captain. He glared disdainfully at Katharina. "You simply do not understand such things. I have been a man of this sea for nigh on twenty years, now. I know full-well what needs a doin'."

Nicklaus ignored the captain. He was too focused upon attempting to redirect the head of the child. But, it seemed as if the little one was fighting back. He ... or she ... would not budge. Nicklaus groaned in frustration.

The captain finally yelled in his thick, Scottish-tinged voice, "Damn it, man, you have done enough, already! 'Tis a lost cause! Now, stand aside and allow us to do our jobs. We must throw the wench overboard. Neither she, nor her bastard child will survive this night. Let us end her misery! 'Tis the merciful thing to do!"

"There is still time!" Nicklaus responded vehemently. "I can save them!"

"Aww ... you're dreamin', man! Now, get out of me way so's I can do my job."

Once again, Nicklaus ignored the officer.

"Stand aside, Dr. Schell. That is an order." The captain stomped through the putrid water and reached for the girl's leg. His associate, Simon Clark, followed his lead.

Quick as a flash, without even thinking, Nicklaus grabbed a medical bistoury knife from his instrument dish, spun around, and lunged at Captain Hawk. He kicked up a splashing wave of seawater as he made his sudden move toward the officer. Nicklaus pinned the man against the wall and held the blade of the knife against his neck. Only a thin layer of skin and muscle separated the seaman's carotid artery from the wafer-thin blade of razor-sharp steel.

Nicklaus growled threateningly, "If you touch her, you *Scheißkopf*, I will slit your throat!" Just at that moment, another a huge wave slammed against the bow of the ship, knocking both men off balance. The tip of the surgical knife pierced the captain's skin, drawing a trickle of blood from his grimy, water-soaked neck. Captain Hawk winced from the sudden, stinging pain.

"Careful now, Doctor," urged Mr. Clark. "There's no need for violence." He glanced at the captain and saw a stream of blood staining Captain Hawk's filthy neck sock. "You must unhand the captain, immediately." Moments later, a dull click echoed throughout the suddenly silent room. Mr. Clark had drawn and cocked his pistol. He placed the muzzle against the back of Dr. Schell's head.

Nicklaus did not respond. He maintained pressure against the man's chest with his left forearm and, with his right hand, continued to hold the blade against his neck. Captain Hawk slowly reached upward and dabbed his finger against his blood-stained collar. He withdrew his hand and glanced at the crimson stain on the tip of his finger.

"Well, well, Dr. Schell. What would Hippocrates think of your actions on this day?" he chided sarcastically. "I do believe that, despite your oath to the contrary, you have done me a measure of harm."

Katharina Schell's trembling voice interrupted the violent confrontation. She was terrified and worried for her son. "Nicklaus! Leave him be. You must tend to your patient. This girl is fading quickly."

Dr. Schell ignored the plea of his mother as he continued to glare hatefully at the ship's captain. "You will survive your wound, Mr. Hawk. But, I promise you ... if you lay one hand on that girl without my permission, Mr. Clark and his minions will be tossing both of our dead bodies over the rails before sunrise. *Verstehen Sie?*"

"Oh, I understand very well, Dr. Schell. Just like I understand that you will answer for your unlawful actions on this night," hissed the captain.

"I can live with that. And upon our arrival in America ... if we ever get there ... I will enlighten the authorities as to your maleficence and criminality throughout this hellish voyage. I will see to it that you never command another seagoing vessel."

The captain's eyebrow raised incredulously. "So, it is like that, then?"

"Yes, Captain. It is like that. Such is my promise to you. We shall ruin one another." He paused, narrowing his eyes into a piercing stare. "Now, you can either stand here against this wall in silence, or you can get the hell out of my infirmary."

Just at that moment, the bodies of one of the dead men floating in the tepid seawater bumped against the back of his leg. Nicklaus glanced downward. He hissed, "If you are truly so desperate to throw someone overboard, you could do us all a favor and remove these bodies that are floating about."

The men glared hatefully at one another for a most uncomfortable span of time.

"Please, Dr. Schell. Let him go," urged Mr Clark. "Look ... I am putting my firearm away." The man released the hammer on his pistol and swiftly tucked it back into his belt. "We shall put aside this entire affair. There is no need for violence."

"Nicklaus!" his mother urged. "Forget them! This girl needs your help!"

Nicklaus maintained his stare as he relaxed his arms and then stepped away from the captain. The muscles in his broad chest remained tense. A sweat of fury and conflict soaked his brow. He trembled imperceptibly from the surge of adrenaline elicited by the confrontation.

Suddenly, a fluidic gurgling noise emanated from behind him. It was *Fraulein* Etelwein. Katharina sloshed through the shin-deep water toward the girl. She lowered her ear to the patient's mouth as she placed her hand on her chest. There was no sound. There was no movement, at all. The top and sides of the crate upon which she lay were soaked with dark, gelatinous blood.

"Nicklaus, she is dead!" his mother wailed.

He dashed to the girl's side to confirm his mother's declaration. She was correct. The breath of life had departed the pitiful young woman. The room fell into a deep, mournful silence. No one spoke or moved, despite the din of the raging storm and seas that consumed the boat.

Katharina suddenly gasped. "Nicklaus! The child!"

She pointed at the dead girl's abdomen. Her belly was wiggling and surging. The unborn infant was thrashing about inside the girl's womb. It was still alive! But, with the cessation of its mother's heartbeat, the infant was starving for oxygen. It was suffocating.

Nicklaus ordered, "Quickly, mother! Towels!" He motioned to the captain. "I need light. You two! Bring those lanterns close."

"What are you going to do?" demanded the captain.

"I have no time to explain. Hurry! Bring the lights!"

Captain Hawk and Mr. Clark fetched two tin ship's lanterns from their hooks and carried them timidly toward the pale body of the dead girl.

Nicklaus ordered, "Stand near her feet. Hold the candles close."

Curious, the two men did as they were told. Nicklaus leaned forward over the girl's belly. Using his left hand, he applied pressure against the wiggling child, pushing it away from the mother's pubis. He reached across her body and placed his bistoury knife against the gray skin just below the fold of her belly.

"Good God, man! Surely, you are not going to desecrate the dead!" wailed the captain.

Nicklaus exhaled, frustrated. "Shut up, you imbecile, and hold the light steady! I must be able to see!"

He then swiftly and skillfully made a shallow cut from one side of her pelvis to the other, following the contour of her rounded belly. There was very little blood.

"Good heavens!" groaned Mr. Clark, as he made the sign of the cross on his chest. "Father, forgive him!"

Nicklaus ignored the man. He quickly spread the separated skin open with his fingers, exposing the thin tissue beneath.

"I need more light! Come closer!" he demanded.

The men stretched their arms forward as far as they would go, but refused to move their feet. They were both equally mesmerized and terrified by the surgeon's actions.

Nicklaus moved his head to one side to allow more of the light to enter his field of view, and then applied the blade again. He cut inside his previous incision, more slowly this time. The tissue popped open and there was a sudden release of blood and fluid from inside the punctured uterus. Then, quite surprisingly, a skinny purple foot and leg popped out of the cut. The leg immediately began to move. The child was kicking!

"Jesus, Mary, and Joseph!" exclaimed Captain Hawk. Imitating Mr. Clark, he, too, made the sign of the cross on his chest, only much more slowly and fearfully.

Nicklaus finished the cut. It was an eight-inch incision, which lay open the dead girl's uterus. He tossed his knife into the instrument pan, quickly pulled the incision open, and grabbed the baby's leg. He felt inside for the other leg. Finding it quickly, he instantly and effort-lessly pulled the child from the womb. He lay the baby on its side on its mother's flattened belly.

It was a boy. His tiny, wrinkled body was covered with a pasty, white coating tinged with blood. His color was a slightly purplish-blue. A faint steam of humidity drifted upward from his moist, warm skin into the cold air of the cabin. The tiny fellow was jerking his arms and kicking his legs, but he was not breathing.

Nicklaus quickly inserted the forefinger of his left hand into the infant's mouth, scooping out the mucoid contents from his throat. He then picked up the child quite violently and held it upside-down, swatting it smartly on the behind. The baby coughed and gagged, then unleashed a wailing cry.

"Quickly, *Mutter*! We need wraps!"

He unceremoniously flopped the howling, purple-faced baby onto his dead mother's chest and then quickly tied a piece of string around the umbilical cord about an inch from the little one's belly. He retrieved his bistoury knife again and cut the cord just as Katharina arrived with a stack of dry cloths.

His mother took the child and gently wiped the various substances from his skin. He wailed even louder. Katharina chuckled with joy. The boy's color was beginning to change to a healthier-looking pink. The boy was strong, and so very alive! She quickly wrapped the baby snugly in swaddling cloths. She held him against her chest and spoke soothingly in her native tongue.

"What shall we do with him, *Mutter*?"

Katharina responded resolutely, "We shall give him to *Frau* Mahler. The poor wretch still has milk. Indeed, her breasts are swollen and aching from it. This little one will help relieve both her pain in body and her pain in spirit. He is a tiny miracle, I tell you!" She stared at her son with admiration. "And it is all because of you, Nicklaus. I have never seen anything so amazing as what I have witnessed on this night. You are a healer, my boy ... an instrument of God, Himself."

"Amen to that," mumbled Captain Hawk from across the room.

Nicklaus cut a disbelieving glance at the captain. The officer nodded and grudgingly showed the doctor a grim smile of admiration.

"Mr. Clark will go and fetch Mrs. Mahler forthwith. Whilst he is gone, I will gather a detail and get these bodies out of your infirmary." He glanced toward the dead mother, still lying blood-soaked on top of the crate. "If you will prepare and wrap the young woman, we will bury her for you, as well. Whenever you are ready, Doctor."

Nicklaus returned the captain's nod. "Thank you, Captain Hawk. *Mutter* and I will see to it."

The captain and his assistant turned and trudged toward the doorway of the hold. A wave of seawater and rain swept through the threshold when they opened the door. They quickly stepped out into the storm and then wrestled the heavy portal closed behind them.

~

Six Days Later

THE *BETSEY* LAY at anchor in the Delaware River. She was one hundred yards off-shore, directly across from the immigrants' quarantine hospital. Captain Hawk and two of his sailors paddled their small launch toward the hospital's dock. Three men stood on that dock, awaiting their arrival. Dr. Schell was the only other passenger in the launch. He stared wistfully toward the north at the distant shroud of smoke that hung low over the treetops. It was the haze from the morning fires of Philadelphia. The sun had been up for less than an hour.

A high-pitched, educated British voice invaded his peaceful thoughts. The voice spoke with confidence and authority. "Hold your position! Proceed no further! I am Dr. Henry Ward, chief inspector and administrator of this facility. What vessel is this?"

The captain and his men used their paddles to bring the boat to something of a stop. The tiny craft drifted gently in the creeping flow of the river. "The *Betsey*, out of Rotterdam and Cowes," Captain Hawk responded.

"Ah! I thought that was you, Mr. Hawk. But, that layer of filth you're wearing makes you a bit unrecognizable!" He chuckled at his pitiful effort at jest. "Didn't Dr. Holbrook make the voyage with you?"

"He did, indeed, sir."

"And where might that old scoundrel be? We have much reacquainting to do. Though, I shall, no doubt, have to hide my supply of rum before he comes ashore."

"He is somewhere on the bottom of the cold sea, sir," Hawk replied matter-of-factly. "Dr. Holbrook died of fever only a couple of weeks out of Cowes."

There was an awkward silence. Dr. Ward's face turned downcast.

"How unfortunate. So, am I to assume that you have had a difficult voyage?"

The captain was growing impatient. "Indeed, we have, sir. And if you would be so kind as to allow us to make landing, we can give our report and bring this nightmare to an end." He pointed southward. "The current is beginning to takes us back downstream."

The physician nodded. "Very well. Is there any illness, at all, on board your launch?"

"Everyone on board this rowboat is perfectly healthy," Nicklaus responded curtly.

Dr. Ward was clearly surprised by the sound of Nicklaus' distinctly German voice. "And, who might you be, sir?"

"I am Dr. Nicklaus Schell, a native of the village of Ibersheim, on the Rhine."

"Are you engaged by the naval service?"

"No, Doctor. I am merely a passenger. My skills were required after the death of the ship's surgeon."

"How fortuitous, indeed. And where, may I ask, did you take your medical training, sir?"

"At the University in Leiden."

"Leiden? In Holland? How exemplary! Oh, I would love to visit Amsterdam again someday! I have such fond memories!"

"I do not care for that particular city, myself," remarked Nicklaus matter-of-factly.

"To each his own, I suppose." The doctor onshore sniffed arrogantly. His face betrayed a measure of incredulity. "I hear that Leiden is a fine medical school. That would seem to be quite a journey for you to make from the Palatinate in Germany, *Herr* Schell."

Nicklaus exhaled, somewhat exasperated. "It is only a few days by river boat, I assure you. I have made the voyage many times. May we make our approach, Doctor?"

"Of course! Of course! Make your landing. I shall receive your full report."

Captain Hawk and his men swiftly guided the launch toward the dock. One of the men tossed a line to a silent dock hand, who expertly tied the craft to a large piling.

Hawk and his men clamored out of the craft quickly. Nicklaus was the last one to step onto the dock. The sensation of the solid, unmoving structure was disconcerting. He had been at sea for so many weeks that his body had grown accustomed to the constant motion beneath his feet. His knees buckled beneath him, but Captain Hawk quickly grabbed him by the arm.

"Steady, there, Dr. Schell. You'll need a short while to get your land legs about you. Just hold on to me or one of the lads until we can get you to a chair."

Nicklaus nodded his thanks.

"Please follow me," invited Dr. Ward. "I will examine each of you, first, and then receive your report."

The exhausted travelers followed the doctor and soon stepped off of the small dock. They trudged along a dusty, weed-infested path that led toward a rather unimpressive brick building.

THE RED-FACED Dr. Ward jubilantly slapped his hand on the heavy table. "Is this true? Surely you jest!"

Captain Hawk shook his head and raised his eyebrows as a testimony of his sincerity.

Dr. Ward stared at Nicklaus in unexpected admiration. "How extraordinary! You actually delivered a caesarian birth on a dead female, lying on top of a shipping crate, and in the midst of an Atlantic gale?"

Nicklaus shrugged and nodded. He had little desire to regale in the memories of the voyage ... especially that particular event. In his heart, there was nothing to celebrate or memorialize. It was a hellish journey, and he was anxious to put the memory of it all behind him.

Captain Hawk chimed in, "I don't know what you call it, but Dr. Schell cut that dead lassie's belly open and pulled the little fellow right out by the legs, big as you please! He whacked the boy a time or two, and soon he went right to wailin'! Brought tears to this old sailor's eyes, I promise ya' that!"

Dr. Ward shook his head in disbelief. "And the baby is well?"

Nicklaus nodded. "There was another woman who had lost her baby, and her husband, only a couple of days before. She still had milk. She has taken the little one as her own."

The English physician smiled broadly and raised his glass of rum. "A toast then ... to Dr. Nicklaus Schell! Our miracle-worker of the Atlantic!"

"Here! Here!" affirmed Captain Hawk and his men. They each took an enthusiastic drink.

Nicklaus grinned emptily and took only a tiny sip from his glass. He sighed. "Are we finished here, Doctor? I am anxious to get my mother and my sick patients ashore."

"Indeed, indeed. I am anxious to meet this amazing woman," Ward responded. He reached out his hand to shake with Nicklaus. "You did a most admirable job, considering the circumstances." He smiled warmly. "I will instruct my people to prepare for the arrival of your passengers. You will be quarantined here for a minimum of two weeks, perhaps more, depending upon the diseases that present."

"What about the pox?" inquired Nicklaus.

"We shall get everyone else ashore first and then examine the men of whom you have spoken. But, if they have not yet erupted with the bloody pustules, I sincerely doubt that they are infected with the pox. Regardless, we have a special building for just such cases. They may have to remain in our facility a bit longer."

Captain Hawk cleared his throat. "I shall be anxious to get these folk to Philadelphia, sir. I have to collect my payments."

"Indeed," mumbled the doctor. "As I am well aware. Rest assured, there is an endless market for the indentured ones there, Mr. Hawk.

There have been no other ships for the past three weeks. You will have an enthusiastic chorus of clients awaiting you. Meanwhile, though, whilst I am bringing your cargo back to a state of health, I shall task you and your crew with the cleansing of your ship from all filth and disease. From the sound of it, you have much work to do. I shall not release a single soul to the docks in Philadelphia until your ship passes my personal inspection. Do I make myself clear?"

Captain Hawk nodded grudgingly. "We shall get to work immediately. I will need some help."

"There are ample workmen here on my staff. They are accustomed to such tasks. But, you shall have to reimburse them for their labors. It is not my responsibility to pay for the cleaning of your ship."

Again, Captain Hawk nodded.

Nicklaus quickly rose to his feet. "Thank you, Dr. Ward. We shall get to work immediately. The day grows short."

"No ... thank you, Dr. Schell. You are a surgeon *par excellence*. In fact, once we get all your patients ashore and in quarters, I should like to discuss a position with you. I could use a physician with your skills."

"A position? Here?" Nicklaus asked in disbelief.

"Yes, here in this facility. You could help me take care of your immigrant countrymen and become adjusted to life in America. Philadelphia is only a short carriage ride away. It is a very good and sincere offer, I assure you."

Nicklaus stared in disbelief. "I never thought I would find such opportunity, especially right off of the boat." He shook his head. "But, before I even ponder such a position, I must consider my mother's well-being and desires."

Dr. Ward grinned broadly. "I should like to hire your mother, as well. We have a great need for skilled nurses and aides. From the sound of it, she will likely be in charge of this place in a week or two." He chuckled lightly. The sailors, thinking the notion humorous, joined with him in laughter.

Nicklaus' face became downcast. "But, there is the matter of our passage ... I owe payment to Captain Hawk ..."

Dr. Ward waved his hand reassuringly. "Do not waste another moment of worry about that. I shall be honored to pay passage for both you and your mother. We will consider all of that this evening as we negotiate the terms of your contract."

Nicklaus gulped in disbelief. "I do not know what to say, Dr. Ward."

The Englishman patted him on the shoulder. "No words are necessary. And please, Nicklaus ... call me Henry." He patted his shoulder again, a little more enthusiastically. "Now, away with you all! You have work to do. Nicklaus, we shall discuss everything over dinner this evening. Please bring your lovely mother. Seven o'clock, at my residence." He paused and grimaced slightly. "But, please find a bath before you come."

Nicklaus grinned and nodded. "I shall do so, and I shall see you at seven. Thank you, sir."

The sailors all drained their glasses, slapped them happily on the table, and then quickly departed the office. They returned their hats to their heads as they stepped outside the door. Nicklaus followed. The slightly-drunken entourage trudged carefully back down the path toward the dock.

"I cannot believe that just happened," Nicklaus mumbled in disbelief.

Captain Hawk threw back his head and chuckled merrily. "Welcome to America, Dr. Schell!"

4

INTERSECTION

December 16, 1774
City Tavern - Philadelphia

"Raise your glass, Nicklaus! 'Tis a night to drink to liberty!" declared Dr. Benjamin Rush. The middle-aged doctor stood to his feet, lifted his glass of port high into the air, and exclaimed, "To our oppressed brothers in Boston!"

The room erupted with shouts and cheers. Men lifted their glasses and tankards high, then drank enthusiastically. Philadelphia's City Tavern was filled to overflowing, and the clientele seemed to be a bit more rowdy than usual. It was neither the frigid air nor the hot, satisfying food that lured the throng of men into the warm, smoky tavern on this winter's night. Something else was afoot. Dr. Nicklaus Schell was growing accustomed to the nightly tavern discussions of taxes, liberty, rebellion, and war. But, there was something different about this particular evening. He did not quite know what to think about all of the raucous, unrestrained merrymaking.

Nicklaus offered no verbal sentiments in response to the good doctor's toast. He did not wish to offend his new supervisor and colleague. He merely smiled, somewhat embarrassed, at the slightly inebriated state of his mentor, and then took a humble sip from his own glass. He savored the delicious burn of the port. It was sweet, with just a hint of a nutty, caramel flavor. Nicklaus preferred slowly enjoying the aroma and taste of the fine wine. He considered guzzling such an expensive beverage in quick and copious gulps to be quite foolish, indeed.

The man across the table from Nicklaus, a very dignified-looking gentleman by the name of Charles Thomson, drained his own twisted-stem wine glass and then tossed the empty vessel into the nearby fireplace. The fragile glass shattered and tumbled into the scorching coals, releasing a brief wave of sparks. He stared, mesmerized by the glowing coals and yellow-orange flames of the dancing fire.

The fellow slowly shifted his gaze from the fireplace to the face of Dr. Nicklaus Schell. He had a very long, distinguished, and pointed nose. His wig was perfectly powdered and styled with a single curl above the ears on each side. He had the appearance and the attitude of a very powerful, influential man. He had piercing eyes. The reflection of the flames in those eyes made them resemble the deep crimson color of his coat. His devilish stare and red eyes were disconcerting, to say the least. Nicklaus shifted nervously in his seat. He did not know this man. He was not certain that he liked this man.

The gentleman declared in a slightly Irish-sounding brogue, "Ben, your friend does not seem to be reveling with us in our celebrations tonight. Might we have one of King George's loyal amongst us?"

Dr. Rush chuckled. "Charles, I can assure you that young Dr. Schell is no agent of King George. He is a Dutch-trained physician from the Rhineland-Palatinate, and a citizen of these Colonies for nigh on ..." He glanced at Nicklaus. "How long has it been, young man?"

Dr. Rush's unexpected query caught Nicklaus mid-drink, and with a mouthful of wine. He swallowed quickly, coughed, and then responded, "Six years."

"Yes! Six years off of the boat, and freshly released from a five-year medical indenture under Dr. Henry Ward. I am quite pleased to have him on our staff at the Pennsylvania Hospital. His interest and expertise in midwifery are much-needed in our facility."

"Henry Ward, you say? The master of the immigrant hospital out on that horrid island?" Thomson's left eyebrow raised in suspicion. "Dr. Ward is one of the King's men, for certain." The man leaned toward Dr. Rush and growled, "Are you positive about this man's politics, Ben?"

Nicklaus declared, "I have no politics to speak of, Mr. Thomson."

The man grunted. "Apolitical, eh? Most unlikely. Especially in times such as these."

Nicklaus stared confidently at the man. "Apolitical would, indeed, be a good word to describe me at this particular stage of my life. I have had little time for such things. Since I could not afford my own passage to America, I spent five years in servitude, practicing medicine amongst the newly-arriving immigrants. I rarely traveled into the city during that time. Since my employment under Dr. Rush at the Pennsylvania Hospital last month, I have been consumed entirely with my work and learning my new position."

"And he came to us with his very capable mother in tow!" Dr. Rush added. "That woman is a wonder, I tell you. A real firebrand, and quite skilled in patient care. If young Nicklaus ever decides to leave us, I may have to retain his mother." The kindly doctor winked at his young colleague.

Mr. Thomson continued to glare at Nicklaus with a searching stare. "Then, you bear no allegiance to King George, nor his uncle, Frederick II of Hesse-Kassel?"

Nicklaus chuckled lightly. "Hesse-Kassel? Not likely. That state is a distant journey from my native lands, Mr. Thomson. You can rest assured of that. I can barely understand their coarse, unpleasant dialect. No, I have no allegiances to Prince Frederick. And my only fidelity to King George, and sole mention of his name, for that matter, was in the wording of the oath that I swore before the magistrate when I arrived six years ago. As I said before, I have no significant political leanings, sir. I am a physician, and live only to serve my fellow man."

"As do we all, Dr. Schell." Dr. Rush patted his back affectionately. "As do we all." He winked at Mr. Thomson. "Perhaps, Charles, we can talk a little treason, and sway young Dr. Schell in our direction?"

Charles Thomson grunted. "Perhaps. We shall see."

Nicklaus, somewhat confused and anxious to change the subject, inquired, "So, what is *your* profession, Mr. Thomson?"

"Oh, I have many professions and interests, Dr. Schell. I am a writer, foremost. I have authored many essays and pamphlets. I work regularly as a tutor at the prestigious Philadelphia Academy. Lately, however, I have made use of my literacy in serving as a governmental secretary."

"Governmental secretary?" Nicklaus echoed. "What does that entail?"

Thomson nodded mischievously to the bar wench as she placed a fresh glass and another bottle of port on their table. The young girl scurried away before receiving any unwanted attention from her customer. Thomson grabbed the bottle and clumsily poured his glass full, spilling some of the tangy wine on the crusty tablecloth.

"My duties are quite ordinary, Dr. Schell. I record minutes, make notes on debates, and perform whatever other duties are assigned to me by the president."

"President?" Nicklaus asked, confused.

"He is speaking of the President of the Continental Congress, Nicklaus. A fellow from Boston by the name of John Hancock," explained Dr. Rush.

"I have heard of this group," Nicklaus declared. "It is comprised of delegates from all of the Colonies, correct?"

Dr. Rush nodded. "That is correct. We formed our Congress to address our grievances to the King, and to enable better governing and communication throughout the Colonies. I serve as a delegate from Pennsylvania. And Mr. Thomson is being quite modest in describing his duties. He is our distinguished secretary, record-keeper, negotiator, and, on occasion, our arbiter during our numerous enthusiastic disputes. Our body met in September and October and will, no doubt, convene again in the coming months."

Dr. Rush gulped more wine, and then reached for the newly-arrived bottle.

"It all sounds very practical and quite appropriate," Nicklaus declared, taking another sip of his tasty port. "Though I have no experiences beyond Philadelphia, I am told that life is quite different in the other Colonies and regions, especially on the frontier. Such a Congress would seem to be a wise approach to a common governance."

Dr. Rush nodded enthusiastically. "That is exactly the point, Nicklaus. We are actually seeking to build a system of self-governance. Common sense dictates that a Congress in these United Colonies is better suited to govern its people than a foreign King and an unknowing, unconnected Parliament somewhere across the distant sea."

Nicklaus raised an eyebrow at Dr. Rush's last statement. Though he knew little of politics, he fully understood the nature of a deeply treasonous statement. He offered a comment, formulated as a question. "And I suppose that King George might take issue with such a gathering?"

"We shall see," declared Mr. Thomson. "We closed the Congress at the end of October and sent our correspondence to the King immediately after. We included some very strongly-worded petitions of our various redresses to the unwise policies of taxation and oppression exacted upon the Colonies over the past decade. Obviously, there has not been enough time to receive any a response. Hopefully, we will hear something in the spring of next year."

"Was that the full extent of the actions of the Congress?" Nicklaus inquired.

Dr. Rush responded, "No! Not at all! We made some very strong economic and military decisions. We created the Continental Association, which is a general agreement amongst the Colonies to boycott goods from Great Britain."

"And then there was our military declaration," added Mr. Thomson.

"What was that?" asked Nicklaus, somewhat shocked at the mention of military matters.

Thomson responded. "All of the other Colonies pledged to support Massachusetts if it is attacked."

A moment of silence descended upon the table as the men pondered the solemn topics of their conversation. Each man sipped his wine and stared into the fire.

Nicklaus' mind reeled a bit. The notion of a British attack upon one of its own colonies caused a chill to creep down his spine. He could scarcely imagine such a prospect. Indeed, it was unthinkable that the English military might take up arms against its own people. He had heard many stories about Boston and the British army that occupied the city. He had heard about atrocities, the removal of people from their homes, rapes, and murders at the hands of British soldiers. But, Boston was a distant, unknown city, and far outside the realm of Nicklaus' thoughts or concerns. Frankly, he did not understand the extent or implications of Colonial politics.

Nicklaus broke the silence. "Those seem like very strong actions, indeed, especially since they were taken by an unsanctioned legislature. What if King George does not appreciate your efforts? Indeed, what if they meet with his stern disapproval?"

Nicklaus stared at Mr. Thomson, eager to hear his answer. The man's face reddened and formed into a bit of a scowl. He offered no response.

"We shall cross that bridge when we come to it," Dr. Rush answered for him. "But ... enough of this talk of Congresses and Kings. This is a night for celebration and remembrance." Once again, he stood and raised his glass. "To liberty, and to salty tea!"

The room exploded in a huge cheer. Men drained their tankards and glasses. Somewhere across the room, a violin launched into a familiar tune. The men began to sing a distinctly Irish song known as, "*The Parting Glass.*"

Nicklaus leaned toward Dr. Rush to confirm the wording of his toast. "Salty tea?"

"Yes, my young friend. Salty tea! This night marks the one-year anniversary of a little event down in Boston. It was quite a party, I assure you. And, somehow, three hundred and forty-two chests full of the King's highly taxed tea wound up floating in Boston Harbor." He winked.

Nicklaus suddenly realized the event to which Dr. Rush was referring. He had read about it in the Gazette the previous winter.

"But, I thought that attack was perpetrated by natives."

Both Dr. Rush and Charles Thomson chuckled gaily as they raised their glasses to one another.

"No, Nicklaus. Those were not natives. They were only dressed as such. They were friends of ours, out to teach the King a lesson in economics."

Nicklaus stared at Dr. Rush, surprised and somewhat confused.

Charles Thomson picked up the half-empty bottle of port, leaned across the table, and topped off Nicklaus' glass. "Dr. Schell, Ben and I are participants in a small but distinguished group of Patriots who share a common cause of justice in these Colonies. Perhaps we might tell you about it."

Dr. Rush placed his hand cautiously on Nicklaus' knee. "Dr. Schell, have you ever heard of an organization called the Sons of Liberty?"

February 18, 1775
Upper Milford Township - Northampton County, Pennsylvania

IT WAS GOING to be a brilliant, sunny day. The air was crisp and cold. The clear, purple-pink sky of dawn was cloudless. There was not even a hint of snow or sleet. It was a perfect day for a quick expedition into Philadelphia.

The Yeisleys were flush with bolts of linen, wool cloth, and cases of thread. Their inventory was substantial. They had been busy on their looms for the past three months. Such was the life of a weaving family in winter. But, as the frigid weather lingered on, they were becoming somewhat strapped for cash. Nicklaus and his son, Michael, needed to make a quick sale to carry the business through until springtime, which was still at least six or eight weeks away.

"Why must you go, Papa?" whined five-year-old Elizabeth Yeisley. "I do not want you to go!"

The heartbroken little girl stood in the open doorway of the family cottage, wrapped snugly in her wool cloak and clutching her ticking-cloth doll close beneath her chin. There was a hint of a tear glistening in the corner of her left eye. Three-year-old Mary stood silently at her side.

George Yeisley chuckled at the little girl's impassioned plea. He tossed a loose rope to his big brother and the two men busied themselves securing the load. Michael cut a quick glance at his daughters. The kitchen fireplace glowed orange and gold behind them, silhouetting them in the warm light. Their appearance was angelic. He longed to step back into that warm room and spend his entire Saturday playing with his little girls. But, alas, he could not. He had work to accomplish, and goods that had to be sold. He pulled the rope tightly across the substantial load of textiles that lay safely covered in his wagon beneath a waterproof canvas.

"That should do it," George declared.

Michael nodded. He turned and trudged through the shallow, partially melted snow toward the door. He knelt in the threshold. His daughters melted into his embrace.

Again, Elizabeth begged, "Please stay home, Papa! You do not have to go!"

Michael sighed. "Elizabeth, we talked about this last night. I must go with Uncle George to Philadelphia to sell our goods at the market. I will be home on Wednesday."

The little girl whimpered, "That is forever, Papa! You do not have to go. Uncle George is big. He can go by himself."

Magdalena Yeisley appeared suddenly from inside the kitchen. She was holding an iron spatula in her right hand and had her youngest daughter, nine-month-old Catherine, pinned precariously against her hip with her left hand. Her belly, greatly swollen with child number four, pressed her linen pinner apron upward and outward.

She wagged the spatula threateningly and declared, "What a

horribly selfish thing to say, Elizabeth Yeisley! Do you sincerely wish for your Uncle George to make the journey to Philadelphia all by himself? And would you have him do so in the dead of winter?"

The little girl grumbled unashamedly, "Yes." She then buried her head in her father's shoulder and wept.

Magdalena groaned in frustration. "Michael Yeisley, do something with your child!"

Laughter erupted from deep inside the kitchen. Magdalena's father, Heinrich Mueller, stepped into the doorway behind his daughter. He was smiling ear-to-ear. A glistening dab of butter decorated his upper lip. He was holding a half-eaten *Brötchen* roll, smothered with butter and blueberry jam, in his right hand, and a steaming cup of tea in his left.

The wise grandfather intervened. "Now, now, *mein Mauszähnchen!* You must cease this whining! You know that your father has his work to do. He will be back in a few days. Besides, I need some help with the chickens and the geese this morning. Will you be my assistant today? You would like to help your tired old *Opa, ja?* I will let you collect all of the eggs."

The child sniffed and nodded ever-so-slightly.

"*Gut. Komm bitte rein.* It is too cold to be outside without your heavy coat. Kiss your papa, and allow him be on his way."

The heartbroken little girl wrapped her arms around her father's neck and hugged him with a powerful squeeze. Michael returned the strong embrace.

"Thank you for that good hug, Elizabeth. Now, obey your *Opa* and go inside. I need to talk to Mama."

She hugged him again. "*Ich liebe dich, Papa.*"

"I love you, too, my little Elli. You must obey your mama and *Opa* whilst I am gone."

The child pulled back from the hug, touched her papa's face lovingly with her tiny hand, smiled and nodded, then turned and darted back inside the warm house. Michael stood upright as Magdalena stepped forward and occupied the little girl's place.

"My turn, now?" she inquired somewhat sarcastically, though smiling warmly.

"It is always your turn, *mein Liebling*. This home is full of girls, but you are always the first for me."

Michael pulled her close and kissed her warmly on the lips. She smelled like the bread that she was baking. Her lips tasted sweet. Her body was warm. Michael placed his hand on her swollen belly.

"Perhaps you can bring a little bit of change to our home soon? A boy would be nice. I need a fellow member of my species to help me endure the raging female emotions and constant complaining in this household. I need someone who might actually enjoy a little silence and peace with me."

Magdalena playfully pushed him away from the embrace. "You have Papa to keep you company. And you can visit George at any time. He only lives next door." She grinned and looked over Michael's shoulder at his younger brother, locking eyes with the young man. "George, I would appreciate it if you would return my husband to me, unharmed, and in a timely manner. We need him around here."

George lifted and tipped his straw hat. "*Ja, Frau* Yeisley."

She kissed her husband again ... slowly and deeply ... then leaned back and stared into his deep blue eyes.

"Come back home to me, Michael Yeisley."

He grinned and then kissed her lightly on the nose. "I shall always return to you, Magdalena Yeisley."

❧

Near Dusk – The Next Day
Peter Matson's Ford on the Schuylkill River

"THIS IS NOT what I was expecting," George declared, staring dazed at the swollen Schuylkill.

Michael did not respond. Instead, he scrutinized the swiftly-moving water. His soul was foul with impatience and disappointment.

Thus far, nothing had gone as expected on their journey to Philadelphia. They had to stop in Plymouth on the previous afternoon to seek repairs for a cracked wheel hub. The front left wheel would not make it all the way to Philadelphia. The hub had to be replaced.

The Quakers in Plymouth Township were most friendly and very helpful, but they needed considerable time to make the repair. It required an overnight stay. The wheelwright offered them a hot meal and shelter in his barn, which Michael and George gladly accepted.

An unexpected weather front struck during the night, dumping four inches of fresh, wet snow on the Pennsylvania landscape. Michael knew that the precipitation would make their travels more difficult, especially once they reached the heavily-traveled Bethlehem Turnpike. They departed shortly before noon with a brand-new wheel hub and their bellies full of smoked sausage sandwiches, courtesy of the wheelwright's generous wife.

They made good time for the first two hours. But, as expected, the busy Bethlehem Turnpike was a quagmire of thick, sticky mud. Most wagoners seemed to be abandoning the route for the less-traveled Butler Pike that led southwest toward Peter Matson's ford.

The brothers followed their lead and opted for the less-traveled road. They altered their journey toward the southwest. Things had been going well until late afternoon, when a dark gray cloud bank rolled in and the temperature dropped considerably. Snow began to fall about two hours before dusk, but it was very different from the heavy, wet snow of the previous night. It was dry and fluffy. Temperatures had fallen well below freezing.

The Yeisley brothers could contend with winter's temperatures and snow easily enough, but the unusually high river was another proposition altogether. Michael sat stoically and considered his options. They could wait it out and try crossing the following day, but that would require them to re-trace their progress back three miles to the nearest tavern. With the unexpected inclement weather, none of the taverns in the area were likely to have empty beds or floor space.

George's voice interrupted his brother's thoughts. "What do you think, Michael? Do we cross here, or do we go back?"

Michael shook his head. "I am not certain."

"Well, we have to cross somewhere. It might as well be here. The river is not going to be lower upstream or down. And, besides, Matson's is the shallowest ford in the region. Our best opportunity to cross safely is right here." He paused and frowned. "But it does not look very safe, does it?"

Michael did not know how to respond. He was deathly afraid of the water. He always had been. He could not swim. He never had any desire to play in the ponds and creeks with the other children of his family. His mother often teased him for it, and proposed that his disdain for the water was rooted in his birth at sea.

Michael had absolutely no desire to cross this river, but he had little choice. There were no suitable fords or bridges for ten miles in either direction. Sundown was approaching rapidly. The snow was piling up quickly, and there was no way that they could make it into Philadelphia before dusk. They had to get across and find shelter for the evening.

"We must cross now," Michael declared resolutely. "If we turn around, we will be spending the night out in this snow." He nodded toward the river. "The water appears swift, but that is because it is so very shallow. Mr. Matson has placed deep layers of rock and planks at the crossing. I do not think that it is deep enough to enter the wagon."

George nodded. "Let us hope not. I will get in the back and watch over the cargo." He grinned. "I will let you know if my feet get wet."

Michael did not smile in response. He merely replied, "I hope you lined the bed well with those oilskins. We can ill afford to lose this load."

"Your precious linen is well-protected, big brother. But, I cannot guarantee its safety if you tip us over into the water."

Michael smiled thinly. "I shall endeavor to avoid such an outcome."

He snapped the reins and whistled shrilly at his horses. The wagon eased forward, moving very slowly. The animals were spooked by the water. They stepped gingerly into the current, but quickly gained confidence when they felt the smooth boards of the ford beneath their feet.

When they were half-way across the river, Michael called out, "How is it looking back there?"

George leaned over the side of the wagon on the upstream side. "The water is two or three inches below the wagon bed. It is good!"

A pulse of confidence surged through Michael. They were at the very deepest point in the ford. It appeared that they were going to make it, and keep their cargo dry. Again, he whistled loudly at the team. The animals responded by picking up the pace. Minutes later they neared the far bank.

"Almost there!" Michael announced to his brother. "We just have to get up the embankment. It is a bit steep, and the snow has drifted."

He was thrilled when the horses' feet touched the mud on the bank. The crossing was done, and their cargo was intact! The animals strained forward, digging their hooves deeply into the mud as they pulled the fully-loaded wagon up the hillside. Finally, the wagon cleared the water. The rig was in the dry. The deed was done!

Just as the wagon crested the embankment, there was a thunderous, cracking pop from beneath the rig. Somewhere beneath the wagon, a portion of the wooden structure had failed. The front left corner of the wagon dropped suddenly. The sound also spooked the horses, causing them to lurch forward with a tremendous jerk. They began to run, pulling the wagon forward, dragging it away from the river. The front left corner seemed to move even further downward. There was a scraping sound of wood against pebbles and stones.

George yelled excitedly from the rear of the wagon, "Whoa! Whoa! Whoa!"

Michael, already off-balance from the sudden leaning of the wagon, completely lost his footing when the horses broke into their clumsy gallop. He fell forward and to his left, tumbling from the seat of the rig. As he fell, he caught a glimpse of the wheel, which was turned outward and at a strange angle. He knew, in an instant, that the new hub had given way.

His final thought was one of anger at the Quakers for such a poor repair. Then, there was a loud, resounding thump. His face and head felt cold and numb ... then there was nothing. His entire world went dark.

~

February 24, 1775
Pennsylvania Hospital – Philadelphia

MICHAEL FELT THIRSTY. Parched. His head pounded with pain. He struggled to open his heavy eyelids. As he attempted to reach up with his left arm to feel his throbbing head, pain surged through that member, as well. He could not move the arm at all. It was immobilized.

He finally willed his eyes to open. He quickly discerned that he was lying on a cot. He stared, confused, at the stained, gray ceiling. It was an unfamiliar place. The room where he lay was bathed in light from many windows. It was daytime.

Michael struggled to lift his head, but his stiff neck resisted the movement. He slowly stretched his neck to the left. There was an empty cot beside him. He was in a very large room. Somewhere, beyond that empty cot, he heard voices.

He called out in a scorched, dry voice, "Help!" But, little sound came. He could not seem to coax a single utterance from his sore, dry throat. Again, he called, "Help!" But, he could barely hear his own voice.

He checked the movement of his right arm. He was relieved to find that it was still functional. He reached to his right and felt a wooden table. He tugged at the table and shifted his weight, attempting to sit up and get a better look at his surroundings. The table tilted and scooted across the floor. There was a very loud sound of shattering glass, followed by a splash of liquid onto the floor.

Suddenly and sternly, a female voice shouted, "*Mein Gott!* Just look at this mess! Just what I wanted to contend with today ... a floor full of piss!"

Michael turned his head to discern the source of the voice. He was quite shocked to hear such vulgarity emitted by a female. The declarant of the verbal consternation was a handsome older woman, clothed in a gray short gown and petticoat. She wore a light gray linen pinner apron over the top of her garments. A simple, white mob cap decorated her head. She was standing with both hands on her hips. The woman appeared to be quite displeased.

"*Herr* Yeisley, I would appreciate it if you would refrain from making such a mess of my ward! It is difficult enough, as it is, without the addition of shattered urine bowls."

But, almost instantly, her countenance transformed from displeasure to warmth.

"Welcome back, *Herr* Yeisley. It is good to finally meet you."

Michael mumbled, "Water ..." His voice remained scorched and almost silent.

"Yes, of course. You must be very thirsty." The woman darted toward a nearby table. As she walked, she called toward the far end of the room, "Inga! Bring towels and a mop! *Herr* Yeisley has shattered a full bourdaloue!" She scolded, "Perhaps cleaning this mess up will help you remember to empty them more often!"

She quickly poured several ounces of water from a stoneware pitcher into a tin cup. She scurried back to his bed, careful to avoid the puddle of stale urine in the floor. She helped him to sit upright, then held the cup up to his dry, cracked lips. Michael drained the refreshing liquid voraciously.

"Where am I? What happened to me?" he moaned.

She responded reassuringly, "You are at the Pennsylvania Hospital in Philadelphia. You were in an accident several miles north of town. But, you are in good hands. You are young and strong and well on the mend."

"Who are you?" he asked, still confused.

"I am Katharina Schell, the matron in charge of this ward. My son, Nicklaus, is the surgeon who has been caring for you since your arrival."

"How long have I been here?"

She fluffed his flattened pillow and replied, "Four days."

"Four days?" Michael shrieked, almost gagging. "How? Why?"

"You struck your head, *Herr* Yeisley. It was a powerful blow. My son will explain everything to you."

A noisy young girl in stained, threadbare clothes appeared at Michael's bedside. She was lugging a very old, stained mop and a wooden piggin full of steaming water. She attacked the smelly puddle beside Michael's bed. She intentionally avoided eye contact with both the head nurse and her patient.

Michael continued his questioning. "I cannot seem to move my left arm. What happened to it?"

"The bone was broken during your fall. Again, my son will tell you all about your various injuries as soon as he returns."

Michael suddenly remembered his brother. He glanced around the room, and then demanded, "Where is my brother, George?"

Mrs. Schell smiled. "Your brother is well. He has returned home to bear the news of your accident to your wife and daughters. He did not want your family to worry unnecessarily about you. He should return in a couple of days."

"You seem to know much about me," Michael observed.

"Young George was quite the conversationalist."

Michael was surprised by such a description of his brother. George barely spoke, at all, during the normal course of life back home.

Michael quipped, "That does not sound like my brother. Are you certain we are talking about the same fellow?" He grinned.

"He was simply worried about you. He remained at your side for the first day and a half. The poor lad would scarcely even eat. We finally convinced him to take care of his affairs and then return home."

"So, then, he sold our goods? He transacted our business?"

She nodded. "I believe so. Though, I have no knowledge of the details, of course."

The sound of heavy footsteps invaded their conversation. A young man who appeared to be only a few years older than Michael arrived at the foot of his bed. He was dressed in an immaculate charcoal-gray coat, with matching breeches. A clean, brilliantly white shirt peeked out from the collar of his coat, and perfectly matched his white stockings. His sandy blonde hair was pulled back into a braided queue, and he sported two large, fancy curls above each ear. He was most distinguished and handsome. Upon the man's arrival, the cleaning girl quickly finished her work, grabbed her mop and bucket, and scurried away.

The fellow seemed pleasant enough, but his face appeared tainted with anxiety. He nodded to Michael as he examined a paper in his hand. "*Herr* Yeisley, it is good to see that you have awakened. I am Dr. Nicklaus Schell. I have been tending to your care since your unfortunate arrival here. I see that you have met my mother."

The doctor had an accent that seemed very familiar to Michael. It was hauntingly similar to his father's. Michael assumed that he was from the Rhineland, or from very close by.

"Yes, Doctor. She has been most kind and patient with me."

The doctor grinned, amused. "If she were only the same in all of her interactions with me."

Katharina slapped her son playfully on the arm. "That will be enough of your insolence, Doctor. You may be the surgeon in this ward, but everyone knows who truly runs the place." She winked playfully at Michael.

Dr. Schell's eyes opened wide with amusement. "Indeed." He turned his attention to Michael. "I assume that *Mutter* told you about your injuries."

"Only a little. She deferred to you to explain the details."

"Very well." He stepped forward and took a small looking glass from his pocket as he leaned toward Michael's head. He used the mirrored glass to examine Michael's eyes. "Do you remember what happened to you?"

"I remember something breaking on the wagon and tumbling off of the seat. But, that is all."

The doctor nodded. "I am pleased that you remember even that much detail. You landed on the very top of your head on the stones of the embankment. You have a large lump on your skull. I have been quite concerned about the possibility of injury to your brain. But, it seems that your body has repaired itself well, all things considered. You are young and strong. No procedures of blood-letting or purging seemed necessary. You have had no fevers or signs of other illness. It appears that all you truly needed was an extended period of sleep. I daresay you should be well enough to travel home in a couple of days."

"And my arm?" Michael asked.

"I believe the bone was broken as a result of the fall. I set the arm nice and straight and then wrapped it tightly. You will need to keep it wrapped thusly and immobilized for many weeks. I recommend that you seek a local surgeon upon your return home who can help you continue care for the broken bone."

"But, Doctor, I am a weaver by trade. How can I do my job with my arm tied up like this?"

"You cannot," declared the doctor matter-of-factly. "At least, you will be unable to perform the operation of a loom, or anything else that requires the use of both of your hands. You shall have to make yourself useful to your business in other ways ... for a couple of months, at least. However, I am quite confident that you should be healthy and able to resume your normal activities by the summer."

Michael's face became downcast.

"Do not fret your outcome, *Herr* Yeisley," Dr. Schell encouraged him. "You could have died beside that river. A few months of limited activity is a small price to pay, indeed."

"'Tis true, *Herr* Yeisley," Katharina confirmed. "You must count it a blessing that you survived such a treacherous fall."

Michael nodded. "*Danke, Frau* Schell."

She grinned. "*Bitte.*"

The doctor extended his hand toward Michael. "Well, if I have answered all of your questions satisfactorily, *Herr* Yeisley, I will take my leave. I have other patients in the north hall who require my attention."

"*Danke*, Dr. Schell. I am in your debt. But, I must confess ... I do not care for physicians or hospitals. I hope that I shall never be in need of your services again."

Nicklaus chuckled and pumped Michael's hand with a vigorous handshake. "Such is the nature of my business, *Herr* Yeisley. Perhaps, the next time we meet, it will be under different and better circumstances."

"I certainly hope so," Michael agreed.

Katharina interrupted the parting handshake. "What are the orders for this patient, Doctor?"

"Keep the arm bound tightly. Check his scalp for any signs of swelling. I do not believe that a trepanning procedure will be necessary. But, if unexpected expansion of his head presents itself, please inform me immediately. And please see to it that *Herr* Yeisley has something to eat. Nothing heavy. Some soup or stew ... and some hot tea with sugar. I want him to remain here for two more days. You may release him on Saturday, unless he exhibits any further complications."

"Yes, Doctor. I shall attend to his every need."

Dr. Schell leaned toward his mother and kissed her affectionately on the cheek. "*Mutter*, I shall see you at supper. I am looking forward to your *Hasenpfeffer und Kartoffelkloesse* this evening."

She pinched his cheek. "It shall be waiting for you when you get home."

He turned once more and nodded to Michael. "*Auf Wiedersehen, Herr* Yeisley."

"*Auf Wiedersehen*, Dr. Schell."

As the young doctor turned and strode confidently toward the door, Michael wondered if their paths would ever cross again.

5

BUNKER HILL

May 25, 1775 - Philadelphia

"But, Nicklaus! I simply do not understand!" Katharina wailed at her son. "You have a position here, and many responsibilities. You have absolutely no business going to Boston!"

Dr. Nicklaus Schell continued placing his shirts and stockings inside his large leather portmanteau. He did not respond. He refused to make eye contact with his mother. He continued to focus upon the task of packing his clothing and belongings.

"I will not allow you to simply ignore me in this manner, Nicklaus. You owe me more respect than that."

He continued his work in silence. Moments later, Nicklaus heard a disturbing *whack* and felt a sudden, numbing blow to the back of his head. He reached his right hand upward, toward the wounded spot on his skull, and just as he was about to turn around, felt another resounding blow across his knuckles.

Nicklaus shouted, *"Verdammt, Mutter!"*

He spun around and faced his mother. The diminutive woman held one of his leather shoes menacingly in her right hand. Her face was beet-red. Tears crept down both of her cheeks.

"Do I have your attention now, boy? I will not be ignored!"

Nicklaus was stunned. The blow to his head had been slight. He was not injured significantly. What confused him was the fact that his mother had actually struck him in violence. She had never done so before. Indeed, he could not recall receiving a single spanking from her during his childhood. Physical discipline had never been a part of her relationship with her son, or her philosophy of parenting.

Nicklaus rubbed the tender spot on the back of his head and stared in disbelief at his mother. The longer he gazed, the more amusing the spectacle of the tiny, shoe-wielding woman appeared to him. He could not control his urge to smile. Soon, his smile yielded to a chuckle.

"Really, *Mutter* ... you look ridiculous!" He pointed toward the shoe. "Do you have further intentions with that deadly weapon?"

She wailed, "Oh, Nicklaus!" She tossed the shoe onto the floor and tumbled, weeping, into her son's arms. Nicklaus spoke soothingly and attempted to calm her. He turned his body slightly and nudged his bag aside. He authoritatively sat his mother on the bed, then knelt on the floor in front of her.

"*Bitte, Mutter*. There is no need for all of this. I shall return in a matter of weeks."

"But, there is danger in Boston! The entire colony of Massachusetts seems hell-bent on starting a war!"

"I am not going there to take part in any war. I am merely going as an observer. I have been charged to study the hospitals and medical conditions associated with the armies and militias that surround the city. The Congress recently voted to establish a Continental Army. Dr. Rush is keenly interested in the impact of medical facilities and care upon such an endeavor. He is concerned that the Congress has not given enough thought to the medical care of an army. He wants an advocate who might observe and report from the field."

"So, then ... Ben Rush is the one who has put you up to this?"

Nicklaus patted his mother's hand. "No one has required me to make this journey, *Mutter*. I volunteered. It is proper that I am the one who should go."

"Why?" Katharina demanded. "Because you are young and have no family?"

Nicklaus shrugged. "The fact that I have neither wife nor child makes me the sensible choice for such a fact-finding mission."

"But you have a mother in your charge!"

Nicklaus quipped, "Speak truthfully, *Mutter*. You know that I am the one who is truly in *your* charge."

Katharina mustered a thin smile.

He grinned back at her. "I promise you, I will only be inspecting the hospitals and field clinics. I will be outside Boston proper, and shall not come in contact, at all, with the British armies. I will be under the watchful eye of the Colonial militia."

"So, then ... you admit it ... you *are* going into the path of danger."

"*Ja, Mutter*. There may be danger there. There are armies and weapons and a history of recent hostilities at Lexington and at Concord. But, I am no fool. I am simply going to observe and then report back to Dr. Rush. He will, in turn, report to the Congress."

Katharina sniffed. Nicklaus reached into the pocket of his weskit and removed a handkerchief, which he handed to his mother.

"And when will you return?" she inquired, somewhat resigned to the fact that her son was, indeed, going to Boston.

"In a month or so. Perhaps six weeks. I want to present a thorough report to Dr. Rush."

Katharina sighed. She stared helplessly into her son's dazzlingly blue eyes. She saw in his angular, handsome, manly face the gaze of the little boy that she had long ago reared in the Rhineland. She lovingly reached down with her right hand and cupped it beneath his chin.

"You must exercise all caution, Nicklaus. You are important here. Our hospital cannot operate efficiently without you." She paused. "And I need you. I have none other but you, my son. Please, do not abandon me."

Nicklaus took his mother's hand in his own. "I will be home in time to plant our summer garden. I promise."

~

June 16, 1775 – Charlestown – Near Boston, Massachusetts
Late Evening

THE SHEER SPECTACLE of humanity mesmerized Dr. Nicklaus Schell.
The fields, pastures, and meadows surrounding Boston were quite
literally crawling with soldiers. Thousands of tents dotted every hilltop. Likewise, innumerable cooking fires leaked their lazy, drifting
wisps of smoke upward into the humid summer air. Across the waters
of the Charles River, he could see the numerous city lights of British-
occupied Boston.

The siege of Boston was in full force. The entire region had the
look ... and all of the accompanying odors ... of deployed armies. The
air was heavy with the stench of smoke, feces, and decaying flesh.
The latter was, no doubt, the result of numerous dump piles filled
with the rotting, buzzard-covered carcasses of slaughtered livestock.
Such putrid piles could be found on the outskirts of every militia
encampment. Nicklaus made a mental note to write about this
unseemly, unwise, and thoroughly unsanitary practice. He intended
to include it in his report to Congress.

The road north out of Cambridge was thick with troops on the
march. Nicklaus thought it odd for the army to be maneuvering in the
darkness of night. Indeed, the sheer volume of humanity on the roads
and highways made travel quite difficult. He had desperately wanted
to reach the home of Dr. Isaac Foster before nightfall. Dr. Foster was
the physician in charge of all military hospitals in the quadrant north
of Boston. But, alas, the numerous checkpoints along the highway
had slowed travel considerably. It was well over an hour past dark
when Nicklaus' hired carriage arrived on the narrow peninsula that
was the location of the quaint, sleepy village known as Charlestown.

Nicklaus leaned out of the window of the vehicle to address the
driver. "Henry, how much further? I am famished, and aching in my
bones!"

The young fellow responded, "We are but a mile from Charlestown, Dr. Schell. I shall have you at the Foster home in just a short while."

Nicklaus sighed. "Very well." He was just about to duck back inside the window when another query popped into his mind. "Why are there so many soldiers near Charlestown?"

"I am not certain, Doctor. But, something is afoot. Of that, I am certain. Breed's Hill is covered with men. I can see their silhouettes in the campfires. And I can hear the sound of digging."

"Fortifications?" Nicklaus inquired.

The young driver nodded. "No doubt, sir. This is something new. The heights above Charlestown provide an excellent view of Boston. I also saw a big gun being pulled by horses down one of the side roads just a few moments ago."

"Artillery?" Nicklaus replied, shocked. "Here? At Charlestown?"

"Yes, sir."

Nicklaus shuddered a bit. He had not counted upon being housed near any military encampments. The reason that he had chosen to travel to Charlestown was because of the relative quiet and safety of the peninsula. He hoped that the presence of all of the soldiers and the increased military maneuvers were not a harbinger of impending hostilities.

The carriage jostled along the bumpy road toward the south. The waters of Mill Pond and the Charles River reflected the lights of Boston to the southeast. Within minutes, Nicklaus caught sight of the lanterns and candles of Charlestown. The driver, Henry, led the carriage several blocks into the town and soon turned toward the east. Nicklaus was quite relieved when he felt the carriage descend in speed and then come to a sudden halt.

Nicklaus felt the carriage jostle slightly as Henry climbed down. The boy's boots crunched in the dry soil of the road as he rounded the carriage and approached the door. Almost immediately, the tiny half-door swung open.

"We have arrived, Dr. Schell. Welcome to Charlestown proper. If you will go on up to the house, I shall be pleased to fetch your baggage."

Nicklaus grunted, "Thank you, Henry."

He climbed, stiffly, through the door of the carriage. He was most relieved to finally be at his destination. He attempted to evaluate his surroundings, but the night was moonless and very dark. Glancing at the house of Dr. Foster, he noted a handful of candles burning in several of the rooms. He was relieved that his host had not yet retired.

As Nicklaus trodded slowly up the walkway to the house, the front door opened and a man emerged onto the porch.

A voice called from the darkness, "Who goes there?" The dull click of a pistol's hammer accompanied the question.

Nicklaus stopped in his tracks. "I am Dr. Nicklaus Schell, surgeon from the Pennsylvania Hospital in Philadelphia. I am making the rounds of the medical facilities near the city of Boston. I have been tasked with making a report on military medicine to Dr. Benjamin Rush, for presentation to the Congress."

"A German, eh? Most intriguing. So, then ... it was Ben Rush who sent you?"

"I was born in the Palatinate, but have been here for many years. Yes, Dr. Rush is my mentor and supervisor," Nicklaus responded.

There was a prolonged period of silence. The man of the house finally responded, "I find it peculiar that you would come in the dark of night, and without announcement, Dr. Schell."

Nicklaus' heart dropped. Obviously, his preparatory letter had not arrived.

"I posted a correspondence to you over a week ago, Dr. Foster. You did not receive it?"

The pistol clicked again as the man standing in the doorway released the hammer.

"The local postal deliveries have been somewhat infrequent because of this damnable siege. There is no telling where your correspondence might be. But, no matter! Come on inside, Dr. Schell. You are most welcome. Your driver may leave your baggage on the porch, and then report around back to the kitchen. The cook will see that he is fed and has adequate accommodations in the shed. After you rest and sup, we will enjoy a glass of my good port and then do some acquainting. I am anxious to hear of the situation in Philadelphia."

Nicklaus felt a tremendous sense of relief. As he took a step forward, he answered, "And I am most anxious to hear of the medical situation in the army that surrounds Boston."

"Well, come on out of the dark night, then. We have plenty of time to swap stories and lies before bed." He chuckled at his own joke.

Nicklaus climbed the steps to the porch. Dr. Foster greeted him with a warm handshake.

"Welcome, Dr. Schell. Let's get you washed and find you some food, and then we shall talk."

Nicklaus gladly stepped into the warm glow of the humble doctor's home.

~

4:00 AM – June 17, 1775
Home of Dr. Isaac Foster - Charlestown

SOMETHING RIPPED Nicklaus from a deep sleep. He was confused. He glanced at the window near his bed. It was pitch dark outside. In his disoriented state, Nicklaus had forgotten his whereabouts. The room was thoroughly unfamiliar to him. But, soon, the memories of the evening emerged in his mind.

The two doctors had been up to almost midnight. They consumed copious amounts of pastries, brandy, and port. Indeed, Nicklaus had been quite drunk when he stumbled into the darkness of his bedchamber. He had not even bothered to remove his waistcoat and breeches. He had simply kicked off his leather shoes and tumbled, exhausted, into bed.

So, Nicklaus was quite surprised to find himself awake in the wee hours of the morning after such a late, alcohol-filled evening. What could possibly have roused him from such a deep, exhausted slumber?

Suddenly, there was a very bright flash of light outside his window. Seconds later, the flash was followed by a dull boom. The house trembled slightly. The glass in his window rattled. Nearby, on his dressing table, a cup danced lightly within the round bowl of its accompanying saucer. Then, there was another flash, and another explosive rumble. It sounded and felt like it was a little closer to the house than the first.

Nicklaus leapt from his bed and sprinted into the hallway. He almost slipped and fell as his wool stockings found little traction on the slick, polished wood floor. The front door of the home was standing open. There was another explosive, golden flash in the distance, followed quickly by yet another rumbling boom. Nicklaus saw Dr. Foster on the porch, silhouetted in the glistening lights of the artillery. The man stood stoically, staring toward the east.

Nicklaus quickly joined his host. He hissed, "What is happening, Dr. Foster?"

The doctor pointed toward the explosions in the distance. "They are firing on Breed's Hill."

"Who is?"

"The British. The firing is coming from the east. It must be one of their ships patrolling on the river. But, I do not understand why they would be firing on our hill."

"It is crawling with men, Dr. Foster. They were digging fortifications when we crossed nearby last night."

"Here, on our little island?" Dr. Foster challenged incredulously. "Why did you not mention this bit of information during our many discussions last evening?"

Nicklaus stammered, "I ... well ... I assumed that you already knew."

"You assumed wrongly, sir." Dr. Foster seemed disgusted. "Our little city has been untouched by the armies and their siege up until now. I had hoped that we would remain so." He paused. "How many soldiers do you reckon are up there?"

"Henry said there were hundreds. Perhaps, even, a thousand. The roads were filled with troops on the move. Henry said that the men on the hill were digging feverishly. And he saw a cannon."

Dr. Foster's back stiffened. "A cannon ... on Breed's Hill." He exhaled deeply and slowly. "General Howe will not allow this to stand. Our little hills have a most excellent view of Boston proper. They make for perfect artillery positions, and place the entire inner city in jeopardy." He turned and faced Nicklaus. "I fear that you may get more from your inspections than you bargained for this day, Dr. Schell. The British will, almost certainly, attack that hill."

"You actually believe they will send an army? Here?" Nicklaus groaned in disbelief.

A huge explosion illuminated the night, followed quickly by another.

"I have no doubt. And as the principal surgeon of Charlestown, and a member of the Committee of Safety, I must organize the hospital and medical personnel. Might I count upon your assistance?"

Nicklaus experienced a shudder of fear mixed with excitement. He bowed slightly and proclaimed, "I am at your service, sir."

Near Breed's Hill – Two Hours After Dawn

THERE HAD BEEN NO MORE rumbles of artillery for at least an hour. It was a pleasant respite. The less frequent artillery fire that had awakened Nicklaus in the middle of the night grew into a crescendo of explosions at dawn. Well over a hundred guns from the ships in Boston Harbor and the Charles and Mystic Rivers had joined in the fray. There was even sporadic fire from the British cannons atop Copp's Hill in Boston. All of their rounds were focused upon the tiny fort on top of Breed's Hill.

A short time after the barrage ended, a messenger arrived in Charlestown. He declared, breathless, that someone had been hit by cannon fire at the fort and that a surgeon was required. Since Dr. Foster was busy supervising hospital preparations, Nicklaus volunteered to go to the site of the injury. His host gladly loaned him a horse and sent him on his way.

Nicklaus was thrilled to have a break from the dull monotony of the morning. He had quickly grown weary of marking checklists, arranging beds, and counting bandages. He needed fresh air and sunshine. The cross-country morning ride provided both. As he guided his mount toward the distant hill, he was somewhat surprised at the extent of the fortifications. The top of the hill was scarred by freshly-dug earth. It bristled with timbers, bales of hay, and men. To his right, he saw more men digging an entrenchment that extended down the crest of the hill toward the waters to the north.

It took only a few minutes to reach the breastworks. Nicklaus tugged at the reins and reared his borrowed horse to a smooth halt near a cluster of soldiers. The sweaty, dirty men were busy digging an entrenchment and piling the earth into a mound on the southern periphery of the trench. Focusing intently upon their work, they paid little attention to the new arrival.

Nicklaus cleared his throat and announced, "I am Dr. Schell, dispatched by Dr. Foster. We heard that someone was wounded. Where is the afflicted man?"

One of the men stood erect and rested on his shovel. He spat on the ground and declared, "You're a bit late, Doc. You couldn't have done anything for that boy, anyhow. The ball from that ship snapped his head right off of his neck. They say it popped open like a ripe melon and scattered his brains in the wind."

Nicklaus gulped. "Ghastly."

The men digging in the trench chuckled at his sophisticated response.

Attempting to change the subject, Nicklaus inquired, "Was anyone else injured?"

"A couple, I suspect. You can check with Colonel Prescott. He's around back, working to get that dead fellow buried. He or one of the other officers can present you to the wounded." The man glanced over his shoulder. "I had best get back to work, before I get in some trouble." He tipped his hat to Nicklaus, indicating that his part in the conversation was done.

Nicklaus left quickly and guided his horse around the redoubts. He quickly located a cluster of men to the northeast. They appeared to be hovering around a body that lay covered on the ground. A lone officer stood twenty paces away, supervising the event. Nicklaus dismounted and walked over to the officer.

"Colonel Prescott?"

The man turned and faced Nicklaus. "Aye. Who's asking?"

"I am Dr. Nicklaus Schell. Dr. Foster sent me up from Charlestown to check on the wounded."

"We have scant few wounded, Doctor, and their wounds are minor. There is no helping that headless lad over there. His mates are saying their final words right now."

Nicklaus removed his hat as a show of respect. "What was his name ... the dead man?"

"Asa Pollard. He's a local chap, from up in Billerica. The poor man was in the wrong place at the wrong moment. He never knew what hit him, thank God." The officer paused. He appeared to be a bit annoyed. "Can I be of any further service to you, Doctor?"

Nicklaus shook his head. "No, sir. But, the surgeons want you to know that we are preparing to offer medical aid to you and your men. Hospitals and stations are being prepared and staffed in Charlestown."

Colonel Prescott nodded. "We shall put you to work this day, no doubt." He turned and scanned toward the south. He lifted his hand to shade his eyes and peered toward Boston. "I can see their boats forming up now. They will be coming soon, and in force. We are going to have to fight to hold this hill." He growled, "Damn them! Damn them all to hell!

Nicklaus mumbled, "Yes, sir." He did not know what else to say.

The officer did not make further eye contact with Nicklaus. "You had best be on your way, Doctor. There's no need for you to come up here in search of the wounded. They will be coming to you soon enough. Hurt men will find a doctor when they need one. Before this day ends, you will treat more wounded men that you should ever hope to."

Again, Nicklaus mumbled, "Yes, sir."

The colonel shot him an irritated glance. "Get about it, then, Son! I have no more time to waste on conversation with you!"

The officer started walking toward the top of the hill, leaving Nicklaus standing in numb silence. The good doctor quickly returned to his horse, leapt into the saddle, and then pointed the animal in the direction of Charlestown.

3:00 PM - Field Hospital at Fairweather House, Charlestown

THE BARRAGE HAD BEEN relentless since noon. The British trained every large gun in their naval and land arsenals upon the exposed top of Breed's Hill. Searing hot cannon balls screamed over the heads of the people of Charlestown village. The rumbling of the ground on the peninsula was continuous. Dishes rattled within the cabinetry of the homes. Occasionally, glassware vibrated and danced across the furniture and tabletops until it eventually tumbled onto the floor and shattered.

Tragically, some of the British cannon rounds fell short of their intended targets. Several dwellings in Charlestown were burning. The shouts of the village men and the desperate screams of women were becoming more and more frequent within the Charlestown limits. The surgeons had already treated patients with significant burns. Nicklaus thought it ironic and somewhat unjust that the first casualties of this great battle were the helpless civilians of the town.

The first British troops finally arrived ashore and established a beachhead camp around 2:00. It appeared that the King's army was delaying for some reason. The soldiers certainly made no move toward the hilltop. They seemed content to allow the artillery to do its work.

Nicklaus peered through a borrowed spyglass toward the crimson-coated soldiers in the meadow to the east. They were a curious sight, indeed. Over a thousand men were reclining in the tall grass. They appeared to be relaxing and enjoying a meal.

"What are they doing?" demanded Dr. David Townsend, a local physician on duty at the hospital. He was busy on the far side of the room, skillfully wrapping the burned hand of a local resident.

"Nothing exciting," Nicklaus replied, shrugging. "I think they are eating."

"Eating?" exclaimed Dr. Townsend. "Enjoying dinner on the green? I sincerely doubt that the Lobsterbacks rowed across this bay just to have a picnic in the sunshine."

"Agreed," Nicklaus affirmed. "Nevertheless, they are eating, talking, and laughing. They seem to be in fine spirits. It also appears to me that they are waiting."

"Waiting for what?" asked Townsend.

"For the cannons to stop, perhaps?" He moved the direction of his spyglass toward the top of Breed's Hill. Explosions continued on that hilltop, and on Bunker Hill, the taller knoll behind it. Nicklaus could also see explosions at the northwest end of the peninsula, at the spot where the road from Cambridge crossed to Charlestown. Clearly, the British were bombing the road. He turned and looked out the opposite window, in the direction of Boston. A terrified chill ran down his spine. Dozens of boats, all filled with red-coated soldiers, bobbed in the bay. The boats were headed in the direction of Charlestown.

Nicklaus declared, "More soldiers are coming. Reinforcements, I believe. Their boats are moving directly toward us. They are full of soldiers."

Dr. Townsend gave a low whistle. "It shall not be long, now."

The shrill, frantic voice of a woman echoed up the stairs. "Casualties! Doctors! We need you down here! Casualties have arrived!"

Nicklaus closed the spyglass and quickly placed it back on the desk. He darted toward the door. Mary Ellsworth, a local volunteer and self-appointed mistress of the hospital, stood red-faced at the bottom of the stairway. Her hands rested authoritatively on her hips. She roared, "You surgeons need to stop your dawdling and get to work!"

"From whence have they come?" Nicklaus demanded. He bounded down the stairs. "I have been watching with a spyglass. I saw no movement from Breed's Hill. There were only the artillery explosions. The men appeared to be under cover."

She replied, "They've come by boat. It is only a few of them right now, but the men assisting them say that many more will follow."

Nicklaus was confused. "By boat? That makes no sense!"

"It makes perfect sense," she retorted. "The safest evacuation was to the rear. They moved the wounded men down to the water and placed them in skiffs and rowboats. They landed on the beach at the southwest edge of town."

"What manner of casualties?" Nicklaus inquired as he stepped through the doorway into the yard.

"The blown up, wailing, bleeding kind," the headstrong woman responded. "Now, put your skills to work."

Nicklaus could scarcely believe the sight that awaited him on the sunny lawn. A dozen men lay bleeding. Women wailed and attended to their husbands. Blood was everywhere. The clothing of the men was soaked in it. Great puddles of the life-sustaining fluid formed beneath the stumps of severed legs and shattered arms. Nicklaus fought the urge to vomit.

He scanned the lawn as he attempted to discern the person who was in greatest need. Three other surgeons were already at work. They were directing orderlies to move some of the wounded indoors. It appeared to Nicklaus that at least two of the men on the lawn were already dead.

He gasped when he looked up and saw a young officer being carried onto the lawn. The wounded man was seated in a chair. Two gigantic, muscular soldiers held the chair suspended across their interlocked arms. The unconscious man's head flopped loosely on the top rung of the ladder-back chair.

One of the men carrying the chair locked eyes with Nicklaus. He wailed, "Please, Doctor! Help our lieutenant! He's been hit by cannon fire in the chest!"

Nicklaus pointed to the shade of a nearby tree. "Place him over there, and lay him flat on the ground!"

Nicklaus grabbed his surgical bag from the porch and approached the wounded officer. He knelt beside the man and made a preliminary examination. He leaned his ear forward and placed it over his mouth. He could hear the faint sound of shallow breathing. The soldier was alive, but barely. The doctor turned his attention to the man's chest. A layer of congealed blood soaked his torn waistcoat and shirt.

He demanded, "How long ago did his injury occur?"

One of the soldiers wailed, "How long ago? Hell, if I know! It was a long damned time ago! We took him to the house where the hospital was supposed to be, but they told us that it had been moved. We've been running all over this cursed village looking for you people!"

"Calm down!" Nicklaus ordered. "You did just fine. But, why did you bring him in a chair? Why not use a litter?"

"A litter?" the man responded incredulously. "There are no litters! We've been carting men off of that hill in wheelbarrows, Doctor! They're stringing threadbare blankets between discarded muskets and calling them litters ... and only the highest-ranking officers get those! We did the best that we could. We did not know what else to do, so we took the lieutenant's chair from his tent and brought him to you. How about you stop with all of your damned worthless questions and patch the man up?"

Nicklaus did not say anything else. He grabbed both flaps of the man's bloody waistcoat and ripped it open. The wool-covered buttons popped from their threads and scattered into the grass. He then tore at the linen shirt beneath. He gasped when he saw the wound in the center of the man's chest. His sternum was cut in two. Pieces of exposed bone protruded through the skin. A large, pointed piece of iron was imbedded in the center of the shattered bone.

Nicklaus' heart sank within his own chest. He knew that he could not treat this man. It was a mortal wound to the vital organs. Of that, he was certain. Even if he could remove the projectile from the man's chest, there was no medical procedure to make a repair. He placed his hand over the wounded officer's mouth again. There was no more sign of breathing. The lieutenant was already gone.

"I am sorry, gentlemen, but there is nothing that we can do. This man is dead."

One of the lieutenant's companions wailed, "If we had only found the hospital sooner!"

Nicklaus placed a reassuring hand on the despondent fellow's shoulder. "Young man, your lieutenant was dead the moment this projectile entered his chest. It was a fatal wound. No doctor or hospital in the world could save him. I am truly sorry."

"What do we do now?" the other man asked.

Nicklaus glanced down the street that led to the waterfront. Dozens of men approached. They were carrying and dragging more wounded soldiers.

"You should take him with you and see to his body in whatever manner pleases you. I fear that he might be misplaced, otherwise. There are sure to be many dead soldiers in Charlestown today."

Both young fellows nodded. They rose to their feet and then reverently lifted their dead commander back onto his chair. Nicklaus stared, sadly, as they struggled to carry the body back down toward the boats.

The shrill, venom-tainted voice of Mrs. Ellsworth invaded Nicklaus' moment of reverence. "'Tis no time for a break, Dr. Schell. There are many wounded men who demand your attention. Hop to!"

Nicklaus nodded reluctantly, and then rose to search out his next patient. Suddenly, the cannonade stopped. Almost in an instant, the heavy guns of the ships fell silent. From the east came the sounds of shouting officers, drums, marching, and rattling metal. The British force was beginning its infantry assault on Breed's Hill. Moments later, the field to the east erupted in musket fire, followed by the occasional boom of an American cannon from the hilltop.

The battle of Bunker Hill had begun in earnest.

Sunset

NICKLAUS MARCHED, exhausted, in front of a tired squad of bayonet-wielding British soldiers. They had arrived only minutes ago at the makeshift hospital in Charlestown. Their mission was to draft all of the surgeons and physicians for service to His Majesty's army. The wounded Colonials, they decreed, would be left bleeding and dying as they lay. The soldiers had no interest in the rebels. By force of arms, they commandeered every available physician for the care of their own wounded. Within minutes, the six impatient soldiers were prodding ten weary doctors westward down the crowded boulevard.

The doctors moved slowly and reluctantly toward the battlefield. Theirs was not a philosophical resistance. They were simply exhausted. Their legs and feet were numb. Dr. Isaac Foster, Nicklaus' host, was a much older gentleman. He walked stiffly beside Nicklaus, who held tightly to his arm. He relied upon the younger man to help him across the ditches and gullies that lay between Charlestown and the battle-scarred field. Nicklaus gazed upon the old doctor with admiration. He knew how physically spent that he, himself, felt after the three-hour surgical marathon that afternoon. He could only imagine the state of fatigue of the older men in the group.

Nicklaus took a moment to glance down and examine his own clothing. He was encrusted in dried blood. Every stain reminded him of one of his pathetic, desperate patients. He had actually stopped counting the number of men he treated within an hour after the initiation of small arms and musket fire. He eventually lost count of the ones who died on his table. He attempted to block from his mind the pile of amputated arms and legs that lay discarded outside the parlor window of the Fairweather home. He shuddered at the memory of the enormous pile of dead bodies that lay in the shade of the trees behind the house.

As the group topped a small rise, an audible gasp echoed through the cluster of physicians.

"My God!" exclaimed Dr. Foster. "How can this be?"

Nicklaus offered no comment. He merely stared at the carnage that lay sprawled before them. He could scarcely believe the scope of it. Hundreds upon hundreds of British troops lay dead and dying on the south-facing slope of Breed's Hill. Dozens were crawling about on the ground in a vain attempt to find assistance. Others moaned, wailed, and waved their arms for help. It seemed that no one was actively tending to any of them.

Several boats were beached at the southern end of the peninsula, near the base of Breed's Hill. Troops were busily escorting civilian-clothed Colonial prisoners toward the boats. Prison cells and encampments awaited them across the water in Boston. As Nicklaus watched, one of the captives yelled something at one of the British soldiers. The recipient of the verbal abuse swiftly lifted his musket and drove the stock into the defiant man's skull. The fellow collapsed onto the ground. Three other soldiers instantly joined the first in kicking and beating the helpless, fallen, unarmed man.

Nicklaus felt a warming sensation of defiant rage growing within his breast. The flicker of anger in his soul increased into a vigorous flame. He discovered a sudden and thorough disdain for the soldiers of King George's army. He looked left to the top of Breed's Hill. British soldiers were swarming throughout the fort. The bodies of the defenders of the breastworks were scattered awkwardly across the earthen berms. The Lobsterbacks were busily tossing those bodies over the tops of the walls of the bastion. Several tall pillars of thick, black smoke climbed upward into the purple sky. A huge Union Jack, the national flag of Great Britain, flew arrogantly in the stiff breeze. Further north, behind Breed's Hill, another identical flag adorned Bunker Hill.

Clearly, the British had taken the fort, and the field, but at an unimaginable and immeasurable cost in life and blood.

Dr. Foster mused, heartbroken, "What manner of king could do this?" He turned and faced the soldiers who were escorting them.

"What manner of king would attack his own people? What manner of king would order the slaughter of his own army?"

The soldiers offered no response. Nicklaus, however, spat defiantly on the ground in front of him.

"This I know, Dr. Foster ... such a man shall no longer be *my* king!"

PART II

PATRIOTS

6

A REGIMENT OF GERMANS

May 12, 1776
Upper Milford Township - Northampton County, Pennsylvania

Heinrich stared at his son-in-law, grinned, and shook his head in total disbelief. He could not fathom how the young man could remain absolutely calm and aloof in the midst of the daily storm of confusion, emotion, and activity that so often typified the Yeisley house.

The two youngest daughters, Catherine and Barbara, were both confined to their cribs and crying hysterically. Mary Magdalena, the precocious four-year-old, was tugging at her papa's waistcoat and begging for attention. Six-year-old Elizabeth had somehow managed to dress a neighbor's cat in a baby's gown, and actually had the animal sitting comfortably in a child's feeding chair at the end of the table. The youngster was allowing the cat to lap milk from her breakfast spoon ... in between bites of her own porridge, of course. Michael's wife, Magdalena, seven months pregnant with child number five, was noisily attempting to flush two stray geese from the kitchen with her broom. The simple-minded animals refused to be directed toward the door to the back yard.

Despite the bedlam that surrounded him, Michael Yeisley sat calmly at the breakfast table, sipping his tea and reading his newspaper. It was the latest edition of the *Pennsylvanischer Staatsbote*, the largest and most influential German-language paper in the American Colonies.

Michael exhaled in disgust and slapped the table top, violently jostling the breakfast dishes. He exclaimed, "Heinrich! Can you believe this?"

"Believe what, Michael?" Heinrich asked, feigning interest. He was actually more concerned about his breakfast. He smacked his lips and enjoyed yet another hearty bite of sausage and bread.

Michael growled, "The Holy Roman Empire is supplying troops for hire to King George! Parliament has elected to employ thousands of German troops for service here in America!" He lowered the newspaper and stared at his father-in-law. There was a mixture of rage and disbelief in his eyes. "Can you imagine? German troops are coming here to fight for England!"

"What would possess the German lords to do such a thing?" Heinrich mused.

"Money, Heinrich! Money! Listen to this ... *'the government received from Germany 1,800 Jaegers. The Landgrave of Hessen-Cassell gave 12,000 men, and the Duke of Braunschweig committed 5,000.'*" He folded the paper and slapped it angrily against the table. "Our German nobles are now sending their soldiers to wage war against the peasants of these Colonies. I tell you, Heinrich, it will not stand! We shall not allow it to stand! Our German brothers in Pennsylvania must take up arms and join in this war!"

The thunderous, violent honk of a goose echoed through the kitchen, followed by a resounding thud. The men turned and observed Magdalena standing over the flopping body of a very large goose. She was holding the iron fireplace poker in her hand. She raised her weapon high in the air and struck the animal in the head once more, delivering a fatal blow. The very pregnant woman stood menacingly over the bird, surrounded by a thin, hovering cloud of downy feathers.

Michael exclaimed, "Magdalena, what in Heaven's name? That was my favorite goose!"

"And it had no business being in my kitchen, Michael Yeisley! There are plenty of others like it on the lawn, where geese actually belong. Since you men-folk are so absorbed in your newspapers and talk of war, I had to resolve the matter as I saw fit. Now, your favorite bird shall be our supper." She pointed the poker at her husband. "And if you do not take it outside at once and get it plucked and prepared for the oven, you'll have grander things than a war to concern you, Michael Yeisley. You shall be making your bed amongst the cows in the barn this night!"

Michael pushed his chair back from the table. He mumbled, "*Ja, meine liebe.*"

"Do not try to sweet-talk me, husband," she retorted. "Just get it done. Or you shall have a war in this household that will keep your attentions fully occupied. *Verstehen sie?*"

"*Ja, ja, ich verstehe.* Consider me on goose duty." Michael rose and walked toward the dead bird.

"Place your dishes in the tub, first!" Magdalena barked, hands on her hips.

Michael spun back around, grabbed his cup, saucer, plate, and utensils, and then reverently deposited them in the wash tub.

As he walked past his wife, he grabbed her in a surprise embrace and hugged her close. He teasingly asked, "May I pluck your goose now?"

She placed her hand in his face and pushed him away. "I rather think you have plucked my goose a few too many times, don't you?" She rubbed her tight, round belly and grinned.

Michael growled and kissed his wife playfully on the neck. Elizabeth and the younger Mary Magdalena giggled at their parents.

Magdalena pushed Michael away, once again. "Off with you, now." She seemed serious this time. "Be sure to keep every feather, especially the down. I am saving up for some fresh pillows for winter. And pluck the wing feathers carefully. I can sell them for quill pens in the town market."

"Of course, my dear. Your every wish is my command." He executed an overly-dramatic bow. The little girls giggled again.

~

July 9, 1776
Milford Township Market

THE CROWD of townsfolk was uncharacteristically silent. The people were numb with a mixture of excitement, fear, and confusion. The reader of the newly-signed Declaration of Independence, a German-speaking rider dispatched from Philadelphia, folded his brand-new copy of the *Pennsylvanischer Staatsbote* and tucked it back into his satchel. He quickly trudged toward his horse, climbed atop the animal, and then guided it toward the north. His next stop was Northamptontown, where he would read the text once again to the next group of German-speaking citizens. He would repeat this process in many Pennsylvania villages in the coming days.

Nicklaus, Michael, and George Yeisley were seated among dozens of other men and boys on a low stone wall in front of the Reformed Church. Nicklaus reclined between his two oldest sons, resting comfortably against the wood siding of the building. Nicklaus' youngest son, Henry, a lad of only eleven years, sat cross-legged on the ground at the feet of his big brother, Michael. No one spoke a word. Michael drew slowly and deliberately on his clay pipe and pondered the words that he had just heard.

It was George who finally broke the silence of the moment. "What does it all mean, Papa?"

At first, Nicklaus did not acknowledge his son. He was too stunned and consumed with his thoughts to offer an answer to the young man's question.

Michael, too, was astounded beyond words. The very name of the document that had just been read to them was shocking, in and of itself. It was entitled, *"The Unanimous Declaration of the Thirteen United States of America."*

And the passionate, moving words read by the herald were still ringing in his ears:

We, therefore, the Representatives of the United States of America, in General Congress, Assembled, appealing to the Supreme Judge of the world for the rectitude of our intentions, do, in the Name, and by Authority of the good People of these Colonies, solemnly publish and declare, that these United Colonies are, and of Right ought to be Free and Independent States; that they are Absolved from all Allegiance to the British Crown ...

Michael knew that the fervor for war had been expanding throughout the northeast, but he had never imagined that the end result would be the formation of a new country. Lowered taxes and expanded rights, perhaps ... but certainly not a new nation. And, yet, the deed was done. The thirteen formerly British Colonies were now the thirteen independent United States.

George prodded his father and then kicked Michael's boot. He asked once again, "Papa! Michael! What does it mean?"

His father responded quietly, reverently, "The Congress has broken with England. We are no longer English subjects. We are citizens of the United States, now. We are a country of our own."

George shook his head, confused. "I still do not understand. What does it mean to us ... here in Milford? What does that mean for the German people of Pennsylvania?"

Michael drew deeply on his pipe, but received no smoke. He grunted in mild disgust and quickly tapped the ash from the bowl. He answered, "It means that we have to choose a side, George. Philadelphia is now the capital of a new nation. The British will surely want to make an example of its rebellion. The war is coming to us, and we have to decide whether or not we Germans, as a people, will fight."

His brother pondered those words for a moment. "All right. So, then ... what will *we* do?"

Nicklaus wrapped his arm around his inquisitive son's shoulder. "George, I am too old to fight, and little Henry here is too young." He affectionately and playfully reached down and nudged Henry's straw cocked hat forward to cover his face. The boy giggled and pushed his hat back up onto the crown of his head. "But, you and Michael are of age. You will have to choose your own paths. There is no militia in Pennsylvania, so you will not be impressed into service. Therefore, you will have to decide what you intend to do."

"What do you wish us to do, Papa? Should we join their army?" George inquired rather innocently.

Nicklaus grinned. "I wish for you to always stay home, near me, and far from this war. Such is a father's wish. I want my sons and daughters and grandchildren to remain close to home." He paused. "But, it is not up to me. And, ultimately, you may not have a choice."

"What do you mean?" demanded George.

Nicklaus clarified, "Should the war come to us, you may be compelled to fight to protect your home and our family."

Michael grunted. "I agree, Papa. I fear that this war will eventually come to us ... to the very doorsteps of our homes. The British have already occupied York City. It is only a matter of time before they move down the coast. Philadelphia will, most certainly, be in their sights."

Nicklaus nodded almost imperceptibly. "So, you've made up your mind, then?"

"I have, Papa." Michael took a deep, thoughtful breath. "I will fight for this new country."

$\sim$

August 7, 1776

MAGDALENA HELD HER THREE-DAY-OLD DAUGHTER, Eva, lovingly against her left breast. The newest daughter in the Yeisley home nursed contentedly. Simultaneously, fourteen-month-old Barbara nursed voraciously from her right breast. The other three Yeisley daughters toddled about the house, laughing, playing, and filling their time as only children can do.

Magdalena sighed. She was happy, content, and fulfilled in her motherhood. If not for her husband's impending departure, her joy would be complete.

Michael was on the far side of the room, busily packing a goatskin knapsack and shoulder bag with clothing and supplies. He had delayed his departure long enough to see his fifth daughter born and ensure his wife's physical well-being. But, now, the birthing was done, and it was time for him to go.

Magdalena had given up on trying to convince Michael otherwise. For the past two days, she had attempted every tactic in her arsenal to change the mind and intentions of her husband. She tried reasoning with him regarding the needs of the family business. She referenced the elderly status of Michael's parents. She pleaded with him about the needs of their five little girls. But, in the end, nothing had worked. And with her recent childbirth, she was in no condition to utilize her ultimate, intimate female weaponry to influence her husband's decision-making. She had no choice but to resolve herself to Michael's decision. He was going to join the Continental Army.

"Where will you go?" Magdalena inquired sullenly. "How does one join an army?"

Michael stuffed a linen sack of dried beans deep into his bag. "I am told that there is a captain recruiting men in Reading for a regiment made up entirely of Germans."

"So, then ... you just sign a paper?"

Michael nodded as he continued packing. "*Ja*. I believe so."

"And will they pay you?"

Michael grinned. He could always count on his wife to be thinking of family financial matters.

"I am told that there is a bounty of ten dollars to sign up, and then eight dollars a month in pay. I will be able to allocate a portion of that pay to be reserved for you and the girls."

"Spanish silver?" she asked hopefully.

He shook his head. "Continental dollars, issued by the Congress."

"I do not know what that means," she declared. "Is it a new silver coin?"

Again, he shook his head. "*Nein*. Paper script."

"So, then, it is worthless," she growled with disgust. "As usual, we will have to rely upon our business skills and our wits for our livelihood."

Michael exhaled, somewhat frustrated. "Let us hope not. I will give my service as a soldier, and trust that the government will reciprocate and fulfill its obligations to me."

"And what are those obligations, exactly?" Magdalena challenged.

"Food, clothing, shelter, pay. A government provides for the necessities of its soldiers. It meets its obligations. Otherwise, there would be no army." He sighed. "You should not worry about such things, Magdalena. I will be fine. You and the girls will be fine. George and Heinrich will keep the looms and manufactory running smoothly. I am quite certain that business and profits will be good in the coming months. People will always need thread, woven cloth, and garments, especially in a time of war. George will bid on government contracts, should the opportunity arise."

Michael tied his knapsack closed and placed it on the dining table. He walked over to his wife's bed and sat in the chair beside her. He gently and lovingly stroked the arm that cradled his newborn.

"Will you go alone?" she asked wistfully.

"No. Abraham Price and Conrad Traywitz are joining up with me. We are to meet at the church in one hour. George is taking us to the enlistment place in Reading."

"So soon?" She choked back her tears.

Seeing that she was so upset, Michael spoke gently. "I cannot tarry. I am told that the company forming there is scheduled to depart for training in a day or two."

"Where will this training be?"

"Philadelphia. The regiment will be in barracks there for a while, I am certain. It will require some time to secure officers and equipment. It is a brand-new and as yet non-existent regiment, recently authorized by the Congress."

Magdalena seemed somewhat relieved. "Then, you will not be going to York City to join Washington and his men?"

Michael shook his head. "No, I do not think they will throw us directly into the fighting so quickly. They must drill and train us first. The Congress will have to secure uniforms and equipment. Like I said, it is a completely new and unorganized regiment. Many matters must be resolved before it will be combat-ready. We must learn to march, drill, and maneuver as a regiment."

She nodded. Her face was somewhat stoic and without emotion. But, almost immediately, her blank expression morphed into despair. She began to weep openly. Her chest heaved. Her hollow, broken sobbing reflected her inner feelings of helplessness and hopelessness. Michael felt tears welling in his own eyes.

"Whatever would we do if something happened to you?" She glanced downward at her nursing babies. "These poor girls are so very young. None but Elizabeth would even remember their father." She cried without reservation or shame.

Michael moved from his chair onto the bedside. He wrapped his arms around his wife and baby daughters. "Oh, my darling! Nothing is going to happen to me. You will see. God shall protect me."

August 9, 1776
German Reformed Church - Reading, Pennsylvania

THE MORNING WAS humid and stifling hot. Most of the men in the township of Reading had abandoned their coats shortly after breakfast. Though the skies overhead were clear, an ominous gray hue painted the horizon to the west. The heavy air smelled of rain.

The boisterous men who filled the lawn did not seem to care about the weather or the incoming rain. The yard of the German Reformed Church was a busy beehive of activity. Over a dozen men were hovering about, arranging their belongings and saying their goodbyes. Men were tending to horses and loading wagons. There was an air of excitement and anticipation. The new recruits' departure for Philadelphia was imminent.

Michael Yeisley stood with his brother, George, behind one of the military wagons. His off-white linen shirt and gray weskit were soaked with sweat and humidity. He reached forward and carefully tucked his brown wool coat inside the handles of his large leather bag. He knew that he would need its warmth in the coming fall and winter.

"I shall miss you, Michael," George declared. "Are you certain this is the right thing to do?"

Michael pushed his portmanteau deeper into the bed of the rather rickety wagon. He removed his black fur-felt cocked hat and wiped a river of perspiration from his brow. He grinned at his brother. "It is too late to reconsider now, George. I have already pledged my oath and signed the papers. I am now a soldier of the German Regiment of the Continental Army."

"For how long?"

"Three years."

George grunted. "That is a very long time. Much can occur in three years."

Michael shrugged and shook his head. "I will simply follow orders and do my duty. Surely, this war will not last for three more years."

"Let us hope not." George's voice trailed off to almost a whisper.

Michael glanced toward the front steps of the church. He saw his captain, a serious fellow named Benjamin Weiser, directing two other men toward a nearby wagon.

"It is almost time, George. We are about to depart." Michael grabbed his younger brother and embraced him in an emotional hug.

"Before you go ... I have something for you," George declared as he pulled away from the embrace. He walked quickly to the Yeisley wagon and retrieved a long linen sack that he had concealed beneath a blanket in the vehicle's bed. It was, obviously, a weapon. As he walked back toward Michael, he removed a long, shiny gun from the sack. He smiled broadly as he presented the gun to his brother.

Michael's eyes were wide with shock. "What is this?"

"A new musket for you, Michael. I could not have you going off to war with that beastly old Jaeger rifle. It misfires on every third shot. Besides, you will be hunting men, not birds. You need a true soldier's gun."

"But, I have never seen such a musket!" He glanced at the writing on the lock plate. "From whence did it come?"

George smiled. "It is a French Charleville ... a .69 caliber. The design is positively genius. These bands have release clips, and they slide off so that it comes apart easily for cleaning. I believe it will serve you well in the field."

Michael stammered, "George, I ... I do not know what to say." He admired the gun. "Where did you get it?"

"I traded for it at the market in Philadelphia last month. There was a fellow there all the way from Quebec City. He had about a dozen of these amongst his wares. I picked out the very best one in his inventory."

"I hope it did not cost you too much." Michael winked. He continued to admire the gun. He held it up and sighted down the barrel. The weapon felt solid, and very balanced.

"Do not worry about the cost. I got a fair deal. I have a box in the wagon that you will need to take, as well. Magdalena packed some things ... clothing, food, and such. I put in some powder and lead, and a nice leather cartridge box. It is homemade, but will serve you well." George grinned. "I convinced the Canadian fellow to include that in our little trade agreement. It is actually a belt box, but I added a hemp strap so that you can wear it over your shoulder. That will make it a bit easier to use, I think."

"I am truly grateful, Brother. Again ... I do not know what to say." Michael choked back his raw emotion. "And I am so glad that you will remain home to help care for my family. My little girls truly adore their Uncle George."

"I shall watch over them as if they were my own. Still, they need their Papa. So, do not do anything brave or stupid. Just do your duty, and then hurry up and come home."

Captain Weiser's commanding voice interrupted their exchange. "To the wagons, gentlemen! Glory awaits!"

Men began to clamor into the seats and beds of the four army wagons that were scattered throughout the church yard.

Michael nodded grimly. "I must go. *Auf Wiedersehen,* George."

He reached his hand forward to shake with his brother. George took his hand and gave it a single tug.

"*Auf Wiedersehen,* Michael. Until we meet again."

⌣

September 24, 1776
Philadelphia – Guardhouse, German Regimental Barracks

"WE'VE MADE a big damned mistake, Michael," declared Abraham Price. "We should never have joined this God-forsaken cause."

"The army will sort this out. Congress will fulfill its promises. I know it will," Michael replied hopefully. "And Captain Weiser will get us out of this gaol."

"Your optimism is admirable, but foolish, *Mein Freund.*" Abraham spat through the bars of the window. "We've been in this shite-hole for fourteen days, and not a sign of our dear Captain Weiser!"

"Or a hint of anything to eat," added John Portner.

The men ached from hunger. Conditions were appalling in Philadelphia. The men of the German Regiment had received very little food since their arrival in the putrid, fly-infested city. Not once had they received the lawfully required daily allowance of one pound of beef or fish, one pound of flour, one pint of milk, and one quart of beer per day. Instead, they had received only an occasional sack of Indian meal ... ground corn ... and the German soldiers had little tolerance or taste for it.

Clothing had become an issue, as well. The men of the regiment came into the army with only their customary clothing from home. They had fully expected the government to clothe them in a military fashion. Many of the poorest soldiers arrived in Philadelphia with very little in the way of clothing. Indeed, a handful of men in one of the Maryland companies were clad only in hunting shirts. They had no breeches, stockings, or shoes. They were practically naked. Each day, concerned family members appeared from the various towns and villages of Pennsylvania and Maryland, all of them bearing token gifts of clothing and meager rations for their beleaguered husbands and sons.

The first sign of angst and rebellion amongst the Germans appeared on September 1, the initial regimental muster and pay. The men of the regiment fully anticipated receiving their allotment of eight dollars for a month of service. Instead, they received only six and two-thirds dollars in Continental script. The army had retained the difference as a fee for military clothing. Colonel George Stricker, temporary commander of the regiment, called it a "stoppage." He assured the men that it was a common military practice. The only problem, however, was that the army had not provided a single thread of military clothing for the men. The soldiers were being forced to pay for uniforms that had never been issued.

The men of the regiment already hated Colonel Stricker. He was a pompous, arrogant arse. He strutted around the barracks and acted very military, but it was quite clear that he had neither the attitude nor the skill set to command a regiment of troops. He focused his military attention entirely upon marching, and little else. And he was obsessed with respect for the officers. It seemed, to the men, that he cared little as to whether they could actually maneuver, or shoot, or fight. But, as long as they saluted and showed courtesy and deference to the officers, they were a "proper military unit."

Colonel Stricker had a motto that he repeated often. He entered it in the regimental logbook almost every day. He declared, "*Vigilance, sobriety, and good order!*" This motto had quickly evolved into a mocking greeting and private joke among the enlisted men.

Two days after the payday fiasco and near-mutiny, as the lack of food persisted, Captain Weiser decided to take matters in his company into his own hands. He dispatched six of his men into the countryside to the north of the city in search of provisions. It was a simple supply run. His idea was to appeal to the German residents outside the city for help in feeding their countrymen languishing hungrily in the barracks of Philadelphia. Michael Yeisley, Abraham Price, and four of their comrades had gladly taken on the task.

But, when Colonel Stricker discovered their absence at roll call that evening, he lost his military mind. He had given no such order for a foraging party, and he absolutely refused to listen to Captain Weiser's explanation or defense of his men. Colonel Stricker declared that all six soldiers were deserters and wrote warrants for their arrest. If they ever returned, they would be placed in the stockade as examples for the other men.

When they returned victoriously seven days later, driving two wagons laden with meat, ale, and flour, they were summarily arrested and thrown into the regimental blockhouse. That was two weeks ago. They had been confined in a dank, flea-infested, rat-filled room for fourteen insufferable days. They had not enjoyed a single mouthful of the food that they had scrounged from the countryside. Their diet had been a small daily ration of moldy bread and tepid water. Michael was beginning to wonder if they would ever be released back to their company ... or if his hunger would ever, again, be satisfied.

So, the six prisoners were quite pleased when a large melee erupted outside the jail. The men crowded around the tiny window of their cell to observe the scene of bedlam on the company parade ground. The men of the German Regiment were gathered in a bold demonstration of protest. They were cursing the army, the Congress, and Colonel Stricker. The regiment seemed to be on the verge of a mutinous frenzy.

"The boys certainly are putting on a show, today," declared John Christman, a member of Captain Weiser's company and fellow prisoner in the battalion jail. "I wonder what has them so worked up?"

"They are tired of aching, empty bellies!" declared Abe.

"And tired of the army taking away more than it is giving in return," echoed Ben Servey, another of the prisoners.

All six of the men grunted and moaned in agreement. Suddenly, a cluster of soldiers ran past the jail. They were headed toward the already-crowded parade ground.

Abraham called out to one of the men, "Peter! *Was ist los?*"

Peter Lesher, a private in Captain Weiser's company, stopped and ran back toward the window. He seemed giddy. The red-faced private exclaimed, "Colonel Stricker has done it now! He has declared that men who do not make formation or perform their duties to his standards will not be fed! He has cut off all rations!"

"Well, it is not as if they were being fed that much to begin with," Abraham replied.

"True. But just the notion of cutting off all rations has really set the men off. There is talk of a general mutiny. They are calling for Major Weltner to take command."

"If only that were possible," Michael wished out loud.

Major Ludwick Weltner was, in the eyes of the men, the only high-ranking officer of the regiment who was worth his salt. A former breeches-maker from Maryland, Major Weltner was a soldier's advocate. He was a good, down-to-earth man. The troops of the regiment respected him. They secretly longed for him to displace the tyrant, Stricker, as commander of the unit.

"I must go, boys," Private Lesher declared. "I do not want to miss the action!"

Their friend turned and sprinted toward the parade ground. Well over two hundred men were gathered there. They shouted and waved their fists in the air. Then a chant erupted, "*Satisfaction or mutiny! Satisfaction or mutiny!*"

The men were in a general state of disorder, and appeared to be nearing a riot, when a single gunshot pierced the clamor of voices. The shot was followed by the shrill cry of a whistle. Two dozen men, all armed with muskets, sprinted through the gate and scattered around the periphery of the parade ground. They held their weapons at the ready and stared menacingly at the crowd of German soldiers.

The chanting ceased. Silence descended upon the grounds. The door to Colonel Stricker's officer opened and he stepped outside onto the edge of the parade field.

He shouted authoritatively, "I order this unlawful assembly to disperse immediately! I consider this demonstration to be nothing short of a mutiny! You have until the count of ten to return to your barracks, or I will order the guards to open fire!"

The men stood silently. They stared in disbelief. No one moved.

Colonel Stricker shrieked, "Make ready!"

The armed soldiers reached up and pulled the hammers of their muskets to the fully cocked position.

Then, amazingly, Colonel Stricker began to count. "*Ein!*" He enunciated the number clearly, slowly, and deliberately. He offered a dramatic pause.

No one moved.

"*Zwei!*"

Confusion gripped the men. They began to murmur.

"*Drei!*"

Bedlam ensued when he reached the number three. The crowd dispersed suddenly and quickly. The parade ground was empty in seconds. The men disappeared inside the brick buildings that surrounded the drilling ground. The crisis was averted. Michael could see the relief on the faces of the men in the musket detail. One by one, they each released the hammers on their guns and assumed a more relaxed position. Colonel Stricker turned and strutted victoriously back inside his office, slamming the door behind him.

"Well ... that was interesting," declared Abraham.

Late Evening – The Next Day

THE SOUND of rattling keys echoed down the hallway. Moments later, the door to the cell swung open. Lantern and candlelight invaded the dark room. Captain Weiser stepped into the glow and crossed the threshold. The six men rose slowly to their feet.

Michael spoke for the group. "Captain. We are very happy to see you."

The officer grinned. "Are you boys ready to go back to the barracks?"

"Are we to be released?" Abraham inquired excitedly.

"You are, indeed."

"How did you manage that, Captain?" Michael asked in disbelief.

"The colonel is in a bit of a tight spot right now. Major Weltner lodged a complaint against him this afternoon in the Congress. He has, quite suddenly, discovered that the withholding of rations from the soldiers under his command is not only immoral, but unlawful. After receiving a thorough chastisement from the president of the Congress, he ordered everyone to be fed. The major also convinced him that it was not a good idea to cashier his soldiers and incarcerate them for following their captain's orders to forage for food. So, you gentlemen are henceforth free and will suffer no further consequences or punishment from this unfortunate incident."

Michael nodded. "We are most grateful, Captain."

Weiser shook his head. "It was not my doing. I am only the bearer of the good news. We can all thank Major Weltner for bringing about some much-needed change."

"I wish he was in command of this regiment," Abraham proclaimed rather insubordinately.

Captain Weiser nodded knowingly. "As do we all, Private. But, it will not matter much longer."

"What do you mean, sir?" Abe asked.

"We have received word that a new colonel is on the way. His name is Nicholas Haussegger. Congress has appointed him as commander of the regiment."

Michael declared, "Let us hope that he arrives very soon. I do not know how much more we can suffer under Colonel Stricker."

"I do not think the colonel will be causing us much trouble, anymore. He has heard of some threats against him and has developed a sudden fear for his health and well-being. The man has surrounded himself with armed guards and is hidden away inside his office. We shall not see much of him during the coming transition."

"Even more good news," observed Abe.

The captain sighed. "Well, enough of this idle talk. Let us retire to the barracks. We have much work to accomplish tomorrow. We shall begin bayonet training."

"But, we have no bayonets," objected Michael.

"A wagonload arrived late this afternoon. And we were informed by the commissary that official army uniforms will be delivered by the first of November."

"Continental coats?" asked Michael in disbelief.

The captain shook his head. "No. We shall be uniformed in heavy white hunting frocks and breeches. Our leggings will be blue striped. Everyone will wear identical black cocked hats. They say that we will even receive our winter blankets. We shall make a very smart regiment, indeed!"

Michael Yeisley grinned broadly.

~

December 2, 1776

Philadelphia - German Regiment Parade Ground

IT WAS time to enter the fray. The men of the German Regiment were going to war. They had received their orders to join a retreating General Washington at the front. Their destination was Trenton, New Jersey.

The disciplined, well-groomed soldiers stood at attention. Colonel Haussegger sat tall atop his horse and gazed proudly upon his men. Many members of the Congress and dozens of other civilian and government officials stood along the walls of the barracks that surrounded the grounds, watching the nation's first officially designated ethnic regiment on parade.

The regiment looked most impressive. It numbered almost four hundred and fifty men fit for duty. The eight companies each wore matching white or off-white linen hunting frocks and breeches. They sported blue and white striped leggings below the knee. A black fur felt cocked hat adorned each head. Bayonet and cartridge box straps crossed each man's chest, forming a perfect "X." On their backs, they wore an assortment of knapsacks, blankets, folded tent shelters, and tarps. The only pieces of essential equipment that were not uniform among the men were their firearms. Each man carried the weapon he had brought from home, or whatever weapons that their captains could procure in Philadelphia. The regiment was armed with an odd assortment of muskets, fowling guns, and rifles.

The training and equipping of the German regiment had improved dramatically since the arrival of Colonel Haussegger. Unbeknownst to the men, they were now the strongest and best-equipped regiment in the Continental Army. They had long-since shed their reputation as an ill-mannered, underdressed, mutinous rabble. They were an impressive and imposing regiment, and ready to perform their duties in the field.

Private Michael Yeisley was very proud. At long last, he truly felt like he was a part of something important. He was ready to go into battle and fight for his new country. The taut, puffed-out chests of the other men of Captain Weiser's company indicated that they shared the same pride.

Colonel Haussegger barked an order. "Officers, prepare for march!"

Major Weltner echoed the order, "Companies, prepare for march!"

Captain Weiser joined the other company commanders and shouted, "Shoulder arms!"

Major Weltner then called out, "Left face!"

The men of the regiment immediately and crisply faced left.

Haussegger crowed from horseback, "Captains! By companies! Forward! March!"

The men of the German Regiment moved out smartly. They marched toward the brick archway that led onto Green Street. The lead elements turned northward onto Third Street. The gravel of the thoroughfare soon gave way to the muddy rural road that led north toward Germantown. The men marched confidently toward the battle front in New Jersey.

7

THE NIGHT OF ALL NIGHTS

December 20, 1776
Washington's Camp – Newtown, Pennsylvania

"Shut the damned door, you imbecile!" Abraham Price howled from his relatively comfortable spot near the fireplace. "Were you reared in a barn?"

George Strouss, a young private from Captain John Woelpper's company, had just entered the drafty house. He was returning from a temporary duty assignment as a messenger and runner at Washington's headquarters. The young fellow had been outdoors for most of the day. He was cold, tired, and ravenously hungry, and he was in absolutely no mood for a scolding. He slowly, deliberately, and tauntingly placed his fowling gun against the wall. Before he reached to pull the rickety door closed, he removed his homemade wool mitten from his numb left hand and raised his middle finger defiantly at Abe.

The soldiers of Captain Weiser's company, Abe's buddies, growled in ominous disapproval at the gesture. George's comrades from Captain Woelpper's company howled and whistled their encouragement. This brewing conflict was the most interesting form of entertainment that the men had witnessed for many hours. They were bored beyond description. A good fight, be it verbal or physical, would be an excellent distraction from the dull monotony of the encampment.

"You had best put that finger away, George," Abe warned. "I am hungry enough to roast it over this fire and eat it."

The three dozen men who were packed into the cramped room erupted into raucous laughter.

"If I thought cooking it would make it warm once again, I would gladly surrender it to you," Private Strouss retorted.

The laughter grew even louder. Abe grinned and winked at his friend. Private Strouss grinned back, hurled his glove playfully at Abe, and then stepped over two of his reclining comrades to close the door against the invading December chill.

In reality, the mangled assemblage of wood that leaned crookedly within its crumbling frame was a door in name only. It hung loosely on its hinges, and had wide cracks that had formed decades earlier between its thin, ancient boards. The twinkling light of the outdoor campfires, as well as the howling winter winds, flowed freely through those cracks in the wood and around the partially rotten, poorly constructed door frame. Still, it provided a meager but welcome deterrent against the invasive cold.

Night had fallen on yet another unremarkable day in the Continental Army. The men of the companies of the German Regiment commanded by Captains Weiser and Woelpper were bivouacked in an abandoned farmhouse on the outskirts of Washington's camp. The General had his army deployed temporarily in the tiny township of Newtown, Pennsylvania.

The American forces had recently abandoned all military operations in New Jersey and retreated across the Delaware River. The British and their Hessian allies controlled all ground in New Jersey, on the eastern side of the river. The Continental forces controlled Pennsylvania to the west. Washington and his men remained camped near the waterway in the hope that their presence would deter a potential winter incursion by the enemy. The commanding general had actually ordered all boats burned and sunk for several miles north and south of Newtown to prevent such an invasion. Now, the soldiers of the Continental Army were strategically positioned and keeping vigilant watch toward the east.

In warmer weather, the men would have complained about being in the horribly cramped quarters of their abandoned house. However, in the current winter conditions, the packed quarters were a blessing, indeed. The close proximities of bodies, bedrolls, and blankets ensured extra shared warmth against the cold. Besides, considering that most of Washington's army was sheltering inside of tiny two-man tents, no one would dream of complaining about having an actual roof over their heads, regardless of its questionable condition. A functional fireplace for cooking and keeping warm was an added bonus.

Two days prior, Colonel Haussegger had assigned these two companies sentry duty on the outer periphery of the camp. They were charged with monitoring traffic along the road that led northeast from the village toward McConkey's ferry, the nearest boat crossing over the Delaware River. However, the weather was far too cold and unpleasant to post sentries out of doors for any length of time. Instead, the captains cleverly devised a schedule for keeping watch through a small window on the second floor of the house. It provided a perfect view of the road and the approach toward Newtown. When not keeping watch, the soldiers spent the remainder of their time sleeping and attempting to keep warm and somewhat fed.

"What news have you from the outside world, George?" Michael Yeisley inquired. "Any excitement at headquarters today?"

Private Strouss joined Michael and several other men near the fireplace. He stretched his frozen hands toward the crackling fire. Michael poured him a pewter mug full of hot, freshly-brewed tea.

Michael apologized, "I am sorry, but there is no sugar."

"Sugar? What is that?" George quipped. He smiled and took a grateful swig of the hot drink. After a brief pause, he replied to

Michael's question. "Well, there is some news. Men are pouring into the camp. Lots of men."

"Indeed?" Yeisley responded. "How many?" He leaned forward and reached toward the large pot that dangled beneath a fireplace crane. He stirred the contents vigorously with an iron ladle. He grabbed a pewter bowl and spooned out a measure of the soupy concoction.

George responded, "General Sullivan arrived mid-day with almost 2,000 well-outfitted troops. General Gates arrived unexpectedly from Fort Ticonderoga only an hour ago. He brought about eight hundred men."

Abraham let out a low whistle. "So many! And they could not have come at a better time. We have been losing men by the droves to desertion. And most of the fellows who fought in York City and are still on the rolls have enlistments expiring at year's end."

George nodded. "The general seemed very pleased, indeed. He knows full well that his men are abandoning him in great numbers. Morale is very low. Honestly, I think the general's morale is low. He seems broody and distant. This influx of fresh troops should help keep the army intact through the winter."

Michael handed the soldier a bowl filled with hot peas flavored with tiny pieces of pork. "Do you believe that we will remain here for winter quarters? Did you hear any talk of it amongst the officers?"

Private Strouss sniffed the bowl. He smiled. "Thank you, Michael." He took a quick bite, and then responded, "No, I do not think we shall remain here. Something else is afoot. I believe that General Washington has some action in mind."

"Where?" Michael demanded apprehensively.

Strouss shrugged and took another bite. "I cannot be certain. But, I have heard talk of Trenton. Reports show that there are over 1,000 Hessians stationed there, quartering for the winter."

"*Mein Gott!* Those will be experienced troops from the New York campaign. So, you're saying the man is considering an attack with Christmas upon us and in this ungodly cold and wet weather?" Abe wailed.

Strouss nodded. He chewed noisily as he spoke, "And from the whispers that I heard, it will be very soon. His Excellency wishes to make a move before the enlistments are up for all of his original regiments."

"What a wonderful sentiment!" Abe mocked. *"Merry Christmas, boys! Hurry up and get killed before you go home.'* And just think! Our enlistments have barely even started. We have only just arrived in camp, and we are already staring at the possibility of winter battle."

"Look at it this way," Michael teased. "If you get killed now, you will be spared the cold of this winter's encampment."

"That is most definitely the case for you, Abraham," declared Private Strouss as he chewed his soft peas and stared thoughtfully into the warm, crackling fire. "Should you be killed, the fires of hell will, most certainly, be much warmer than New Jersey."

The men in the crowded room exploded, once again, in laughter.

Mid-Morning - Christmas Day, 1776
Washington's Headquarters

HIS EXCELLENCY, General George Washington, was busy at his field desk. He despised the burdens of paperwork and letter writing that consumed the lion's share of his time as commander of the army. He sighed wistfully and stared longingly at the five-candle stand that glowed merrily on his desk. It reminded him of Mount Vernon at Christmastime. His thoughts wandered to that magical place. He wondered what his beloved Martha was doing at that very moment. Closing his eyes, he tried to imagine being back home. He lost himself in the memories of the sights, sounds, and smells of home and Christmas. He scarcely heard the rustle of linen when the door to the tent opened.

"Taking a nap, are we now, George? That is no way to command an army!"

The general's heart leapt with joy at the familiar, welcome voice.

"Benjamin Rush! What, in the name of Heaven, are you doing here?"

The commander of America's armies rose quickly and stepped from behind his desk. He offered a warm handshake to his old friend. Dr. Rush was accompanied by a younger, distinguished-looking fellow, unfamiliar to the general.

"And who is this?" General Washington inquired.

"George, allow me to introduce Dr. Nicklaus Schell. He is a colleague of mine from Philadelphia. The lad is considering service with the army. He was at Breed's Hill last year and treated countless wounded."

General Washington shook Dr. Schell's hand. "Indeed? How did you come to be at such a place, Dr. Schell?"

"Happenstance, General. I was on a fact-finding tour for Dr. Rush. I was visiting at a home in Charlestown when the British attacked. Unfortunately, I received a rather rapid and most thorough course of training in battlefield medicine."

"Of that I have no doubt, sir," the General responded. He motioned to two chairs in front of his desk. "Please, gentlemen ... sit. I will have my orderly fetch us some brandy. Do you require food?"

Dr. Rush shook his head. "No, George. We enjoyed dinner at a tavern on the way from Philadelphia. Besides, we do not wish to tarry long. You have much business, no doubt, to which you must attend."

The general knit his brow and nodded. "'Tis true, I am afraid. We are on the verge of an action that is demanding all of my attention at the moment."

"Indeed? Where?" Dr. Rush inquired.

General Washington chuckled, "You know that I cannot divulge such information to a civilian, Ben ... even one who is a member of the Congress. You could be captured on the way out of camp or on the road to Philadelphia. Spies abound in this country. I must maintain the tightest security. I trust that you understand."

Dr. Rush flushed from embarrassment. "Of course, George. Please forgive me for being so intrusive regarding your military affairs."

General Washington smiled. "Think nothing of it. Now, tell me, why have you come to my encampment on Christmas Day?"

"To cheer you up, George! And to bring you this." He reached into his satchel and removed a pamphlet. "It is a brand-new publication from Thomas Paine. He has called it, '*The American Crisis.*' The fellow's words inspired and moved me. I hope that it will do the same for you and for your men. In fact, I brought several dozen copies for you to distribute amongst your officers."

The general glanced at the cover of the pamphlet. He mumbled the words of the first sentence. "*These are the times that try men's souls: The summer soldier and the sunshine patriot will, in this crisis, shrink from the service of his country; but he that stands it now, deserves the love and thanks of man and woman.*"

The general paused and took a deep, emotional breath. Dr. Rush could almost swear that Washington daubed a tear from the corner of his eye.

"Ben, I am most grateful. I have not even finished the first paragraph, and I appreciate it already. I promise that I will study the text after your departure. I will give it every consideration for a reading before the men."

"Excellent!" Dr. Rush proclaimed. "Allow me to leave these other copies with you."

He rose and removed the thick stack of papers from his leather bag. He placed the documents carefully on the general's desk. As he tarried near the desk, he saw a scrap of paper with three words scribbled on it. The paper read, '*Victory or Death.*' Dr. Rush pointed at the note.

"That is a most interesting combination of words, George."

The general quickly covered the paper with a small satchel that was lying nearby.

"I would ask you to pretend that you never saw that, Ben. I would hate to have to change tonight's challenge and countersign." The general grinned.

"Your secret is safe with us, General."

Just at that moment, there came a dull knock upon the post beside the entrance to the tent.

"Who is there?" the General called out, somewhat annoyed. "And where is my orderly?"

"Private Yeisley, German Regiment, sir. I have the regimental report from Major Weltner. I believe that your orderly is in the privy, sir. I saw him running rather enthusiastically in that direction."

Dr. Rush chuckled lightly and then quickly covered his mouth. Dr. Schell grinned. The general shook his head and rolled his eyes.

"Enter!" Washington commanded.

Michael Yeisley parted the linen privacy curtain that covered the doorway. He strode confidently into the commanding general's tent. He respectfully placed his cocked hat under his arm and then nodded as a courtesy to the officer.

He announced smartly, "Your report, sir." He extended the rolled-up papers in the general's direction.

"Place it on the orderly table, Private, and then be on your way."

"*Ja, Herr General.*"

Michael stepped toward the table on the opposite side of the room. As he placed the document on top of a stack of similar papers, he stole a glance at the visitors seated in front of the general's desk. The younger fellow looked very familiar to Michael, but he could not seem to remember where or when he had made the man's acquaintance. As he walked back toward the door of the tent, he quite suddenly remembered who the fellow was. It was the doctor who had treated him in Philadelphia after his unfortunate fall while crossing the Schuylkill River.

Without thinking of any potential breech of etiquette or consequence, he spoke out, "*Herr Schell? Sind Sie das?* Is that you?"

The young physician rose to his feet. "*Ja. Ich bin Nicklaus Schell.*" He appeared confused.

"I am Michael Yeisley. You were my physician last winter. I experienced a fall from my wagon while crossing the river near Philadelphia. Your precious mother took care of me in the hospital."

Dr. Schell experienced a sudden recall of the event. "*Ja! Herr Yeis-*

ley! I remember, now. You had a harsh blow to your head, as I recall, and a severe injury to your arm. But, I thought that you were a weaver from one of the northern townships. Why are you here with the army?"

Michael grinned. "I was a weaver. I mean ... I still am a weaver. But, I serve in the army now. I must do my duty for my country."

Dr. Schell nodded. "Indeed. What regiment?"

"Das Deutsche Regiment, Herr Schell."

General Washington cleared his throat. "Perhaps you gentlemen could take your conversation outside, so that Dr. Rush and I might continue our visit."

Michael popped to attention. "No, sir. I mean ... that will not be necessary, sir. I shall depart immediately. Please pardon my rude intrusion."

Dr. Schell offered Michael his hand. "It was good to see you again, *Herr* Yeisley."

"Likewise, *Herr* Schell. Perhaps our paths will cross again soon."

Dr. Schell smiled. "Of that I have no doubt."

Michael nodded respectfully, once again, to his general, turned quickly, and made his exit. Dr. Schell returned to his seat.

"So, there is a German Regiment in your army, General Washington?"

"There is, indeed, Dr. Schell. It is fresh on the field. The men have been here less than three weeks, but they have every appearance of being a fine regiment. However, we must first see how they perform under fire."

Nicklaus nodded thoughtfully. "Is this German Regiment, by any chance, in need of a surgeon?"

Dr. Benjamin Rush beamed with satisfaction and pride.

∾

Noon – Christmas Day
German Regiment Headquarters

"GENTLEMEN, we have received our orders. We are moving out late this afternoon," Colonel Haussegger declared. He smiled grimly as he looked upon the faces of the assembled troops of the German Regiment.

The men were not surprised. They had been hearing various rumors of a coming action. Still, with the onset of winter, they found it a bit difficult to believe that the army was abandoning its camp and moving to engage the enemy.

"What is our destination, sir?" inquired Captain Weiser.

"Trenton. General Washington is determined to strike the Hessian forces wintering there. Intelligence shows that, even though there are over a thousand troops in the town, there are no fortifications. The village appears lightly and incompetently defended."

"What, exactly, are our orders, sir?" asked Major Weltner.

The colonel held up a dispatch from Washington's headquarters. He cleared his throat, and then read authoritatively:

You are to see that your men have three days' provisions ready cooked, everyone fit for duty, except a sergeant and six men to be left with your baggage. You will parade with arms, accoutrements, ammunition (40 cartridges) in best order and with provisions and blankets. No man is to quit his division on pain of instant punishment. Each officer is to provide himself with a piece of white paper stuck in his hat for a field mark. You will order your men to assemble and parade them at 4:00 PM in the valley immediately over the hill from McConkey's Ferry, and remain there for further orders.

The colonel paused and eyed his officers, who were seated in the front. "The parole for this operation is 'Victory.' Countersign is 'or Death.' That is all, gentlemen. Mark your hats as instructed. See to your companies. We depart precisely at 4:00. There will be a six-mile parade to the ferry site, a tedious river crossing, and then a very long and arduous march toward Trenton. It shall be a most taxing night for our army. Please take all precautions to prepare your men for foul weather. My shoulders and my knees are aching. I fear that a storm is upon us." The colonel turned and strutted back toward his quarters.

In the rear of the formation, Abraham turned and stared disbelievingly at Michael. "*Victory or death?*"

Michael nodded solemnly. "*Sieg oder Tod.*"

Abe rolled his eyes. "How reassuring."

~

9:00 PM – McConkey's Ferry Crossing

"If that man reads that damned pamphlet one more time, I shall ram it down his gullet!" declared a tempestuous Abraham Price.

The corporal droned on. He was reading, for the fourth time, from the words of Thomas Paine's, *The American Crisis*. General Washington distributed the document to all of his officers and ordered it read to the men as they waited to cross the river.

"Wait! Wait!" exclaimed Private John Snyder. "This is my favorite part!"

The corporal proclaimed, "*Tyranny, like hell, is not easily conquered; yet we have this consolation with us, that the harder the conflict, the more glorious the triumph.*"

"Doesn't that sound grand?" Private Snyder reflected.

"Whatever do you mean?" challenged Abraham Price. "Why is that your favorite part?"

"It mentions hell," Snyder answered.

"Huh?" Abe was genuinely confused.

Private Snyder exhaled, frustrated. "Hell, I say! Hell, Abraham! Hell! The part about hell sounds wonderful." He grumbled, "At least it is warm there."

The men of Captain Weiser's company chuckled half-heartedly at John's wit. But, truth be told, the men were in no mood for humor. The afternoon started off tolerable enough, but after dark the temperature had dropped precipitously. Within the last half-hour, a cold, misty rain had begun to fall.

So, the men of the company huddled together for warmth. There were no buildings or evergreen trees to provide shelter for the men waiting to cross the Delaware River. They protected themselves from the cold and rain as best they could. Most of the soldiers had already strapped a protective layer of makeshift wool coverings over the exteriors of their leather shoes. Since there were no waterproofed tarpaulins or oilcloths to be had, the men sought what little protection they could find beneath their wool blankets. However, it did not take long for the absorbent wool to become soaked from the rain.

The men of the German Regiment, like all of the other men waiting with them on the western side of the river, or floating on board the Durham boats and ferries, or gathered on the eastern bank in New Jersey, were thoroughly cold, wet, and miserable. And the night had only just begun.

"Look!" Michael Yeisley exclaimed. "Major Weltner is coming."

The major approached the group of men. He waved in a friendly manner and then squatted beside the blanket-covered cluster of frozen soldiers.

"How are you fellows holding up?"

"We are quite cold, sir," Michael declared. "How much longer will we be waiting for our crossing?"

Weltner shook his head in disgust. "Quite a while, I am afraid. Getting across this icy river is taking longer than expected. The cannons and horses are quite difficult to load on the ferries, and we have precious few boats for moving troops. We are numbered amongst the second-to-last division scheduled to cross, so you boys must make the best of it. We still have at least a couple of hours to wait before we get our turn in the boats."

"When is the attack scheduled?" one of the men mumbled from beneath his blanket.

"General Washington wanted to attack near midnight, but there is no way in this frozen hell *that* is going to happen. Once we get across, we still have a ten or eleven-mile march south to Trenton."

"Ten or eleven miles?" Abraham exhaled in disbelief. "In this weather?"

Major Weltner shrugged. "This was the only crossing available to us, Private Price. What would you have us do? Attempt to transport 3,000 men at the Trenton crossing, in full view of the Hessians and under fire from their muskets and artillery?"

"I suppose not," Abe replied sheepishly.

"No, I suppose not, indeed." He slapped Abraham encouragingly on the shoulder. "But, keep your spirits up, men. We will likely attack at daylight. The Hessians should not be expecting us. Our spies tell us they do not have any patrols out tonight. The weather is simply too bad. It should be a rout!" He stood and glanced toward the water. "Just hold on as best you can. I will come and fetch all of you when it is our turn in the boats."

As the officer walked away, Abe Price tugged his blanket closer beneath his chin. He declared to no one in particular, "If ever we live that long."

~

December 26, 1776 – Just After Midnight
Crossing the Delaware River

AFTER ALMOST SIX hours of waiting, the men of the German Regiment were finally loaded in the boats. Though they were not, at all, anxious to be on the other side of the river, they *were* anxious to get moving. Anything was better than sitting still and suffering in the midst of a relentless winter storm.

The dull rain that began falling before dark had eventually changed to sleet. There were moments when the ice pellets were so large and fell so hard and fast that they were akin to small hailstones. The wind was howling from the north. The temperature continued to drop. The men all knew that they were under the assault of a fearsome winter nor'easter. What had started as an unpleasant night had quickly become bitterly cold and impossibly torturous.

Michael and his friends were among twenty-five men from the various companies in the German Regiment, all huddled in the bottom of one of the low-riding Durham boats. Two men from the Pennsylvania Navy were actually in command of the small vessel. The sailor on the bow used a long pole to probe for the bottom. The fellow on the stern steered the craft with his oar. The navy men had assigned oars to four soldiers on each side of the boat. The other men seated along the periphery were responsible for bailing the frigid water and accumulating sleet from the bottom of the craft with small buckets and piggins.

Everyone else seated in the center of the boat received a very simple assignment. They were the "ballast." The boat captain ordered them to remain as still as possible and help ensure that the boat did not tip over from all of the activity of the oars and bailing buckets. The captain was determined not to lose a single man from his boat into the deep, icy waters of the Delaware.

There had already been a handful of mishaps during the crossing. The men of the German Regiment had heard the frantic commotion coming from the direction of the dark river each time a man had fallen overboard. Over 2,000 troops were already on the eastern side of the river. Unfortunately, roughly a dozen of that total had gone into the river. They had survived, but all those who entered those icy waters were almost certain to fall ill with chills and fever from the exposure.

Though the current was strong, and the water choppy from the howling wind, the sturdy Durham boat carrying Michael and his mates plowed its way steadily through the dark water. Michael was surprised at how very low in the water the boat was riding. The gunwale was only a few inches above the frothy waves. There was also some surface ice to contend with. Though the river was not frozen over, there were still large, dangerous sheets of ice riding the current downstream. The men handling the oars fought a constant battle against the ice. The heavy chunks impacted against the port side of the boat and attempted to push the vessel downstream and off-course.

Michael was suffering tremendously from the foul conditions. Despite putting on a good front for his fellow troops, he was actually in pitiful shape. The wool wraps over his shoes did little to combat the water and cold. His leather buckle shoes were filled with water and his feet were thoroughly soaked. He had lost all feeling below his knees long before midnight. A couple of his comrades had to support him and help him reach the loading area. After the process of walking to the point of embarkation rejuvenated his circulation and awakened the nerves in his ice-cold feet, he immediately wished that they had remained numb. It felt as if razors were slashing and carving away the flesh from his bones. Silently, Michael's heart and members screamed from the agony of the cold and pain.

After waiting for so many hours, the actual crossing of the Delaware River proceeded unexpectedly quickly. Within minutes, the men of the German Regiment caught sight of the troops on the New Jersey riverbank. Several hundred yards to their left, they spied the dim glow of campfires.

Michael leaned forward and whispered to Abraham, "I must get near one of those fires. I need to change my stockings and thaw my feet, or I shall never reach Trenton."

Abe nodded. "I must warm myself, as well. Worry not. I will get you to a fire, my old friend."

They pressed on toward the muddy bank. Moments later, they heard the underside of the boat scrape against the rocky river bottom. Men standing along the shore grabbed the bow and held the boat steady against the slight eddy that swirled within the landing area.

The officer in charge of the boat began shouting orders. "Disembark immediately! Do not leave behind any weapons or equipment! Help the man in front of you! Proceed quickly, men! We have many more trips to make! Help your comrades who are unable to move! Do not tarry! Time is wasting!"

Michael struggled to his feet. He used his Charleville musket as a crutch to help straighten his stiff knees and enable him to stand upright. As he attempted his first step, he felt his knees buckle slightly. Abe grabbed him by his right arm.

"Steady, now, Michael. Our river crossing is done. Now is not the time to fall into the water, here in full view of all of these godless Virginians. These backwoods farmers may consider eating you!"

Despite his pain and discomfort, Michael grinned at his friend's levity. He did not understand how Abraham could remain so unaffected by the wet, frigid night.

Abe handed his Jaeger rifle to a man on the riverbank. He snatched Michael's musket from his hands and passed it to the same fellow. He then clamored over the bow and found solid footing in the thick mud.

"Someone help me!" he implored. "My comrade is frozen solid. He cannot move his legs."

Two other fellows immediately helped Abraham extract Michael from the boat. They retrieved their weapons and then fell in with the line of frozen men making their way toward the fires. Michael leaned heavily upon his friend. No matter how much he willed them to move, his legs were reluctant to respond.

Captain Weiser's voice soon penetrated the frozen soldiers' grumbling, murmuring, and griping. He was somewhere to the left, off of the path. "Weiser's company! Formation!"

The Germans followed the sound of their captain's voice.

"Is everyone here?" he demanded.

The men glanced throughout the gathering. There was no way for them to see everyone or get an accurate count in the dark. There was no moon, and the night was black as pitch.

"*Scheisse!*" Abraham declared. "It is dark like a cave out here. How in hell are we supposed to know if everyone is present?"

The captain exhaled. "*Verdammt!* This is useless. We have to get near some light."

"We have to build some fires, Captain," Abe responded. "Yeisley here is frozen severely. He cannot feel his feet. Some of the others are almost as bad."

"I agree, Private. We stand in much danger of suffering injury from this cold." He scanned the area where the fires glowed. "The other men of the army are gathered beyond that stone wall. I have been informed that there are some large haystacks near a barn to their north. We can, likely, find some dry hay in the center to kindle our fires."

"Is it safe to display so many campfires?" inquired First Lieutenant Jacob Bower.

"We are ten miles from Trenton, Lieutenant. We could set these haystacks afire, and the Hessians would remain unaware. Still, we must exercise proper caution. We will make every effort to conceal our flames."

"How long before we march on Trenton, Captain?" another of the soldiers asked.

"At least two hours ... perhaps three. There remain almost a thousand men left to cross, which gives us plenty of time to dry out a bit and get warm. Let us not tarry. We must claim one of those haystacks, string up some tarps for cover, and get our fires going."

The men needed no further encouragement. They moved quickly toward the prospect of warmth.

∿

Three Hours Later – 4:00 AM

MICHAEL AWAKENED to a stinging slap on his right cheek. When he finally willed his eyes to open, he was staring into the wet, scraggly face of Abraham Price.

"Yeisley! Wake up! Christ, Almighty, I thought you were dead!"

Michael pushed himself up onto his elbows. He could not believe that he had fallen into such a deep sleep. "What time is it?" he moaned.

"Time to go. The army is forming on the Ferry Road. We are commencing the march."

"How long have I slept?"

"Two hours," Abe answered. "Most of us napped with you. We are reasonably well-rested, compared to most of the army." He grinned mischievously. "I hope you do not mind ... I climbed up inside that warm hole and cuddled against you. But, I assure you, my intentions were honorable."

Michael smiled and retorted, "I thought I smelled an odd stench in here."

"'Tis all those mushy peas that we have been eating!" Abe rose and kicked Michael in the shin. He wrapped his wool blanket around his shoulders and then strapped his knapsack across his back.

"Michael, you had best cover your shoulders with your blanket, as well. I dried yours as best I could. You will need it to help keep the snow and ice off of your cartridges and equipment."

Michael groaned and then began to crawl from his warm cave inside the haystack. He hated to leave the warmth and comfort of the soft hay. Abe had hollowed him a spot inside the stack whilst searching for dry material for the fire. Michael's loyal friend had also attended to his soaked, frozen feet. He had removed Michael's shoes and placed them on a rock beside the fire. He had even removed his soaked stockings and hung them to dry, replacing them with a fresh pair.

Michael felt like a new man, indeed. He stared at his cold, aching feet. Abe had already returned his semi-dry shoes back to their proper place. He had also wrapped Michael's lower extremities with makeshift woolen foot-mittens and stuffed those wool wraps thickly with dry hay. Michael grinned at their strange appearance. He stole a glance at the other men of Captain Weiser's company. All of the men, including the captain, had wrapped their feet thusly.

Captain Weiser chirped, "We must make haste, gentlemen! His Excellency is on the move!"

The men groaned. Minutes later, the German Regiment was formed, by companies, on the Upper Ferry Road. Soon, the order came for silent march. There were no drums or fifes or songs. The general wanted stealth as his army approached Trenton. He was counting upon the element of surprise.

Silently, and without fanfare, the southward march began.

7:00 AM – Northwest of Trenton

THE SNOW CEASED JUST before dawn. The men of the German regiment were flanking the town, marching southeast through the fields toward the road to Princeton, on the far side of Trenton. They had been given a most inglorious assignment. They were tasked with securing the road and preventing any reinforcements from relieving the Hessians once the attack began.

The troops of the German Regiment were thoroughly disgusted. After suffering through a most intolerable and stormy night, and after marching over fifteen total miles through mud, ice, and snow, they would not be joining the assault upon the town. The attack was being left to the "more experienced" troops under Generals Sullivan and Greene.

The men marched silently. As they walked, their bulky, wool and hay-wrapped feet dislodged the snow and trampled upon the tall, ice-coated grass that lay beneath. The long blades of thick, icy grass snapped, emitting a soft, muffled chime akin to the high-pitched sound of shattering glass. It was a most curious sound, indeed. Hundreds of feet created a jingling chorus of shattering ice.

The regiment came upon the crest of a small hill and spied the Princeton Road below and to the south.

Major Weltner called quietly, "Halt! This is the spot, men! We shall occupy this high ground and maintain watch over the road. Spread out! Captain Weiser, take your company and occupy that knoll on the far side of the road. Move one hundred yards toward the west and maintain watch toward Trenton. We cannot allow any messengers or runners to escape. Remember, our task is to prevent reinforcement from Princeton."

"Yes, sir." Captain Weiser waved to his troops. "Let us go. Across the road, men! *Schnell!*"

Most of the three hundred troops of the regiment scattered across the hilltop and spilled over into the shallow valley below. Captain Weiser's company lumbered through the wet snow toward the roadway. They paused and knelt near the ditch before crossing. The captain checked carefully in both directions, then guided his men across. They moved toward their right one hundred yards, per the major's instructions. They quickly took up positions on the back side of a small hill that provided an excellent vantage point over the highway.

"Get low on the ground, men!" the captain commanded. "Intervals of three yards. Watch that road. Shoot anything in a Hessian uniform."

The men groaned. No one had any desire to lie in the snow.

"*Scheisse*, Captain Weiser! We don't even know what a Hessian uniform looks like!" complained Private Jacob Lorash.

"Shut up! And do as I say!" the Captain barked sharply. "I want no silhouettes. Make yourselves invisible." He stared stonily at Private Lorash. "I fear that you will find out what a Hessian looks like soon enough."

All thirty men dropped reluctantly onto the ground. Their wool blanket wraps crackled and popped as the men fell to their knees. The snow and ice had actually frozen into solid sheets on their backs. The men began to dig down into the thick snow. They worked together to cover one another's backs with blankets, tarps, and tents. Minutes later, the field was quiet and still. Captain Weiser was worried about the visibility of the dark, gray blankets and tarps against the milky white snow. Their position was entirely too visible from the east. However, he would not have to worry for long.

The wind continued to blow briskly. A wave of dark precipitation began to blow in from the northeast. Soon, the men heard the unmistakable drumming sound of sleet. The huge pellets of ice assaulted the field and the men who lay flat on the ground beneath their blankets and cloths. Huge, fast-falling flakes of snow intermingled with the ice pellets. Almost immediately, the Germans were covered and thoroughly concealed beneath a camouflaging blanket of ice and snow.

"The enemy will not find us now," Michael whispered to Abraham.

"It is not as if they are looking, my friend. I quite think that everyone in New Jersey is still asleep," Abe retorted sarcastically.

Michael grunted. "Except for us."

"Except for us," Abraham echoed.

Seconds later, the unmistakable sound of musket fire erupted in the west. It was sporadic at first, but grew in intensity. Then came the thunderous rumble of General Washington's cannons. At least a dozen deep booms echoed through the valley. Curiously, Michael could feel the ground vibrate beneath his belly.

"It sounds as if General Washington has delivered a belated Christmas greeting," he observed.

Abraham chuckled. "And I suppose that our Hessian brethren are awake, now."

8

VICTORS AND TRAITORS

They could hear the battle raging in Trenton. The barrage of gunfire continued without abating. The men of Captain Weiser's regiment maintained careful vigil toward the town, watching for retreating Hessians. Suddenly, a rider appeared on the road, moving fast in their direction.

"Captain!" Michael exclaimed. "Someone is coming! One man, on horseback!"

"Make ready your weapons!" the captain commanded.

A chorus of clicking hammers echoed across the snow-covered hilltop. When the rider was a mere fifty paces away, Captain Weiser rose from concealment and declared loudly and authoritatively, "Halt!"

The rider tugged at the reins of his mount in an effort to bring the galloping animal to stop. The mare's hooves skidded haphazardly in the snow, and it appeared that the horse was in danger of tumbling from the roadway. Just before careening into the ditch, the horse managed to gain some traction in the rocky mud beneath the ice, and slid to a grinding stop. A long, white piece of paper peeked from behind the cockade on the rider's hat. It was the sign of a Continental.

Captain Weiser challenged, "Victory!"

The man smiled and responded, "Or death!"

The Germans on the hilltop relaxed. There could be no doubt. The man was a fellow Patriot.

Captain Weiser demanded, "State your purpose, young man."

"I am here under orders of General Washington. Are you of the German Regiment?"

Weiser nodded. "I am, indeed. Captain Benjamin Weiser."

The man nodded respectfully. "Captain. I am Lieutenant Horace Andrews, bearing orders from His Excellency. Your regiment is being recalled immediately. Command no longer fears reinforcements from Princeton. The battle appears to be all but won, yet we are in danger of a large number of the Hessians making their escape to the east. The general has ordered your regiment to proceed forthwith and advance upon the town. You are charged with 'closing the back door' of Trenton, sir. The general wants prisoners."

"Should we expect action against the enemy?" Captain Weiser inquired hopefully.

"Heavy action, sir. The entire Hessian force will be moving in your direction."

"We are departing immediately. Inform General Washington."

The rider tipped his hat, then turned and guided his horse off of the road toward the northwest. His mount kicked up a spray of slush and mud as it grinded its way across the open field.

Captain Weiser nudged one of his soldiers with his foot. "Private, inform Colonel Haussegger and Major Weltner of our new orders. Our company will depart immediately. The remainder of the regiment must follow as quickly as possible."

"Yes, sir!" The private clamored to his feet, grabbed his blanket, and then ran along the road toward his comrades who lay concealed behind the nearby hills.

The captain clapped his hands and urged his troops, "Get up off your arses, boys! We are getting into this fight!"

~

MICHAEL COULD SCARCELY BELIEVE IT. He actually had sweat on his brow. The perspiration trickled down from his forehead and dripped from the end of his nose. He was panting for air. And, for the first time in over fourteen hours, he was not thinking about his frozen feet. He was not thinking about the cold and snow. He was not thinking about the gnawing hunger in his belly. He was not thinking about pain. Like the other men of the German Regiment, he thought only of the explosions and gunfire somewhere ahead in the snowy fog and haze. The din of the pitched battle grew louder and louder with each step he took toward Trenton.

Michael and the other soldiers of Captain Weiser's company lumbered awkwardly along the snow-blanketed road. They had been running, despite their cumbersome wool and hay-wrapped feet, for almost a half-mile. Michael was relieved when he caught sight of the rooftops of the town. However, simultaneously, his heart filled with terror and fear from the deafening explosions and pillars of billowing, flame-laced smoke rising into the air.

Suddenly, an officer in a brightly-colored blue and white Continental uniform appeared in the middle of the road. He waved excitedly at the Germans and pointed to their left, guiding them onto the southern side of the highway. Michael recognized the man. It was the Frenchman, Matthias Alexis Roche de Fermoy, a brigadier general in Washington's army. He was the commander of the brigade that included the German Regiment.

The general called frantically and in a heavy French accent, "Are you the Germans? This cannot be all of you! Where are the others?"

"*Oui*, General. I am Captain Weiser. We are the lead element of the regiment. The remainder of our men are following close behind. What are your orders?"

The general pointed into the haze. "There is a small creek approximately one-quarter mile this way. Two regiments of Hessians have escaped the town and taken refuge in a large orchard of apple trees directly south of the canal. You must deploy along that creek and engage the enemy in the trees. General Stephen's men will join you, but I am having trouble locating them in this horrid weather. You must proceed quickly. We must surround these Hessians and convince them to surrender."

The two officers heard the dull chomping of feet treading through brittle, ice-crusted snow. They glanced to the northeast and saw the remainder of the regiment approaching at a slow run. Almost two hundred and fifty men churned up the wet, sloppy snow, exposing the mud beneath. Major Weltner was in the lead. He was the first man to arrive at the improvised parley in the middle of the Princeton Turnpike.

Captain Weiser made the introduction. "General ... this is Major Weltner, our second in command."

The major nodded. "General."

"Where is Haussegger?" demanded General Fermoy.

Major Weltner answered matter-of-factly, "He insisted that a horse be located for his use. He is standing in the roadway, to our east, awaiting a suitable animal."

Captain Weiser shook his head in disbelief. There was a moment of stunned silence.

The general grunted his displeasure. "So be it, then. Major, you will lead the blocking force. Captain Weiser has my instructions and will brief you as you go. Please deploy immediately!"

Weiser grinned. He pointed in the direction of the as-yet unseen apple orchard. Major Weltner called over his shoulder to the soldiers of his regiment, "Follow me, men! Keep silent! *Schnell!*"

Abe Price poked Michael in the ribs and muttered, "*Sieg oder Tod.*" It was the German translation of the challenge and response for the day, and General Washington's motto for this battle ... "*Victory or Death!*"

THE SNOW WAS DEEPER in the thick grass of the meadows near the town. It slowed the men considerably, but they soon reached their assigned area. The creek that the general mentioned was actually little more than a ditch. The bare, scraggly limbs of an orchard were barely visible in the glade beyond, shrouded in a frozen mist. The officers deployed their men in a long line that followed the pathway of the shallow ditch. They stood peering into the orchard, attempting to discern if any enemy soldiers were hiding there. They could see none.

The sudden, unexpected call of a German voice from deep in the icy fog verified the enemy's presence. The voice proclaimed, *"Feuer frei!"*

Hessian muskets flashed and barked in the distance. Tiny geysers of snow and mud leapt into the air in front of the German Regiment soldiers. The enemy's bullets landed on the far side of the ditch. Clearly, the Hessians were "firing blind." They had no real bearing on the position of the Continentals. The flash of their muskets, however, provided an ideal aiming point for Major Weltner and his German Regiment.

"On the firing line, men! Make ready!"

The muskets, Jaegers, and fowling guns of the German Regiment clicked to the ready. The men held their guns sideways and upright in front of their chests to demonstrate their readiness to the commander. Major Weltner inspected the line. He smiled proudly.

"Use their flashes and smoke as your targets. Aim high. We are at a considerable distance." He took a deep breath. "Level!"

The men raised their guns high and then took careful aim into the orchard.

"Fire!"

Almost three hundred guns exploded simultaneously, unleashing a hail of deadly lead into the orchard. Screams of indignation and pain pierced the smoky, frozen mist. Some of the balls had found their targets. The German Regiment had drawn its first blood.

Michael was numb from the thrill of it all. He had just fired a shot in battle. He felt proud and excited, as did the other men of the regiment.

Major Weltner ordered, "Clear all misfires! Prime your firelocks!"

The soldiers frantically began the process of reloading their weapons. Michael jerked open the flap of his cartridge pouch and grabbed at one of the paper tubes. In his excitement and haste, he fumbled the cartridge and it tumbled from his aching, frozen fingers into the damp snow. The powder was ruined.

He cursed, *"Verdammt! Scheisse!"*

He pawed at another cartridge and lifted it to his mouth. He tore open the powder end and daubed a small pile into his pan. He instantly flipped the frizzen down and then dropped the buttstock onto the ground. He quickly poured the remaining powder down the barrel, then crammed the paper and ball into the muzzle.

More fire erupted from the orchard in front of him. This time, the shots approached a bit closer, but still fell short of their mark. Most impacted near and into the ditch in front of the regiment. After a brief pause, Michael ripped the ramming rod from beneath his barrel and tamped his load, then quickly returned the rod to its place. He lifted his musket to the ready position. He glanced left and right. Most of the men appeared ready to fire.

Major Weltner shouted, "Prepare to advance! Ten paces, on my order! Advance!"

The soldiers marched forward into the ditch. A handful of men slipped and fell into the water, unleashing a chorus of curses up and down the line. Their comrades helped them to their feet and the regiment proceeded forward in a somewhat ragged formation. Ten paces later, the men heard Major Weltner's commanding voice once again.

"Halt! Clean up this rank! I want a straight line!" He paused to allow the men to follow his order. He then shouted, "Extend ranks! Firing by twos!"

The captains repeated his command for their respective companies. Every other man stepped forward, forming two parallel lines. Michael stepped up and took his place in the first rank. The men awaited the next order. Meanwhile, the enemy soldiers peppered sporadic fire in their direction.

Michael's adrenaline flowed. His legs and knees were beginning to ache from the excitement. He heard enemy lead impacting the ground nearby. He thought that he heard one round whistle near his left ear. However, he could not be certain, since both of his ears were still ringing from the first volley that he and his fellow soldiers had fired. He could feel the ground vibrating beneath his feet from the impacts of cannon fire in the village to his right. The battle was reaching a frenzied pitch. He could hear shouts and screams in the distance, both in the town and in the orchard ahead of him.

"First rank, make ready!"

Firelocks clicked into action.

"Level!"

Michael brought his musket down and took aim. He was shocked when he saw the mist dissipate for just a fleeting moment. He observed the figure of a man, about fifty paces in front of him, kneeling beside a tree. He aimed directly at the man's chest.

"Fire!"

Michael pulled the trigger. His musket roared and kicked violently against his shoulder. The smoke and fire blinded him temporarily. A gray and white haze of exploding gunfire lingered over the battlefield, obscuring everyone's vision. Michael was frustrated that he could not see if his shot had found its mark.

"Second rank, five paces forward! First rank, clear all misfires and prime your firelocks!"

The second rank stepped forward between the members of the first and occupied their new position in the front of the line. Moments later, they followed the same instructions as had the first, as they unleashed their concentrated volley upon the surrounded Hessians. Whilst they were firing, Michael's rank reloaded their flintlock weapons. They moved more swiftly and efficiently than they had during the first reload. The repetition of their training had taken over, counteracting the fear and confusion of battle. The first rank was ready to fire in less than thirty seconds. Major Weltner directed Michael's rank forward and ordered them, once again, to open fire.

Michael's excitement continued to build. He had just fired his third shot in battle, and his regiment was closing fast on the enemy. He reached down and felt for his bayonet, confirming that it was still safely tucked inside its leather frog. He dreaded the notion, but he knew that the command to fix bayonets could be coming very soon. He wanted to be prepared.

In front of the German Regiment, there was a haunting din of wailing and screaming from deep inside the mist and smoke. Then, there came an echoing call from the enemy position. It was a single word that the Continentals longed to hear. Somewhere, on the far side of the apple orchard, an unseen officer exclaimed, "Quarter! Quarter!"

Major Weltner responded, "*Ergeben Sie sich!* Drop your weapons!"

Weltner's men joined him in the call. Every voice in the German Regiment demanded, "Drop your weapons! Surrender! Surrender immediately!"

Dozens of voices echoed in response, "*Nicht schießen. Ich ergebe mich!*"

Major Weltner spoke confidently, "Prime all weapons! Maintain vigilance, men! Move forward!"

The soldiers of the German Regiment eased ahead, weapons at the ready. They soon discovered their foes. The Hessians were standing amongst the apple trees, their hands high in the air. Muskets, blades, and equipment, along with dead and wounded men, littered the ground.

Michael walked to the spot where he had glimpsed the enemy soldier during the battle. His heart sank when he discovered, beside the tree, a Hessian private. He was sprawled backward with arms outstretched. His musket lay near his head. His legs were curled awkwardly beneath his body. He was but a lad, no more than seventeen or eighteen years or age. There was a perfect, round hole on the right side of the boy's chest. Clotting blood oozed from his lifeless mouth. His eyes were fixed open and staring, empty, into the gray sky above.

Michael was overwhelmed with emotion. He had taken a life. Yes, this young man was the enemy, but he was also a fellow German. And he was dead. There was nothing that Michael could do to bring him back ... to undo what had been done. He dropped down on his knees beside the Hessian, reached forward, and closed his lifeless eyes. He silently uttered a prayer for the boy's eternal soul.

Nearby, to the south, the Continental soldiers heard other calls for quarter and surrender. Then, quickly and quite unexpectedly, all musketry and cannon fire dwindled and then ceased.

The battle was won. Trenton had been taken with minimal losses. The German Regiment, in its first combat action, had just captured over six hundred enemy troops.

Abraham walked over to Michael and placed his hand on his friend's shoulder. "It appears that today is not our day to die, my friend. Today, we have victory."

Michael smiled grimly and replied, "Not death." He glanced regretfully at the body in front of him. "Not for us, anyway."

~

December 27, 1776
Philadelphia

"YOU UNDERSTAND, of course, that I cannot assure you an assignment to the German Regiment," Dr. Rush explained. "Though I am an officer in the Hospital Department, I cannot accomplish my every wish and whim. I do have my limitations."

"My true desire is to serve amongst my countrymen," Nicklaus declared.

Dr. Rush nodded. "I understand that fully. I know that our glorious victory at Trenton has done much to lift the spirits of our people. I also know that it has greatly elevated the German Regiment's reputation in the army."

"Yes, sir." Dr. Schell nodded.

"Are you certain that you wish to join our forces at this time?"

Nicklaus nodded. "Now is the perfect time. The influx of wounded and sick into our city is appalling. Men are dying by the dozens each day. We have neither the facilities nor the personnel to care for them properly. If I join a regiment as a surgeon, perhaps I could make a difference in the field. Hospitals closer to the battlefield would, obviously, be a wiser and more effective strategy for treatment."

"I agree, of course." Dr. Rush removed his glasses and dropped them onto the stack of papers that littered his desk. He leaned back in his chair and interlocked his fingers atop his somewhat portly belly. He yawned loudly. "My apologies, Nicklaus. I am exhausted. And I am sorry that I have so little time to devote to your request. I depart in the morning to join our forces in New Jersey."

"And I intend to accompany you, sir," Nicklaus announced firmly.

Nicklaus' supervisor closed his eyes and contemplated for a moment. "I have heard rumors that another regiment will be forming this spring. It is to be commanded by Colonel Thomas Hartley. It will be populated by men of Pennsylvania, mostly Germans. Does such a regiment as this appeal to you?"

Nicklaus' eyes twinkled with excitement. "It does, indeed!"

"Even if you have to wait a few months for your official assignment?"

"Absolutely, sir!"

"Very well, then. I will escort you to the office of the Hospital Department this afternoon and present you to Dr. John Morgan. That inept, arrogant bastard will soon be departing from our ranks, God willing. It is my sincere hope that Dr. William Shippen will take his place very soon. Still, Morgan remains in charge for now. We shall stand before him and get you sworn in today. Then, hopefully, Dr. Shippen can get you assigned to Hartley's Regiment upon our return from New Jersey."

"'Our return,' sir?"

"You said that you wanted to accompany me, did you not?" He grinned affectionately. "Now, be gone with you! Pack your bags and prepare for the cold. We will join the Pennsylvania troops in the field in short order. But first, meet me for dinner at the City Tavern at noon. We shall dine on stew and fresh bread and then take care of the paperwork and formalities. I want you on Congress' payroll by day's end."

"Yes, sir!" Dr. Schell beamed with excitement. He darted from the doctor's office. Taking a deep breath, he headed in the direction of the soldier's ward. He had yet to inform his mother of his plans. Nicklaus knew that she would less than be pleased.

"AND YOU ARE certain that this is what you must do?" Katharina Schell inquired in an uncharacteristically dispassionate voice.

"Yes, *Mutter*. I must join the cause."

Katharina shook her head in an effective non-verbal scold. "I fail to see how you can serve the American cause any more faithfully than you already are. There are countless thousands of sick and wounded soldiers right here in Philadelphia. You are needed here. Indeed, your skills are essential here."

"You simply do not understand, *Mutter!*"

"Then, help me to understand, Nicklaus! Why must you go off to a battlefield in New Jersey in order to be a doctor, when you can serve the same soldiers right here in this city, and sleep in your own bed at night? Men are dying in our hospital every day, and yet you want to leave this place and abandon them to their fates? It defies all reason!"

Tears welled in her son's eyes. "You were not there, *Mutter*. You did not see what I saw."

Her face became stoic and still. "You are speaking of Boston, and Breed's Hill."

"Yes, *Mutter!* Breed's Hill. I saw the resolve of King George and the British soldiers. They killed hundreds of Colonists and sacrificed many hundreds of their own in the effort. They aim to keep this continent and rule it beneath a blanket of tyranny and blood." He paused and drew a deep breath. "And I cannot let that stand. I am now a citizen of these United States of America, and I intend to serve my country in its army. I shall be a regimental surgeon."

Katharina sighed, frustrated. "Then, it is settled. It does not matter what more I say."

"Of course, it matters, *Mutter*. But, you shall not change my mind. My resolve is as stone. I *will* join the army."

"And Dr. Rush approves of this?"

"He is escorting me to the Hospital Department this afternoon. I leave tomorrow morning to accompany him to the battle front in New Jersey. I will assist him in supporting the Pennsylvania troops until I receive my permanent assignment."

She choked back a sob. "Well, I suppose we have many preparations to make. I must gather, launder, and mend your clothing. And I will prepare foodstuffs for you to take with you. I hear that horrid General Washington is barely feeding his army." She wiped her nose and eyes with a dingy handkerchief. "What else do you require?"

"Nothing, *Mutter*. Only your blessing, and your prayers."

"I will offer my prayers liberally and freely, my son, but you shall have no blessing of mine. I will wait and worry, as all mothers of soldiers do, until your safe return to our home. No matter what you say, I remain convinced that *this* is where you *truly* belong." She paused. "You shall not change my mind. My resolve is also as stone."

"Then we must agree to disagree."

"Indeed, my son. We must agree to disagree."

"*Ich liebe dich, Mutter.*"

"And I love you, my one and only son."

Later that Afternoon
Continental Army Hospital Department

DR. JOHN MORGAN, Hospital Department director, stood in front of Dr. Nicklaus Schell with Bible in hand and a serious look upon his face. He stared impatiently as Nicklaus scrutinized the paper on his desk. When Nicklaus finished reading, he took quill in hand and added his name to the oath. He also recorded the word, "Surgeon," in a blank near the bottom of the paper. He nodded to Dr. Morgan.

The chief of the Hospital Department cleared his throat. "Your pay, as a Junior Surgeon, will be the sum of two dollars per day, plus four daily rations. Do you understand these terms?"

"Yes, sir."

"Dr. Schell, are you prepared to verbalize the words of your oath?"

"I am, sir."

"Very well, then. Dr. Rush and I will serve as your witnesses. You may proceed. Please place your right hand upon the Holy Scriptures as you declare your oath."

Nicklaus did as he was instructed. He raised the parchment high in his left hand.

"I, Dr. Nicklaus Johann Schell, do acknowledge the United States of America to be Free, Independent, and Sovereign States, and declare that the people thereof owe no allegiance or obedience to George the Third, King of Great Britain; and I renounce, refute and abjure any allegiance or obedience to him; and I do swear that I will to the utmost of my power, support, maintain, and defend the said United States, against the said King George the Third, his heirs and successors, and his and their abettors, assistants and adherents; and will serve the said United States in the office of Surgeon, which I now hold, with fidelity, according to the best of my skill and understanding."

"So help you God?" Dr. Morgan clarified.

Nicklaus nodded resolutely. "So help me God."

Dr. Morgan lowered his Bible and placed it reverently on his desk. He offered his right hand to Nicklaus.

"Welcome to the Hospital Department and to the Continental Army, Dr. Schell. I know that you will serve your nation valiantly. We will find you a permanent assignment as soon as it is practicable. Meanwhile, I understand that you will be accompanying Dr. Rush to the Jerseys?"

"Yes, sir. We depart tomorrow morning."

"Excellent. Good luck, and Godspeed. I shall look forward to hearing the accounts of your contributions to our glorious cause." Dr. Morgan nodded to Dr. Rush. "Teach him well, Benjamin."

"Of that, I have every intention." Dr. Rush bowed subserviently to the director. "By your leave, sir."

"You are both dismissed."

Drs. Rush and Schell departed quickly. As they walked down the long, narrow hallway, Dr. Rush declared, "You know, Nicklaus, I only did this to secure your mother's allegiance to the cause. She is a wonderful cook, and a much better physician than you. I am of a mind to leave you here in Philadelphia and take her to the Jerseys with me."

Nicklaus cut a pretending glance of offense at Dr. Rush. "If you understood how angry she truly is about my service in the army, you would, without doubt, choose a different strategy."

The older fellow shook his head and chuckled.

~

December 31, 1776
Near the Highway to Princeton, New Jersey

"IF WE CROSS that damnable river once more, I am going to request naval service pay," Abraham growled. His voice overflowed with disgust. The men at his side, all enjoying a vigorous campfire and bowls full of steaming salt pork stew, groaned in agreement.

As the men pondered their foul luck and griped about their circumstances, as soldiers always do, the company fifer, a fellow named Peter Miller, teasingly began to play a happy rendition of *"Over the River to Charley."* His choice of tunes did not sit well with the men, who instantly hurled curses and snowballs in his direction. Peter giggled at their indignant reaction, until an unusually large wad of snow hit him solidly in the center of his face, effectively separating the shrill fife from his pursed lips. The men howled and cheered in joyous victory.

The German Regiment was encamped in a small thicket of trees about a mile outside Trenton. Along with the remainder of Fermoy's Brigade, the regiment was charged with guarding the turnpike that led to Princeton. Over nine hundred men were dispatched amongst the fields and hills that lined the well-traveled road. The German Regiment was on the outer line, furthest from town, and closest to the as-yet invisible enemy. They secretly hoped that the British and Hessians would remain, warm and cozy, inside the homes and barns of Princeton.

The men of the Continental Army had just experienced seven very exhausting, frustrating days. Following the Christmas night river crossing and decisive victory at Trenton on December 26, Washington immediately ordered his army back across the Delaware River into Pennsylvania.

The post-battle return across the water was a daunting task, indeed, because of the sheer volume of captives and cargo. The men of the army had to disarm, document, process, and transport over nine hundred Hessian prisoners of war. In addition, the raid upon Trenton had also yielded a treasure trove of goods and supplies. The Continentals discovered a warehouse in the town that contained all of the winter provisions for the Hessian armies in the region. There were tons of flour and dried meats, along with barrels of salt-cured meats, ale, and liquor. Another building yielded wagons full of European-manufactured shoes and boots, wool uniform coats, and blankets. These supplies were a most welcomed find and would help sustain Washington's ill-equipped army throughout their upcoming winter encampment.

But, with all of the added passengers and booty, the return crossing proved a long and arduous endeavor. The task of moving men and supplies required the exhausted army to make multiple trips back and forth across the river on ferries and in Durham boats. These crossings continued all day on the 26th and throughout the following night. The job finally complete, the last group of cold, exhausted, hungry, sleepless men tumbled into their bedrolls and tents in Newtown on the morning of December 27.

Once the men were rested, many of them made their preparations to depart for home. Over two thousand of the men of Washington's original army had enlistments that were set to expire on December

31. The general was desperate to keep his army intact, so he launched an intensive re-enlistment campaign throughout the camp. He spoke passionately to the departing soldiers and called upon their patriotism and duty to country. He used every emotional tool that one could imagine to appeal to the hearts of the men. When such appeals failed, he resorted to good, old-fashioned money. He offered a bounty of ten dollars, in addition to regular pay, for all who would extend their service by a mere six weeks. Washington's bribery worked. It convinced over 1,200 men to remain and help him finish the New Jersey Campaign.

Amazingly, the commanding general ordered another crossing of the Delaware on December 30. Though that particular crossing was accomplished during daylight hours, it was even more treacherous than the nighttime endeavor before the battle at Trenton. With the sustained low temperatures and ample precipitation, the river had become clogged with enormous, boat-crippling blocks of ice. Somehow, the army crossed, once again, intact and without any deaths or serious injuries.

So, the German Regiment was back in New Jersey. The men had enjoyed a restful eighteen hours at their current location. Since the British already knew that the Continentals were deployed in a defensive perimeter around Trenton, there was no need for light or sound security. The men enjoyed campfires and larger bonfires, songs, music, and entertainment. They pitched their tents and constructed lean-to's. Indeed, they hoped that Washington might even call for winter encampment at Trenton. If so, they might be able to enjoy the cold months inside the sturdy homes and beside the warm hearths of the quaint little town.

But, that was not to be. The voice of Captain Weiser interrupted the soldiers' merriment and thoughts.

"Prepare to break camp, gentlemen. We move out within the half-hour."

"Why, Captain? Where are we going?" inquired Private John Snyder.

"The entire brigade has been ordered toward Princeton to scout the disposition of the enemy. We are to locate, engage, and delay any movement upon Trenton. Our regiment will be in the lead. Prepare for action, and check your weapons. Full cartridge pouches for every man."

⌒

One-Half Mile Southwest of Princeton

"WHAT THE HELL is this fool doing?" Major Weltner muttered.

Captain Weiser responded, "I do not know, sir, but someone needs to take action. We are almost upon an enemy stronghold."

The German Regiment had progressed far beyond their assigned rally point. The regiment formed the lead element in the reconnoiter column. It was charged with occupying a position at the Five Mile Run Bridge. However, Colonel Haussegger had led his men beyond that point and continued northeast on the road to Princeton. Three miles later they bypassed the village of Maidenhead and then continued on past the Stony Brook. They were almost upon the outskirts of Princeton.

It made absolutely no sense to the other officers of the regiment. Their travels had far exceeded their orders. The other regiments in the patrol were many miles far behind. They were standing post at their appointed positions. The Germans were alone. Colonel Haussegger trotted proudly on horseback about forty yards ahead of the men.

"Major, we have to do something ... say something," Captain Weiser implored. "I have spotted a couple of rooftops in the distance. Princeton is just around that bend."

"I agree," Weltner responded. "Captain, I would be honored if you would accompany me."

"Gladly, sir."

"Climb on with me, Son." Major Weltner reached down with his right arm and hoisted Captain Weiser onto his horse. The captain settled onto the saddle behind his major, who kicked the sides of the large animal and urged it forward. It took less than a minute for them to cover the distance to their colonel.

Major Weltner wasted no time. "Colonel Haussegger, sir ... a word, if you please."

The colonel halted his horse and turned. "What is it, Major?" The officer seemed surprised to see another man accompanying the major. "Captain ... I am sorry, what is your name?"

"Weiser, sir."

"Ah, yes! Captain Weiser. Of course. How might I help you two gentlemen?"

"What are you doing, sir?" Major Weltner demanded.

"I do not understand your query, Major."

"Very well, then. What the *hell* are you doing, sir?" The major greatly emphasized and exaggerated the word, "hell."

"I do not appreciate your tone, Major. You are being wantonly insubordinate."

"And you are not following our orders, Colonel."

"How can that be, Major, since I am the one who gives the orders in this regiment?"

Major Weltner stared stonily at the colonel. "I read the dispatch from headquarters, sir. We were tasked to reconnoiter this road to the Five Mile Run. That was every bit of five miles ago. The rooftops of Princeton are now in view. Therefore, I ask again, what the *hell* are you doing, sir?"

The colonel sniffed proudly and puffed out his chest. "It is my intention to enter and occupy Princeton, to the glory of this regiment."

Major Weltner's eyes widened with shock. "Are you daft, sir? We know that British forces currently occupy Princeton."

"We know of no such thing," the colonel retorted.

"Sir, are you somehow in possession of intelligence to which not even His Excellency General Washington is privy? If so, I would love to see it!"

The foot-soldiers of the regiment had all caught up with the conversing officers. They ceased marching to observe the dramatic confrontation between the regiment's two senior commanders. The colonel, realizing the public nature of the argument, assumed a supremely authoritative air.

"I am acting upon my military acumen and instinct, Major. That is something that one does not develop whilst sewing breeches in Maryland. Now, shut your damned insubordinate mouth and get these men back into columns. We are going to enter this town."

Captain Weiser and Major Weltner climbed down from the major's horse. Weltner proclaimed, "No, sir. We are not."

"I beg your pardon!"

Major Weltner spat and then wiped his mouth on his glove. "Let me put it this way. There is no way in hell that I am going to allow you to take this regiment into that town."

"'Allow me,' you say?" the colonel thundered. "'Allow me?'" He was livid. His voice elevated almost to a scream. "You do not 'allow me' to do anything. I am in command of this regiment, and you will do as I order!"

"No. I will not follow this order, sir. It is unwise and foolish. Indeed, I believe it is in direct opposition to the orders given you by our army's commander. And I will, most certainly, not allow you to jeopardize the lives of these men on such an errand of folly."

The men of the regiment stood and stared in disbelief. The major was firm and resolute. The colonel's face flushed red with rage.

"This is mutiny! I will have you shot!"

"Call it what you wish, Colonel. But, we are not taking another step on this road, unless it is back toward Five Mile Run."

The colonel pointed at a young officer standing behind Major Weltner. "Young man, what is your name?"

"Lieutenant Hubley, sir."

"Hubley, you will take Major Weltner's horse and select ten men. You will accompany me on a patrol into Princeton. We shall claim this glory for our regiment!"

Major Weltner wrapped the reins of his horse tightly around his right hand. "You will stand fast, Lieutenant Hubley. You shall *not* have my mount."

Michael Yeisley could not believe what was transpiring before his very eyes. Major Weltner, an officer greatly respected and well-loved by the men, was committing an act of mutiny against the aloof, arrogant Colonel Haussegger. It was very frightening and exciting, all at the same time.

Michael stood to one side of the confrontation, in the field on the northwest shoulder of the road, amongst a cluster of men from his company and a handful of Marylanders. He glanced at his regimental comrades. They all appeared as equally shocked as he.

Suddenly, and quite unexpectedly, the colonel drew his sword and guided his horse toward Michael. He and the men standing nearby dodged to their right to avoid the animal and the blade. The colonel used the tactic to effectively cordon off a cluster of twelve men from the regiment. The separated group included six men of Captain Weiser's company. They were Michael Yeisley, Jacob Garesh, John Bishop, John Snyder, Joseph Manst, and Conrad Traywitz. The remaining six men were from a Maryland company.

"You twelve men will accompany me into Princeton. If you refuse, I will run you through!"

Michael looked fearfully and questioningly at Captain Weiser and Major Weltner. The major nodded grimly. He grumbled, "It is all right, boys. Do as you have been ordered. We will be waiting for you when you return."

The colonel eased his horse sideways toward Major Weltner and pointed his sword menacingly. "I shall see you dangling from a rope for this mutiny, Major."

"Probably so, Colonel. But I should think that General Washington has plenty of rope to spare for the both of us."

The colonel spat at the major's feet and then wheeled his horse in the direction of the town. The twelve-man squad trotted on foot behind him. Major Weltner and the others stood silently and watched them disappear around the bend.

"What do we do now, Major?" Captain Weiser inquired.

"We go back to Five Mile Run," he replied, disgusted. "Those poor lads are lost."

Princeton appeared deserted. Though smoke wafted from every chimney, there was no one outside. There were no horses, no dogs, and no people. It was spooky. Something was wrong, and the men knew it.

"What, in God's name, are we doing, Michael?" Jacob Garesh groaned. "We are walking into an ambush!"

Michael hissed, "Remain silent and watch the buildings!"

The colonel guided his horse slowly down the main thoroughfare. A few minutes later, he eased to a stop in front of a large brick house. He climbed down from the horse and tethered the animal to a post. He turned to the fellows in the patrol and declared, "You men wait here."

"Where are you going, sir?" Michael inquired nervously.

"Mind your own business, Private. Simply remain here and await further instructions."

The soldiers stared in disbelief as the colonel removed his gloves and then proceeded through a small gate. He ambled along a wide brick walkway that led to the house. He rapped soundly on the door. It opened, and an African servant girl appeared at the threshold. She bowed to the officer, then disappeared back inside the house. Moments later, a Hessian officer stepped into the doorway. The Hessian smiled broadly and offered a friendly hand to Colonel Haussegger.

"*Mein Gott!*" Michael exclaimed. "We are all dead men. Our colonel has turned coat."

At that moment, three dozen Hessian soldiers poured out of two adjacent houses. They quickly surrounded the twelve German Continentals.

"What do we do?" Private Joseph Manst moaned. He gripped his musket tightly. The lad was terrified.

"Easy Joseph," Michael warned. He bent down and placed his Charleville gently on the ground at his feet, and then slowly raised his hands. "We have no choice. We must surrender."

9

FINDING REFUGE

January 2, 1777
Mercer's Headquarters – A Farmhouse Near Trenton

General Hugh Mercer eyed Dr. Schell skeptically. He inquired in his characteristically thick Scottish brogue, "Where did you say this laddie hails from, Benjamin?"

Dr. Rush grinned and winked at Nicklaus. "Philadelphia, General."

General Mercer grunted. "I ken full-well that the both of ya ere from Philadelphia, ya sharp-tongued prick. I meant his family home." He turned to Nicklaus. "Tell me the place of your clan. Schell is a German name, is it not?"

"It is, indeed, sir. I grew up in the Palatinate, near the border with France, *Herr* General."

General Mercer tossed back a hearty swig of brandy. "Then, you've no allegiance to these Hessian thugs, hired by their German cousin?"

"German cousin, sir?" Nicklaus was thoroughly confused.

"Aye, boy! Their German cousin!" General Mercer fumed. "Are you daft, laddie? Surely, you don' think that lunatic, George, to be a true Englishman? That entire pack of imposters of Hanover are German usurpers of the worst order. They stole the throne of Britain from the rightful heirs, the Stuarts!"

Nicklaus finally grasped what the man was inferring. "You mean the Jacobites, of course."

"Aye! The Jacobites!" He became silent and stared, wide-eyed, into the crackling fire in his fireplace. His mind searched for a nostalgic memory of times long past. "I was a soldier of the Bonnie Prince, don' ya ken? 'Twas a surgeon for an army of slain men." He sniffed. "And I survived the slaughter at Culloden." He poured another dram and downed it quickly. "Those red-coated bastards murdered my brethren by the droves, and then hunted me down as if I were a worthless cur. To hell with the lot of them!"

Dr. Rush's eyes twinkled mischievously. "Are those not the same red-coated bastards that you served alongside in the war against the French fifteen years ago?"

The general exploded, "That was an altogether different context, and ya bloody well ken it! I'll not have ya teasin' and makin' light of my travails here in my own house, Benjamin Rush!"

Dr. Rush laughed out loud. "Put a lid on that temper of yours, Hugh. I was only having some fun. Surely, a couple of old, gray doctors such as ourselves can enjoy some levity at one another's expense."

The general smiled thinly and nodded. "Aye, I suppose we can. Though 'tis nay many that I would allow to speak to me so, Benjamin." He leaned toward his old friend and attempted a stern face. "I s'pose I'll not have ya shot this night. But there's always tomorra' mornin'."

Both men slapped one another's shoulders and laughed as only old friends do.

The general finally got down to some business. "Now, tell me, truthfully, Ben ... why have you brought this German boy to me on such a cold, inhospitable night?"

"General, I would like to assign Dr. Schell to your brigade on a temporary basis. I just brought him over from Philadelphia. He recently pledged his oath as a Continental surgeon, but has no regimental assignment at this time. I shall remain with General Washington, of course. But, there is no need for the both of us to be at the headquarters. I thought that, surely, your men could use a good physician during this campaign."

"A decent surgeon is always welcome, Ben. But, we depart soon after midnight for Princeton. I am certain that we shall face the enemy with the risin' sun of the mornin' ... and not just Hessians. Cornwallis is only miles away. We shall be fightin' Regulars, as well." He shook his head. "No, Ben. I am neither willin' nor able to play wet nurse for a doctor who has never even cast an eye upon a man wounded in battle."

"Oh, but he has treated on the battlefield before, Hugh. The boy was at Breed's Hill last year. He was near Boston examining medical facilities for me when the British made their attack. He treated dozens of battle-wounded men."

"Is that so?" The general was, obviously, surprised.

Nicklaus nodded grimly.

"Breed's Hill," the general moaned quietly. He stared at Nicklaus. "'Twas a ghastly, wicked sight, wasn't it, laddie?"

Nicklaus gulped as the memories of that bloody day flooded his mind and heart. He nodded. "It was, indeed, *Herr* General. It is the reason I pledged myself to this cause, and why I am here today. Sir, I would be honored to support your brigade in the field during the New Jersey campaign, or until the Hospital Department determines my permanent assignment elsewhere."

The general slowly turned his face back toward the fire. He stared, silently, for a moment and then took another drink of brandy. "'Twill be an honor to have you with us, Dr. Schell. Let us pray that your skills be aplenty and your patients few."

～

January 3, 1777
Near Princeton

GENERAL HUGH MERCER, his orderly, and his staff rode proudly on horseback beside the three hundred and fifty men of the brigade. The fellows marched smartly, but quietly. There were no drums or fifes. General Washington had ordered a silent march. He wanted the attack upon Princeton to be a total surprise.

"Where are we going, *Herr* General?" Nicklaus inquired of his commander. "The army is surrounding Princeton, and yet, we are going in the opposite direction. Are we headed back to Trenton?"

The general chuckled. "No, laddie. We are mos' definitely not goin' to Trenton. The ground betwixt there and here is teemin' with Lobsterbacks. We are headed back to the Stony Brook, 'bout a mile below Princeton. Despite all of George's well-laid plans, the army is a bit behind schedule. The sun is up. The general is worried that the British will discover our absence from Trenton. He does nay wish Cornwallis to bring his 5,000 troops up this highway to strike us from the rear. So, we've been ordered back to the turnpike. We must destroy the bridge over the Stony Brook. That should slow Cornwallis down well enough, I'm a thinkin'."

Nicklaus nodded his understanding. He had no knowledge, whatsoever, of military tactics or movements of armies, but he could see the wisdom in removing a bridge on a major thoroughfare. The wet, muddy fields that surrounded the road and a deep, fast-flowing creek with no bridge would prove a significant obstacle for an enemy force of 5,000 troops.

The general smiled and declared, "You look very smart, indeed, in your uniform, Dr. Schell."

Nicklaus smiled and stole a glance at his brand-new Continental attire. He was thankful that the general had provided him with such a fine coat. He had absolutely no idea how the man had procured a perfectly new, unsoiled regimental wool coat. The body of the garment was a deep navy blue. The facings and cuffs were not truly buff in tone, but more of an olive-gold. It was an unusual color, but Nicklaus did not care. His buff-colored breeches and weskit matched the overcoat perfectly. He looked every bit the Continental surgeon.

Nicklaus declared, "I shall wear it proudly, General Mercer."

"I know ya will, boy. You just take good care of my men, and you and me'll be all fine and dandy. But, don' make me have to abandon my generalin' and fall back to my doctorin' ways." He smiled warmly.

The brigade crunched quietly across the wet rocks of the small roadway. Suddenly, an alarm rose from the front of the column. Men shouted and pointed toward their right. General Mercer craned his neck to see in that direction, but his vision was obscured by a thick cluster of trees.

He growled, "What the bloody hell? The men are supposed to remain silent!"

A lieutenant from the front of the column spun his horse around and trotted back toward the general.

"What is the damned problem, Levtenant Fraser? I ordered a silent march!"

"It's the British, sir. We can see the turnpike from our position in the front. The road is covered with troops. They are already across the bridge and proceeding north toward Princeton."

"Damn! Damn it all! We've been discovered! How many are there?"

"I count roughly one thousand men, General."

"It can nay be Cornwallis. His force is five times that number, and some more. It must be Mawhood, maneuverin' out of Princeton." He stood up high in his stirrups. "Halt the march! Rest the men!" He turned to the lieutenant. "Go back and inform General Washington of the situation. Tell him that Mawhood is out, and that the road is filled with enemy troops. I can nay take the bridge. I shall await his new orders."

"Yes, sir!" The lieutenant kicked his horse and galloped northward.

"What do we do now, *Herr* General?" inquired Nicklaus.

"We wait, laddie. We wait for instructions from Washington."

So, General Mercer's brigade lingered near the roadway. The men were anxious and restless. They smoked their pipes and huddled in small groups. A few sat or reclined in the soft grass alongside the road. Thankfully, they did not have to delay for very long. Less than ten minutes later, the lieutenant returned, red-faced and breathless with excitement.

General Mercer barked, "Report, Mr. Fraser!"

"General Washington orders you to column right and engage the enemy immediately." He pointed toward a small orchard to the south-west. "You are to lead the brigade through this orchard, attack the enemy on the road, and take every measure to protect the exposed flank of the main army."

The general nodded. "Inform my company commanders. Prepare to engage. Instruct Major Wilson to deploy his cannons on that small knoll. Commence fire immediately, and at will. We will attack on my command."

THE FIGHTING WAS FURIOUS. Mercer's artillery engaged first, but the British troops quickly swarmed from the highway toward the orchard. Mercer's brigade was outnumbered three to one. The men took cover behind a dilapidated split-rail fence. Though the fence was low and provided meager concealment, the ancient structure still offered a small measure of protection from the enemy's gunfire. From this fixed position, Mercer's riflemen unleashed a hail of deadly and accurate lead into the scarlet-clothed troops.

General Mercer was no longer on horseback. He dismounted and released his horse the moment that the first cannon opened fire. The bold, proud commander pranced throughout the orchard, waving his sword and encouraging his men. He soon turned and strutted toward Nicklaus, who was crouching behind a thick, stubby apple tree.

"Dr. Schell, I want ya to remain on the western side of the orchard and see to our wounded. Do ya ken a suitable location for your hospital?"

The young doctor almost laughed out loud at the general's question. The notion of a "hospital" suddenly appearing out of nothing-ness in the midst of a pitched battle was nothing short of an absurdity.

Nicklaus glanced to the rear. There was a small stone shed on the eastern edge of the apple trees. He pointed. "I will establish an aid station behind that shed. The men must bring the wounded to that location."

The general smiled and lifted his sword in a friendly salute. "Very well, then. I shall have Levtenant Fraser inform the officers. Good luck to ya, boy."

"And to you, sir," Nicklaus responded.

The general turned his attention back to the action in the orchard. The British were forming firing lines. Moments later, hundreds of round balls from the British Brown Bess muskets tore through trees, mud, and men. Mercer's riflemen attempted to reciprocate, but the rate of fire from the British musketeers was staggering. The redcoats were executing three volleys for every one shot from Mercer's troops.

Then came the methodic stomping of the British light infantry soldiers. Their booted feet pounded the ground as they marched forward in perfect step. The shiny steel of their bayonets glistened in the morning sun. It was a bayonet charge. Over one thousand enemy troops advanced through the muddy field toward the Continentals.

The British rapidly overran General Mercer's outnumbered brigade, many of whom turned and ran in the face of the British blades. The enemy troops quickly captured the American cannons. They immediately turned the barrels upon the fleeing Patriots and opened fire. The effect was catastrophic. Men fell by the dozens.

Nicklaus gazed, horrified, upon the one-sided battle from his place of concealment behind the stone shed. He was completely surrounded by British infantrymen. Still, he was in a good hiding place, and had not been spotted by the enemy. He considered running, like the other Americans. It seemed foolish to remain, alone, behind the shed. There were no wounded soldiers for him to treat. The location of his aid station had not been made known to the officers in a timely manner before the British overran their position. He was, without doubt, going to be captured if he remained at his location.

Just as he was about to make his run through the orchard, he heard a chorus of British voices screaming, "Surrender! Surrender you damned rebel!"

Nicklaus peered through the trees. He gasped when he saw General Mercer, surrounded by roughly a dozen red-coated soldiers. The grizzly old fellow had his sword drawn.

"I shall nay surrender to the likes o' you!" he declared resolutely.

One of the British soldiers threatened, "Surrender, or we will run you through!"

General Mercer growled a barbaric, rebellious yawp. "I claim the vengeance of my Scottish countrymen, and my clan! Damn you all to hell! You and that German imposter you call King! Remember Culloden!" He slashed madly with his sword.

The British were upon him in an instant. One of them used the stock of his musket to deliver a crushing blow to the side of his head. The general collapsed, stunned, to his knees. Another gunstock smashed his skull from the rear. The disoriented, bleeding officer fell forward onto his belly. He quickly rolled over onto his back and attempted to protect his head with his forearms and hands. The British soldiers beat him viciously with their gunstocks, then they bayoneted him. They drove the spikes deep into his belly and chest, twisting the torturous, triangular blades violently with each deadly thrust. Then, they were gone. The enemy soldiers left the general for dead and ran in pursuit of the retreating Continentals.

Nicklaus stared, heartbroken, at the fallen general. His sorrow quickly turned to disbelief when he saw the officer's arm move. The general was not dead! The wretched man attempted to push himself upward off the ground. Blood poured voluminously from his multiple stab wounds.

Nicklaus shot from behind the shed and ran to attend his commander. The general lay only thirty paces from his position of concealment. He covered the distance in seconds.

"Lie still, General!" Nicklaus hissed as he approached.

The officer attempted to talk, but he could not form any words. His face was distorted beyond recognition, pounded into bloody meat by the stocks of the British muskets. His teeth littered the muddy ground around his head. His tongue was cut almost in half and dangling by a thread from the swollen, gaping hole that was once his mouth.

"Shh!" Nicklaus implored. "Do not attempt to speak. You are severely injured, sir. I must get you to cover."

The doctor knelt above the general's head and grabbed him beneath his arms. He tugged at the large-bodied man, pulling him toward an expansive oak tree that stood on the other side of the split-rail fence. It took much effort. Nicklaus slipped in the thick, wet mud several times. He also had to remove some of the boards from the fence to clear the way. But, finally, he managed to get the general out of the open ground of the orchard, and into the limited concealment provided by the tree.

Nicklaus knelt beside the officer and forcefully ripped open his bloody coat and shirt to inspect his wounds. General Mercer suddenly began to cough and growl. A mist of blood spewed from his mangled mouth and nose.

"Please, sir, remain calm and quiet."

The general groaned and attempted to lift his arm.

"General! I must see to your wounds!"

Then came a dull, resounding thud. For the shortest of moments, Nicklaus felt the painful blow against the back of his skull. Then there was nothing but darkness ...

⁓

Shortly After Noon
Two Miles East of Princeton

THE GERMAN REGIMENT prisoners huddled together beneath a single threadbare blanket. Their bodies ached and longed for warmth that could not be found inside the cold, damp, dark basement of the old stone farmhouse. Their British captors had deposited them in the horrid hole two days prior, and had paid little attention to them since.

Only one of their number was absent. Private Conrad Housman, of York County, had been selected as the traitorous Colonel Haussegger's personal attendant. At first, his comrades did not know whether to envy him or pray for him. But, considering their current circumstances, they had little doubt that Conrad was enjoying much better conditions than they.

Thankfully, the men had access to clean water in the below-ground cistern that held the home's underground supply. But, their only food was two loaves of stale bread that the British had thrown down the stairway shortly after their arrival. They rationed the dry morsels carefully, for they had no idea when they might enjoy another meal.

Though their bellies ached from hunger, their minds were consumed with the morning's battle. From the sound of it, the fighting was intense. The thunder of cannons rumbled and shook the ground throughout the early morning hours. But, the artillery and gunfire had been silent for quite some time. The farmhouse above was eerily quiet.

"I wonder who took the field," Jacob whispered.

Michael Yeisley shook his head. "There is no way to tell. But, the fighting sounded fierce, indeed. Even more so than Trenton."

"Do you think it was a battle for Princeton?" Conrad mused.

"I suspect so. As best I can tell, we are east of the town. The distance and direction sounded right for Princeton," Michael declared.

John Bishop observed, "It is very quiet up above. I wonder where the lobsterbacks are."

"Perhaps they have been run from the field," Joseph wished out loud.

"And are still running," added Conrad. "All the way out of New Jersey!"

"That would be bad," Michael declared.

"Why, Michael?" Conrad asked, confused.

"Because no one else in New Jersey knows we are in this basement!"

The men in the group, cold and hungry as they were, chuckled and laughed. Then, they heard the sounds of an army in the distance. There were numerous fifes and drums. Soon, there came the echoes of shouting voices ... officers and sergeants barking orders at their men. Those voices were distinctly British.

"Well, it seems that our friends are back," John Snyder moaned.

Moments later, the iron latch rattled on the doorway above. The door opened, allowing a column of warm, yellow light to invade the stark blackness of the basement.

The raspy English voice of the sergeant of the guard called from above, "Stand clear of the stairs!"

"We are clear," Michael responded.

"We need food, Sergeant Andrews!" Conrad wailed.

"You shall have food after the King's soldiers are fed, and not a moment sooner," the sergeant responded. "But, I do have a visitor for you."

The stairs creaked and popped as soldiers descended. There was one private in front, holding his musket and bayonet at the ready. Sergeant Andrews followed closely behind, carrying a lantern and two blankets. Then came two other privates. They carried the heavy, limp body of a wool-coated Continental Army soldier. One man gripped the fellow beneath his arms. The other held tightly to his ankles. They deposited him respectfully against the stone pillar in the center of the basement. The man lay on his side, facing the stones. The back of his head was stained with dried blood.

"You will render aid to this man, as you are able," the British sergeant ordered. "We shall return and retrieve him for interrogation tomorrow morning."

"Who is he?" Michael demanded.

"We do not know. He is a rebel officer, taken just outside of Princeton. Obviously, he received a rather severe blow to the head. He has not awakened since the battle. He may die. Our surgeons are preoccupied with our own wounded, so you must care for him."

"You have many wounded, then, do you?" Conrad grumbled.

"The battle must not have gone your way. Pity that you had to go and lose such a fine town as Princeton."

The sergeant grunted pridefully. "The events beyond these stones are of no consequence to you traitorous rebels. You need only concern yourselves with the prison ship that awaits you in York City." He glanced at the unconscious man. "Still, I expect you to render care to this man. Do I make myself clear?"

Michael responded spitefully, "We have no supplies with which to care for him, Sergeant. No medicine. No blankets. No food."

"You shall have food. I did not lie to you before. As soon as His Majesty's soldiers are fed and cared for, I shall order the cooks to bring down soup, bread, and ale. Meanwhile, I will leave these blankets for you. You may fashion bandages from one of them. And I shall leave this lantern and two extra candles." He glanced at Michael. "Do I have your word, as a gentleman, that you will not use them to set fire to this house?"

Michael replied tersely, "We have no desire to burn your headquarters down on top of our own heads."

The sergeant sighed. "I shall take that as your word, then."

He placed the lantern and blankets beside the unconscious soldier, then nodded to his men. The four British soldiers quickly ascended the stairs. The door slammed shut and the latch rattled back into place, once again sealing the cellar prison.

"I hope he is telling the truth about that food," Conrad declared wistfully. "My belly is beginning to gnaw at the rest of me."

"I believe the sergeant to be a man of honor," Michael reassured him. "He will keep his promise to us. Now, let us have a look at this man."

The Germans gathered curiously around the new arrival.

"'Tis odd," Michael declared. "He is wearing no insignia of rank."

"Then, how do they know he is an officer?" Conrad questioned.

Michael shrugged. "His coat is quite fancy, and looks new. Perhaps they assumed that only an officer would be dressed thusly."

Michael quickly inspected his head wound, and then developed a plan.

"Jacob, tear some bandages from the poorest of the two blankets. We shall keep the other one for warmth. And make a couple of wash cloths, as well. John, fill that bowl with water and bring it to me. Conrad, light the other two candles so I can have more light. Joseph, check his pockets. See if you can find anything that might reveal his identity."

The men moved quickly. It took only a few minutes to wash and bandage the wound. It was not particularly deep or bloody, but the fellow had an enormous knot on his skull. Michael prayed that he would survive the injury.

"Make a pillow with the torn blanket," Michael directed. "Let's roll him over and have a look at his face."

The men did as Michael instructed. Conrad grabbed the lamp and brought it close. The man's face was covered with mud and grime. Michael dipped his makeshift washcloth into the blood-stained water and then cleaned his cheeks and forehead. He gasped.

"*Mein Gott!*"

"What is it, Michael? Do you know this man?" Conrad asked.

"*Ja.* I saw him in Washington's headquarters in Newtown, just before Trenton. He is Nicklaus Schell, a doctor from Philadelphia."

Six Days Later - January 9 –Walnford, New Jersey

THE TWELVE PRISONERS had been very busy for the past three days and nights. They had finally managed to pry a wide floorboard away from the joists beneath. Their clandestine mission was almost complete. It was time to make their escape!

The captives squeezed through the narrow gap into the crawl-space below the house. They concealed themselves in the shadows and tarried. Their hearts pounded with excitement and fear. Each of the men could almost taste the freedom that awaited them in the nearby woods. And yet, each of them also realized that they could just as easily receive a slug from a Brown Bess in their backs. But, they were committed. There was no going back now.

John Bishop had discovered the loose floorboard entirely by accident. It revealed itself shortly after their arrival in the village of Walnford, where their British captors elected to confine them in the windowless storeroom of a local house. When John sat down to recline against the wall of their new "home," the loose board rotated slightly, giving him a painful, bloody pinch on his arse.

His fellow prisoners examined the board and recognized that it was an opportunity. It was just wide enough that, if they could pry it loose, they might squeeze through the hole and then steal away into the forest. They instantly initiated their escape plan.

It took seventy-two painstaking, covert, tedious hours to chisel away the crud in the joints adjacent to the eleven-inch wide pine floorboard and then pry it away from the joist. They had finally achieved success just after dark. Nicklaus knew that they could not wait another day before attempting escape. Just that afternoon, they had heard the guards discussing the impending departure of prisoners the following morning. Their ultimate destination was a prison camp near York City. That was deep in the enemy's territory, and escape from such a location would be all but impossible. But here, in a remote New Jersey village, they stood a decent chance of reaching freedom.

"This is it, men," Nicklaus whispered. "Just before the guard changes, the soldiers meet for evening report in the front of the house. Once they are all out front, we must cross the rear lawn quickly. Stay low, and remain quiet. We will meet deep in the forest when we are well away from the house."

Michael placed a cautious hand on the surgeon's arm. "Are you certain that you are ready for this, Dr. Schell? You had a serious injury less than a week ago."

Nicklaus smiled warmly at his friend. "I am quite well, Michael. And please, do not make me say it again ... I want you to call me Nicklaus."

Michael nodded, but said nothing else.

Nicklaus looked searchingly to the other men. "So, then, are we ready?"

Each man nodded his assent.

"Excellent. I will go first. Keep the man in front of you in sight. Follow me until I stop. Once we are clear of the village, we will divide into groups of three and then make our way back toward the river. We must cross and get back into Pennsylvania."

"Are you certain that we should split up?" Conrad moaned.

"We discussed this already, Private Traywitz. Twelve men running blindly about in the woods is a recipe for disaster. We might all escape, but in such a large group, we are more likely to be apprehended again. If we separate, we have a much greater chance of at least some of us getting to safety. Are we agreed?"

Again, the men nodded their understanding.

Michael hissed, "The evening guard is at the front steps!"

Nicklaus glanced around a brick footer to confirm Michael's observation. He saw the legs of both guards. They were standing on the front walkway that led to the house. "All right, then. We go now. Do as I instructed."

Without another word, the doctor shot from beneath the house and sprinted silently toward the woods. Michael followed only steps behind. The distance to the tree line seemed like a thousand miles. He ran and ran and ran, but it did not feel as if he would ever reach the trees. Finally, he dove through the hedges and then sprinted into the tall oaks beyond.

Michael ran breathlessly behind Dr. Schell. He could hear the footfalls of the others running behind him. He prayed that the British sentries could not hear their steps. The men ran into the dense woods for what Michael estimated to be a quarter-mile. When Dr. Schell stopped, Michael nearly stumbled over him in the middle of the trail. The last three soldiers in the line actually did tumble and fall over their comrades.

Nicklaus lifted his finger to his lips and made a motion with his other hand toward the ground. All of the men fell prone and silent on the forest floor, listening for any response from the British. Amazingly, there was none.

"I think we made it!" Jacob Garesh mumbled in disbelief.

"I believe you are correct," Nicklaus affirmed. "Let us stick to the plan. Follow your assigned directions. Get to the river and then cross by any means possible. Be careful, men. And good luck to you all."

The twelve soldiers took a brief moment to shake hands and embrace. Quickly, clusters of three men peeled away from the gathering and disappeared into the woods. Dr. Schell remained until the last, along with the other men of his trio. He slapped Michael and Conrad on their shoulders.

"Are you boys ready to go find General Washington?" He grinned. His perfect teeth glowed in the moonlight.

"I would rather go home," Conrad groaned.

Nicklaus ignored Conrad's spurious statement. He stood to find his bearings, and then headed south. It was his plan to bypass Princeton and Trenton entirely and make their crossing at Bordentown. He hoped that the weather would cooperate with his plan.

Several Days Later – Near Crosswicks, New Jersey

THE NIGHT WAS TERRIFYINGLY DARK. The snow seemed to capture and multiply what little light was available, casting a dull gray glow upon the landscape. A stiff wind howled through the tall trees. The three men pulled their collars tight and continued walking westward. Fine, stinging snow assaulted their exposed faces and hands. The fluffy ice had accumulated several inches. It spilled over the tops of their leather shoes, soaking their already-frozen feet. None of the men had hats, so the snow soaked their heads, as well. A shallow coating began to accumulate on top of their unkempt, matted hair.

The temperature had dropped dramatically since nightfall. Nicklaus, Michael, and Conrad were in danger of freezing to death. The doctor was faring a bit better than the others. He enjoyed the protection provided by his heavy wool coat. But, the thin linen hunting frocks worn by Michael and Conrad offered little insulation against the moisture and cold. The men were also famished. They had not eaten in three days.

"I cannot go much further! We must find shelter!" Michael shouted into the deafening wind. "I can feel neither my hands nor my feet!"

Nicklaus turned and placed a steadying hand on Michael's arm. "There is no cover here, my friend. We must continue on. We will locate shelter soon. I promise. Stay close. Do not get separated from me."

The doctor turned and quickly trudged forward into the deepening show. Michael and Conrad struggled onward behind him. They continued their blind trek into the merciless winter darkness.

It was roughly an hour later when Nicklaus turned and announced, "I see something up ahead. It appears to be a structure. Perhaps it is an old barn."

The promise of shelter against the wind and snow awakened new life in their frozen members. They each increased their pace. Moments later they stumbled into a deep snow drift, piled high against a dull gray, wooden wall. The structure was large. It blocked the wind significantly. Snow drifted lazily over the roofline and added its volume to the expanding drift.

"It is, indeed, a barn!" Nicklaus announced excitedly. "We must find entry. Follow me."

The men worked their way toward their right in search of a door. They inspected the entire eastern wall, and then turned the corner around the northern side of the building. Moments later, they discovered a split door. The bottom portion would not budge, but the top half swung outward with minimal force.

Nicklaus reached for Michael and shoved him toward the door. "Inside! Quickly!" He grabbed Michael around the waist and tossed him over the closed lower portion of the doorway. He hoisted Conrad over in similar fashion and then quickly climbed in behind them. He reached out and pulled the upper door closed behind him. It took a few moments for their eyes to adjust to the darkness inside.

"This is a working implement barn, Nicklaus. Look!" Michael exclaimed.

Near the far wall was a plow. Harnesses and other equipment dangled from nails above. Everything appeared very organized, clean, and well-kept. There was a stall at the far end of the barn. The heads of two curious horses extended over the gate of the stall. One of the animals grunted and snorted, blowing a cone of vapor from its nose into the freezing air.

Conrad whined wishfully, "There must be a home nearby. They will have a hearth and fire. And food! We must go and knock!"

Nicklaus shook his head. "We cannot risk it. The British may be here. Or, these people could be Tories. Our bellies will have to wait until morning, when we can get a better view of things. Meanwhile, we must get warm. Look for something that we may use to cover ourselves. We need cloths, tarps, and straw. We must make a bed and huddle together to share our heat. Move quickly!"

Conrad found a large mound of hay in a nook directly across from the horses. Michael soon discovered four very old wool blankets hanging on nails near the horse stall. As he reached to remove the blankets, one of the animals nudged him playfully with its nose and then nibbled at the frayed threads on the collar of his hunting frock. Michael quickly rubbed the horse's nose, then returned to his friends. Conrad and Nicklaus were busy leveling off a spot in the hay.

"I found these old horse blankets."

Nicklaus nodded excitedly. "Excellent! Let us spread one on top of the hay beneath us. We will cover with the others and then add a layer of hay over the top. We should warm up very quickly."

The exhausted men worked together to prepare their nest for the night. Within minutes, they were comfortably wrapped inside a cocoon of wool and hay, oblivious to the howling winds and winter's snowy assault against the sturdy barn. Sleep came instantly.

≁

MICHAEL AWAKENED WITH A START. He glanced at his friends. Both were still fast asleep. Light was streaming in through the cracks between the boards of the barn. It was daytime. The world outside was silent. The wind had ceased.

Michael rubbed his temples vigorously. His head pounded from a raging headache, and his knees and feet were dreadfully sore. But, the primary source of discomfort was his bladder. Michael had to relieve himself, and quickly. Though he hated to leave the warm comfort of the makeshift bed, he had to step outside and relieve the burning pressure in his pelvis.

Michael crawled from beneath the blankets and hay, stood, and stretched. He scurried toward the main door of the barn and peered between the cracks for any sign of movement outside. Seeing none, he tugged at the leather thong to release the outside latch. Opening the door slightly, he stuck his head out into the cold and inspected toward his left and right. He spied a small farmhouse to the left, about forty yards from the barn. A lazy trail of tan smoke drifted into the dull gray winter sky. He saw no signs of activity.

Moving quickly, he pushed against the door. A tall drift of snow had formed against it during the night. Michael easily forced it open. Making a crack just wide enough to step through, he darted outside and around the corner of the barn, out of view from the house. His bladder was on the verge of exploding. He fumbled awkwardly with the buttons on his breeches and finally loosened them just enough to open the flap and take care of his business. He sighed contentedly as his warm urine burned through the dry snow and formed an ever-widening puddle of yellow slush.

He quickly re-buttoned his breeches and then stepped back around the corner of the barn. Instantly, he froze in his tracks. Ten paces away, there stood a small boy holding two piggins full of water. The lad's eyes were wide with terror. The two of them stood, unmoving, and staring fearfully at one another.

Michael spoke reassuringly, "It is all right, boy. I am a soldier ..."

Instantly, the child dropped both piggins onto the ground. The tiny buckets tumbled sideways, emptying their water into the snow.

The lad screamed in terror and then took off running toward the house.

The boy screamed, *"Papa! Papa! Diebe sind in der Scheune!* ... Thieves are in the barn!"

Michael waved frantically. *"Nein! Nein! Ich bin ein Soldat!* ... I am a soldier!"

Suddenly, the door of the house opened and a man appeared on the porch. He pointed an ancient fowling gun at Michael.

Michael shouted, *"Nicht schießen! Nicht schießen!* ... Don't shoot!"

The man with the gun screamed, "Hessian bastard!"

Michael's heart raced. "No! I am not a Hessian! I am a Continental soldier!"

The flintlock exploded, engulfing the shooter in a cloud of sparks and smoke. The little boy screamed again.

Michael felt searing fire tear through his left cheek, arm, and chest. He looked downward and saw several tiny holes and expanding rings of crimson on his white hunting frock. The warm blood emitted tiny wafts of steam as it leaked from his body into the frigid winter air.

Michael's eyes rolled back into his head and he collapsed, unconscious, to the snow-covered ground.

10

REUNIONS

N icklaus and Conrad burst through the door of the house, carrying their unconscious, wounded friend. The man who shot him and his terrified little boy followed closely behind. The lad was carrying the gun for his despondent father.

"Quick! Clear the table!" Nicklaus commanded. "My friend is shot and bleeding badly. I must see to his wounds."

The woman of the house collected dishes and other items from the table and dumped them quickly into a basin. As she did so, she wailed, "Alfred, what have you done? You damned fool! This man is a Continental soldier!"

Her husband was numb with disbelief. He could scarcely think, much less move or speak.

His wife scolded him again, "What were you thinking, Alfred? You shot an unarmed man! Why would you shoot at a Continental?"

The man stammered, "I ... I ... did not know who he was, Inga. Eric cried out that thieves had invaded our barn. I saw the man. He spoke German. I thought he was another of those Hessian thugs, coming to steal our horses and potatoes."

"You have had problems with the Hessians?" Nicklaus asked as he leaned forward to examine the bloody spots on Michael's clothing.

"*Ja*. They have taken almost all of our livestock. Even our laying hens." The man frowned. "It shall be a long, difficult winter for us."

"Are there any Hessians or British encamped nearby?" Conrad inquired.

The man shook his head slowly. "*Nein*. I do not think so. We have not seen any soldiers for over two weeks."

"Then why, on earth, would you come at us, guns blazing, without first verifying our identities?" Nicklaus demanded, diverting his gaze to the shooter. "You may have killed this man! A good man!"

"I am sorry! I am so very sorry!" The fellow collapsed onto a bench beside the fireplace and buried his face in his hands. He wailed, "*Mein Gott! Mein Gott!* What have I done?"

Nicklaus actually felt a pang of sorrow for him. Clearly, he was not someone familiar with violence. He had simply overreacted in fear.

Nicklaus cleared his throat. "What is your name, sir?"

"Alfred Jung." He motioned toward his family members. "This is my wife, Inga, and my son, Eric."

Nicklaus nodded respectfully to the woman and boy. He spoke frankly to Mr. Jung. "You can rest assured that I will do everything I can to save this man. I am a surgeon from Philadelphia. Your victim is Michael Yeisley. He is a weaver from Pennsylvania." He nodded toward Conrad. "My compatriot is Conrad Traywitz, a friend and neighbor of Michael's, and a fellow soldier in the German Regiment. I am Dr. Nicklaus Schell."

Nicklaus ripped open Michael's hunting frock to take a closer look at his wounds. Simultaneously, there was a thunderous explosion of pewter plates and cups. Every eye turned toward Mrs. Jung, who had just dropped her entire dishpan of kitchen wares onto the hard-packed earthen floor. The woman stared, wide-eyed, at Nicklaus.

"Is something wrong, Madam?" he demanded.

"Dr. Schell? Nicklaus Schell?" she screeched with great emotion.

"*Ja?*" He was confused.

"It is I, Dr. Schell! Inga! You once knew me as Inga Mahler!"

Nicklaus still did not recognize the woman, at all.

She repeated, "Inga Mahler! From the *Betsey*! You delivered my dead child on that horrid ship, and you cared for my first husband. He died on the journey. Do you not remember?"

The recollection of that voyage of ten years previous flooded Nicklaus' mind. He mumbled, "Inga Mahler?" His mind raced. Then, suddenly, he recalled her face. And he remembered the postmortem caesarian delivery of *Frau* Etelwein's child. He exclaimed, "We gave you that dead girl's baby!"

She clapped her hands joyously and smiled. "*Ja!*" She pointed at the lad standing near the door. "It was Eric! He was the infant that you cut from that poor child's belly!"

Nicklaus stared at the boy, misty-eyed with disbelief and joy.

It was late in the evening. The makeshift surgery was complete. Nicklaus had to remove six pellets of bird shot from Michael's body. Two were in his shoulder and upper arm, three were in his chest, and one was in his cheek. The pellet in his cheek had been the most challenging one to remove. It was embedded deeply in the muscle. The other wounds were superficial. The lead came out of his skin very easily. Nicklaus cleaned the wounds with vinegar and bandaged them well. Michael was sleeping soundly and comfortably on little Eric's pallet in the corner.

Nicklaus voraciously gobbled a third bowl of morning porridge, smothered in a heavy layer of fresh maple syrup. Conrad was on his fourth bowl. Both men washed the hot concoction down with hard apple cider.

Inga and Alfred Jung sat quietly and watched the starving men eat. Alfred's face was wrinkled with worry. Inga's was beaming with joy. Her little boy sat in her lap and leaned comfortably against her breast. The lad was fast asleep.

Conrad inquired between spoonsful, "What is today's date? I have lost track of time. We have been wandering through these woods for many days."

Mr. Jung replied, "Today is January 16."

Conrad glanced at Dr. Schell. "Six days. Did it seem that long to you?"

"Longer." Nicklaus chuckled. "But, I thank God for that warm barn in the wilderness."

Inga declared, "I simply cannot believe that you are here, Dr. Schell."

"Nor can I, *Frau* Jung." He smiled. "What are the odds that I would stumble across your farm in New Jersey, in the darkness, in the midst of a blizzard, and in the middle of a war?"

"Indeed," she replied. "It is the hand of God. There can be no other explanation."

Nicklaus smiled out of courtesy. He did not hold to a similar theological worldview. In order to avoid any religiously-oriented conversation, he decided to change the subject. He glanced at the humble house. "It seems that you have done well for yourself."

"Oh, yes! I found myself a wonderful husband ... at least he *was* wonderful until this morning." She shot the hapless man a stern look. Alfred groaned and covered his face. Nicklaus and Conrad could not help but laugh at his reaction. Inga joined in. Finally, even Alfred could not help but crack a small smile.

Nicklaus assured him, "Michael will be fine. The lead is out. As long as he does not develop a fever, he will do well. Should a fever arise, I may have to bleed him. But, I have no doubts as to his full recovery."

Alfred smiled thinly and nodded. He did not seem very assured.

Inga continued her story. "Alfred and I met on a farm near Trenton, shortly after my arrival. We were indentured by the same family." She frowned. "I was one of the last ones off of the boat, because of the baby, and having no husband. My terms were extreme. I was committed to ten years of service."

"So, then, you were recently released?" Nicklaus asked.

"Oh, no! Alfred earned his freedom only one year after I arrived on the farm. He saved for two more years, and then paid out the remainder of my service. We wed immediately. We have been here, on our own place, for just over five years now." She sighed. "It is a good life. We are blessed in many ways."

"And, since you mentioned it in his presence, I assume that your boy knows the dramatic story of his birth."

Inga gazed upon the sleeping child. "He does, indeed. We have been honest with him about everything. I wanted him to know about his mother and the circumstances in which he entered this world. He understands that, even though I did not give birth to him, he is every bit my son. Alfred is the only papa that he has ever known." She hugged the child close. "We adore our little boy. He is truly a gift from God."

The men finally finished eating. Conrad burped. Nicklaus stared numbly at the fire. Exhaustion, a full belly, a moderate dose of alcohol, and the warm fireplace were all working together to lure their minds and bodies toward much-needed sleep.

Inga barked at her husband, "Alfred! Fetch the blankets and bedrolls. We shall make these men a warm pallet beside the fire." She instructed Nicklaus and Conrad, "I want you both to shed those filthy garments. You can change behind the curtain. I have fresh shirts for you for sleeping. In the morning, I will launder all of your clothes. And both of you need to wash your bodies. You smell akin to skunks. But, that can wait until the morrow."

Nicklaus smiled warmly. "*Danke, Frau* Jung."

"You are most welcome, Dr. Schell. Now, get stripped, both of you!"

Four Days Later – January 20, 1777

"THE BOY IS NOT GETTING any better," Inga observed. "He simply will not eat. He was talking outside his mind throughout the night. The fever is ravaging him."

Nicklaus nodded grimly. "I do not know what else to do. His fever comes and goes violently. The wound on his face has the bloody pus, which is good. It shows that his body is expelling the fever from his glands. Yet, I have bled him thrice, and still the poisons remain in his members. He also has a bad color about him. I am worried."

"And you are certain that the bloody pus is a good thing?"

"That is what I learned in my medical training. It is the philosophy of all modern practitioners of the medical arts."

Inga did not seem convinced. "How can something so foul and nasty pouring forth from a man's face be a good thing? It does not make any sense. I think we should clean that horrid wound with something."

"No. We must leave it alone," Nicklaus declared authoritatively.

The woman stood and walked over to Michael. His body trembled with fever.

"My grandmother always washed wounds with whiskey. She swore by its healing powers. She would actually spread open a cut and pour it in."

Nicklaus was aghast. "That is absurd! Wounds must be left alone so that the body's imbalances can find normalcy on their own. We must continue to bleed him and keep him warm."

"Beggin' your pardon, Dr. Schell ... but it seems to me that we should cool him down. The poor lad is burning up. He is soaking his clothing and bedding. And, for the life of me, I cannot discern any sense in draining a man's blood. Talk about absurdity!"

"Whatever do you mean? Bleeding and expulsion are the standard treatments for all maladies involving fever."

"And, yet, how many of your patients survive such fevers and bleedings?"

Dr. Schell hung his head low. "Roughly one-third."

"One-third," Inga repeated. "Have you ever wondered why?"

"We do not know the answers to such quandaries!" Nicklaus exclaimed defensively.

"Then tell me this, Dr. Schell ... how does one go about killing a chicken?"

He shrugged. "You cut off its head, I suppose."

"And then?"

He stared blankly for just a moment. He was smart enough to discern the direction of her line of reasoning. Finally, he answered, "You drain the blood."

Inga smiled somewhat condescendingly. "You drain the blood. Man has known since the very dawn of time that the way to kill an animal is to cut its throat and drain its blood."

"*Ja.* So?"

The woman planted her hands on her hips. "So ... if the way to slaughter a chicken or a goat or a pig is to bleed it, then why in God's name should you think that bleeding a man is, in any way, beneficial to his health?"

Nicklaus stared in silence. He had no reasonable answer.

"Should we not, at least, try my grandmother's remedy? As I recall, she never lost a single one of her patients."

"It would be foolish and against medical practice."

Inga marched over to her cupboard and fetched a bottle of whiskey. She declared decisively, "I am going to clean his filthy wound."

"I will not allow it!" Nicklaus exclaimed.

"And I will not allow you to order me about in my own home, Dr. Schell. Now, you can either assist me, or you can sit there and remain silent!"

It seemed that the doctor would have to swallow some pride with either choice.

Six Days Later - January 26, 1777

MICHAEL'S FEVER HAD BROKEN. He was out of danger.

Inga's revolutionary treatment method had been quite simple. Each morning and evening, she wiped the pus from the surface of the festered wound with a warm cloth. Then, she spread the flesh open and poured a splash of whiskey into the cut. Michael squealed with pain each time. Nicklaus was outraged and thought her efforts folly, but he did nothing to prohibit her actions.

By evening of the second day, the redness and swelling around the wound had gone down considerably. The following morning, the wound was completely closed and the oozing had stopped. Inga continued to bathe the scab with whiskey. Michael awakened on the evening of the third day with cool skin and a raging appetite. He drank some broth, and finally enjoyed a quiet, restful night of silent sleep.

Though still not completely recovered, Michael had improved dramatically. He was sitting comfortably in a ladder-back chair in front of the hearth. He had a thick wool blanket draped over his shoulders and held a steaming mug of extremely sweet tea in his hand. Inga happily forced another spoonful of hearty venison stew into his mouth.

Michael objected, "*Frau* Jung! *Bitte!* I can feed myself."

"Nonsense!" she retorted. "Only a few days ago, you were at the very cusp of death, Michael Yeisley. You still require much care and tending."

Nicklaus sat in an identical chair on the opposite side of the fireplace. He grinned with amusement and sipped hot tea from a pewter mug. Mr. Jung was sitting on a bench on the opposite side of the room, reading a pamphlet in the meager light provided by the house's only window. Young Eric was outside, playing happily in the snow with Conrad. The entire scene was quite peaceful. It was hard to believe that the region was engulfed in a war of revolution.

Michael nodded to the doctor. "Nicklaus, I am forever in your debt. 'Twas the second time that you saved my life."

"None of that credit goes to me, Michael. You were marching unwaveringly toward the grave before *Frau* Jung took over with her magical whiskey bottle. I removed the lead from you, but she saved you from the fever." He stared thoughtfully into the fire. "She certainly taught me something."

"Then, I am indebted to the both of you," Michael declared.

Inga patted Michael on the hand, rose, and then carried his

empty bowl to the wash basin. The men remained in front of the fire, sipping their tea and basking in the comforting warmth.

Nicklaus sat his mug on the hearth and stretched. "We have some decisions to make, Michael."

"I know. But, truly, what is the rush?"

"There is no rush," Inga declared from across the room. "You boys are welcome to remain here for as long as you like. You may stay the entire winter, if you wish. Alfred and I have already discussed it. We owe you that much, at the very least."

Michael shook his head. "We cannot impose upon you thusly. You were already frighteningly short of supplies before we arrived."

"We shall make it work," she promised. "I have faith."

"*Danke schön, Frau* Jung. But, we must consider our duty," Nicklaus explained. He glanced at Michael. "We know that Washington is encamped at Morristown. The townsfolk informed Alfred of their whereabouts two days ago."

"Morristown is one hell of a long distance from here," Michael retorted. "Sixty miles, perhaps. Being a winter encampment, the men will be in houses and huts, and simply sitting out the cold weather. We can do that anywhere."

"What are you saying, Michael?"

"I am saying that we have no cause to return to the army before the spring thaw."

"But, we have our duty!"

"Our first duty is to ourselves, Nicklaus. We did not desert. We were captured … all of us."

"And we made our escape," Nicklaus added.

"Yes, we did. Still, I do not believe that duty requires us to make a sixty-mile journey north, on foot, simply to rejoin an army that is, in all likelihood, freezing and starving. We would be better off either to remain here," Michael paused dramatically, "or go home."

"Home?" Nicklaus exclaimed. "Why, that would be nothing short of desertion!"

"I disagree. It would be a time of convalescence for me."

Nicklaus sat silently, thinking. He acknowledged, "'Tis true. You have been wounded rather severely, and suffered a terrible fever."

Inga inserted herself into the conversation. "Dr. Schell, surely you could not think of returning this young man to the army at this time. He will need weeks to recover fully from that fever. A nasty army camp is no place for him."

Nicklaus took a deep, thoughtful breath. "An army hospital would not be my recommendation for Michael at this time. They are ridden with disease, and woefully inadequate, both in supplies and personnel. But, still, to return to your home would be almost as far as the trip to Morristown, would it not?"

Michael turned and faced his host. "Alfred, how far is it to Philadelphia from here?"

Mr. Jung lowered his pamphlet and performed a mental calculation. "Thirty miles. It is not a difficult journey. Joseph Kirksbride's ferry at Bordentown is still operational, so long as the Delaware has not frozen over. You could reach Philadelphia in two days, easily, by horse or wagon."

Michael turned to Nicklaus. "We could reach Milford in a week, on foot. If necessary, we could spend some time in Philadelphia and rest along the way."

"You shall not walk anywhere, Michael Yeisley! You are in no condition for such a trek," Inga proclaimed. "Alfred will take you in our wagon, and shall be happy to do so. Won't you, Alfred?"

The man lowered his pamphlet once again. He was a bit reticent to respond. His wife shot him a threatening look and repeated, "*Won't you*, Alfred?"

He smiled thinly, looked over the top of his spectacles, and quickly replied, "Of course, *Mutter*. It would be an honor and a pleasure to deliver *Herr* Yeisley to his home."

"You could just as easily deliver us to the army at Morristown," Nicklaus countered.

Alfred shook his head vehemently. "I shall not take my wagon anywhere near an army encampment. It would be confiscated, and I would never see it again. I am sorry. But that, I cannot do."

"It is settled, then," Inga proclaimed. "You will rest here for another week, and then my Alfred shall deliver you to your home in Pennsylvania."

Michael studied Nicklaus' face. The doctor was clearly struggling with the notion as he stared, once again, into the fire. Nicklaus was an honorable man, conflicted by his duties to his country and to his patient.

Nicklaus drained the last of his tea from his mug and then sat the empty vessel down on the stone hearth. He appeared peaceful and determined. Clearly, he had reached a decision.

"Michael, I will escort you home. As your doctor, I feel that it is my duty. But, once I deposit you safely beneath your own roof, I shall return to the army. That is my *ultimate* duty. Upon my return, I will file a report with your regiment explaining the circumstance of your injury, along with your intent to rejoin your company in the spring."

"And what of Conrad?"

"Conrad will have to decide for himself what he will do."

"It is decided, then," Michael declared.

Nicklaus smiled and nodded. "It is decided."

Sunday, February 2, 1777
Upper Milford Township – Pennsylvania

IT WAS ALMOST SUNSET. Michael was exhausted. The trip had exacted quite a toll on his damaged body. He spent most of the travel days reclining on a soft bed in the back of the wagon. Though he napped and otherwise enjoyed quite a leisurely journey, he was still aching and tired. The muscles around his wounds burned with pain. His jaw ached almost without ceasing, aggravated by the jostling of Alfred Jung's rather ancient wagon.

But, the trek was almost over.

The remaining trio of travelers had just departed Conrad Traywitz's home. The reunion with Conrad's parents had been interesting, to say the least. The boy's mother fainted when she saw him. It was quite a sight. She opened the door to their home, looked into the face of her smiling son, and then simply folded at the waist and collapsed face-first onto the porch. The poor woman suffered a horrible scrape and a most unsightly bruise on her forehead.

The reason for her reaction was that she believed her son to be dead. The family had received word six days prior that Conrad was killed in action near Princeton and that his body was lost. Just that morning, the people of the local Reformed Church hosted his memorial during the morning worship service. There were still several funeral visitors and well-wishers making their calls upon the home when Conrad reappeared. The stonecutter was all set to deliver a memorial tombstone inscribed with Conrad's name to the church graveyard on the following Thursday. The entire community thought that Conrad Traywitz had died valiantly whilst serving his country.

Seeing their son "back from the dead" had been overwhelming. It took over an hour to explain everything about Colonel Haussegger's desertion, their subsequent capture and captivity, and the remarkable tale of their escape.

Michael had also been shocked to learn that the army had officially listed him as a deserter. It was most confounding. All of his friends who had been taken prisoner with him were listed as either dead or missing. He, alone, somehow wound up with the title of "deserter." Such was Michael's luck in the army. Thus far, it seemed that it was destined to be bad.

Michael pointed to his left, indicating the turn onto a side road. Alfred guided the wagon between a small stand of trees and headed north along the rough, wagon-rutted thoroughfare. Michael slapped Nicklaus' knee in joy and excitement. They were less than two miles from his home. His heart thumped from the thrill of it. He had not seen his beloved Magdalena in almost six months. As they followed the road toward Michael's house, Nicklaus brought up the subject of Michael's status with the army. It fouled the euphoric mood.

"Michael, this desertion issue may prove difficult to resolve."

Michael responded bitingly, "You said that you would file a report upon your return that will explain everything."

"Indeed, I shall. But, before, you were simply missing ... likely presumed dead, or a prisoner. But now, you are on a list of deserters. That descriptor is quite dramatic." He paused. "They can shoot you for it, you know. And coming back home has not helped matters, at all. I fear that it will only reinforce the army's accusation."

Michael shook his head. "'Twill be all right. I will explain everything. You will help me."

"I will help you, as well," Alfred volunteered. "I will go before the local magistrate tomorrow and swear an affidavit. That would carry some weight, would it not?"

"Very much so," Nicklaus answered. "That is most generous of you, *Herr* Jung."

The man shrugged. "I owe *Herr* Yeisley so much more than that. I shall go to my grave regretting the moment that I pulled that trigger."

Michael placed a reassuring hand on his shoulder. "Everything worked out, Alfred. You owe me no debts, at all. And I am very grateful for your offer to provide testimony for me. I will accompany you to the magistrate."

"As will I," Nicklaus added. "And when you depart, I would appreciate a ride back across the river, *Herr* Jung. I must return to the army's encampment. Every inch that I can ride in your wagon will benefit my aching feet greatly."

Mr. Jung nodded. "I will take you northward toward Morristown, but not all the way."

"I understand your predicament, sir, and would not ask you to risk this fine rig. I am quite certain that the army would, indeed, conscript it for its own use. But, I do I appreciate any walking that you might spare me."

Michael's emotional excitement interrupted their discussion of travel plans. "There it is! I am home!"

Just over a small rise, there was a series of cottages on the left side of the road. Candle and lamp light glowed through the windows. The place appeared warm, inviting, and peaceful.

"We shall sup at my own table this night!" Michael declared.

"I do hope that your bride has prepared enough to feed three hungry travelers," Alfred answered. "I am famished."

Michael simply grinned.

MAGDALENA YEISLEY LIFTED the lid from her large stew pot and gave the hearty concoction a vigorous stir. Her father was sitting in the center of the floor, covered by a pile of wiggling, giggling girls. He held a small doll high in the air with one hand. The girls busily attempted to climb his body and retrieve the doll. Just when one was about to reach their goal, Heinrich would shift the doll to his other hand, which precipitated a fresh wave of giggles and shrieks from the boisterous children.

"Someone is going to get hurt, *Opa!*" Magdalena warned.

"Nonsense! We are simply having fun, Daughter."

She planted both of her fists on her hips. "Your fun and games always begin with laughter but end with someone in tears. Please be careful with my daughters."

Heinrich Mueller winked at Magdalena. "They are in good hands."

Just at that moment, little Mary tumbled sideways off of his lap and slammed her elbow against the floor. The blow unleashed a torrent of wailing and a veritable river of tears.

"Papa!" Magdalena scolded her father, "What did I just say? My warning still lingers fresh on my lips!"

She darted to the crying child and scooped her up off of the floor. She wiped the little girl's huge tears and cooed soothingly. She wagged an angry finger at her father. "Get the rest of them to the table. Now!"

Heinrich sighed and then slowly climbed to his feet. Both of his knees cracked and popped as he rose from the floor. He grunted from the pain in his joints.

Magdalena rolled her eyes. "You are entirely too old to be rolling around in this floor, Papa."

"Nonsense! I want to enjoy my granddaughters, whilst I still have the energy to do so." He smiled. "I never thought that I could know such joy."

His daughter smiled back, warmly. An unexpected, loud rapping at the door startled Magdalena, causing her to jump. Despite her tears, little Mary giggled at her mother's reaction of surprise.

"Who, on earth, would be calling at this time of the evening?" Magdalena wondered aloud.

She deposited Mary in her chair at the table and then turned toward the door. As she walked across the room, she called out, "Who is there?"

A familiar voice echoed from beyond the door, "Just a few weary travelers!"

Magdalena froze in disbelief. She could scarcely believe her ears.

Heinrich exclaimed, "What are you waiting for, child? Let the boy inside!"

She reached for the door with a trembling hand and slowly lifted the latch. The door swung open on its smooth hinges. Her heart leapt when she saw her husband's scarred, smiling face. At the sight of his bride, Michael reached up and respectfully removed his borrowed, stained cocked hat.

"May we enter this abode?" he asked playfully.

From behind Magdalena, a voice shrieked, "Papa!"

Elizabeth bolted from her dining chair and ran to her father, followed by a gaggle of ecstatic little girls. Michael dropped to one knee and scooped them up into his arms. He wept with joy.

Magdalena stepped forward, slowly. She ran her fingers through his oily, stringy hair and then cupped his chin in her hand. She gently traced the outline of the red, tender wound on his cheek.

"You are home, my husband."

His smile filled his entire face. "*Ja, mein Liebling.* I am home."

THE MOMENTS after their joining were what Michael truly enjoyed the most. He held his soft, warm, sweat-soaked, naked wife close against him, relishing in the euphoria of the passion and pleasure that only she could provide. Magdalena, her left leg draped across his pelvis, sighed contentedly and stroked the mound of curly hairs on his chest.

Heinrich's cottage was bathed in the soft glow of the fire that burned bright in its tiny fireplace. The small, ten-foot-square stone house was well-built and warm. It was the perfect getaway for their marital reunion. Magdalena's father had generously offered his home and its comfortable bed to his daughter and son-in-law. He knew that they would appreciate the privacy on Michael's first night back home. He assured his skeptical daughter that he, Nicklaus, and Alfred would provide ample supervision for the sleeping girls. So, once all of the little ones were finally calmed and down for the night, the couple took him up on his offer. That was over two hours ago. The love-starved husband and wife had been reuniting ever since.

"We may have to crack a window," Michael declared. "It is unbearably hot in here."

"The window does not open. You know that."

"Then, I may have to open the door."

She slapped his chest playfully. "You will do no such thing! Do you wish to show my nakedness to the entire village?"

"Well, it is not as if anyone is still awake in Milford," Michael quipped.

Magdalena reached down and tickled his belly. "Oh, I don't know. With all the strange noises that you have been making, I'm sure that a couple of neighbors may be awake and looking out their windows for wolves and bears right now. Perhaps even a wayward rooster?"

Michael pushed her hand away from his taut belly. His face flushed with embarrassment. "You are a bold, sinful woman, Magdalena Mueller!"

She raised up on her elbow and leaned forward, staring into his eyes. "As well you know it ... and it is Magdalena Yeisley, if you please!" She kissed him tenderly on his wounded cheek. She turned his head slightly and examined the reddened flesh and scar on his face.

"Does it hurt much?"

"No, not lately. It itches more than anything."

"Then, it is healing well," she declared.

"Mrs. Jung said so."

"I am grateful for her, and for Alfred. They must be wonderful people. Together, they brought you back to me." She laid her head on his chest. "And Dr. Schell seems like a good man."

"He is that, and more," Michael declared. "I am honored to count him as a friend."

"I can scarcely believe that he was your surgeon in Philadelphia. Your lives have had these two unimaginable intersections. Happenstance is an amazing thing, is it not?"

"I do not believe it to be happenstance, Magdalena. It is Providential. Only a sovereign God could orchestrate meetings such as ours. I believe that Nicklaus is in my life for a reason."

"Then, you must be in his life for a reason, as well."

"Indeed. I believe with all my soul that God brings people together and joins them with intent and meaning and purpose."

"Hmm," she purred. "I like the sound of that."

She slowly and teasingly kissed his shoulder and chest. The effect was instantaneous. She sighed happily, then climbed on top of her husband and covered his warm body with her own.

Three Days Later – February 5, 1777

"Are you certain that you will not return with me?" Nicklaus asked Conrad.

The young fellow shrugged and grinned. "Dr. Schell, the army has declared that I am dead. Who am I to argue with them?"

Nicklaus pondered the man's interesting question. He did not agree with Conrad's decision to stay. However, ultimately he considered it none of his business. "Well, each man must live with his own conscience. I leave the matter entirely to you."

"Then, you will not report me?"

Nicklaus grinned. "Your secret is safe with me, Conrad. I will make no mention of you in my report."

Conrad offered his hand. "Then, I bid you farewell, Doctor. I hope that someday we shall meet again."

"Indeed. Perhaps we shall. Milford is a quaint, quiet village. It reminds me of my boyhood home. I may visit again someday."

"You are welcome at my hearth anytime, Doctor." He tipped his hat, then turned to Michael. "I shall see you on Sunday, Michael, if not sooner." Conrad turned and walked down the road toward town.

Nicklaus patted the leather satchel on his side. It was a new bag, freshly made by Michael's father-in-law in his small leather-working shop. He promised, "I have all three of the documents, Michael."

"Including mine?"

Nicklaus smiled. "Yes, of course ... including yours. I believe that your captain will gain a full understanding of our circumstances once he reads them all and hears my account. I shall inform him to expect you at some time during the month of April." His face became stern. "But, if you do not report back as you have promised, I will be most disappointed in you."

"You did not seem so disappointed in Conrad," Michael teased.

"He made no such promise to return." He paused. "Besides, I know that you are a man of your word and a man of honor. You have unfinished business in the army. Am I correct?"

Michael nodded slightly. "You are, indeed. I intend to fulfill my duty."

"Very well, then. I will see you in April. I will inform Captain Weiser that you should be listed as an invalid, and on furlough until your return."

"Thank you, again, Nicklaus ... for everything." They shook hands. "And you, as well, *Herr* Jung."

Alfred, already seated on the wagon bench, tipped his hat. "I am sorry that I shot you, Michael."

"I will forgive you this time." He grinned. All three men burst into friendly laughter.

Nicklaus climbed onto the seat beside Alfred.

Michael declared a blessing. "God be with you, gentlemen."

Alfred clucked at his horses and the team lurched ahead. Neither man turned or waved. They faced forward, focusing on the muddy road in front of them. Michael watched until they topped the rise and then disappeared from view. He uttered a quick prayer for them both and then turned and ambled happily toward his warm kitchen.

PART III

THE PHILADELPHIA CAMPAIGN

11

DUTY CALLS

Early Morning – April 17, 1777
Upper Milford Township – Pennsylvania

"How long will you be gone?" asked Magdalena, as she skillfully tied a perfect knot in Michael's white silk neck sock.

"I shall be home by supper. I promise. The journey to Maxatawny is a short one, and the load is light. Still, this sale will make a good profit for our business. It is well worth the trip. I shall make our delivery mid-day and then return immediately."

She cupped his scarred cheek with her tiny, warm, tender hand. "I must confess, husband. I certainly do enjoy having you home."

He covered her hand with his own. "I love being here amongst my girls. My desire is to remain here with you, always and forever." He turned his face and kissed the palm of her hand.

Her eyes betrayed a silent sorrow. "But this joy cannot last forever, can it?"

"No, my dear. The time is drawing nigh for my departure. The snows are gone. The spring days are growing warmer. Washington's army will soon be on the move, and I must be there when the time for the new campaign begins."

"When must you go?" she inquired softly.

"Oh, not as soon as you might think. I quite imagine that I can stretch out my stay a few more weeks. We still have time." He smiled warmly and hugged her close. "But, right now, I have breakfast on my mind. My belly aches for some of your sausage and bread."

Just at that moment, a raucous chorus of shouts and giggles invaded their bedchamber through the nearby wall. The Yeisley girls were awake and active in the adjacent kitchen.

Magdalena sighed, then smiled. "I must feed your hungry pack of girls, as well. We have sausage aplenty and ample eggs. The hens have almost doubled their laying over the past week. I will fry up a batch for the family and boil you an extra half-dozen to take for your dinner on the road today."

Magdalena took a quick moment to check her appearance in her small looking glass. She wrapped a colorful dark green and mustard yellow block-printed scarf around her shoulders, and then tucked the ends inside the bosom of her olive-colored short gown. She quickly donned her pinner apron and mob cap, then stepped into the bedlam that was her kitchen. Michael followed her, grinning broadly at the sight of his boisterous girls.

"And how are my angelic little darlings this morning?"

The brood of girls squealed, "Papa!" They instantly abandoned their grandfather and ran to Michael, inundating him in a wave of hugs and kisses. Heinrich smiled with joy at their celebrative reaction to their father.

"I have poured your tea, Papa," little Elizabeth declared. "I also fixed you a glass of fresh milk. It is still warm and frothy!"

"*Danke, mein Leibling.* You are such a thoughtful little girl." Michael patted her gently on her head.

Michael nodded to his father-in-law. "*Guten Morgen,* Heinrich."

"And to you, Michael. Did you sleep well?"

"Lately, I sleep well every night, *Opa*. Truly, there is no place quite like home."

Heinrich nodded and took a quick sip of steaming tea from his Blue Onion patterned china cup. He pointed to a small, one-drawer table beside the front door. "There is a letter for you on the entry table."

"When did it arrive?"

"It must have come before sunrise. I never heard the postal rider. I discovered the note leaning against the door this morning." He paused. "It looks official."

Michael walked numbly toward the table and fetched the correspondence. It was wrapped in a wide blue ribbon and bore a red wax seal marked with the letter, "*W*." He broke the wax loose from the ribbon and removed the silk loop from the paper. Somewhat fearfully, he unfolded the letter and turned it over to view the message.

> *To Private Michael Yeisley,*
>
> > *Current Status: Leave of Convalescence for Wounds Received*
> >
> > *You are hereby ordered to return to duty with the German Regiment. Due to orders from General Washington and our new regimental commander, Baron de Arent, all furloughs are henceforth cancelled, and all soldiers must report for examination by Hospital Department surgeons. You must present yourself at the regimental headquarters at Morristown by May 1, or you will be henceforth listed as a deserter and subject to all laws and punishments prescribed for such a crime during time of war. I trust that you will act honorably and perform your duty admirably, as is your custom.*
> >
> > *Respectfully,*
> > *Benjamin Weiser, Capt.*
> > *German Regiment, Penn.*

Magdalena walked into the kitchen. She saw the surprised, pained expression on her husband's face. "What is wrong, Michael?"

He carefully folded the letter and returned the ribbon wrap. "Orders, my dear. I have been recalled to the army at Morristown." He frowned. "I must leave within the week."

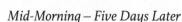

Mid-Morning – Five Days Later

HEINRICH TUCKED Michael's knapsack and bedroll behind the wagon seat. Michael stood and stared with a measure of disbelief at the copious bundles, boxes, and stacks of supplies piled high in the bed of the rig.

"I cannot believe you found room for my bag," Michael quipped.

Heinrich chuckled. "We could always tie it on top, if necessary." He admired the pile of goods, as well. "That daughter of mine is a wonder, is she not?"

"Indeed," Michael agreed. "A blessing beyond description."

He could scarcely believe the amazing feat that his wife had accomplished in less than a week. After the receipt of Captain Weiser's letter, Magdalena decided that she would spearhead an effort to collect supplies for the men of the German Regiment. The project gave her a source of distraction and sense of purpose during those dreadful days leading up to her husband's departure. She immersed herself in the task, dedicating every waking moment to writing notes to local merchants, making appeals to neighbors, and networking through both the Reformed and Presbyterian Churches.

The response was overwhelming, to say the least. The woman had mobilized the entire community to collect clothing, blankets, and non-perishable foodstuffs for the men of Michael's company. She even convinced a rather wealthy old fellow by the name of Hans Becker to donate a dilapidated wagon that had been sitting in his barn, abandoned, for many years. He did so with the full under-standing that the wagon would remain with the army and never return. Magdalena made such a "hero" of the man within the community that he even threw in a pair of old mules to pull the rig.

Two local carpenters repaired the ancient wagon in a mere two days, replacing the deck boards, one axle, and all four of the wheels. The majority of the lumber on the wagon was very old and gray, but it was still solid and roadworthy. And, in less than three days, it was filled to overflowing with supplies for Michael and his friends.

On Sunday afternoon, Magdalena and the ladies of the Reformed Church packed the wagon with three dozen wool blankets, several dozen shirts, and bags full of hand-knitted wool stockings and mittens. There were small barrels packed with smoked meat, tobacco, ale, rum, corn, wheat flour, salt pork, and whiskey. There were even two barrels of gunpowder and several pounds of lead.

The wagon was full. Michael was packed and prepared. It was time for him to depart for New Jersey.

Heinrich peered down the road toward town. "I see that Conrad has not come to see you off." He frowned.

"He probably thinks that I will attempt to convince him to come with me."

Heinrich nodded. "He is ashamed."

Michael shrugged. "His conscience is his own. I cannot make his decision for him. He must do as he feels God is leading him. I must do likewise."

Heinrich pushed his gray felt cocked hat forward and scratched the back of his head. "True. Still, I find it interesting that God has spoken to the two of you with such starkly different revelations." His face displayed a somewhat teasing smile.

Again, Michael shrugged. He tried to appear aloof, but it was only pretense. Michael was very angry at his friend. Actually, he was ashamed of him. He could scarcely believe that Conrad would carry out the falsity of his own death in order to avoid returning to the army. Earlier in the week, Magdalena had encouraged Michael to go and plead with his friend to change his mind, but he had refused. Despite what they had endured together, Michael did not even want to be in Conrad's presence. It was hard to look upon the man and not consider him a coward.

Seeing Michael's pained expression, Heinrich rested his arms on the side board of the wagon and sought to change the subject. "It is good that you visited with your mother and father yesterday. I trust that they are well."

"Yes, indeed. Mother has been sick throughout much of the winter but is much better now. Papa is as strong as an ox. He will outlive us all. He is already preparing his fields for cabbage. He much prefers farming his five acres over spinning and weaving."

Heinrich chuckled. "Your father is a great man. I will forever be in his debt. It is because of him that I enjoy such a wonderful life in America."

"He thinks very highly of you, Heinrich. He misses you."

"I must go for a visit this week." There was a moment of uncomfortable silence. "I wish that you could have seen George once more before your departure."

"I, as well. But, his militia company is patrolling on the western frontier and not due to return for at least another month." Michael sighed. "I pray for him every day. I hope that I shall see my brother again."

"May God keep him safe out there amongst those murdering, scalping heathens," Heinrich declared.

Michael nodded grimly. "Amen to that."

He looked across the lawn at his daughters. The girls were busy running and playing a ferocious game of tag. They were laughing and giggling. The youngsters portrayed a perfect scene of the carefree bliss that only children know.

"I shall miss my daughters, Heinrich. There is no joy that compares to the love of one's children."

"*Ja.* And no such sorrow as when one is lost."

Michael placed a firm, reassuring hand on his father-in-law's shoulder. "May your little Emma rest in peace."

Heinrich's youngest of three daughters had succumbed to a winter fever only two years after his arrival at the Yeisley home. His middle daughter, Anna Emilia, was now twenty years of age, married, and living in Lancaster, where her husband operated a small dry goods shop. Only Magdalena remained as a regular participant in his daily life.

"Emma was a precious little girl," Michael declared. "We all miss her very much and cherish the memories of the woefully brief number of days that we knew her."

"And she was feisty!" added Heinrich. He smiled warmly as he relished an almost decade-old memory of his departed child.

Michael smiled and nodded. "Well, at least you know all of your girls are in good hands. Sweet Emma rests in the arms of Jesus, and Anna has that somewhat tolerable, though odorous, husband of hers." He winked. Heinrich chuckled. "And, of course, Magdalena has the most amazing husband in all of the Colonies."

"States!" Heinrich barked.

"States." Michael nodded slightly. "I stand corrected, *Opa*."

Heinrich looked toward the open kitchen door. "Where is my daughter, anyway? The hour has come for your departure."

"She is in the privy. The poor girl has not been feeling well in her stomach these past couple of days."

"Surely, it is nothing serious."

"No. Most likely, it is Frau Baumann's cooking from the dinner at church on Sunday. Her dish had a peculiar odor about it, as if her mutton was rancid. I could not bring myself to eat it."

"Nor could I. But, then again, all of her cooking smells equally inedible. 'Tis a small wonder that old Jacob has any meat on his bones, at all."

"He feasts at Langor's Pub every day for dinner, Heinrich! If not for that place, the poor man would have starved years ago!"

Both men chuckled at their wretched, perpetually hungry neighbor's plight.

Magdalena's soft voice punctuated their laughter. "I hope the joke is not at my expense."

Michael spun around and faced his bride. The young woman radiated strength and beauty. Wisps of perfect, silky blonde hair peeked from beneath her white linen bonnet. Her eyes fixed upon Michael's and captured him in a longing gaze. Even after bearing five children, her body remained trim and perfectly proportioned in all the right places. In his heart and in his loins, Michael burned to take her, once again, to their bedchamber.

Michael almost whispered, "No one ever laughs at you, sweet wife. Your perfection turns all levity into frivolous folly." Ignoring Heinrich's presence, he pulled her close and kissed her passionately.

Magdalena gasped and pushed him away. "Sir, you embarrass me in front of my father!"

Heinrich chuckled. "Do not be silly, daughter. Do you think me an idiot?" He nodded toward his granddaughters. "I know full-well of your nighttime escapades, and I cannot say that I disapprove." He winked at Michael.

Magdalena flushed a bright crimson. "Papa! You are incorrigible!"

"And you are soon to be without a husband for many months. Allow me to say my farewells, and then I shall leave you to yours."

Heinrich reached his right hand toward Michael, who grabbed it and then pulled him close into a strong embrace.

"I love you, *Opa*. Take good care of my girls."

"Always, my boy." Heinrich patted Michael on the back. He quickly broke away from the embrace and bolted toward the kitchen door. The old man had two long streams of tears flowing down his cheeks.

Magdalena fell into Michael's arms. "You must return to me, Husband."

"I shall always return to you, *Frau* Yeisley."

Michael knew that he could not linger. Prolonging his departure would only make it that much more unbearable. He kissed his wife tenderly on her forehead, squeezed her with one last hug, and then separated himself from her embrace. He climbed quickly onto the wagon seat and grabbed the reins.

"It will be easier if you go inside. I do not want you to watch me leave."

Magdalena did not respond. She turned and ran, sobbing, into the house. Michael choked back his own tears. He closed his eyes and prayed for strength, then snapped the reins.

"Hyah! Go, girls!"

The team of mules leaned into their harnesses and the wagon launched forward. Michael settled in for the long, boring ride. He had gone less than a quarter of a mile when he heard someone calling his name.

"Michael! Michael Yeisley! Wait!"

Surprised, he halted the wagon and turned around in the seat. His heart leapt when he saw who it was. Conrad Traywitz was lumbering awkwardly along the shoulder of the muddy roadway. He was carrying a fat, thickly-stuffed market wallet over his left shoulder and a full snapsack on his right shoulder. He soon reached the wagon and tossed his bags on top of the pile in the bed. He nimbly climbed up onto the seat. Michael stared at him in silence and disbelief.

Conrad looked at Michael and cocked his head. "Well? What are you waiting for? You had best get this rig moving. I do not want you to be listed as a deserter."

"That is most thoughtful for a dead man."

Conrad grinned. "Just drive ... before I change my mind!"

Wednesday, April 30, 1777
Morristown, New Jersey

It was a beautiful, sunny, pleasantly cool spring afternoon. The clear weather made for good travel. The trip had not been particularly difficult. Michael and Conrad made good progress most days. They suffered a cracked wheel hub shortly after crossing the Delaware at Trenton. The only suitable local carpenter was sick with the ague, so the delay cost them three days of frustration and waiting.

So, the journey to Morristown required just over a week of travel. They reached the town about three hours before dusk. The boys were famished, so they stopped to purchase a hot meal at an establishment called Arnold's Tavern. Both were anxious to warm their feet, hands, and bellies. Michael hired a lad at a nearby store to stand watch over their wagon and goods while they were dining.

Because it was between normal meal times, there were only a handful of customers gathered in the serving room. There was one table in a far corner that was occupied by four smartly dressed Continental Army soldiers. The men were clad in spotless blue wool regimental coats with buff facings, collars, and cuffs. They wore red wool weskits and buff linen breeches. Four black cocked hats, trimmed in white ribbon, hung on a pegboard beside the table. Likewise, four shiny Charleville muskets leaned against the wall beneath their hats. The soldiers eyed Michael and Conrad with an air of scrutiny. They seemed to be very watchful. They each sipped hot tea from the tavern's stained china cups. One of the fellows smoked a long clay pipe.

Michael and Conrad nodded to the soldiers and quickly claimed a small table in the opposite corner. They placed their order, and within minutes were enjoying a hearty wooden plate layered with roast venison, onions, and potatoes, along with a small pewter porringer full of buttery stewed turnips. The proprietor included a loaf of dry, dark bread and copious amounts of cool ale with the meal.

While they were eating, the fellows heard a mild commotion near the bar, and then noticed that all eyes were focused on the narrow staircase. Michael turned and was astonished to see General Washington descending the stairs with a lovely and distinguished-looking middle-aged lady. Michael assumed the woman to be the general's wife, Martha.

"Christ, Almighty!" Conrad hissed under his breath. "That is George Washington, himself!"

Michael nodded and whispered, "He must be quartered upstairs."

"What do we do?" Conrad moaned.

"We keep eating. That is what we came in here to do. 'Tis a tavern, Conrad."

"But, it's General Washington!"

"Generals must eat, same as us." Michael grinned.

Suddenly, the four soldiers in the far corner rose to their feet. Two of them darted to a table near the fireplace. The other two made their way toward the stairs and greeted the commanding officer upon his arrival at the bottom step. They escorted General and Mrs. Washington to a table near the fireplace. The general seated his wife in a most gentlemanly manner. As he helped her scoot her chair closer to the dining table, he glanced around the room. Michael tried not to look, but he could not help himself. The general's gaze met Michael's. Mr. Washington leaned forward and whispered something to his wife, then turned and strolled toward Michael and Conrad's table. Two of the blue-coated soldiers followed him. It suddenly dawned on Michael who the four identically-dressed troops actually were. They were the general's escorts and members of his Life Guard.

Michael wiped his lips with his napkin and immediately rose to his feet. Conrad followed his lead. Michael offered a slight, respectful bow to the general. "Your Excellency."

The general returned a courteous nod. "Good afternoon, young men. I cannot help but notice that you fellows have the look of soldiers about you. Many of our men still retain these linen hunting frocks. What is your regiment?"

Michael responded confidently, "We are of the German Regiment, sir."

The general grinned. "My heroes of Trenton, eh?"

Michael nodded proudly. "Yes, sir. We were there ... in the apple orchard."

"Indeed. Are you the captain of a company?"

"No, sir. I am Private Michael Yeisley, of Captain Benjamin Weiser's Company. This is my comrade, Private Conrad Traywitz."

The general raised an eyebrow. "And what brings you into the town, Private Yeisley? Only command officers are quartered here. This area is actually off-limits to the enlisted men."

Michael's heart sank just a bit. He and Conrad had only just arrived in Morristown, and they were already getting into trouble. He scrambled to explain.

"We did not know of the regulation, General. Neither did I know that you were quartered in this inn. We just arrived from my home in Northampton County, Pennsylvania. We have not eaten since yesterday and were much hungered. We only stopped briefly to have a hot meal. I sincerely apologize. We are bearing a wagon load of goods and have every intention of reporting to our regiment after we finish our food."

"There is no need to apologize for hunger, son. It happens." He smiled. He pointed at Conrad. "What about this one? Does he speak?"

Conrad almost choked. "He does ... I ... I mean ... I do, sir. Yes, sir. I speak."

The general chuckled at Conrad's reaction. "Have you fellows been on a foraging expedition?"

"No, sir. I have been on convalescent leave. I was captured at Princeton, and later made my escape, but was wounded in the Jerseys. I made my way home, with the help of some friends, and have been recuperating under my wife's care for several weeks. I received notice of my recall only days ago."

A sudden look of realization washed across the general's face. "Are you the lad that Dr. Schell told us about?"

Michael breathed a sigh of relief. He smiled. "Yes, sir. Dr. Schell is a personal friend. He has saved my life twice now."

"What an amazing tale! The doctor enthralled us with his story of your escapade when Mrs. Washington and I entertained him for dinner last month. Simply incredible! So, you boys were both captured with Haussegger, then?"

Michael's head dropped in shame. "Yes, sir."

"Chin up, lad. 'Twas not your fault. That man was a traitorous fool." He turned to Conrad. "What is your story, young man?"

Conrad's head dropped. "I was with Michael ... I mean, Private Yeisley. I helped him get home. When I arrived, I discovered that the army had declared me dead."

"Really?" The general's right eyebrow raised high. "Surely, the army did not make such a grievous error in its records." He grinned knowingly.

"They certainly made an error with regard to my records, sir. You should have seen the look on my mother's face when she saw me. She fainted, fell flat in the floor, and cracked her head."

Conrad's descriptive declaration caused General Washington to laugh heartily. "Poor woman! But, I trust that she has recovered from her wounds?"

Conrad smiled sheepishly. "She is quite well, General Washington."

"Well, that is good. And now you have come back from the dead to return to your duty with your regiment."

"Yes, sir."

"Well done, Private Traywitz. You are to be commended for finishing out your enlistment. A less honorable man might have allowed the army its mistake and remained at home. I salute you, sir." The general bowed graciously toward Conrad. The young German's face beamed with delight.

General Washington continued his friendly interrogation. "And now you gentlemen have brought back supplies for your comrades?"

Michael nodded and grinned. "Yes, sir. My wife led in a great collection effort. The entire county responded. She even convinced one old fellow to donate a wagon. My company will be the envy of the regiment."

General Washington chuckled warmly. "Well, I am glad that you have answered the call back to duty, Privates Yeisley and Traywitz. Do enjoy your meals. But, you shall need to find your regiment before nightfall. I do not want either of you to be shot by one of our sentries or pickets. Just follow the lane that leads to the southeast. You cannot miss the encampment. If you encounter any trouble, tell them that I sent you." He winked.

Michael nodded again. "Thank you for your kindness, *Herr* General."

"Thank you for your service, *Herr* Yeisley, and for the wounds you have suffered for our cause." The general nodded slightly to Michael, then turned to Conrad. "*Herr* Traywitz." He spun smartly and walked back to his waiting wife. His Life Guard soldiers followed one step behind him.

Michael and Conrad returned to their seats. Michael's legs were a bit wobbly from the nervous thrill of the encounter. His heart still thumped from the excitement of an actual conversation with the supreme commander of the Continental Army. But, when he caught a whiff of the tasty venison, his hunger quickly over-whelmed his excitement. Both men wolfed down the remainder of their meals, drained their pewter mugs of ale, and then paid the bill.

Minutes later, Michael was guiding the rig down the road toward the army's encampment. They traveled the distance in short order, arriving about a half-hour before dusk. Their only interruption was at a checkpoint roughly a quarter-mile from the camp. Michael presented his recall order from Captain Weiser and endured a brief inspection of the wagon and contents. Minutes later, the two comrades were admitted into the Continental Army's first winter encampment.

The soldiers of the army were quartered a few miles southeast of the village, in the beautiful Lowantica Valley. Michael was surprised to look upon such a picturesque site. It was not, at all, what he expected an army camp to look like. The entire valley was shrouded in a gray haze of fog and smoke. A beautiful stream flowed slowly through the center of the encampment, no doubt the source of ample fresh water. Hundreds of log huts lined the field, each belching clouds of smoke from their tiny fireplaces. Many of the dwellings were located in the edge of the woods, just inside the tall trees. There was a large parade ground in the center of the encampment. Despite the rapidly approaching darkness, several companies were still on the field, marching and drilling.

With some assistance from a helpful Virginian, Michael and Conrad soon located the German Regiment's assigned area near the southern edge of the camp. The commandant and staff were head-quartered in a small stone cottage about three hundred yards beyond the last hut. Michael parked his wagon and tied the mules to a post. As he neared the front door of the house, he experienced a measure of conflict within his emotions. He was proud of his regiment and eager to do his duty. But, he just as equally wished that he had stayed at home with his family. He could only imagine how conflicted Conrad's emotions must be. Still, it was entirely too late to reconsider their decisions. The men had arrived in the Continental Army camp. It was time to return to work.

Michael pushed on the heavy oak door and entered the humble cottage. An orderly sat at a small field desk to the right of the door. The fellow nodded. "*Guten Abend*. How may I assist you gentlemen?"

"I am Private Michael Yeisley, of Captain Weiser's Company. I am reporting back from a furlough of convalescence."

"And I am Private Conrad Traywitz of the same company, reporting for duty, as well."

"Captain Weiser is actually on duty here in the headquarters today. One moment, please."

Before the fellow could push back his chair from his desk, Captain Weiser appeared in the open doorway of a side room. "So ... our prodigal son returns!" He was smiling.

"Indeed, sir. Shall we kill the fatted calf?" Michael grinned mischievously.

The captain's smile immediately morphed into a gaze of shock and confusion. "Private Traywitz! But ... but ... How can it be? You ... you are supposed to be dead!"

"That is what I have heard, sir. But, I beg to differ." He grinned.

The captain smiled back. "Good news, indeed. I shall have to hear the entire story." He waved an inviting hand. "Come into my office, both of you. Let us get you back on our muster roll."

The men followed their captain into the office. The officer motioned toward the door. "Close it, please." Michael complied.

"Sit, gentlemen. We have much to discuss."

Michael and Conrad obediently seated themselves in a pair of mismatched, rickety ladder-back chairs. Captain Weiser walked over to a serving table and turned over three matching crystal glasses. He poured a quarter-inch of red-brown brandy into each. He crossed the room and handed each man a glass. He lifted his own drink high to offer a toast. "To your safe return." All three men downed the tasty, scorching liquid.

Captain Weiser walked around his desk and sat down. He pointed at Conrad. "You first, Private Traywitz. I know all about Private Yeisley's predicament. But, you showing up here today has confounded me. I want to know every detail."

For the next hour, Conrad and Michael endeavored to share the story of their capture, escape, and eventual return to Pennsylvania. Captain Weiser listened intently, enthralled by their first-hand account. When they were finished with the entire story, the captain pulled a small stack of papers from one of the drawers in the desk.

"I have maintained a file on your case, Private Yeisley. Somehow, command managed to list you as a deserter after the unfortunate Haussegger incident. Thankfully, Dr. Schell has helped tremendously in setting our records straight."

"You received my letters and affidavits?"

Captain Weiser nodded thoughtfully. "We did, indeed. The doctor included a rather detailed report of your injuries from the gunshot wound and the subsequent complications. Although, I find it curious that he made no mention of you, Private Traywitz."

Conrad's head hung low. "It was my original intention to remain at home, sir. I thought it best to leave things alone and allow the army to live with its mistake. Dr. Schell would never lie for me, but he did consent to leaving my name out of his report."

The captain stared blankly at Conrad. "But, then, later on you changed your mind?"

"Yes, sir."

The captain continued his icy stare. His brief expression of disapproval soon disappeared. "I am quite proud of you for reaching such a noble and honest decision, Conrad."

"Thank you, sir."

The captain nodded. "Indeed. We need not speak of it again. I will correct the rolls immediately and return you to active status, fit for duty."

He sorted through the stack of papers on the desk. He chuckled as he held up one of the documents. "Yeisley, this letter from that poor farmer who shot you is quite an entertaining document. It reads a bit like a confession."

Michael and Conrad both laughed. Michael responded, "I am

sure it does, Captain. He apologized to me without ceasing, right up until the moment he left with Dr. Schell."

The captain smiled and nodded. "Well, once we received all of this corrective information, I immediately changed your status from desertion to furlough. That was on the first of March."

"Then, I am not in any trouble?" Michael confirmed.

"Of course not. You are to be commended for making your escape from the enemy. I am honored to have you under my command. I have noted your return to duty and back-dated your pay to March 1. Legally, that is the earliest date for which I can correct the records. The payrolls through February have already been submitted to Congress, audited, and closed."

Michael was greatly relieved. "I understand. March 1 is good. Frankly, I had not thought about receiving any back pay."

"And me, sir? What about my status?" Conrad asked timidly.

"I will change your records in the same fashion. Your official date of return will be March 1."

"Thank you, sir."

The captain tucked his papers back inside their drawer. "Do either of you require any equipment or gear?"

Michael responded. "I am quite well with regard to personal equipment. However, I lost my prized Charleville upon my capture in January. I need a weapon."

"Same for me, sir," Conrad added.

The captain nodded. "I suspected as much. But, not to worry. We have an ample supply of arms. We still retain a storeroom of weapons confiscated from the Hessians at Trenton." He jotted a note on a small card, then handed it to Michael. "Take this to the commissary. I have noted that each of you are to have your pick of the guns. Make it a good one. Now ... do you have any other correspondence or paper-work for me?"

"No, sir. But, we brought a wagon filled with items for our company. My wife led an effort throughout our county to collect stockings, gloves, and other garments. There is also a considerable amount of food and drink."

The captain's left eyebrow raised in surprise. He appeared very pleased by the news. "It sounds like your bride is quite the Patriot, Private Yeisley."

Michael grinned proudly. "The wagon and mules have been donated, as well, for the regiment's use. I assume that you would like to keep them within our company."

"You assume correctly, Private Yeisley. And the goods, as well, if you do not mind. Let us make sure that our company is equipped and well-fed. If there is anything left, we can turn over any unclaimed items to the battalion quartermaster." He winked. "But I doubt that there will be any unclaimed items."

"As do I, sir."

"Will there be anything else, gentlemen?"

Michael shrugged. "Is Abraham well? Private Price?"

The captain rose from his chair. Michael and Conrad stood, as well.

"Private Price is faring well enough, all things considered. Like the others of the company, he is confined to the barracks area at this time. He should be glad to see you, though. I recall now that you were very close friends. I am certain that he can make room for you in his hut for the night."

Michael was confused. "Why are the men confined to the barracks?"

"Smallpox."

A shudder of fear ran down Michael's spine. "The men have the smallpox?"

"No. But, they were recently inoculated against the smallpox. Most of the men are mildly ill. There are a few with slight fevers, some with rash, and others have been vomiting. But, it is nothing compared to the actual bloody pox. They are almost recovered. You should find them in high spirits. No doubt, the beverages in your wagon will lift those spirits even more."

"I thought the inoculations were forbidden by law of the Congress," Conrad observed.

"They were, but General Washington ordered the procedure.

The entire army has been inoculated over the past two months. It has been a top-secret project, indeed. We were one of the last groups to receive ours." The captain paused and looked over the top of his glasses at Michael. "Have you ever had the pox, Private Yeisley?"

"No, sir."

"And you, Traywitz?"

"No, sir."

"Then you must both receive your inoculations as rapidly as possible. I need you to be recovered and fit for duty when our orders come. I doubt that we will remain at this location for much longer. The weather has broken, and the army will commence operations soon."

The captain took a piece of paper from a small box on the desk. He opened the ink well and took up the goose feather quill from its cradle. He dipped the nib into the ink, daubed the excess from the tip of the feather, and began writing on the paper.

"This will be your pass from camp to go into town tomorrow. I expect you both to report to the hospital, where you will receive your inoculation. But, do not tarry inside the town. Command does not wish for common soldiers to be loitering about."

"Where is the hospital located?"

"It is at the Presbyterian Church. You cannot miss it."

"But, sir ... we are both of the Reformed Church," Michael protested.

The captain rolled his eyes. "Son, you are not going there to give an offering. You're going to get inoculated against the pox."

"Yes, sir," Michael responded sheepishly, humiliated by his own foolishness.

The captain shook his pounce pot over the paper, scattering cuttlefish bone powder over the surface of the ink. After a few seconds, he cupped the paper, tilted it, and returned the ink-stained powder back into the collection bowl on top of the pounce pot. He gave the document a quick shake, examined it, and then handed it to Michael.

"Do not lose this pass. You will need it to cross the checkpoint and depart the camp."

Michael nodded his understanding. "Yes, sir."

The captain reached a friendly hand across the desk. "Welcome back, gentlemen. You have been missed. Now, go ... enjoy your reunion with your friends."

IT WAS A SWEET REUNION, indeed. Michael and Conrad reported to the company huts and discovered their compatriots lounging around an outdoor campfire. It was a pleasant, warm spring evening. They had just settled down for an evening meal of bean soup thickened with ground corn. When Michael and Conrad pulled up in the wagon, the men of Weiser's company erupted into mayhem. Abraham Price greeted Michael with a shriek of surprise and a vigorous hug. Conrad's return from the dead was almost more than the German soldiers could fathom.

Once the initial surprise and onslaught of emotional reunions had subsided, Michael informed Abe and the other fellows about the cargo in the wagon. When he mentioned that there were barrels of ale, rum, and whiskey buried beneath the clothing and food, the cele-bratory mood became almost euphoric. It took only a few minutes for the men to dig the barrels of liquor from the bottom of the pile. Immediately, the drinking, singing, and celebrations began. The men begged Michael and Conrad to tell the story of their capture and escape. Of course, they obliged.

Soon, men from other companies in the regiment began to wander over to investigate the cause of such a grand celebration. With each incoming group, Michael and Conrad had to re-tell their story. They soon grew weary of it. In his rum-tainted state, Abraham Price overflowed with generosity and invited the other companies to join in imbibing the supply of liquor and drink that Michael had delivered. Before they even realized, every barrel was tapped and drained.

The men reveled in the celebration of joy and friendship until long past the time of evening curfew. It took a stern word from Lieutenant Colonel Weltner, the regiment's second-in-command, to shame the boisterous men into going to bed.

The party ended quickly. One by one, the men stumbled toward their log huts. Some of them, being quite inebriated, required assistance. Minutes later, and to the great relief of the hundreds of other inoculation-sickened men attempting to sleep in huts nearby, the small valley fell silent.

Since the temperature was well above freezing, Michael and Conrad elected to make their bed beside the fire that night. It was too late, and the men of the company were entirely too drunk, for them to locate any available bunks inside the dark huts. They used the ample supply of donated blankets in the wagon to construct comfortable cocoons beside the blazing campfire.

Conrad was thoroughly drunk. He simply fell onto his pile of blankets and passed out. Michael, however, had been a bit more circumspect in his drinking. Before going to bed, he went behind a tree to relieve his bladder. He then kicked off his well-worn buckle shoes and climbed beneath the warm covers of his bedroll.

Michael lay awake for a long time, completely alone, staring at the fire and thinking of his family. Though he was happy to be back among his mates, he longed for home. He imagined the faces of his daughters. He pretended that the campfire was his own hearth in his own house, and that his wife would soon be joining him beside the fire to sip hot, honey-sweetened tea. His heart ached for the company of his bride. He cherished in his mind and heart all of the moments that he had enjoyed with her over the past two blissful months in Pennsylvania. He eventually surrendered to sleep. But, in his dreams, he was with Magdalena.

12

UNDER NEW MANAGEMENT

May 22, 1777
Army Hospital - Morristown, New Jersey

Michael stared longingly at the beautiful pair of lead dice lying idle on the tiny table beside his bed. He had carefully carved them from two .75 caliber British musket balls, obtained in a trade from a Scotsman prisoner who had been housed temporarily on their ward. The heavy game cubes were pristine and unused. A layer of dust coated the upper face of each one. Michael doubted that he would ever lure Conrad into a friendly game of hazard.

Instead, he listlessly shuffled the ancient German thirty-two-card deck and prepared to deal yet another mind-numbing hand of *Mariagenspiel*. The game, somewhat popular amongst German families for decades, was a two-card trick-and-draw contest. The name of the game meant, "marriage," and one earned bonus points for uniting the king and queen of the same suit.

Michael hated *Mariagenspiel*. Indeed, most people in the German communities considered it a contest for ladies only. But, it was the only card game that Conrad ever wanted to play ... perhaps, because it was the only one that he seemed capable of winning.

Michael sighed and resolved himself to his fate. Until Dr. Schell declared him immune to the smallpox and released him from care, he was sentenced to long, tedious days filled with Conrad's shallow banter and ceaseless women's card games. He prayed that his seemingly perpetual confinement would end soon.

The one redeeming quality of hospital life was that the food was a bit better than what could be scrounged at the camp. Meals were much more regular, always hot, and greater in volume. Still, despite the semi-decent rations, hospital life was torturously boring. The only real excitement Michael found was in observing the regular influx of new patients. There was always an interesting assortment of various maladies and injuries.

Michael was strangely fascinated by the process of diagnosing a patient's illness. He and Conrad invented their very own game of "diagnosis," and attempted to guess what the doctors would declare to be wrong with each new patient that arrived on the ward. Michael correctly pre-diagnosed the new patients approximately nine out of every ten times. On more than one occasion, Conrad declared, "Perhaps you should be doing the doctoring around here."

Michael was less impressed, however, by the cures that the surgeons prescribed with such predictable regularity. It seemed that, without exception, their almost immediate reaction to every illness was therapeutic bleeding. If not draining blood from the patients, the surgeons always seemed to desire to attempt their second-favorite and most bizarre remedy ... a tobacco smoke enema. That procedure involved using a bellows and a hollow tube to blow clouds of smoke into a sick man's arse. It was a preposterous notion, in Michael's humble opinion, and a tragic waste of good Virginia tobacco.

Michael was thoroughly relieved when a familiar voice interrupted his shuffling and pre-empted the impending chore of dealing the next boring hand of cards.

"*Guten Morgen*! And how are my patients today?"

Conrad and Michael turned and watched Dr. Nicklaus Schell

saunter down the narrow aisle that divided the beds on either side of the small room.

"Fit for duty and ready to be set free from this glorified prison," Michael replied numbly.

"Are our attendants not treating you well?" Nicklaus inquired, confused.

"The behavior of the staff is admirable, Dr. Schell. Michael is simply bored," Conrad clarified. "He is anxious to return to duty at the encampment."

"Sincerely? I thought that you fellows would enjoy the luxury and warmth of our hospital. There is ample food, good fires, and no officers harassing you. That is why I kept you here instead of sending you back to convalesce at your regiment. I thought I was performing a favor on your behalf."

Michael shook his head. "I am losing my mind, Nicklaus. I feel as if these walls are shrinking inward on me. You must send me back to the regiment."

"As you wish. But first, you must allow me one final inspection. Now, lie back. Lift your shirts."

Both men complied. They had performed similarly for at least a half-dozen surgeons over the past three weeks. Dr. Schell leaned forward and carefully inspected the scabbed-over cowpox sores on their torsos and chests.

"Any fever, foul stomach, or vomiting?"

"Not since the first week," Conrad replied.

"And the itching has ceased?"

"Mine never really itched. Not enough that I should notice," Michael reassured him.

"Same for me," Conrad echoed.

"Are your appetites good?"

Michael grinned. "Too good."

"Michael's appetite has always been better than mine," Conrad quipped, smiling.

Nicklaus slapped Conrad on the knee. "Very well, then, gentlemen. You are, officially, free from the pox and inoculated against its future infection. I shall write up your release immediately. You may leave after your mid-day meal. Good enough?"

Michael was elated. "That is wonderful news, Nicklaus."

The door into the room opened and a young surgeon's mate poked his head inside. "Dr. Schell, there is someone here to see you."

"Tell them to wait in my office. I will be along shortly."

"But, Doctor, it is a Continental officer. He is a colonel, I think. He seems to be in quite a hurry. I do not think him to be the sort of fellow who is accustomed to waiting."

Nicklaus rolled his eyes and sighed. "Very well. I am coming." He nodded to Michael and Conrad and then turned to leave. He called over his shoulder as he walked toward the door, "I would not tarry long in town, gentlemen. I hear that the army is soon to be on the move."

"Where did you hear this?" Michael challenged.

Dr. Schell stopped at the door and faced them. "It is simply a rumor. But, unlike most rumors, this one is working its way through many different channels. It seems that His Excellency intends to relocate the winter camp. It has something to do with a surprise attack by the British at a place called Bound Brook."

Michael glanced at Conrad. Both men knew the place. It was to the south, near Princeton.

"We will report immediately to our headquarters," Conrad promised.

Nicklaus nodded and smiled warmly. "Good luck, Conrad. And be careful around Michael. He is always having accidents and foul luck." He paused and smiled fondly. "Until we meet again ..."

Dr. Schell turned and exited the ward. He strolled quickly down the hallway in the direction of his office. This mysterious visitor had greatly aroused his curiosity.

Nicklaus sat, stunned, behind his desk. He was ensnared in a mental and emotional whirlwind. Colonel Thomas Hartley, veteran of the ill-fated invasion of Quebec, was a man of action. He had wasted no time in getting down to business.

"I stand in need of a surgeon, *Herr* Schell, and you come highly recommended. I want you to return to Philadelphia with me today. I depart within the hour."

Nicklaus' mind raced. Deep in his heart he longed to be assigned to an actual regiment. For some months now, he had been without a "home" in the army. He was both respected and valued as a surgeon in the encampment. But, his lack of attachment to a particular command was a matter of personal shame. He was beginning to wonder if he had been forgotten by the Hospital Department, or if any regiment might ever request his service.

"But, Colonel, I do not understand. I thought you already had a surgeon assigned to your regiment."

Colonel Hartley's face registered disgust. "I thought so, as well. I enlisted a fellow named Swope back in February. I secured his commission from the Congress. I thought I had my medical service covered. But, the fellow has disappeared, seemingly, from the face of the earth. I have neither seen nor heard from his since. As you can imagine, I have precious little time to waste in searching for him. I have almost completed the raising of eight of my assigned companies. The army will be on the move very soon, and I must deploy with an able surgeon."

"I thought that I had been forgotten by headquarters and, in some ways, 'put to pasture' here at the encampment," Nicklaus declared.

The colonel shook his head vigorously. "Not at all, sir. I was with General Washington this morning, securing our orders and assignment within the main army. He honored you with his personal recommendation. He shared at great length about your exploits at Breed's Hill, your capture at Princeton, and your subsequent escape. He is quite proud of you." Colonel Hartley leaned forward in his seat. "Dr. Schell, you are young, handsome, gallant, and brave. It is quite obvious that you are a skilled physician. And you are, clearly, a man who is loyal and attentive to duty. You are, most definitely, the man for me and my regiment."

"I am honored by your words, sir ..."

Colonel Hartley cut him off, "I am not interested in the pleasantries of mere conversation, *Herr* Schell. I did not come all this way to flatter you. Will you, or will you not, join my regiment as junior surgeon?" He reached forward and slapped the palm of his hand on the desk. "I must know immediately!"

Nicklaus took a deep, thoughtful breath. This was exactly the news that he had longed for. He smiled, nodded slightly and then rose to his feet. "Colonel, 'twould be my honor to join Hartley's Independent Regiment."

The colonel stood. His face bore a smile of satisfaction. "Excellent. I shall see you on the town green in one hour. I will send my man for your baggage. We will share a coach to Philadelphia. It will give us some time to become better acquainted."

"Of course, sir. I am at your service."

The colonel turned and walked toward the closed door. "Welcome to the regiment, Dr. Schell. You have made a good choice."

He opened the door and strolled confidently through the office beyond. Nicklaus stared after him for quite a while. He prayed that he had, indeed, made a good choice.

New Encampment at Middlebrook – May 26, 1777

CAPTAIN WEISER ANNOUNCED, "Stricker is gone, for good, men. I just received word. It is official."

The soldiers in his company cheered. None of them were sorry to see the former executive officer riding out of the camp. The captain attempted to retain an emotionless expression in the face of their celebration, but he was not successful. He could not restrain his own smile. Like the enlisted men, he was equally happy to see the incompetent officer depart their ranks. He waved a hand to calm the soldiers and continued, "And Major Weltner has been promoted to

Lieutenant Colonel. He is now, officially, second-in-command of the regiment."

The men nodded approvingly. A handful of them clapped. Weltner had been a much-respected and well-loved officer since the early days of the formation of the German Regiment. He was the fellow who, when he stood up to the treasonous recklessness of Haussegger, saved the entire regiment from capture at Princeton.

"What of this new Colonel of ours?" inquired Private Christopher Wiegel.

The captain shrugged. "We do not know much about him. He is a paid soldier from Germany. I heard that he served for over twenty years as an engineer in the Prussian army."

"An engineer?" Wiegel followed. "What use is that to us?"

The captain grimaced slightly. "I do not know, for certain. But, for now, you must rest assured that he seems a most competent commander. He is very organized. He has worked diligently to clean up the various messes left behind by Major Stricker, and thus far he has performed admirably. I am also told that he is very well-connected within the army." The captain paused. "Ultimately, though, the work ethic of our colonel is of no concern to you. Colonel Weltner and the other officers will deal with the commander. If you fellows are attentive to your duties and follow *my* orders, you will be just fine. Understood?"

The men nodded and grunted.

"Good. Now, in other news ... our regiment has been reassigned to another division within the army. General John Sullivan offered us to General Nathanael Greene in exchange for Colonel Moses Hazen's Second Canadian Regiment. It was an even swap. So, now we are part of Greene's Division."

The men sat quietly and digested the news from Captain Weiser. Most had no notion of its implications.

"What does all that mean to us, exactly?" Abraham Price inquired of Captain Weiser.

"Nothing, really. The regiment remains unchanged. We are

simply under a new division commander. And we also have a new brigade commander, freshly appointed by General Washington."

"Who is that?" inquired an anonymous private.

"Brigadier General Johann Peter Gabriel Muhlenberg of Maryland. They call him the 'fighting preacher.'"

The men groaned. Many rolled their eyes.

"Preacher?" Conrad questioned. "What manner of preacher is he?"

"He was ordained as an Anglican but most recently served a Lutheran congregation in Maryland."

Again, some of the men groaned. Captain Weiser waved a hand of caution.

"Make no mistake, men! Peter Muhlenberg is a soldier's soldier. He served in the 60th Regiment of Foot and in the German Dragoons in the war against the French. They called him 'Devil Pete' back then."

"That does not sound like a very complimentary name for a vicar," Michael quipped.

"I do not think you will find him to be a typical member of the clergy." Captain Weiser grinned. "There is quite an amazing story circulating about him."

"Tell us!" Abe Price exclaimed.

Captain Weiser took a deep breath. "They say that last January he stood up in his pulpit and preached from Ecclesiastes chapter three."

"*To everything there is a season ...*" Michael quoted.

"Right. That one. The church folk claim that right after he read the part about, '*a time for war and a time for peace,*' he slammed his Bible closed and proclaimed, '*And this, my friends, is a time for war!*'"

The men were spellbound, mesmerized by the notion of such a declaration from a man of the cloth, standing in the pulpit of his church, no less.

"Well," Captain Weiser grinned and continued, "They claim that he tore off his clerical robe ... right there in the pulpit ... and underneath was the uniform of a Continental colonel. Then, right at that moment, outside the door a drum began to roll. The front doors opened up, and the colonel slowly marched toward the sunlight. All throughout the church, men stood and kissed their wives goodbye, and then walked outside to the recruiting tables and enlisted in the army. In a half-hour, 162 men joined the Continentals."

"Horse shite!" Abe Price retorted.

"No ... really ... that is what I was told!" Captain Weiser vowed. "They say the next day, he marched out of the county with 300 men in all. They are now the 8th Virginia Regiment. They have been in combat throughout South Carolina and Georgia for the past year."

"Christ, Almighty," Conrad wailed. "A fighting preacher, indeed!"

"And a German," Michael added approvingly.

"And he is your new brigade commander," Captain Weiser declared, with a look of satisfaction.

The men were impressed. They looked at one another and nodded with affirmation and pride. It seemed that fortunes might, indeed, be changing for the German Regiment.

~

May 30, 1777
Pennsylvania Hospital - Philadelphia

KATHARINA SCHELL MOVED SWIFTLY through the convalescent ward. Her inspection was quick, but thorough. The girls had done a decent job of cleaning the room, but there remained a handful of tasks yet to be completed. She turned and marched resolutely toward the small gaggle of timid nurses standing near the doorway. The faces of the four teen-aged girls betrayed their dread. Mrs. Schell was never satisfied and always managed to find shortcomings in their work.

Katharina cleared her throat. "Ladies, the floors and beds look excellent. You are to be commended for your efforts."

The nurses exhaled in relief. They could not believe that they had received their first perfectly positive report from the detail-conscious matron of the ward. They were almost giddy with delight.

"However!" she declared. The young girls moaned in frustration.

"The window ledges are dusty and still require cleaning. Your task this afternoon is to remove and launder all curtains, polish all glass windows and fixtures, and clean all doorframes and windowsills. I want this to be the cleanest ward in Philadelphia."

One of the girls, a fair-skinned, red-haired Scottish lass named Elspeth McClelland, timidly raised her hand. "Might we go and fetch our dinner first, Mum? 'Tis almost noontime, and we're a might bit famished."

Katharina glanced at the clock in the corner, which revealed that it was a quarter before the noon hour. She nodded. "Of course. There is no need to hurry, I suppose. The curtains can wait. Off with you, then. But, return to me no later than one o'clock."

The girls darted out the door. They walked quickly down the hallway toward the staircase that led downstairs. Elspeth led the way. She burst through the swinging door that led to the stairway access and ran head-first into a dashingly handsome young man in a Continental Army officer's uniform. The girl stumbled sideways and almost flipped over the railing of the stairs. Instinctively, the officer caught her in his iron-strong grip.

"There, now, *Fraulein*. You must slow down! Speed is dangerous around these staircases. Why are you in such a hurry?"

Elspeth stared into Dr. Nicklaus Schell's captivating, dazzlingly blue eyes. She was speechless at first ... mesmerized by the young fellow's perfect, angular face, his impressively broad chest, and lean, muscular arms. His sandy blonde hair was braided in a thick, lengthy queue, tied at the top and bottom with a string of blue ribbon that matched the blue of his wool greatcoat. He was, without doubt, the loveliest man that she had ever seen.

He chuckled. "Can you not speak, *Fraulein*?"

His verbal challenge broke through her stunned silence. "Aye, I can, I shall, and I do. Beggin' your pardon, kind sir. I was in a rudely fearsome hurry, and I dinna ken you was comin' through the door. I pray you might forgive me my impudence."

The gentleman responded, "It is quite all right, Miss ..." He left the greeting dangling, inviting the pretty girl to share her name.

"McClelland ... Elspeth McClelland, my Lord." She curtsied quickly and sloppily. "Are you a surgeon, sir?"

"I am, indeed."

"Then I must beg your forgiveness, Doctor."

"No, *Fraulein* McClelland, there is no need for such as that. Think nothing else of it. I am merely glad that you were not injured in our ..." He paused and searched for the right descriptor. "Our encounter."

The young woman's ashen, slightly freckled face flushed deep crimson in embarrassment. "Thank you, sir. You are most kind."

He glanced at the other three girls. "Why were you ladies in such a dire hurry?"

Elspeth looked sheepishly toward the floor. "We just received release from our matron to go and fetch dinner. We were simply anxious to depart her presence."

"Why, so?"

"I should not say, sir."

"Why not, pray tell?"

"Because it would be neither proper nor ladylike to speak it, sir."

The young fellow grinned. "Is that so? Now, I *am* intrigued. You *must* tell me!"

The girl sighed. "Very well, then. We simply had to escape that horrid woman's grasp!"

"What horrid woman?"

"Our matron. Oh, sir, 'tis a devilish woman, she is. Every single day, she works our fingers to the blood and bone, with neither a word of mercy nor of grace."

The other three girls all covered their mouths and giggled slightly.

Nicklaus turned his gaze toward them. "Is she truly that bad?"

The three giggling girls nodded, their timid mouths still covered.

The outspoken Miss McClelland continued her rant. "Worse. She treats us as if we were her slaves. If you were to ask her, none of us can do a single right. The woman is headstrong, cold-hearted, and evil!" One of her friends laughed out loud and then covered her mouth with both hands in an attempt to hide her amused, embarrassed smile.

"Elspeth McClelland! You should be ashamed! You are a bold, headstrong girl!" one of the other girls scolded her. "You are speaking ill of this woman, and you do nay even know the man who stands before you!"

The chastised young woman pursed her lips in an effort to harness her disdain. Then, she lowered her face in shame. "Gavina is right. I should be nay a tellin' you such things, Doctor. 'Tis of no concern to you."

"Well, I must declare with all sincerity, that if a lovely *Fraulein* such as yourself is being mistreated within this hospital, then I must make it my concern!"

The girl's face stretched into an embarrassed smile. The man had actually called her, "lovely." The other three girls giggled once more and then began whispering to one another.

"You should nay be a teasin' me with empty words of compliment, sir. 'Tis not kind."

"Oh, I am not teasing you, *Fraulein* McClelland. I mean every single word that I speak. Now, point me in the direction of this demon, and we shall have words, indeed!"

"Oh, no, sir! 'Tis not necessary!" She was beginning to panic.

Nicklaus attempted to appear stern. "I mean business, girls. I intend to have this woman's head on a plate!"

Elspeth pleaded, "Oh, please, Doctor! Do not take any action against her! It could cost us our jobs. And, we would nay want to be the cause of strife between a surgeon and the chief nurse of the hospital."

"Oh, you shouldn't worry yourself about that, *Fraulein* McClelland."

"Whatever do you mean, Doctor?"

"I know how to handle this particular woman." Nicklaus leaned forward and whispered, "She is my mother."

Elspeth stared at Nicklaus in disbelief. He grinned mischievously.

Elspeth hissed, "You are Dr. Nicklaus Schell? The son that she rattles on about each and every day?"

He bowed graciously. "At your service, *Fraulein* Elspeth McClelland."

He took her hand and lifted it to his lips. Her three friends shrieked in dismay and then sprinted down the stairs. Elspeth never moved. She stared without wavering into Nicklaus' eyes.

"Why did you not make your identity known to me sooner?" she demanded.

He shrugged. "I do not know."

"You were toying with me, then. This entire time, you have been toying with me. Well, 'twas rude, indeed," she declared.

He grinned. "Like your characterization of my mother, perhaps."

Her cheeks flushed once again, the redness reflecting the hue of her blazing red hair. "Now, you *are* making fun with me."

"That was not my true intention, I assure you."

"Nonetheless, you have managed to embarrass me greatly, sir."

He waved his left hand toward the stairway. "And yet, you did not run away with your friends."

She stared resolutely. "I am not one to speak and then go a runnin' off in fear and regret. I stand by my words."

"Indeed." He smiled warmly. "I find that to be a wonderfully refreshing quality in a woman."

"I dinna care whether or not you are impressed with me." She cleared her throat. "Might I have my hand back, sir?"

Suddenly, Nicklaus was the embarrassed one. He had not even realized that he still held the young maiden's right hand in his own. Still, he held fast and refused to release her.

"Only on one condition."

"And what is that?" She eyed him suspiciously.

"If I might have permission to call upon you for tea on Sunday."

Nicklaus did not think it possible for a woman's face to turn such a bright red hue. But, Elspeth McClelland's did. And he could almost swear that he saw a bead of nervous perspiration on her forehead.

"I s'pose that could be arranged, if my father is agreeable."

"Wonderful! Then I shall contact him, personally, tomorrow and secure his permission." Nicklaus released her hand, slowly and gently, and then bowed. "I sincerely hope to see you on Sunday."

"But ... how will you even know how to find my father?"

"Do not worry. I will simply ask my mother for your address. I am certain that she retains your record of employment." His face erupted into a teasing, toothy grin.

The Scottish lass did not back down. She smiled back, raising her eyelids teasingly. "Very well, then. But if I hear that you have revealed a single word of our private conversation to your mum, come Sunday I'll be a brewin' you up a batch of bitter weeds instead of tea."

She turned and sauntered proudly down the stairs. Nicklaus watched her until she disappeared from view. He was completely smitten by the bold, self-confident, red-haired damsel. He had to discover more about the beautiful Elspeth McClelland.

"*MUTTER*, you have barely touched your meal!"

Katharina smiled warmly and reached across the table to squeeze her son's hand. "I am simply so very glad to see you. Nicklaus. My heart leapt when you walked into my ward." She shook her head as she speared a small piece of ham with her bone-handled, two-pronged fork. A tear formed in her eye. "My heart almost ruptured when I received the letter from the army that informed me you were missing. I thought, for certain, that I had lost my one and only son."

"But, I survived."

"Yes. And escaped! *Mein Gott*! Such gallantry!" Her smile transformed into a grimace. She slapped him angrily on the back of his hand and scolded, "I am still angry that you did not come to see me when you traveled through Philadelphia whilst taking that wounded boy to his home."

"I told you, *Mutter*. I had no opportunity to do so. I was in the charge of a sick man. And, besides, we did not come directly through the city. We remained to the east and north."

"You could have made a simple turn and come into Philadelphia."

"I had my patient to consider."

"Perhaps. But you also have a mother to consider. What if you have been killed afterward in the New Jersey campaign? What if I had never seen you again?"

"And yet, here I sit before you now ... sipping port and dining in the finest restaurant in Philadelphia." He smiled kindly, warmly. "Tonight, you have me at your complete disposal, dearest *Mutter*. Your every wish is my command."

When Nicklaus smiled, she saw the eyes of her little boy in the face of the man who sat across from her. Her heart melted with pure delight and joy.

"Indeed. Everything did turn out perfectly." She paused, then resumed her characteristic motherly chastisement. "But, I still do not know why you did not send me a note to announce your arrival. You could have given me some manner of notice that you were coming today."

"There was no time. It was less than a week ago when Colonel Hartley recruited me for his regiment. I had less than an hour to pack and make arrangements." He took a sip of delicious Douro Valley port from his long-stemmed glass. "Besides, I knew that I would arrive well before any correspondence. The colonel was most anxious to get back to his regiment."

"So, then ... you are now assigned to Philadelphia?" she inquired hopefully.

"For the time being. The colonel and his officers are still drilling and training the men."

"Tell me about the regiment," she invited.

Nicklaus' face revealed how pleased he was by her interest. "Well, they are over one thousand men strong. There are eight companies, mostly Germans from Pennsylvania and Maryland, though one company hails from Virginia. And he has an entire company of grenadiers! It is most amazing."

Katharina was confused. "I do not know that word ... grenadiers. What does it mean?"

"It describes the men who are tasked with hurling grenades."

"Grenades?" she repeated, still confused.

"They are explosive iron balls which shatter and hurl shards of metal outward."

"And what is their purpose?"

"To maim and kill, of course. A single grenade can fell up to twenty men, or more, in a single explosion. Their effects are devastating."

"How ghastly." Katherine pushed her plate away from her and leaned back in her chair.

"*Mutter! Bitte! Vergib mir!* I did not mean to offend your sensitivities."

"Well, Nicklaus, you must admit that such talk is not appropriate for the dinner table."

"Indeed. You are absolutely right, *Mutter*. I sincerely apologize."

She stared at him for a moment and then waved her hand dismissively. She returned her attention to her plate. "It is quite all right, Son. I suppose I have heard, and seen, much worse ... as well you know."

There was a moment of awkwardness and silence.

Katharina reached for her wine glass and decided to help her son move past the unintended embarrassment of his uncouth conversation. "Where is your regiment being housed?"

"They are in the Philadelphia Barracks, on the northern edge of the city."

"Do you have a room there, as well?"

Clearly, she was fishing for some particular information. Nicklaus grinned. He could see where the conversation was headed.

"*Nein, Mutter*. As a regimental officer, I must procure quarters for myself at a suitable location and within a reasonable distance from our headquarters."

Her face brightened. "Oh! Is that so? And what are your plans?"

His lips curled into a boyish, teasing grin. "You already know my plans, *Frau* Katharina Schell. I intend to stay with my mother and occupy my own bedchamber."

"Is that right? But, what if I have rented it out to a boarder? Must I turn some poor soul out into the street simply because my son returned home unannounced?" Her own face glowed with a playful smile.

"Indeed, you shall. Do I need to procure a messenger now to send word? We must remove the lout immediately! I intend to sleep in my own bed this night!"

Katharina laughed. "Of course, you will. Your room is exactly as you left it. I launder the sheets weekly, in the sincere hope that you might return to me."

"And now I have."

A fat tear formed in her right eye and instantly streaked down her cheek. "Yes. Now you have."

Nicklaus picked up his napkin and reached across the small table to wipe his mother's tear. "There will be no tears this night," he declared. "No more blubbering and sentimental talk. This is a night of celebration!"

Katharina nodded excitedly. "What else shall we talk about, then?"

Nicklaus took a healthy swig of port and then declared, "Tell me about that exceedingly charming red-haired girl who works for you ... *Fraulein* Elspeth McClelland."

∽

July 27, 1777
Morristown, New Jersey

THE MEN of Captain Weiser's company were spent. They had been marching almost non-stop for the last nine days. Muhlenberg's brigade, supported by General William Maxwell's brigade, had been sent north on July 19 to provide a blocking force against a potential move by the British out of York City. The two brigades marched all the way to the Hudson River. They had just arrived on the outskirts of York when they received recall orders from General Washington. His spies on Long Island had gotten a message through to headquarters that General William Howe's army had departed the city by ship on July 23. The British were out of York City.

Washington wanted his entire army near Morristown so that he might react to an anticipated British landing somewhere to the south. So, the entire force turned around almost immediately and marched back to the encampment. The German Regiment, along with the other 1,500 troops of the combined brigades, stumbled, exhausted, into Morristown on the afternoon of July 26. Most of them had been sleeping ever since ... almost eighteen hours.

Michael slept where he fell upon his arrival back in camp. He dozed happily beneath a stand of chestnut trees near the regiment's tents and huts. He wore neither shoes nor stockings. He had removed them the moment he collapsed beneath the trees. His tortured extremities were shriveled from constant soaking in mud, ditches, and streams. His aching feet reveled in the luxury of the extended absence of musty wool and moldy leather.

Hunger, and a full bladder, finally coaxed Michael from his seemingly perpetual slumber. His distressed pelvis and empty, aching gut roused him shortly after sunrise. Only a handful of other soldiers stirred within the German Regiment's camp. Hunger had, obviously, awakened them, as well. All were making fires and preparing pots for cooking.

First, Michael relieved his distended bladder of its urgent burden. Then, he trotted barefoot into the forest to gather wood and tinder for his cooking fire. Once the small cone of combustibles was prepared and stacked, he used a shovel to borrow a few glowing coals from the campfire of a nearby band of Marylanders. He had a crackling fire going within minutes.

While Michael waited for the fire to die down a bit, he retrieved a small cooking pot from his market wallet. He was busy constructing a wooden cooking tripod for the pot when his trusty comrade Abraham Price appeared at his fireside. Abe was quite a sight. He was wearing nothing but his blue and white homespun shirt. His skinny, pale, pasty white legs protruded from the bottom of the huge, gown-like garment. He yawned and scratched his rather shaggy head with one hand and tugged at his privates with his other hand.

Abraham grumbled, "How can I help?"

Michael choked back a laugh. He smiled at his friend. "Well! *Guten Morgen, Herr* Price! I have beans ready to cook, but I need fresh water for the pot. Do you have any meat, at all?"

Abraham nodded as he placed his hands on his lower back and arched backward, stretching the tight, aching muscles above his buttocks. Michael had to look away quickly, as the maneuver exposed Abe's dangling manhood to full, public view. It was a most unpleasant sight ... one that Michael feared he would not soon forget.

Abe yawned once more and declared, "I have a small slab of smoked salt pork. It should flavor your beans nicely."

Michael nodded. "Chop it up. We must get this pot over the fire quickly. I am famished." He paused and grinned. "But wash your hands first. You've been a bit too busy pawing at your bollocks. And after seeing what's down there, I would rather not flavor our breakfast with your rusty twiddle-diddles."

Abraham nodded matter-of-factly. He retrieved Michael's bean pot and stumbled toward his disheveled pile of personal belongings beneath the trees. After fishing his paper-wrapped salt pork from his snapsack, he grabbed his hunting knife and wandered toward the creek to fill the pot with water. He returned a few minutes later, and soon their pork-seasoned beans were suspended and bubbling over the ample fire.

While Abraham prepared a second pot of water for tea, Michael got to work making some "camp biscuits." He mixed flour and water in a small bowl and worked it into a sticky dough. He flavored the dough with a copious amount of salt and a few tiny pinches of fat that he held in reserve from Abe's pork cuttings. He then patted the dough into small, round, flat discs and placed the biscuits on a thin, scorching-hot rock that lay against the coals of his campfire. He toasted the makeshift biscuits until they were brown on one side, then flipped them with a long-handled forged iron spatula, browning the other side.

Abraham had the water boiling in reasonably quick order. Once it was at a rolling boil, he removed the pot from the fire and placed it on a nearby rock. He shook a generous pile of loose tea leaves into a bamboo strainer and suspended it inside the steaming water. Minutes later, the men munched contentedly on the hard, dry, smoky biscuits and washed them down with mugs of strong, steaming-hot tea. It would be at least an hour before their beans would be cooked enough to eat. The bread and tea would have to hold them over until then.

The two friends sat quietly and stared into the fire. Michael soon fished his pipe and bag of tobacco from his haversack and used his pipe tongs to light up a bowl of the fragrant leaf. He tossed his tobacco sack to Abraham, who quickly joined him. They sat, silent and cross-legged, beside the fire as they puffed their tiny clay pipes and sipped their tea. They were content to simply remain still and enjoy the warmth of the fire. Both men closed their eyes and relished in the luxury afforded them by a few moments of peace and rest.

A familiar voice invaded their morning meditation. "Well, at least two of my men are less than determined to sleep the day away." It was Captain Weiser.

Michael nodded. "*Guten Morgen*, Captain." Abraham nodded, but did not speak.

"And to you, *Herr* Yeisley." Captain Weiser joined them beside their fire.

"Would you like some tea, Captain?" Abe offered.

"No, thank you, Mr. Price. I have already had more than my fair share this morning." He glanced around the area. "Where is Conrad? Normally, the three of you are inseparable."

Abraham pointed to an area twenty yards to his right. "He still slumbers beneath yon trees. If he does not awaken soon, I shall have to rouse him. Surely, the boy needs to empty his bladder ... unless he has done so as he lay."

The captain frowned. "We will have to wake all of the boys soon, I am afraid."

Michael and Abraham both felt their backs stiffen with anxiety. Something was obviously afoot.

Michael inquired with some trepidation, "What has happened, sir? Do you have some news?"

"I just came from a briefing with the colonel. General Washington has learned that the British troop fleet was spotted off of Cape May."

"Where is that?" asked Abraham, ignorant of New Jersey geography.

"It is near the mouth of the Delaware River."

"So, Howe could be moving on Philadelphia," Michael observed. "He is coming up the Delaware Bay, isn't he?"

Captain Weiser shrugged. "Perhaps. Or, he could be going further south. The ships were still well out at sea. We simply do not know. He could be headed for the Chesapeake. It also provides a relatively easy approach to Philadelphia. But, no matter where they are going, we will not be staying here. There is no more enemy to fight in the Jerseys."

"When will we leave?" Abe asked disappointedly.

"Soon." The captain leaned forward and lifted the lid from Michael's pot. He sniffed at the contents and grinned. "But, certainly not before a fine breakfast."

～

August 9, 1777
Delaware River – Trenton, New Jersey

ABRAHAM GROWLED as he leaned into the rough-cut, splintery oar. "I had hoped that I would never see this God-forsaken river again."

"You knew we had to cross it to get back home," Conrad chided him.

"Am I to take it, then, that you are not still planning on applying to the naval service?" Michael teased.

"Not likely!" Abraham cursed and spat into the water.

Captain Weiser interrupted their soldierly banter. "This is likely the last time that we shall be required to cross the Delaware, gentlemen. The defense of New Jersey is done. The entire army is moving across into Pennsylvania today."

"Aren't we headed in the wrong direction, Captain?" Conrad inquired. "This feels like a retreat."

"Not a retreat, Private Traywitz ... a redirect. General Washington is repositioning the army to get in front of Howe. We must defend our city."

"So, they are coming after Philadelphia, after all?" Michael asked.

The captain nodded grimly. "I believe so. Most of the other officers do, as well. It simply makes sense. The British surely desire to cut off the head from our rebellion. What better way is there than to take our capital and our Congress?"

Michael stared blankly toward the far bank of the river. "Do you think there is a fight coming?"

"Indeed, I do." The captain also fixed his eyes across the water, gazing upon the beautiful Pennsylvania countryside. "I believe there will be many great and tragic battles before we expel the Lobsterbacks from our shores. Yes, I believe a fight is coming. And it is coming very soon."

13

BRANDYWINE

August 28, 1777
Philadelphia

"Is something wrong with your squab?" Nicklaus inquired. "Is it undercooked? I can fetch the attendant and have something else brought for you."

Elspeth smiled and shook her head. "No, the bird is delicious."

"But, still, you are not eating," Nicklaus protested. "Surely, something must be wrong."

Elspeth shrugged. "I am just a wee bit nervous, is all." She paused. "Perhaps a little afraid, even."

"Pray tell, why would you be nervous or afraid around me?" Nicklaus reached across the table and gently took hold of her soft, warm, pink hand.

"I think you ken full-well why, Dr. Schell."

"Oh, so it is 'Doctor Schell,' now? I thought we were well past such formalities, *Fraulein* McClelland."

"We are, indeed. But, perhaps we should be a bit more circumspect. I have been thinkin' that we should restrain our familiarities." She sighed. "For now, at least."

"Why?" Nicklaus demanded, concerned. "Have I done something wrong?"

"Nay. You've done everythin' right." She chuckled. "A bit too right, perhaps."

"Whatever does that mean?" Nicklaus was becoming frustrated and confused.

Elspeth sighed. "Oh, I doonah ken! Everythin' just seems to be movin' so very fast."

"In what way?" Nicklaus asked softly.

"Well, I did not even ken you a mere month ago. Now, it seems as though we are spendin' every wakin' moment together."

Nicklaus smiled and squeezed her hand. "Now, Elspeth, that is certainly an exaggeration. I am consumed with my daily duties as a regimental surgeon. And we both know that my fearsome mother keeps you very busy for at least ten hours of each day."

Elspeth could not help but smile at his jest. Still, she offered no verbal response.

Nicklaus pleaded softly, "Talk to me! Tell me what is wrong, Elspeth. Please!"

The young Scottish maiden stared into the German doctor's perfect blue eyes. He was the ideal man. He was kind, considerate, and tender. He attended to her every want and need. Despite only a brief, one-month courtship, she loved him desperately. That was what frightened her so. She wished that she could somehow put her feelings and fears into words and make him understand.

She stammered, "I ... I suppose that I am afraid of what might be, Nicklaus."

He shook his head in frustration. "I am confused."

She inhaled a deep, thoughtful breath. "'Tis true ... I have feelings for you. It is neither a secret nor a mystery. But, I am afraid of what that means for me, and for the future." She jerked her hand away from his. She stared numbly and fidgeted with her napkin. "I doonah ken how to express for you what I'm a feelin'. I'm just afraid, that's all."

"Why should having feelings for me make you afraid?" he challenged.

She slapped a hand almost angrily on the table top. The fires of her volatile Scottish emotions were stoked. "It's because of this damnable war, Nicklaus! Just look at the uniform that you're wearing'! You're a rebel, fightin' against King George! I ken all too well what the British do to their rebels. My own grandfather was put to the bayonet at Culloden in '46. My father says they cut him on the ground as he lay there helpless and wounded. They took no prisoners, a'tall!" She appeared on the verge of tears.

"But, what does any of that have to do with me ... with us?"

"Ever'thin'! If they did it to him, they can do it to you! One day, you'll leave me. You'll march off to this God-forsken war with your regiment, and you'll leave me standin' here on the street in Philadelphia ... not knowin' if'fn I'll ever ever cast my eyes upon you agin'." A single tear crept down her right cheek. "And I doonah ken if I can bear it, Nicklaus. 'Tis not enough to simply have you for now. My heart longs to have you forever." She paused and stared deeply into his eyes. "But, this war ... it could extinguish our forever."

Nicklaus pondered her words thoughtfully. Throughout their whirlwind courtship, he had considered only the joys of the moment. For him, life was to be lived in the here and now. He gave little thought to the war or to their potential future separation. Elspeth had given him a glimpse into the heart, mind, and feelings of a woman who loved a soldier. The depth and passion of it all moved him.

"My service in the war truly troubles you that much?"

She nodded and wiped her eyes and nose with her handkerchief. "Of course, it does."

"Then, that can only mean one thing," Nicklaus declared.

"What?" she responded. Now, she was confused.

"It means that you must truly love me."

Nicklaus smiled playfully and stared into her green eyes. She returned his gaze, but said nothing. Tears quickly filled both of her eyes. Her face flushed bright red. It appeared that she might explode, such was her mixture of love, passion, embarrassment, anger, and prideful indignation.

"Is it true, then? Do you love me, Elspeth?" Nicklaus asked softly, tenderly.

She did not hesitate. "Aye. I love you. With all my heart. Madly, I do."

Nicklaus grinned broadly. "Well, then ... that is a *very* good thing ... because I love you, as well." He folded his napkin and lay it across his pewter plate, covering the remaining morsels of his food.

"Oh, Nicklaus! 'Tis such a mess! Whatever are we goin' to do?"

He reached across the table and took her hand in his. "Tomorrow morning, Elspeth, I shall visit your father and ask for your hand in marriage. Is that agreeable to you?"

Her eyes were wide with a mixture of joy, expectation, and fear. She offered no response.

"Well?" Nicklaus asked, smiling. "Is this a good silence or a bad silence? I can never tell with you."

Slowly, sadly, she shook her head. "Papa shall never allow it."

"And why not?" he protested.

"Because, Nicklaus, you are not of the Holy Catholic Church. You are a part of that strange German Church."

"It is called, 'Reformed,' my dearest."

"Yes ... that. And my father would never allow me to be wed to a man outside the Church."

"That is of no concern to me, at all. I will convert at the earliest convenience, if that is what is required of me."

"What?" she almost shrieked. Her voice was entirely too loud for the fine restaurant in which they were dining. The other customers stared at the young couple with a measure of shock and disapproval.

"I will convert," he repeated, "and shall be happy to do so." Nicklaus stood and pulled her to her feet. "Elspeth, I would charge through the very fires of hell to be with you. Do you not know that?"

"But, you scarcely even ken me, Nicklaus! You might not even like me, once you discover all my secrets and flaws," she whined in a low whisper, her voice cracking.

"I *'ken'* you well enough to know that you are the love of my life, and that I do not wish to waste another moment without you."

Tenderly, scandalously, he pulled her close and kissed her on the lips. His emotion and passion raged within him. The tender maiden smelled of sweet lavender and orange blossoms. Her scent and her touch were electrifying. After several seconds, she finally separated herself from his kiss. She glanced around the room, overwhelmed with embarrassment and shame. Every eye was on them. Nicklaus reached up with his right hand and redirected her chin so that their eyes met. He did not care about the opinions of their onlookers.

"Elspeth McClelland, I plan to have that conference with your father tomorrow. But first, I must know your answer. Will you consent to becoming my bride?"

She smiled and cupped her hand on his cheek. With a broken, weeping voice she replied, "Yes, *mo ghràdh* ... my love. Yes, I will be your bride."

Nicklaus was overwhelmed with joy. After he delivered his beloved safely to her father's home, he could scarcely remember a single moment of the late-night stroll back to his own quarters. He did not even notice the carriage parked across the street from his building. He whistled a gay tune as he walked up the stairway to his mother's apartment. He bounded happily through the door.

"*Mutter! Kommen Sie!* I have wonderful news!"

He walked through an open archway into the kitchen and was shocked to discover there a uniformed officer from his regiment. The young fellow was seated at the table with his mother. The soldier instantly and respectfully rose to his feet.

"*Guten Abend*," Nicklaus greeted the man. "How might I be of service to you, sir?"

"Dr. Schell, I am Lieutenant Hans Spiegler."

"I recognize you, Hans. What are you doing here in my home, and at such an unusual hour?"

"I have come under orders from Colonel Hartley, sir." He offered a slip of paper to Nicklaus. "You have been recalled to the regimental headquarters. I am charged with escorting you to the barracks."

Nicklaus scanned the message. It confirmed the young man's words. All officers of the regiment were summoned to headquarters, with orders to make report before midnight.

"I do not understand. What is so urgent that I must leave my home this evening?"

"I cannot be forthright, sir, in front of your mother."

"I keep no secrets from her," Nicklaus retorted.

"No, sir, but the army does." The young fellow paused. "I will explain everything on our way to the barracks, sir. I have a carriage waiting downstairs."

Nicklaus protested, "But, surely it can wait until tomorrow. I have a very important engagement in the morning ..."

"No, sir," the lieutenant interjected. "It cannot wait. My orders are to escort you to the barracks *immediately*." He paused. His voice dropped to almost a whisper. "Doctor, we simply cannot tarry. The regiment will depart at dawn tomorrow morning."

"Depart? Why?" Nicklaus demanded.

The lieutenant cast a furtive glance at Katharina. "We march to meet the enemy, sir."

Nicklaus felt a cold shiver of dread ascend his spine. He looked into his mother's eyes for the first time since having arrived home. The woman seemed despondent. Tears streamed down both cheeks. He stepped behind his mother and placed his hands on her shoulders.

"I need a few moments in private, Lieutenant. I must write a letter to my fiancé."

Katharina's head spun quickly. She stared at Nicklaus, wide-eyed and confused.

He smiled tenderly and nodded. "*Mutter*, I asked Elspeth to marry me at dinner this evening."

The lieutenant removed a gold watch from the left front pocket of his buff-colored weskit. "We have no more than a half-hour if we are to make report before midnight. You must make haste, sir."

Magdalena patted her son's hand and then stood. "Nicklaus, I will organize your clothing and baggage. You will find paper, quill, and ink on the bureau in my chamber. Go in there and write your letter. I will deliver it for you in the morning. 'Twill be all right."

Nicklaus gave her a quick hug, kissed her on the forehead, and then darted into his mother's dimly lit bedroom.

~

The Following Morning
Pennsylvania Hospital

ELSPETH SAUNTERED HAPPILY through the door of the convalescent ward. She was excited to think about the visit that Nicklaus would soon enjoy with her father. In her mind, she played through the various scenarios and possibilities of the encounter between the two most important men in her life. There was, of course, the chance that her father might reject a German suitor. She was convinced, however, that with Nicklaus' willingness to convert to Catholicism, her father would most assuredly give his consent for the marriage.

Elspeth attempted to dispel such thoughts from her mind and attend to her duties. There were only three patients housed on the ward, all recovering soldiers, freshly returned from their deployment in New Jersey. The three men dozed contentedly. She made a quick check of their water basins and bedpans. Everything appeared to be fresh and in order. She heard the creak of the door opening at the far end of the room.

"Miss McClelland, a word, please."

She knew that voice all too well. It was Mrs. Schell. Elspeth turned and peered toward the door. Katharina smiled and motioned for her to join her outside.

Because of her relationship with Nicklaus, Elspeth had managed to quench the disdain that she had once held for the woman.

However, when it came to the workplace, Mrs. Schell's voice still elicited a sense of fear and dread. She uttered a quick, silent prayer for patience and grace and then marched toward the door. Mrs. Schell was waiting for her just outside in the hallway.

"How might I help you, Mrs. Schell?"

"I have a letter for you, my dear. It is from Nicklaus." She removed the folded paper from behind her pinner apron and placed it in the young woman's hand.

"This is most odd, Mum." Elspeth smiled uncomfortably. "Why, pray tell, would he send me a letter?"

"Just read it, Elspeth. You will soon understand."

Her heart felt as if it flipped within her chest. "Is it bad news?"

Katharina placed a reassuring hand on her forearm. "Just read it, Child."

Elspeth's hands trembled as she broke the wax button and unfolded the paper. The note was brief and seemed hastily written. Her lips quivered slightly as she mumbled its words.

My Dearest Elspeth,

I must offer my sincerest apology to you. I am afraid that my visit with your father must be delayed for a short while. When I returned to my home this evening, I discovered a young lieutenant bearing orders of my recall. I have been forced to report to the regimental barracks. Indeed, by the time you read this, I will no longer be in Philadelphia. My regiment will depart before dawn to join Washington's army in his campaign against the enemy.

I know not when I shall return. But, even as I go to war with my comrades, please know that my heart remains here in Philadelphia with you. Immediately upon my return, I will petition your father for your hand in marriage and take whatever actions that he deems necessary in order to qualify myself as your husband. You are well worth any demand or condition that he might place upon me.

Please know that I love you more than my words could describe on this simple scrap of paper. Even now, I miss you more than my heart can bear. I am, and shall always remain, faithfully yours.

Nicklaus

Elspeth lifted her tear-drenched eyes to meet Katharina's.

"Oh, Mrs. Schell! Whatever are we goin' to do? Our Nicklaus is gone to the war!"

Katharina took the young lass into her arms and embraced her. "We shall wait faithfully, Elsepth. We shall pray fervently. And we are going to love our boy from afar until he returns to us."

Elspeth cried in great, heaving sobs. Katharina hugged her tightly and wept, as well.

September 11, 1777
9:00 AM - Chadd's Ford, Pennsylvania

THICK, heavy, cool fog blanketed the southern Pennsylvania countryside. Visibility was less than a quarter of a mile, at most. It would be several hours before the September sun would evaporate the shroud of gray-white mist.

Abe Price tossed a rather large oak log onto his campfire, releasing a brief shower of sparks into the cool, foggy morning air. Michael and Conrad sat in silence, their wool blankets draped loosely across their shoulders. They attempted, as best they could, to ignore their somewhat annoying friend.

"But, we would return before anyone even knew we were gone!" he moaned. "We could be there and back before dinner time."

"You are being stupid," Michael warned. "More so than usual."

"They say it is just across the creek and no more than a mile or so," Abe pleaded. "I heard some of the Virginia boys describe it. There is ample rum and ale." He paused for effect. "And ample wenches, as well." He grinned mischievously, revealing his comically crooked, stained teeth.

"As if one of them would have you!" mocked a comrade seated at a nearby fire. Teasing laughter ensued.

Michael attempted to appeal to Abraham's limited sensibilities. "No one is going to abandon this camp to join you on a foolish escapade to Welch's Tavern. And it is not only one mile away. It is four miles distant, at least. To attempt such a journey is a fool's errand, and one that is likely to get you shot ... either by the British, or by our own firing squad."

Abe stared, frustrated, at the damp, smoky campfire. He grumbled, "I just want to have me a nip and a song."

Captain Benjamin Weiser appeared, seemingly out of nowhere. "We have barrels of ale right here in the camp, Private Price. I know what manner of nip you seek."

The men around the nearby campfires chuckled knowingly.

The captain continued, "You had best get your mind out of your breeches, before some Lobsterback or Hessian puts a ball through it. The only cock that you need to be concerned about is mounted on the lock of your musket."

The men of Captain Weiser's company erupted in raucous laughter. Even Abe Price could not hide his smile.

After the chortling and teasing finally died down, Corporal Frederick Wilhelm inquired, "Is this the day, Captain? Will the British come?"

"I am afraid so, Corporal. Our scouts have seen movement less than a day's ride to the south. They are headed our way."

There was no more laughter, joking, or teasing. The men mulled their captain's foreboding words in stoic silence. Each soldier withdrew into his own thoughts as he sought to prepare mentally for the violence that would soon visit them.

General Washington's army lay in wait for the British and Hessian force that prowled amongst the hills to the south of the Brandywine Creek. Over 11,000 American troops were scattered across eight miles of countryside. Most were concentrated at several well-used fords across the heavily wooded creek. Washington knew that General Howe and his forces were out there. He knew that they intended to seize Philadelphia. The only issue in question was where they would cross the Brandywine.

Nathanael Greene's Division, comprised of Muhlenberg's and Weedon's Brigades, was encamped just to the east of Chadd's Ford, along the Great Road that led to the nearby village of Chester, and then continued on eastward to Philadelphia. Washington's headquarters was just beyond the German Regiment's encampment, about a quarter-mile down the same road to the east. Other brigades stood watch at Pyle's Ford to the south and at Brinton's, Jones', Wistar's, and Buffington's Fords to the north. Washington was convinced that the enemy had to cross at one of these six places. His spies had assured him that there were no other suitable fords to the north.

Washington's army had been waiting, scouting, and preparing for the past two days. The men were well-rested and well-fed. Their powder was dry and their cartridges rolled. They were as prepared as they could be to meet the Anglo-Hessian force that marched in their direction.

Michael craved a smoke. He plucked his clay pipe from between the ties on his cocked hat and fished his tobacco bag out of his blue wool haversack. He was packing his tobacco into the bowl with his pointed, hand-whittled tamp when the reports of musket fire echoed through the fog to the southwest. Somewhere in the distance, beyond the creek, the forward scouts had engaged the enemy. The Battle of Brandywine had begun.

Captain Weiser stood and stretched. "Check your equipment, men. Make sure your guns are cleaned and primed. Make sure you have all of your necessaries on your person. Once we leave this position, depending upon the outcome, we may not return." He paused and looked in admiration upon his soldiers. "Good luck to you all."

10:00 AM
General Wayne's Division Area- Overlooking Chadd's Ford

Muskets barked sporadically across the creek. The American patrols remained engaged somewhere to the southwest. Still, there was no artillery involvement. The officers of the Continental Army were stymied. Was General Howe's entire army getting into position in front of them, or was it just a portion of his forces? And, if he *had* divided his army, where were the remainder of his troops?

Colonel Thomas Hartley was as equally confounded as the other commanders. He was itching for action, but had no real idea of the enemy's location or strength. He surveyed the troops of his line with pride. His Pennsylvanians were positioned exactly where he wanted them. His own Independent Regiment was at the very center. The other four Pennsylvania regiments in his brigade were deployed to his left and right. He positioned Colonel Thomas Proctor's artillery in a sweeping, semi-circular lunette roughly two hundred yards in front of the infantry. The small knoll upon which the cannons rested gave the artillerymen a commanding view of Chadd's Ford.

Colonel Hartley was not simply leading his own regiment's troops this day. Since General Benjamin Lincoln, commander of the First Pennsylvania Brigade, was absent from the field, General Washington declared Hartley acting brigadier and placed him in command of the entire brigade. Hartley was responsible for over 1,000 men ... half of General Anthony Wayne's Division.

Colonel Hartley and Dr. Schell stood side-by-side on a small hilltop in the middle of the brigade formation. The colonel surveyed the far side of the creek through his spyglass. His view was somewhat obscured by the thick trees and foliage. But, he could see well enough to know that the enemy was crawling all over those distant hills.

The good doctor had made the decision earlier that morning to leave the aid station and go for "a short stretch of the legs." Of course, that stroll had taken him to the front line for a quick visit with the troops of Hartley's Regiment.

In truth, Dr. Schell was bored. He had been preparing his makeshift hospital for the past two days. His surgical table and instruments were laid out and prepared for service in a thicket four hundred yards to the rear. His support staff was prepped and ready. He was fully equipped for the amputations that he would, most certainly, have to perform before day's end. He knew that this quick stroll would be his last opportunity to see the field before the coming battle, as well as his last chance to speak to the colonel before the fighting began.

"Do you see anything, sir?" Nicklaus inquired of the colonel.

"Yes, Dr. Schell. I see Hessian troops on the distant hillsides and a few English, as well. They are digging in. It is only a matter of time before they attack across the water."

Almost on cue, enemy artillery commenced. Seconds later, the ordinance of the British and Hessian cannons impacted into the hillsides in front of Hartley's men. The explosions sent clouds of smoke, smoldering grass, and soil high into the air. The artillery rounds rained down without ceasing. The barrage was disconcerting, but ineffective. Incredibly, a runner emerged from the forward artillery position and zig-zagged his way across the open field that was under bombardment, supernaturally dodging one round after another. Amazingly, the fellow arrived at Colonel Hartley's position unharmed and untouched by the cannon fire.

The breathless corporal snapped to attention in front of Colonel Hartley. "Beggin' your pardon, Colonel, sir. But, Colonel Proctor is requesting orders."

"Requesting orders?" Hartley barked back in disbelief. "Is he deaf, or stupid, perhaps?"

The corporal appeared thoroughly confused. "No ... no, sir. I do not believe so."

Hartley rolled his eyes. "Good God, man! Inform the colonel that he is to commence fire! Immediately! I want those enemy guns silenced!"

"Yes, sir!" The corporal stood perfectly still and continued to stare questioningly at the colonel.

"What is it, Son?" Hartley demanded.

"Is that ... is that all, Colonel, sir?"

"Yes! Damn it, you idiot! Go and tell him! Commence fire!"

The boy turned and began running back toward the artillery position. Colonel Hartley did not wait for the lad to deliver his message. He stood tall on top of a stump and waved ahead to the artillery officers. He used hand gestures and stomping feet to get his message across. Seconds later, the Continental cannons roared to life.

Nicklaus could scarcely believe the sound of it all. He had been in the midst of battle at Breed's Hill and Princeton, but it was nothing like this. He had never before been on the giving or receiving end of cannon fire. The din was deafening ... and horrifying.

Colonel Hartley turned and gave Nicklaus a somewhat disapproving look. "I think it is high time you return to your hospital, don't you, Dr. Schell?"

"Yes, sir."

The colonel offered Nicklaus his hand. "Good luck, Doctor."

"Good luck to you, as well, Colonel Hartley."

Nicklaus turned to head back toward the rear. The colonel grabbed him by the arm and halted his departure.

"Dr. Schell, if our lines collapse, just do whatever you can to help the men."

"How will I know if the lines have collapsed?" Nicklaus asked, confused.

The colonel frowned grimly. "You will know it by the flood of soldiers running past you. You shall have to decide, then, whether or not you will fall in with them."

A cold shiver overcame Nicklaus. He stood, immobile, almost staring through the colonel. He could scarcely imagine such an outcome for the brave army that guarded this hilltop.

"Off with you, Boy! And keep your head down. I shall see you tonight, if not sooner."

Nicklaus nodded, turned, and then trotted in the direction of the field hospital.

4:00 PM
Reserve Holding Area – General Nathanael Greene's Division

"WHY ARE WE STILL HERE, marking time by this road?" Abe griped.

The battle had been raging for hours. It began mid-morning with the musketry beyond the creek and the artillery barrage at Chadd's Ford. But, during the afternoon, intense fighting had erupted several miles toward the north. It seemed that every other division was engaged in the huge battle, except for Greene's. So, the men of the German Regiment waited tensely as they remained in reserve.

Abraham Price fidgeted with his musket and stared toward the north. Columns of gray and black smoke climbed high into the sky. The faraway popping of muskets was ceaseless, as were the screams and cries of men. Their voices resonated in the low hollows between the nearby hills.

"There is fighting all over the damned county, and here we sit on our useless arses!" Abe lamented.

"You should be careful what you wish for," Michael cautioned. "There are men dying out there in those fields. You should not be so anxious to join them."

"General Washington knows what he is doing," Conrad declared hopefully. "He will send us where we are most needed."

Quite unexpectedly, General Washington and his command staff appeared along the Great Road. The distinguished officers were on horseback and moving quickly. They stopped briefly as Washington conferred with General Greene. Two riders peeled away from the group and rode swiftly in the direction of Chadd's Ford. Moments later, General Washington and his entourage spun to their right and galloped through the woods where Greene's men were positioned. They rode toward the north.

A call echoed through the trees, "German Regiment! On your feet!"

Lieutenant Colonel Ludwick Weltner emerged from the trees on horseback to rally the men. He was accompanied by Colonel d'Arendt.

Weltner declared, "The entire brigade has been ordered into action! At the double time! Follow Weedon's men!"

The officers spun their horses and led the animals northward across the hills, following the same path as Washington and his staff.

Almost instantly, the men of Weedon's and Muhlenberg's Divisions emerged from the woods and thickets beside the Great Road, all of them running northward. Weedon's Division was further in that direction and naturally took the lead. Over 2,000 troops sprinted toward the sound of the guns.

Intense cannon and gunfire continued to their left, less than a quarter-mile away, from the vicinity of the crossing at Chadd's Ford.

"Where are we going?" Conrad called to his friends, exasperated and confused.

"We are finally going to the fight!" Abraham answered excitedly.

"But, there is fighting right here beside us!" Conrad protested.

Michael did not bother to engage in their idle musings. Like his friends, he knew nothing of battlefield tactics or the deployment of soldiers. Truly, it was a waste of time to worry over such things. The common soldier needed only do what he was told, and quickly so. Michael focused only upon running and following the commands of his officers.

In truth, Michael was having some difficulty keeping his footing in the tall, thick grass. His left shoe was loose and seemed in jeopardy of flying off of his foot at any moment. He had to wedge his toes deeply into the front of the shoe to avoid losing it. The awkward positioning of his foot threw him into a slight limp. He clutched his musket in his right hand and attempted to hold his cocked hat in place on his head with his left hand. Wherever they were going, he just hoped that they did not have to run very far.

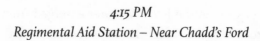

4:15 PM
Regimental Aid Station – Near Chadd's Ford

THE BATTLE RAGED along Brandywine Creek, four hundred yards to the east. The ground beneath Nicklaus' feet shook with each explosion of artillery departing from or arriving upon the adjacent ridge. Incredibly, there seemed to be even more fighting far to the north.

But, that was none of Nicklaus' concern. That action involved other brigades and regiments, each with their own surgeons. Dr. Nicklaus Schell already had more wounded men than he was able to handle.

He dumped a half-bucket of water onto his makeshift surgical table. A wave of pink water, blood clots, and shredded cloth washed over the side of the old, cracked wood onto the blood-stained grass below. The ground surrounding the hastily constructed sawhorses that supported the table was littered with blood-soaked, discarded clothing. The aid station reeked of blood, butchered meat, and human urine and feces. It was a loud, filthy, confused nightmare of a place.

Nicklaus was overwhelmed. The opening hours of the battle had not been difficult. Many of the injuries were minor, requiring only bandages or stitching. By noon-time, though, he had been forced to turn away all such trifles. Major battlefield wounds took precedence over more trivial injuries. For the last four hours, he had been consumed with removing bullets, halting arterial bleeds, and performing amputations. Such was the nature of medicine on the battlefield.

Two anonymous soldiers plopped one of their wounded comrades onto the wet slab of wood. The unarmed soldiers did not tarry. They fled immediately. Curiously, they did not run back toward the creek. Instead, they ran to the east, in the direction of Dilworthtown. There seemed to be many other souls running in that direction, as well.

Nicklaus glanced at his attendant. "John, have you heard the order of retreat?"

"No, Doctor."

"Then, where are those men going?"

His helper shrugged. "Not all men will wait to hear such an order, I s'pose."

The wounded boy in front of him screamed in agony. It was a pitiful, wretched, screeching wail. Over and over again, he cried out, "Make it stop! Make it stop! Make it stop!" The lad thrashed wildly, kicking his legs in violent spasms and yanking at his hair with his hands. Clumps of the matted, bloody hair protruded from between his fingers.

Nicklaus barked, "Hold him still, please. Grab his legs."

The attendant instantly grabbed the boy by the ankles and then lay across his legs to weigh them down.

Nicklaus was focused on the fellow's damaged belly. The writhing boy's entire torso was a mangled mass of linen, wool, and blood. Nicklaus needed to get a better look at the profusely bleeding wound. He used a small patch knife to cut open the Pennsylvania soldier's weskit. The experienced physician gasped when he glimpsed the decimated flesh beneath. The lad's belly had been shredded by artillery. His mangled intestines hung loosely over his left side, completely outside his body cavity.

Nicklaus looked at his surgeon's aide and shook his head. "John, place him in the shade with the others. Do we have any more laudanum?"

"No, sir. We ran out about an hour ago."

"Then, give the boy whiskey. All that you can pour into him."

The young attendant nodded grimly. "Yes, Doctor." He called to one of his comrades, "Henry! Help me move this one!"

The two strong young men whisked the dying fellow from the table and placed him in the shade beneath a sprawling oak tree. There were a dozen others just like him ... mortally wounded soldiers, each awaiting a lonely, agonizing death in a whiskey or opiate-induced stupor. Nine lifeless bodies lay nearby, their faces covered respectfully by their hats or coats.

Colonel Hartley appeared quite suddenly through the haze of artillery smoke that hovered over the embattled ridge, galloping full-speed toward the hospital. Dozens of men on foot followed him. They were all fleeing the field. Interspersed throughout the horrified men were horse-drawn wagons, as well as other horses and mules that were pulling cannons. The artillery pieces still had smoke and steam wafting from their scorched barrels. The colonel rode his horse right up to Nicklaus' operating table and slid to a stop. The poor animal was wide-eyed with terror. Its mouth and neck were covered with sweaty foam.

"Time for you to go, Dr. Schell! General Wayne has ordered the retreat!"

Nicklaus pointed toward the high columns of smoke in the distance. "But there is still fighting to the north."

Hartley shook his head vigorously. "The battle is lost, Doctor. The Hessians are across the Brandywine. They have overrun most of our artillery and are in the process of turning it against us. You must retire with all haste to Dilworthtown. It has become a casualty collection point. Establish your hospital and treat the wounded there. Wayne's Division is in retreat to the east, toward Chester. I will escort the brigade there. Once everything settles down, I will send one of my officers to fetch you back to the regiment."

"But ... what of my wounded here?"

The colonel glanced around the area, noting the dozens of bloody men reclining beneath the trees. He frowned. "You must leave them for the enemy's surgeons."

"But, Colonel!"

"Do not question me, Son, or *you* will soon be in the hands of the enemy ... and I need my surgeon in service. I have no more time to entertain your questions or protestations. I must go and see to whatever remains of my brigade. Simply grab whatever equipment you can and find a horse. Get to Dilworthtown. Now!"

The colonel wheeled his horse to the left and then rode back toward the action at the creek. Nicklaus gasped at the carnage atop the nearby hill. Red-coated British soldiers, accompanied by throngs of strangely uniformed Hessians, engaged the defenders in fierce hand-to-hand combat. The men flailed at one another with bayonets, swords, and knives. Some used their muskets as clubs. A few wielded nothing but large sticks. The fighting was primal, fierce, and bloody.

The surgeon's attendant, John Hardy, disappeared into the woods and soon emerged atop an abandoned horse. The animal was bleeding from a wound in its flank. The boy shouted over the din of battle, "We must go, Doctor! There is no more time! The enemy is upon us!" He reached down and offered a hand to Nicklaus.

Dr. Schell scanned the area and soon spied his medical bag resting against nearby stump. He ran to grab his bloody bone saw and amputation knife, and then tossed them into the bag. He quickly took hold of the orderly's hand and clawed himself onto the back of the suffering animal. Moments later, they were riding swiftly toward the east.

~

5:30 PM – Greene's Division
One-Quarter Mile West of Dilworthtown

THE MEN of Muhlenberg's Brigade were exhausted. Greene's entire division had sprinted over four and a half miles, in full gear, in just under forty-five minutes. The general positioned them on either side of the narrow road that led into Dilworthtown. Weedon's Brigade was to the north, in direct line of the advancing British. Muhlenberg's was several hundred yards to the south, taking cover inside the shadows beneath a thick growth of trees.

The crimson-coated British troops marched in a perfect, mighty, unstoppable wave toward the men of Weedon's Brigade. Their bayonets were affixed to their muskets and glistening in the late afternoon sun. Ahead of the British, hundreds of terrified Continentals were fleeing eastward. Many of them were empty-handed, having abandoned their weapons on the field. The men of Weedon's Brigade parted ranks temporarily, allowing the retreating soldiers to pass through.

Weedon's regiments quickly reformed and faced the enemy. Seconds later, they stretched their ranks and unleashed their first rounds into the approaching Redcoats. The disciplined Patriots poured volley after volley into the oncoming bayonet charge. The enemy soldiers fell by the droves, but still, the wave of humanity continued onward against the resilient defenders. The British progress, however, was noticeably slower.

"*Mein Gott!* Can you believe that?" Michael groaned. "Their men drop dead like flies, and still they move onward! What manner of resolve is this?"

Captain Weiser walked through the small clearing in front of his men. He encouraged them, "Steady, boys! They may turn in our direction!"

"When do we get in this fight?" Abe Price demanded. "And why are we hiding out in these damned woods?"

"Our brigade has been assigned the rear guard, Private Price. Our orders are to remain here and cover the retreat."

"Then, the battle is lost?" Michael inquired dejectedly.

"*Ja*, Michael. 'Tis lost. We will cover Weedon's Brigade and then follow them into Dilworthtown. If the enemy pursues beyond the town, we will continue to cover the retreat to the east."

The men stood and watched, helplessly, as their comrades in Weedon's Brigade continued their orderly retreat. Dozens of their dead and wounded lay scattered throughout the grassy pasture. A half-hour later, the brigade disappeared into the trees one hundred yards northeast of the German Regiment. Almost at that exact moment, a messenger appeared with a report for the officers.

"Remain here," Captain Weiser commanded. "I shall be back shortly."

He sprinted to a position roughly thirty yards to the rear where many of the officers were gathered. Meanwhile, Michael, Conrad, and Abraham, along with the rest of the mates of their company, stared at the carnage of death in the grassy field. Though the British were in a state of disarray, their officers seemed to be doing an admirable job of organizing the ranks and consolidating the ground taken.

Captain Weiser ran up behind the men of his company. "This is it, men! We have orders to fall back to the east side of Dilworthtown. On your feet! Move out in an orderly fashion. Take all of your equipment. Help anyone who is injured."

Michael cast one last glance at the field. The sun had just disappeared below the tree line. The beautiful pre-sunset light cast a warm, orange glow over the lush green fields and trees. Michael's heart ached from the tragedy of blood and death that tainted such an otherwise breathtaking vista.

"Come along, Yeisley," Captain Weiser urged. "We must go."

Michael turned and followed his captain and despondent friends through the woods. The American army had lost the battle at Brandywine ... and the German Regiment hadn't even fired a single shot.

14

OUR CITY IS LOST

Michael and the men of his company emerged from the woods on the far western outskirts of Dilworthtown. The sight that greeted them was disturbing, to say the least. The Continental Army was in state of disarray. Frantic mobs of soldiers were running through the streets of the town. Discarded weapons and equipment littered the ground. Dozens of wounded men limped slowly in pursuit of their more able-bodied compatriots. Several poor souls were so severely wounded that they could not walk. Abandoned by their comrades, they crawled helplessly along the rocky roadway.

Though Weedon's Brigade had fought valiantly and executed a well-organized, orderly retreat from the battlefield, their withdrawal through the town seemed anything *but* orderly. The men were beaten, discouraged, and afraid. The British were in close pursuit. So, they ran. The fervor of flight quickly infected Muhlenberg's men, as well, and they joined in the chaotic eastward exodus through the town.

Captain Weiser quickly established a rally point beside a small barn. Roughly half of the men in his command were present. The remainder had already fled amongst the crowd of other troops.

Desperate for some manner of direction and leadership, about a dozen soldiers from other companies of the regiment fell in with the captain.

Michael searched the group for his closest mates. He quickly spied Abe Price. His affable friend was leaning comfortably against a dilapidated stone fence beside the barn. Michael worked his way around the edge of the group to join him.

"Where is Conrad?" Michael hissed, concerned.

Abe shook his head grimly. "I lost sight of him the moment we received the command to retreat. The lad was moving fast and not looking back. He is likely half-way to Philadelphia by now."

"Surely, we will find him on the other side of the town," Michael declared hopefully. "Command will reorganize the army at Chester."

"I hope so. But, if we don't move our arses and join them soon, we might find ourselves in a British camp tonight."

The men could hear the cracks of the enemy's drums and the pounding of their shoes on the hard-packed ground. Then came the shouts of the British and Hessian officers from beyond the trees. The enemy was still on the move and approaching the town. Captain Weiser was well-aware of the danger of tarrying near the battlefield. He quickly assessed the situation and then issued orders to the small contingent of German Regiment soldiers.

"We are the last ones out, men. I want an orderly withdrawal through this village. That means no running off on your own." He nodded toward the highway. "And I want these wounded men off of the road. Use whatever means necessary to move them. We must get them to our surgeons at the town tavern. Now, make haste!"

The Germans dispersed quickly as the men darted toward the wounded soldiers. Abraham spied the handle of a hand cart peeking from the open doorway of a nearby outbuilding. He trotted over to the building and gave the handle a tug, pulling the rig out onto the lawn. The cart appeared to be relatively new and in good service. Someone had recently sealed the wood with a fresh coat of yellow-orange paint.

Michael nodded. "Good thinking. That will do nicely."

He tossed his musket into the bed of the cart. Abraham did likewise. They each grabbed the handle and pulled the rig onto the road. They guided it toward the nearest wounded soldier. The fellow's left arm was shattered and bloody. The stricken lad was clawing frantically at the road in a futile attempt to escape the enemy. He held a bent bayonet in his right hand, which he was using to propel himself. He did so by stabbing the point deeply into the soil and, once anchored, pulling himself forward. As ingenious a method as it was, the poor boy was moving only inches with each excruciating tug.

Michael and Abe rolled the cart up to the boy and stopped. The horrified soldier flipped over onto his back. Clearly, he thought that his rescuers were the enemy. He wielded the bent bayonet menacingly. His left shoulder was oozing dark blood and his left arm dangled loosely. He appeared to have shrapnel wounds in both of his shins and knees.

Michael waved his hands in defense. "Easy there, my friend! We are here to help you!"

Michael's slight German accent startled the man. He groaned, "Are you Hessians?"

Abe chuckled. "No, you daft prick. We are Pennsylvanians. German Regiment."

Relief washed across the soldier's face. He began to cry.

"We are going to get you out of here," Michael promised, as he grabbed the fellow underneath his good arm. "What is your name?"

"Daniel Harper, 10th Virginia."

"I suppose we can help a Virginian," Abe teased. He wrapped his arm around the man's waist, winked, and grinned. "But only if he has some good tobacco to share."

Together, they hoisted the rather heavy fellow into the cart. The poor man wailed from the pain in his shoulder. They scooted him to one side of the cart, against the side rail, so that they might have room for more passengers.

"Rest easy, Mr. Harper. We are going to grab a few more of your friends and then get you to the hospital."

The wounded soldier nodded gratefully. "I cannot thank you boys enough. I thought I was captured, for sure."

Michael and Abraham wasted no more time on pleasantries or small talk. They grabbed the handle and tugged their somewhat heavier cart toward the next wounded man. He lay thirty yards down the road. Within minutes, they had collected four immobile, severely wounded soldiers in the bed of their cart.

Abe knelt down to examine the rig's axle. "This iron is bowing a bit, Michael. And the block on your side is cracked. We cannot add any more weight to this cart."

Michael surveyed the area. It appeared that their regimental comrades were escorting all of the remaining wounded men from the roadway. Everyone who needed assistance was being helped. Their mission was complete. They needed only to deliver the men in their charge to the surgeons.

"Our job is done," Michael declared. "We must locate the tavern. It cannot be hard to find. This village is very small. You take the handle in front. I will push from the rear."

Abraham nodded and then ducked underneath the handle assembly. Michael stepped around back and took hold of the rough boards of the wagon bed. Both men leaned forward into their heavy load of over six hundred pounds of man-flesh and lumber. It was difficult to get the rig rolling at first. Soon, however, they were able to gain some momentum, and the large wooden wheels began to turn quite easily over the packed dirt and rock of the roadway. Minutes later, Abraham spied a sign that read *Dilworth Tavern*.

6:30 PM - Dilworth Tavern

"Your men must wait their turn. It is as simple as that. There is no need for argument or negotiation. Now, please leave, sir. I have much work to do."

The Continental officer was livid. "Young man, I am George

Mathews, colonel of the 9th Virginia Regiment! I will *not* have you speak to me in such a manner! I want the men of my regiment treated immediately! That is an order, sir!"

Nicklaus had neither the time nor the patience to deal with the troublesome colonel. He was already thoroughly overwhelmed by the impossible task that confronted him. He understood that the distraught officer was simply seeking to ensure the prompt care of the soldiers under his command. But, Nicklaus could not offer them preferential treatment at the expense of the other wounded men in his charge. He had an oath to fulfill. That oath required him to triage the wounded according to the severity of their injuries.

"Colonel, your rank is not pertinent to my duties. There are dozens of wounded men both inside and outside this building. I am the only surgeon here. I will treat my patients based upon their status and the critical nature of their wounds. There is no other criterion. Your men will have to wait their turn in line, just like the others. Now, sir, please vacate these premises immediately. I have my duties to perform and can no longer entertain your interruption."

"I cannot believe such insolence! What is your name, boy?"

Nicklaus did not bother to look the colonel in the eye. He simply continued to focus upon the young man lying sprawled across the tavern's bar that now served as his makeshift operating table. He dug his already-bloodied amputation knife into the thigh muscles of the unconscious patient, slicing until he hit bone.

"I am Dr. Nicklaus Schell of Hartley's Regiment. You may speak to Colonel Hartley directly, if you desire to lodge a complaint against me." He paused. "You will find him in Chester, a couple of miles to the southeast. Please, do go there and have your conference with him. But, as acting general of the Pennsylvania Brigade, I seriously doubt that he will be much impressed with an officer who displays such wanton disregard for the men of the army's other commands."

The colonel stomped one foot and grunted. "You have not heard the last of this, Dr. Schell. I *will* have my satisfaction!"

"Perhaps. But, not today. Now, get out." Nicklaus moved his eyes temporarily away from his patient and leered at the colonel with an icy, authoritative gaze.

There was a brief, awkward pause. The colonel's eyes wandered around the room and surveyed the mass of groaning, bleeding, suffering men who littered the floor. He glanced at the open flesh and exposed bone of the man lying on Nicklaus' operating table. He grimaced, then swiftly turned and stormed out of the room.

Nicklaus exhaled in relief and frustration. He glanced at his orderly. "John, do not bring another wounded man into this room without my approval. For now, make sure only the amputations and head injuries are brought to me. Everyone else must wait outside."

"Yes, sir. I have already organized the wounded men thusly."

Nicklaus smiled and nodded. "Good work, John."

He turned his attention back to his patient and quickly completed the ongoing amputation procedure. He tied off the major arteries and veins in the leg and then sawed through the dense femur with his overworked bone saw. Seconds later, the leg was ready for bandages and wraps.

Nicklaus' strained muscles in his lower back were torturing him. He turned around and leaned back against the front of the bar, rubbing the aching muscles against the smooth edges of the wood. His legs were wobbly from fatigue. His boots were most uncomfortable, causing his feet to cramp and throb. Glancing down at his hands, clothing, and apron, he gagged at their filthy, bloody state. Nicklaus desperately desired to wash his hands, fetch a drink of fresh water, and relieve his pressured bladder.

"John, I need a moment. I am going outside for some fresh air and water. Bind this boy's stump for me, please, and then get the table ready for the next man."

John Hardy, his orderly, smiled grimly and nodded. "There is a rain barrel on the west end of the building, Dr. Schell. The water is cold and fresh. And take this. You look like you need it." The young man handed Nicklaus a small bottle of whiskey.

Nicklaus shook his head. "I cannot, John. We need all of the liquor for the men."

"There is enough whiskey in the basement of this tavern to pickle our entire army," John reassured him. "Sincerely, Doctor, there is plenty to spare. Have yourself a dram now, and save the rest for later."

Nicklaus considered the bottle in the palm of his trembling hand. He was thoroughly exhausted and mentally strained. He knew that a nip of the strong alcohol would help calm his spirit and nerves.

He nodded thankfully. "I am grateful to you, John. I shall return soon."

"I will have your next patient ready, Dr. Schell."

Nicklaus stepped carefully over the mass of wounded men and made his way toward the open doorway of the tavern. Outside, the faint glow of twilight bathed the town with a soft, purple-orange hue. Nightfall was approaching rapidly. It would have been a lovely evening, if not for the fifty bloodied, wounded men sprawled across the lawn.

Ducking around the corner of the building, Nicklaus soon located the rain barrel that John described. There was already a wash bucket nearby, with a chunk of soap on the ground beside it. He filled the bucket, then dropped down on his knees and used it as a makeshift sink to wash his hands. Once he had achieved a modest state of cleanliness, he dumped the filthy water and then hid behind a nearby tree to drain his bladder. After drinking two dippers full of water from the drinking barrel, followed by a large gulp of the fiery whiskey, he felt somewhat refreshed. He tucked the liquor bottle inside the waist of his breeches as he stepped from the alleyway and rounded the corner of the tavern. He was approaching the front steps when he heard a familiar voice call his name.

"Nicklaus Schell! Is it really you?"

Nicklaus halted and spun to look toward the road. He could scarcely believe his eyes. There remained just enough light for him to recognize the face of an old friend. It was Michael Yeisley, standing in the roadway next to a cart loaded with wounded men.

"Michael! I did not know that your regiment was here!"

Nicklaus waded through the crowded lawn to reach his friend.

They shook hands warmly. Nicklaus spun Michael around and gave him a quick examination.

"Are you well, Michael? Are you injured or wounded?"

"No. We were held in reserve for the entire battle and did not see any action today." He nodded toward the wagon. "But, we have brought you these wounded men. We collected them on the way through the town."

Nicklaus frowned and tilted his head toward the tavern. "There are many more like them, I am afraid. You will have to leave them here. We will attend to them as soon as we are able."

The distant, steady thumping of British drums increased in volume, accompanied by the sound of crunching rock. Horrified, Michael turned and looked down the dim road to the west. Very little of the day's light remained, but he could still see the droves of Redcoats that were spilling onto the highway.

"We have to go now, Michael," Abraham urged. "We will be made prisoner if we do not depart immediately!"

Nicklaus shook Michael's hand again. "Go, old friend. Make your escape."

"But, what about you?"

"I shall be fine, Michael. My skills will be in much demand over the next few days. Physicians are afforded a special status in captivity. The British will treat me quite well." He glanced toward the west. The soldiers were approaching. "Now, go! You must not tarry!"

Michael and Abe grabbed their muskets from the wagon, tipped their hats to Dr. Schell, and then sprinted down the road toward Chester. Nicklaus watched them disappear around a bend in the narrow highway.

Suddenly, the enemy troops on the western edge of the town dispersed across the roadway and formed firing lines. Then came the commands of their officers. They were preparing to open fire on the town! The wounded Continentals shouted an alarm. Helpless, stricken men ducked for cover wherever they could find it. The gravely wounded could only remain still and pray that the enemy lead would not strike them where they lay.

Moments later, the British unleashed a volley of fire into the village. Their round balls tore into the wood of the buildings and shattered the glass in the windows. A poor, pitiful horse fell, whinnying in agony, at the far eastern end of the main thoroughfare. Unimaginably, their second rank stepped past the first and immediately unleashed a second volley.

Nicklaus heard the wailing cries of the already wounded as the lead tore into their helpless, immobile bodies. He ran into the middle of the street before the enemy soldiers could reload and raised both of his hands high into the air.

"*Nicht schießen! Nicht schießen!* Do not shoot! This is a hospital! There are only civilians and wounded here!"

The musketry ceased immediately. The British officers quickly and skillfully recalled their soldiers into a marching formation. Without hesitation, they entered the town and dispersed to search the homes and outbuildings. A young officer approached Nicklaus. He looked at the doctor's bloody apron and disheveled clothing with an air of disapproval. He bowed slightly and tipped his hat.

"Doctor, I am most grateful that you took action to prevent further unnecessary violence. I am Levtenant Uriah Abbott, of His Majesty's 2nd Battalion Grenadiers, at your service."

"I am Dr. Nicholas Schell, Hartley's Regiment of the Continental Line. Where are your surgeons?"

"They have established a casualty collection point and hospital at the Birmingham Church, roughly three miles to the west."

"Then, they will not be coming here?"

"Not tonight, Doctor. I think it likely that His Majesty's troops shall remain in their current locations now that darkness has fallen."

Nicklaus nodded. "Of course. Well, if you will excuse me, sir ... I must tend to my wounded."

"Of course, Dr. Schell. Do return to your work. But, know that you and all of these other rebels are now our prisoners. And if any of His Majesty's wounded are transported to this town, you are to give them the utmost priority."

"Are you saying that I must treat *them*, at the expense of my countrymen?"

"Precisely." The British lieutenant did not bat an eye.

Nicklaus stiffened his shoulders and back. "Very well, sir. I am, after all, your prisoner."

The lieutenant grinned haughtily. "I am pleased that you see things my way, Doctor. And, with your ongoing compliance, I am quite certain that your visit with us will be most pleasant." The officer turned and directed some of his men toward the adjacent buildings. "If you will excuse me, I must find suitable quarters for our officers. I will check on you again and inspect your hospital within the hour."

Nicklaus did not respond. He simply nodded, turned, and walked proudly back into the tavern.

~

September 23, 1777
Northwest of Philadelphia

THE MEN of the German Regiment were exhausted and much in need of an extended period of quiet and rest. They had been on the move for almost two weeks, caught up in a seemingly endless game of "cat and mouse" with the British army under General Howe. Finally, it seemed, they had received a duty assignment that would allow them a most welcomed time of respite.

Washington's most recent strategy involved blocking deployments at the major fords along the Schuylkill River and its tributaries. His chief goal was to prevent any British crossing and thereby use the rivers to keep the Redcoats out of Philadelphia. It appeared that Howe was making a move to the north, and that he might attempt a wide, sweeping maneuver to enclose the city. Washington countered the move and shifted his forces northward.

So, the German Regiment was several miles to the northwest of Philadelphia and comfortably encamped on the banks of the lovely Perkiomen Creek. They enjoyed ample food and clear, refreshing water. The past two days had been almost like a holiday. The men hunted the nearby fields for turkey and deer, fished in the creek, and napped beneath the trees. They hoped that their luck would hold, and that they might enjoy an extended stay at this luxurious location.

The men of Captain Wesier's Company were reclining next to their fires and enjoying the evening's twilight with pipes full of tobacco and mugs full of ale. It would have been a perfect evening were it not for the annoying banter of Conrad Traywitz.

"Do you realize how close to home that we are?" Conrad moaned. "Twenty miles! Only twenty miles due north! We could be there by dinner tomorrow." He closed his eyes and smacked his lips. "I can almost taste my mother's schnitzel."

Michael offered no response. He rested lazily beside his campfire. He was well-fed and somewhat content. He normally tried not to think too much of home. To do so made his heart heavy, because he so desperately longed to be there. But Conrad's musings served to fill his mind with memories and his heart with a sickness for that peaceful, blessed place. He closed his eyes and imagined his children playing in the yard. He pictured Magdalena sitting beside the fireplace, knitting a scarf or mending some stockings. As his thoughts dwelled upon his lovely wife, his imagination led him into their bedchamber and to the bliss of their private, intimate moments. The memories of such pleasure were more than he could bear. He shook his head to clear away the tempting thoughts.

"The apple trees are just now beginning to bear, you know," Conrad continued. "That means there is fresh cider to be had! Oh, come on, boys! We must go home for a quick visit!"

"Shut up, you idiot! If you do not, the army could be listing you as dead once again!" Abe Price angrily hurled a musket ball at his friend. The heavy projectile struck the side of the lad's head with a resounding thump.

Conrad wailed in pain and protest. He pressed his hand against the throbbing lump on his skull. "Why the hell did you do that?"

"To silence that stupid mouth of yours," Abe replied. "We are all tired of hearing it! We are content right here as we lay. If we're lucky, we shall remain here for a while. Now, stop torturing us with all this useless talk of home!"

About a dozen grunts and groans from other nearby soldiers affirmed their agreement with Abe's sentiments. The other men of the company wanted peace. And they, most certainly, did not wish to torture themselves unnecessarily with impossible, sentimental thoughts of family, hearth, and home.

"That is some excellent advice, Private Traywitz," declared Captain Weiser as he joined his men beside the fire. "None of us will be going home at any time in the near future. It is best you stop thinking about it."

"Good evening, Captain," Michael greeted him. "Do you bear any news?"

"Indeed, I do." He paused and tossed a small log into the fire. "The regiment is in for some big changes."

"How so?" Michael asked.

"Well, for starters, Colonel Arendt is gone."

"What?" the men all shouted. Most sat up in surprise.

"Gone where?" asked Abe.

The captain removed his cocked hat and rested it on his knee. "He has been transferred. Washington, it seems, is worried about a naval move against Fort Mifflin, below Philadelphia. He has ordered the colonel to go there and assume command of its garrison and lead in the defense of the harbor."

Abe nodded, somewhat impressed. "When will he go?"

"He has already left. He departed shortly after dinner today."

"So, now, what does that mean to us?" asked Michael. "Do we wait for a new colonel?"

The captain shook his head. "No. Our officers must advance within the regiment. Lieutenant Colonel Weltner is now in command."

That news brought a rumble of relief from the soldiers. Ludwick Weltner had been with the regiment from its inception. He was very respected and well-loved by all the men.

"Will we be moving out soon?" Abe asked, fishing for more information.

"We do not have any orders, yet. Colonel Weltner informed me that he intends to stay right here on this creek until we are forced to move."

More satisfied, relieved grumbles ensued. It was wonderful news and a great relief to the weary men. Their brief moment of joy was interrupted, however, by a gunshot and shouting to the south. The men craned their necks in an attempt to identify the source of the commotion. The darkness of dusk obscured their vision. Still, they heard more shouts and then the steady thumping of hooves against the hard-packed soil. Soon, a horse thundered into the camp. It wheeled to a stop next to the German Regiment's fires.

The rider, a young lad of no more than twelve or thirteen years, shouted in a high-pitched, prepubescent voice, "To arms! To arms! Howe is across! Howe is across!"

Captain Weiser stepped forward and grabbed the boy's bridle. "Where has he crossed?" he asked suspiciously.

"Swede's Ford!" the breathless lad exclaimed. "He crossed the Schuylkill at Swede's. He is marching on Philadelphia now!"

Silence descended upon the camp. The men could scarcely believe it. General Howe's supposed swing to the north had, obviously, been a diversion. He had intended to cross the river in closer proximity to the city all along. The cunning Englishman had outwitted General Washington ... again.

"*Mein Gott!*" Abe muttered. "Our city is lost!"

"Who sent you, boy?" Captain Weiser demanded.

"The parson from the Plymouth Meeting House sent me out to tell General Washington. I have a correspondence for him. Do you know where I might find him?"

"Come with me. I will take you to the general."

Captain Weiser trotted in the direction of George Washington's command tent. The boy messenger dismounted, handed the reins of his horse to a nearby soldier, and eagerly followed the captain.

Abe glanced at Michael and sighed. "I suppose we had best pack our haversacks. I think our luck just ran out."

~

September 27, 1777
Pennsylvania Hospital – Philadelphia

EVERYTHING HAD CHANGED. Philadelphia was shrouded in the silence of abandonment. Howe's army entered the city a few hours after making his crossing over the Schuylkill. The British controlled Philadelphia and its people, though few citizens remained for them to govern. Most of the folk who lingered in the city were concealed within the safety of their homes. Only the most ardent Loyalists dared wander the Redcoat-infested streets.

The three days leading up to the British occupation had been nothing short of chaotic. Fearing the impending invasion, the members and staff of the Continental Congress fled to the city of Reading on September 24. Once the governmental leaders evacuated, pandemonium ensued. Independency-minded Americans followed by the droves. There was a constant flood of refugees headed northward, all attempting to escape before the British army arrived. People departed in wagons and carriages, on horseback, and on foot. Most took as many of their personal possessions as they could carry or fit into their meager modes of transportation. Clearly, few held little hope of ever returning to the city.

The Pennsylvania Hospital, though filled to overflowing with sick and wounded, was barely managing to function. Only a remnant of the hospital's staff remained on the job. Most of the surgeons, nurses, and laborers had departed amongst the mass exodus of refugees. Katharina Schell, however, had nowhere else to go. She felt that her ultimate duty was to her patients, so she never even entertained the notion of leaving. She fully intended to report for work in the same manner in which she had done so for the past twelve years. Despite the presence of enemy soldiers, she donned her daily uniform and walked four blocks through the eerily quiet streets to reach her workplace.

As Katharina climbed the stairs to the third-floor ward, she dreaded taking the customary morning roll of her staff. Most of her medical aides had fled before the British arrived. They had been disappearing on a daily basis. She topped the stairs and peeked down the main hallway. She was greatly relieved to see the trusty Elspeth McClelland seated in the nurse's chair outside the door to the ward. The older woman's tired, wrinkled face erupted into a huge smile.

"Elspeth, my dear! Good morning to you!"

The young woman rose respectfully to her feet. "And to you, Mrs. Schell. 'Tis as good a mornin' as can be expected, I s'pose."

"Yes, dear. Quite so." Katharina looked hopefully in both directions along the hallway. "Where are the other girls?"

"'Tis only I, Mum. The rest are departed."

Katharina sighed. It was as she expected. Still, the reality of her expectations did not lessen her disappointment.

"Well, if there are only two of us, then we have precious little time to waste. I hope you are well-rested and prepared for a very busy day."

Elspeth appeared somewhat despondent. "To be honest, I slept very little last evenin', Mrs. Schell. My father's house 'twas a lonely, spooky place. I kept hearin' noises outside. And those soldiers constantly prowlin' about in the streets all the long night was almost more that I can bear."

"Why, pray tell, is your house so lonely?"

The girl's head hung low. "Papa and my sisters are gone." She began to sob.

"Oh, dear child! I did not know!"

Katharina reached for Elspeth and hugged her affectionately. The Scottish lass snuggled like a helpless little child into the older woman's arms. She sobbed uncontrollably. The mother's heart inside Katharina's chest broke for the poor girl. She was only nineteen years old and all alone in the huge, enemy-occupied city of Philadelphia.

"I am so very glad that you have remained here to help me, Elspeth."

The young girl spoke through her mournful sobs. "I could nay leave, not knowin' where Nicklaus may be or how he is doin'. Have you heard anythin' ... anythin' a'tall?" she begged.

"There is still no word, I am afraid. But, I must believe that, since there has been no news of his death or injury, then he *must* be well. He is simply somewhere in the field with his regiment and unable to write to us at the present time." She smiled reassuringly. "Do you not agree?"

Elspeth nodded as she pulled away from the woman's embrace. She seemed somewhat ashamed of her childlike behavior. "Yes, of course, Mum." She was, obviously, not as confident as Mrs. Schell.

Katharina placed both hands on Elspeth's shoulders and stared into her eyes. "Well, this I know, Elspeth McClelland ... you shall not spend another night alone in your father's house. You must come and stay with me."

"Oh, I cannot do that, Mrs. Schell. I do not wish to impose upon you."

"'Tis not an imposition," Katharina interrupted her. "I insist. In fact, once our shift is done this afternoon, we shall go to your house and collect your clothing and belongings."

"Are you certain?" Elspeth asked timidly.

"Most certain."

Elspeth pondered. "There is quite a bit of food from our storage that Papa could not fit into his wagon. Should we not collect that, as well?" She sounded more hopeful.

"Indeed, we should! This city is now occupied by the enemy. There could be 10,000 troops housed here for the winter. Shortages are coming, to be sure. Since your family is gone, we should salvage everything that is useful."

"We have no wagon," Elspeth confessed. "There remain only two hand-carts in the carriage house."

Katharina patted her on the hand. "We will use them as many times as necessary to get the job done. But, we should probably move quickly. These British soldiers are almost certain to begin quartering inside the city's abandoned houses. We should get your house emptied of all things useful before the Redcoats have the notion to take it all for themselves."

Elspeth wiped her face and smiled. It seemed that Katharina had done much to convert her previous state of despondency into one of promise and hope.

"We shall have time to make all of our plans this afternoon," Katharina declared. "Right now, we have much work to do."

"Yes, Mum."

"Very well, then. First, you must go and wash your face and freshen up. All that sobbing has left you a bit of a mess. Come and join me on the ward once you have composed yourself."

Elspeth gave the woman a quick hug. "Yes, Mum. Thank you, Mum." She darted past Katharina and disappeared into the wash room.

Katharina checked her own appearance and then marched through the doors into the soldier's ward. The floor inside the large room was crowded with beds, cots, and pallets. Over forty wounded men were housed there, most of them survivors of the battle at Brandywine Creek. She immediately launched into her work of checking bandages on the soldiers' wounds and emptying their chamber pots.

Katharina was on her knees behind one of the beds, dumping the contents of an unusually full chamber pot into her disposal bucket, when she heard the door hinges creak. Assuming that it was Elspeth returning from the wash room, she did not even bother to look toward the door.

"I've not touched the other side of the room, dear. Start with those chamber pots. You will need another bucket. Mine is almost full. Bring that large one from the storeroom."

Katharina was shocked when the response to her command was the low-pitched sound of a man clearing his throat. Then, a distinctly British voice replied, "I beg your pardon, Madam."

Katharina peeked over the edge of the bed. She was dismayed to see three crimson-coated officers standing just inside the door. She climbed slowly to her feet and then walked in their direction, wiping her hands on her pinner apron as she approached.

"How might I be of service to you gentlemen?"

The soldier nearest her bowed at the waist. He was a very distinguished-looking, middle-aged fellow. His black cocked hat, trimmed in gold ribbon and decorated with an ostrich feather, was tucked neatly beneath his arm. His immaculate red uniform had bright yellow cuffs and facings. On his head, he sported a powdery white, double curled wig with a long, wrapped queue down the back.

"It is I who have come to serve you, Madam. I am Major Jethro Benthram, chief surgeon of His Majesty's 49th Regiment of Foot. General Howe has assigned me charge of this facility."

Katharina bowed slightly. "Major. I am Katharina Schell, head nurse of this ward."

The major surveyed the room. "Tell me, where are your helpers? You seem to have many rebel wounded recovering in this room. Surely, you are not caring for them all by yourself."

"I have but one assistant remaining, sir. She is in the wash room."

"And the others?" the major demanded.

"They fled Philadelphia prior to your arrival."

The major chuckled slightly. "That seems to be the case in much of this city. Oh, well. It simply gives us fewer enemy insurgents to weed out during our occupation." He smiled and inquired teasingly, "You have no such rebellious inclinations, do you, Madam Schell?"

Katharina did not smile in return. She was in no mood for humor. "I am but a humble nurse, Major. My only desire is to serve my fellow man as best I can."

"Indeed." The major smiled. "How noble. It seems that you are doing a quite admirable job, considering the circumstances. I am afraid, however, that your work is about to become a bit more ... shall we say ... inconvenienced."

Katharina's face registered confusion. "Whatever do you mean, sir?"

"All of the wounded rebels in this hospital are being relocated to your floor as of today. They will be housed in this ward and in the adjacent empty room. We will make room in the hallway, if needs be. The remainder of this facility will be dedicated to the care of His Majesty's soldiers. Ultimately, it is my intention to relocate all of the rebels to alternative housing as soon as is practicable. I need every bed for our wounded."

"But, sir, the other room to which you refer is nothing more than storage space," she protested.

"I will see that it is cleaned and made usable for your patients posthaste. I will have my troops haul away any unnecessary or unwanted materials. I have an ample labor force for such tasks."

"Be that as it may, I have no such similar labor force, Major. There is only myself and one young woman who serves as my assistant."

"No need to worry, Mrs. Schell. I have brought you a staff. I have in my custody a rebel surgeon, captured on the battlefield. There are also five rebel orderlies who will serve with him. Together, you will provide the care for *all* the remaining rebels under my roof. Do I make myself clear?"

"Yes, Major." Katharina despised the pompous man's repeated use of the word, 'rebel.'

"And can I count upon you to continue to serve diligently and faithfully under *my* supervision as administrator?"

"Of course, Major. My dedication is to the patients. I care not who resides in the administrative chair."

"Most excellent!" He turned toward one of his accompanying officers. "Levtenant Owen, will you bring up the surgeon to meet Madam Schell?"

The officer bowed slightly. "Of course, sir."

The young lieutenant marched confidently toward the door. He grabbed the knob and pulled just as Elspeth was entering the room. She lost her balance and tumbled forward into his arms. The officer caught her and quickly helped her right herself.

The handsome young man exclaimed, "Begging your pardon, Mistress! Are you quite all right?"

"Aye, sir. I am fine." She checked her bonnet and apron to make sure her garments were intact and undisturbed.

"Again, I am so very sorry. Please forgive my boorish clumsiness."

"'Tis quite all right, sir. No harm's been done. I should pay more attention to where I'm goin', I s'pose."

"Please ... after you." The officer stepped to the side and held the door open for Elspeth to enter the room. Once she was safely inside, he turned and exited swiftly.

Katharina saw the confused, fear-filled look upon the young girl's face. She reached out her hand to Elspeth and protectively pulled the girl to her side.

"Major Benthram, this is Miss Elspeth McClelland. She is my assistant. Elspeth, the major is the new British supervisor of this hospital."

The major bowed. "Miss McClelland. A pleasure, indeed."

"Major." She nodded, but said nothing else to the man. She looked pleadingly at Katharina. "I do nay understand. What has happened?"

"The English have taken over our hospital, my dear. That is all. We will remain here, on our floor, and see to the care of all the *Patriot* soldiers in our charge." She deliberately emphasized the word, 'Patriot.'

The major clearly did not care for Katharina's use of that particular term. His face curled into an angry grimace. He was just about to reprimand her when the door behind him opened. The British lieutenant entered, followed by another young man clad in a brown wool civilian coat. The fellow's gaunt, tired eyes met Katharina's.

"*Guten Tag, Mutter.*" He smiled. "Elspeth, *Mein Liebling.*"

Katharina could scarcely speak. She mumbled, "Nicklaus ... how can it be?"

Elspeth did not say anything, at all. Her eyes rolled back into their sockets and she collapsed, unconscious, onto the cold floor.

15

GERMANTOWN

October 4, 1777
One Hour Before Dawn – North of Philadelphia

A dense covering of fog blanketed the land. Though no one could see it yet, the sun was just beginning to climb upward toward the eastern horizon. Somewhere to the south, a hopeful rooster crowed. The people of Germantown would be waking soon. Tragically, they did not know that a ferocious battle was about to erupt amongst their homes.

The sleep-deprived troops of the German Regiment crept toward their assigned position north of the village. Taking advantage of the fog and the pre-dawn darkness, they darted silently across the Lime Kiln Road. The muffled crunch of dirt and rock beneath the soldiers' feet was the only sound that penetrated the night. The men moved swiftly across the shadowy roadway and took refuge in a cluster of tall trees.

"Take a moment, gentlemen," Captain Weiser urged. "Rest here. I must find the colonel and make sure that we are in the right place. No smoking. No fires. Remain quiet and keep an eye the road." He turned and then darted quickly and silently into the darkness.

The soldiers needed no further urging. They were weary to the bone. Washington's army had been on the march, without rest or reprieve, for over ten hours. The men had covered almost twenty miles during the night and were deprived of both sleep and food. Most of the Germans sat and removed their shoes in an effort to find some relief for their aching, blistered feet. Some munched hungrily on bread, sausage, or cheese. Several reclined on the hard ground and fell immediately into the deep sleep of exhaustion.

Michael Yeisley placed his blue wool haversack on top of a small boulder to create an improvised pillow. He lay flat on his back, musket at his side, and covered his face with his cocked hat. He was teetering on the edge of semi-consciousness when Abraham Price interrupted his somewhat futile attempt at rest.

"Where the hell are we, Michael? I have been lost all night long. I simply cannot get my bearings in this fog and darkness."

"Near Germantown, I think."

"Just north of Philadelphia?"

"Yes. I saw a sign about an hour ago and recognized the crossroad. I have been through this area many times before. The Schuylkill is just a mile or two to the southwest."

"So, do you believe the British are near?"

"I should think so. I doubt that George Washington marched us all the long night so that we might nap in these woods."

Conrad Traywitz was seated against a nearby oak tree. He fiddled with the slip of white paper that protruded from the twill tie on his hat. Every man in their army sported an identical paper marker on his head. He declared, "Well, we all know what these papers are for, do we not?"

Michael folded his arms across his chest and yawned. "It feels a bit like Trenton, doesn't it?"

"It does, indeed," Abe confirmed. "Except for the fact that there is no ice on our backs, we can still feel our feet, and our bollocks haven't frozen off."

Michael chuckled. "Thank the good Lord."

Captain Weiser appeared suddenly from the fog. "On your feet, men! We are out of position. The divisions to the west have already advanced to the edge of the town. Somehow, we have lost Stephen's Brigade altogether. There is no sign of them, at all."

"How, in God's name, have we lost an entire brigade?" Abe complained bitterly.

"'Tis not difficult, it seems," the captain responded. "Darkness, fog, and fatigue. But, no matter. We must move immediately. The regiment is heading south and following this road."

Flashes of yellow light illuminated the thick fog, followed seconds later by dull booms. The Continental artillery had commenced. The fog muffled and distorted the explosions and made it difficult to pinpoint the direction of the cannons. But, it appeared that the action was to their southwest.

"Sullivan and Wayne have engaged," Captain Weiser declared. "We must make haste. We are supposed to link with the 9th Virginia and advance on a mill somewhere to our south. On your feet, boys! Follow me!"

THE MEN of Captain Weiser's company marched steadily along the shoulder of the road. The dense fog glowed gray-white in the brightening dawn. Visibility improved only slightly with the sunrise. Though the sounds of battle reached a frenzied pitch to the southwest, General Greene's brigade still had not encountered the enemy.

The German regiment comprised the lead element of Greene's column. Weiser's company was at the tip of the advance. The fog-shrouded silence that greeted their every step was terrifying. The minds of the men raced with many disturbing, unanswered questions: *Where are we? Have we gone too far? Where is the enemy? Do our officers know what they are doing?*

Michael glanced to his right. Abe and Conrad marched parallel to him, each man gazing intently into the fog. He turned and looked to his left. He could only see one man ... a quiet, lesser-known lad named George Fick. The fellow literally trembled with fear. Michael could not see any other soldiers to Fick's left. The fog was simply too thick. He prayed that he and his friends were not separated from the rest of the company and lost on the battlefield.

Private Fick stopped quite suddenly and rested the butt plate of his musket on the ground beside his feet. He groaned, "*Verdammt!*" He then pawed, frustrated, at the strap on his snapsack where it crossed over top of his left shoulder.

Michael stopped and hissed, "What is wrong, George? You must not stop. You have to stay in formation and keep moving."

"Something is wrong with this strap, Michael! It feels like a needle is digging into my shoulder. I cannot tolerate it a moment longer."

Michael exhaled in frustration. "Let me look."

He rested his musket in the crook of his left arm and stepped behind George's back. He lifted the strap up off of his shoulder and peered beneath. He spotted the problem instantly. There was a long, thin splinter protruding from the flap of George's linen hunting frock. Michael plucked the invasive shard of wood and held it out victoriously for his compatriot to see.

"'Tis nothing but a splinter, George. Problem solved. Now, we *must* keep moving."

George grinned. "Thank you, Mich ..."

He never finished his words of thanksgiving. George was dead before the next syllable could exit his mouth. His smile never left his lips, even as the upper part of his face imploded into an unrecognizable mass.

Michael heard the dull thud of the lead projectile striking George's skull. The ball impacted the man's right cheek just below his eye socket, pulling the skin and muscle of his face inward, through the bone and into his brain. As the lead exited his skull in the rear, fragments of shattered bone and gelatinous brain matter exploded into his felt hat, sending it flying from his head. Death was instant.

A pink mist of brain, blood, and shattered bone coated Michael's face and chest. The momentum of the bullet's impact tossed the young man's lifeless body backward and onto Michael. He attempted to catch the lad, but the dead weight knocked him off balance. He tumbled backwards onto the ground. George's body landed squarely on top of him.

Muskets barked along the German Regiment's line as the Continentals returned fire. The invisible British, hidden somewhere behind the impenetrable wall of fog, commenced pouring concentrated, deadly fire into the Patriot advance.

Michael, however, was not advancing. Neither was he firing. He was pinned, immobile, to the ground, and he could not see. His vision was obscured by a slimy, warm coat of blood and fluids. He tasted the metallic tang of blood and felt tiny, sand-like grains of bone upon his tongue. Michael vomited. The meager contents of his empty stomach erupted from his mouth, adding the foul, stinging taste of bile and acid to the sickening flavor of blood and raw flesh.

Abraham was upon him in an instant. He was frantic. It appeared to him that his friend was gravely wounded. "Michael! Michael! Where are you hit? How bad is it?"

"Not … my … blood …" Michael gagged. He turned his head to spit the foulness from his mouth. "Get him off of me!"

Abraham leaned into Private Fick's dead body and rolled it off of Michael. He inspected his friend for wounds. The battle continued to rage around them. Lead projectiles hummed and hissed past their heads. A few bullets ricocheted off of the rocks in the road, screaming a peculiar, high-pitched squeal. Incredibly, a random musket ball thumped into George Fick's body. It tore a large gash in the dead man's back and sent a thin cloud of shredded, dusty linen flying into the air.

Abraham ignored the enemy's fire. He focused all of his attention upon his friend. "Are you absolutely certain that you are not hit?"

Michael spat once more. "No, I am not wounded. But I cannot see for all of this damnable blood." He attempted, in vain, to wipe the coagulating blood and bits of tissue away from his eyes.

"You are only making things worse, Michael. Lie back. Let me wash them out."

Michael nodded and complied. Abraham guided his friend

slightly to his left in an effort to help him avoid the puddle of blood, brains, and vomit that coated the ground beneath him. Abraham grabbed Michael's oak canteen, pulled the stopper, and dumped cold water into Michael's blood-soaked eyes. He used his own linen haversack as a cloth to wipe away the water and blood. After several rinses, Michael could finally see.

The din of musket fire had moved about a quarter-mile down the road. Fewer and fewer projectiles were impacting in their vicinity. Abraham was growing worried. It was never a good thing to be alone and isolated on a battlefield.

"We must go, Michael. The regiment has moved forward."

"We need to get George's equipment and belongings," Michael urged.

Abraham nodded. Together, they quickly removed their dead comrade's cartridge pouch, haversack, shot bag, and snapsack. Michael checked all of George's pockets for personal items. Abraham located a letter from George's wife tucked inside the liner of his cocked hat. It was coated with the poor fellow's blood. He sullenly revealed the folded paper.

Michael frowned. "Take it, I suppose. We should return it to her, or perhaps burn it. It is a bloody mess, to be sure. But, we certainly do not want any Lobsterbacks to read his personal correspondence. 'Twould not be right."

Abraham nodded in agreement. He removed his own hat and safely tucked the letter inside. He picked up George's musket and examined it. The weapon was still operational. He nodded. "Let's go, old friend!"

They each grabbed their own muskets and then trotted toward the sound of the guns. The din of the battle was tremendous, but they could see nothing. The fog and smoke remained thick and limited their visibility to less than twenty feet. Soon, however, they heard some familiar Pennsylvania German voices ahead and to their right. They veered in that direction. As they neared the firing line, a frightened private spun wildly and aimed his musket in their direction.

Abraham waved his hands in alarm. *"Nicht Schießen!* We are friend, not foe! Watch where you are pointing that thing, *dummköpfe!"*

The terrified soldier appeared greatly relieved.

"Which company is this?" Michael demanded.

"Graybill's. Who are you looking for?"

"Captain Weiser."

The soldier pointed. "He is to the right, about a hundred yards. Colonel Weltner deployed the regiment across this field when we encountered the first skirmishers."

Michael tipped his hat. "Thank you. Good luck, friend."

The fellow did not respond. He merely turned and emptied his musket into the fog. Abe shrugged at Michael. They sprinted toward the west, following the firing line. Moments later, they located Captain Weiser. He was stomping behind line, encouraging the men and directing fire. The captain was visibly startled by Michael's bloodied appearance.

"Yeisley, are you injured badly? Do you need to report to the surgeon?"

"'Tis not my blood, sir."

The captain glanced, confused, at Abraham.

"Michael was standing right beside George Fick when the lad took a ball in the brain," Abe explained. "He's wearing Fick's blood. It took us a while to wash Michael's eyes clean. He was quite the mess. That is why we were a bit late in joining you, sir."

Captain Weiser nodded. "I am glad you boys are well. I was worried that you had fallen in that first volley. The bastards caught us by surprise."

"What are we doing now, sir?" Michael asked.

"Holding this position. We overran their first outpost. They have pulled back to the mill. We are waiting for General Greene's orders to proceed." He pointed toward an open spot in the ragged firing line. "Join the men. Shoot at will. I want suppressing fire in the direction of the enemy."

Abe held up Private Fick's musket. "I grabbed George's gun. What shall I do with it?"

"I will take it. Private Killman received a ball in his hammer lock. It rendered the weapon unserviceable. He will be glad to get a new one." The captain received the musket from Abraham. "Now, you boys get going."

Michael and Abe darted to the line and knelt beside their comrades. They quickly opened fire into the fog. They went through the loading and firing process thrice more, shooting blindly each time.

As they reloaded after their fourth shots, Abe proclaimed, "This is stupid. We are wasting powder and lead. We are not receiving fire, at all."

Almost at that exact moment, Colonel Weltner's voice echoed through the fog. "Formation! Formation! Prime your firelocks, and prepare to march!"

The men scrambled to their feet and quickly formed ranks. Some of the slower loaders struggled to prepare their weapons while simultaneously finding their assigned places in the line. The captains stepped in front of their companies and directed their men, preparing them for the coming advance.

Colonel Weltner yelled, "We are attacking an entrenched enemy, men! They shall not desire to relinquish the ground! Combat will be in close quarters! Fix bayonets!"

The captains echoed, "Fix bayonets!"

The metallic clank of steel blades rattling against the barrels of muskets sounded all along the regimental line. There was a chorus of clicks as each bayonet rotated over its lug and then locked into place.

Abe cut his eyes at Michael. "This is bad."

Michael nodded. His face clouded with stress and fear. "We must stay together, Abraham."

"I agree."

The colonel shouted, "Present arms!"

The captains echoed the command up and down the line. The men lifted their muskets and held them at the ready across their chests.

Then, the colonel thundered, "Charge bayonets!"

Again, the captains echoed the command. The men lowered their muskets to their right hips, placing the buttstocks against the sides of their legs. Hundreds of bayonets pointed menacingly in the direction of the enemy.

"March!"

The German Regiment stepped forward into the blinding fog. They progressed almost a hundred yards before they began to receive fire. The enemy was disturbingly close. The shots erupted from a range of less than fifty yards. A handful of the German Patriots fell, screaming, to the ground.

"Battalion, halt!"

The men took two steps and stopped as ordered.

"Present arms!"

The men lifted their weapons to their chests.

"Make ready!"

The soldiers brought their weapons to full cock.

"Take aim! Fire!"

The German regiment unleashed a thunderous volley into the enemy. They could hear the British officers through the fog, barking commands to their men. Sporadic fire peppered the ground in front of the Germans.

The captains ordered, "Clear all misfires! Prime your firelocks!"

Up and down the line, the soldiers swiftly and expertly primed their pans and loaded their muskets. Intense return fire poured into the German lines. Tragically, soldiers fell wounded and dead.

Colonel Weltner shouted from behind the lines, "At the double-time! Charge bayonets!"

The captains echoed the command. The men of the German Regiment ran at the enemy, bayonets at the ready. Michael's heart pounded from adrenaline and fear. He was charging the British army with a musket and bayonet. He was somewhat in a state of disbelief. These Redcoats were the most powerful and highly-trained army known to mankind. Michael felt numb. He was so frightened that he could scarcely move his feet. He glanced to his right. Abraham ran beside him. The presence of his friend gave him some manner of solace.

As he turned his attention back toward the fog in front of him, his heart leapt in surprise when he unexpectedly found himself face-to-face with a British soldier. The young man was standing in front of a stone fence and was hastily reloading his Brown Bess. The Englishman appeared equally shocked when he looked up from priming his pan and saw Michael charging full-speed at him. The young man's face converted from surprise to horror as he caught a glimpse of Michael's blood-streaked uniform and face. The soldier paused, stunned, for just a moment. It was a costly delay.

There were numerous other British soldiers to the left and right, but Michael paid no attention to any of them. His entire focus was upon this lone Englishman. *This* man was his enemy. Theirs was a struggle of life and death. In that moment, nothing else on that battlefield mattered. In the next few seconds, one of them was going to die.

Michael never slowed down. He reached the Redcoat just as the fellow was lifting his musket to his shoulder to fire. Michael parried the move by catching the muzzle of the soldier's Brown Bess inside the angled joint of his bayonet. Michael thrust his enemy's musket barrel upward. The Englishman pulled his trigger, but the deflection of the barrel caused the shot to go high above Michael's head. Because of the awkward angle, the flash of the powder in the musket's pan exploded in a cloud of fire and smoke directly into the Redcoat's face. It scorched his eyebrows and temporarily blinded him. He screamed, dropped his musket, and lifted his hands defensively toward his fire-seared eyes.

Michael continued the upward motion of his own musket, and, shifting his weight, drove his buttstock into the man's right jaw. It was a savage blow. Michael felt the bones of the man's face shatter. The fellow howled from the pain. Michael recovered from the move, drawing his musket back and angling his bayonet at the enemy's midsection. He screamed with rage and fear as he pressed the weapon forward and buried the bayonet into the man's belly, just below his ribcage. The wounded soldier stumbled to his left and caught himself against the stone wall as Michael forced the triangular blade deeper into his flesh and organs. The bayonet came to an abrupt halt. Michael felt, and heard, the steel impact something harder ... something resistant. The tip had penetrated through the man's back and struck the stone wall behind him.

The stricken Englishman pawed at his belly in disbelief. He grabbed at the barrel of the invasive musket. Michael gave the gun a savage twist and then yanked his bayonet from the man's torso. The sharp edges of the triangular blade sliced through the fleshy palms of the dying soldier's hands. Dark, black blood poured from the gaping wound. Michael's bayonet had sliced open his liver.

The fellow dropped to his knees. He tried to say something, but his jaw was so badly broken he could not make an intelligible sound. He clawed at his scorched eyes with bloody hands, but his blindness remained. He was a shattered man. He was a dead man.

Michael's spirit was suddenly overwhelmed with pity. He dropped his musket on the ground and knelt beside the man. He spoke reassuringly. "'Tis all right, friend. Let me help you."

He gripped the man's shoulders and gently lowered him to the ground, laying him on his left side in the soft grass. The fellow's breathing was quick and labored. Death was inevitable and near. He was bleeding out quickly. It seemed, though, that he was no longer in pain. Michael had to look away. He simply could not watch the man die.

He grabbed his musket and stood. Glancing to his right, he saw Abraham kneeling over a fallen comrade. It appeared that the German Regiment soldier had a puncture wound in his upper thigh. Abe was pressing down on a bandage. Though the fog remained thick over the battlefield, Michael could see that the combat had moved well beyond the stone fence. The Germans had driven the enemy's pickets from the mill. Only a handful of Continentals remained behind the fence, reloading their weapons, securing equipment, and tending to wounded.

Michael called out, "Abe, are you all right?"

"I am, indeed. Just tending to young Albert, from Maryland. The lad has a cut in his leg."

Michael peered intently over the stone wall. Visibility had improved to about thirty yards, but still, he saw no other soldiers. He could hear shouting and shooting further past the mill. A cannon boomed from somewhere in that direction. It was the first artillery that he had heard in their sector of the battlefield.

Michael walked over to Abraham. "We need to keep moving, Abe. The regiment is far beyond the mill, I think."

"Michael, this is Albert Moser from Baltimore. I have bandaged a hole in his leg. The lad took a blade in the thigh, but he shall live. Help me move him to the wall."

Michael and Abe grabbed the boy beneath his armpits and dragged him approximately fifteen feet to the concealment of the stone wall. They propped him comfortably against the rocks. Michael placed the boy's canteen in his lap. Abe handed him his musket and rested his disheveled cocked hat on top of his head.

"Albert, you must rest here. We are going to follow the regiment. Help will come soon."

The frightened boy stammered, "Don't ... don't you leave me here!"

"We have to go. But someone will be back for you."

The boy's face betrayed his fear. "I don't want to be alone!"

Abe knelt beside him and patted his shoulder. "You will be fine. The British have moved south. We have taken this ground. Once the fighting is done, they will evacuate all of the wounded to our surgeons. So, all you have to do is sit here and wait for someone to arrive. You will be sleeping in a clean hospital cot this night! I am almost jealous." He winked and smiled reassuringly at the frightened boy.

"Will *you* come back for me?" Albert wailed.

"If you want me to. Once the battle is done, I will come back to check on you. Satisfied?"

Albert nodded slightly. He did not appear to place much confidence in Abraham's promise.

"We must go!" Michael urged. He grabbed his musket, turned, and walked swiftly toward a break in the stone fence. Abraham followed closely behind.

IT TOOK ONLY a short while for Michael and Abe to locate their company and rejoin the advance. They quickly found their trusty friend, Conrad Traywitz, and fell into formation beside him.

Colonel Weltner had his men on the move, progressing steadily against a somewhat sporadic British resistance. The German Regiment maneuvered alongside the 9th Virginia toward the Market Square, a major crossroads in the heart of the village of Germantown. They fired and advanced in good order and seemed to have the enemy on the run. Suddenly, artillery and musket fire poured mercilessly into both flanks of the column. Bullets and grapeshot raked through the American formation. Men fell by the dozens. Greene's Brigade had marched blindly into a trap. They were enveloped inside a deadly crossfire.

"Get down!" Captain Weiser screamed.

The men of his company fell prone in the thick grass. They clung low to the ground, attempting to crawl below the deadly wave of lead that swarmed overhead. Men screamed from fear and pain. All over the field, there were the sickly thumps and thuds of metal striking meat.

Conrad's voice punctuated the din of battle. "I am hit! I am hit! *Mein Gott!* They have shot me in the arse!"

Chunks of dirt and grass landed on Michael's neck and back as the British lead tore into the ground beside him. He realized that he needed better cover. He was on a small knoll and entirely too exposed. He quickly spotted a small depression in the ground, about six feet to his right. He rolled in that direction, tumbling rapidly until he landed face-up in the shallow hole.

He lay still for a moment, thankful that he was able to secure a place of relative safety. As he stared upward into the blanket of fog, he was mesmerized by the strange disturbances in the low-hanging cloud. He could see tiny waves and distortions created by the hail of projectiles that ripped through the vapors. It had the appearance of a deadly swarm of bees. Michael suddenly realized that this was not just an ambush. It was a well-planned and executed killing field.

Somewhere, in the midst of the onslaught of enemy fire, one of the captains of the German Regiment made a dramatic decision. Indeed, it was the only reasonable decision that one could reach in light of their inescapable and deathly dilemma. That officer's voice echoed throughout the field. "Retreat! Retreat! Retreat!"

It was the command for which all of the men had been waiting ... and praying. No doubt, some amongst them had already taken flight without waiting for such an order. Still, the men remaining on the field were greatly relieved. They repeated the call up and down the line. "Retreat! Retreat! Retreat!"

The enemy's fire diminished somewhat. Michael flipped over onto his belly and spun around to face back toward the direction of the mill.

Abraham shouted, "Michael! We must help Conrad! The boy is wounded!"

Michael crawled about twenty feet to reach his friend. He took a quick look at Conrad's buttocks. He had, indeed, been shot. But, it appeared to be only a grazing wound. He could not tell, for certain, without a better inspection.

"I believe it is just a scratch, Conrad. You will be fine."

"Are you ... certain?" Conrad's voice was shaky and broken.

"He is certain," Abe reassured him, appearing suddenly at Conrad's other side. "Still, it might hurt to shite for a day or two." He grabbed the wounded man's collar. "Come on, we need to get out of here. Conrad, I know it hurts, but you need to use your arms to help us. You must pull yourself along the ground."

"What about my musket?"

Abe grabbed the weapon and drew the sling over the top of his head. He flopped the musket onto his back, positioning it beside his own. "I will carry it. Do not worry. Now, move!"

All over the battlefield, the call continued, "Retreat! Retreat! Retreat!"

Michael, Abraham, and Conrad crawled through the grass, stubble, and stones. Abe and Michael tugged their friend along as best they could. Conrad helped propel himself by clawing at the ground with both hands. They moved toward the north, back in the direction of the mill. They had gone about forty yards when it seemed that the majority of the shooting was far to their rear.

"Let us go on foot now," Michael urged.

Both uninjured men helped Conrad to his feet. He rested his arms around their shoulders. The three soldiers hobbled northward. Soon, the stone wall of the mill came into view.

"We have to get Albert!" Abraham exclaimed.

"Someone else will help him," Michael countered. "We cannot possibly move two wounded men."

"We will figure something out. I am not going to leave the boy here. He could fall into the enemy's hands."

Abraham guided the trio through a break in the wall. They turned to the right and moved toward the area where they had left young Albert Moser. They soon spied him, reclining against the wall.

Abraham called out, "Albert! Are you ready to go, boy?"

The lad did not respond. They walked closer.

"Albert! I told you I would be back! Now, collect your things. We must go!"

Again, there was no response. As they neared the lad, they soon discovered the cause of his silence.

Albert Moser's head was tilted awkwardly to the right. His eyes were fixed wide open. Blood oozed from the corner of his mouth. His belly and chest were punctured by no less than a dozen bayonet wounds. Blood soaked his uniform, forming a thick puddle in his lap. The boy was dead.

Captain Weiser appeared unexpectedly through the opening in the wall. About a dozen men of the regiment were following him. Michael whistled and waved. The captain trotted in their direction.

"We have to go, boys. The battle is lost. The entire 9th Virginia is done."

"Done?" Michael echoed, confused. "Are they all dead?"

"Many are. But, most have been captured. The British surrounded and took the entire lot of them. Sullivan and Wayne's Brigades have been turned back. General Greene has ordered our entire brigade to retreat. Washington will, no doubt, have to order a general retreat for the army. We have lost this field." He glanced at the bludgeoned German Regiment soldier beside the fence. "Who is this?"

Abe growled, "Albert Moser. He is but a lad ... a boy from one of the Maryland companies. I bandaged his wound just a while ago. But, it seems that the enemy had used him for bayonet practice. The bastards!"

"Leave him. You must go. I will remain here for a short while and organize the stragglers. We will rendezvous north of the creek near Chestnut Hill. Good luck, gentlemen."

The captain turned and sprinted back into the fog. The three friends tarried for just a moment. Clearly, Abraham was pained. His heart ached for the dead boy. He kept staring at the body, his eyes welling with tears. Michael glimpsed to his left and saw the British soldier that he, himself, had killed in hand-to-hand combat. The man's body lay in a huge pool of thick, congealed blood. Michael experienced his own pang of guilt and regret. It was, after all, his bayonet that had drained the life from the young Englishman.

Michael sighed. "Death knows no country or nationality, Abraham."

"But, they murdered him!" Abe hissed. "He was done! He was just sitting here, and helpless!"

"I suppose, then, that I murdered that fellow over there." He pointed at the body. "He, too, was done. But, I still stuck him."

"That is different, Michael! That was in the midst of a battle. This lad was no longer in the fight. He was a threat to no one."

"Perhaps. Still, there is nothing we can do for either of them now. They are dead. We are alive. Let us keep it that way. We must take their things and go." He patted Conrad's back. "Can you stand on your own for a bit?"

Conrad nodded. "Just stand me over there by the wall."

They quickly carried Conrad to a suitable spot and leaned him comfortably against the stone wall. They moved quickly to retrieve the equipment and accoutrements from the dead. Abraham stripped off the Marylander's bags and sundries. He grabbed the boy's musket and added it to the other two already strapped across his back. Similarly, Michael relieved the dead Englishman of everything of value, including his musket.

"Take the Redcoat's shoes!" Conrad urged. "I need new shoes."

Michael complied.

As he was preparing to leave, Abe reached over reverently and pulled Private Moser's eyelids downward to close them. He mumbled, "I am truly sorry, Albert. I hope you know ... I did come back for you."

"Let's go," Michael urged.

Both men rose to their feet and retrieved their wounded friend. Together, they helped Conrad limp across the field toward the north. They had several miles to travel in order to reach the rendezvous point. Their battle at Germantown was over.

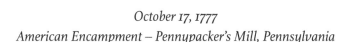

October 17, 1777
American Encampment – Pennypacker's Mill, Pennsylvania

"Michael, can you fetch me some more of that coffee?" Conrad begged. "My cup is empty."

Michael retrieved the horn cup from his friend and poured him a generous portion of the thick, black liquid.

"Make the lazy bastard get his own drink!" Abraham Price hissed.

Conrad's face flushed red. "Mind your own business, Abe!"

"This is my business! You have been milking that scratch on your arse for all that it is worth, *Private* Traywitz. I am surprised that you have yet to ask one of us to wipe it for you."

Several of the men around the campfire chuckled in agreement.

"No one asked for your opinion," Conrad mumbled.

Abe grunted, seemingly disgusted. "I am free to make my own observations, am I not? It is, after all, *freedom* for which we fight. And I currently observe that you are a lazy, worthless lout. Ever since that round ball grazed your arse, you have been as worthless as bird shite on a hat."

The men surrounding the campfire exploded in laughter.

"I was wounded in battle!" Conrad protested.

"A ball bounced off of your arse. I carried your sorry sack of bones almost two miles from that battlefield, and when I saw that bloodless scrape on your buttocks, I was tempted to shoot you myself."

Once again, the men howled with laughter and jeers.

Conrad was almost in tears. "Michael! Make him stop! This is not dignified."

Michael shrugged. "I am not getting in the middle of this. Abraham is merely saying something that has gone unsaid for far too long." He handed Conrad the horn cup filled with coffee. "So, do not ask me to fetch another thing for you. 'Tis high time you tend to your own needs."

Conrad stared in disbelief. He sullenly received the cup. He grumbled, "Some friends you are."

Colonel Weltner's voice boomed throughout the German camp, interrupting Conrad's fireside humbling.

"Formation! Company commanders, assemble the troops!"

Abe exhaled in disgust. "So much for our quiet evening."

The men of Captain Weiser's company gathered in their assigned area.

"To the right ... dress!" Captain Weiser ordered. "Stand at attention!"

Over three and hundred and fifty members of the German regiment dressed their ranks and then stood perfectly still. Seconds later, a wagon pulled into the clearing in front of the formation. The driver parked in the center of the field. His passenger, regimental commander Colonel Ludwick Weltner, climbed over the seat and stood tall in the wagon bed.

"Men of the German Regiment, I have news of great importance! I have just received word by messenger that forces under General Horatio Gates engaged British General John Burgoyne at Bemis Heights, in New York, ten days ago. The outcome was most extraordinary. General Gates and his forces took the field!"

A great cheer erupted throughout the regiment. The men burst forth with the patriotic chant, "Huzzah! Huzzah! Huzzah!"

The colonel waved his hands to calm the men.

"Gentlemen ... please return unto me your attention. You must hear the remainder of my announcement."

The roar of celebration dissipated. The colonel continued his speech.

"General Gates did not only win the field. He took Burgoyne's entire army. Over 1,000 of the enemy were killed or wounded. In all, over 6,000 British and Hessian troops were captured. None of Burgoyne's forces escaped."

The euphoria of victory could not be contained. Men chanted, cheered, hugged, and wept. It was the army's first taste of victory since Trenton. The boisterous celebration continued for several minutes. Colonel Weltner finally brought it under control by firing his pistol into the air.

"I can see that you men are as pleased as I. We will celebrate thusly. First, our chaplain will come and bring for us a prayer of thanksgiving. At dusk, the entire regiment will present itself, under arms, so that we might fire a *Feu de Joie* in honor of General Gates and his victorious army. Finally, after supper I shall have two barrels of ale delivered to each company. Tonight, we celebrate!"

The men cheered, danced, and sang soldier's songs. It had been so very long since the Continental Army had prevailed in battle. Even though the men of the regiment had not taken part in the surrender of Burgoyne, they still felt the pride of a victorious army.

The crowd finally calmed enough for the regimental chaplain to climb into the wagon and word a prayer of thanksgiving. Following the prayer, the men continued to congratulate one another as they walked back toward their campfires.

Abe soon spied Conrad Traywitz dancing and celebrating amongst his brethren. He walked over to his friend and teased, "The chaplains should have tarried a bit longer. Look! We have ourselves a miracle in the camp! Conrad has been healed!"

He playfully swatted his wounded friend on his sore behind. Conrad cursed and acted as if he were going to strike back. But, instead, he grinned sheepishly and grabbed his compatriot in a friendly embrace.

The commemorations and celebrations of the German Regiment, and every other regiment in Washington's army, continued late into the night.

~

December 19, 1777
Twenty Miles Northwest of Philadelphia

As usual, the men of the German Regiment were exhausted. Most were hungry. Many were woefully deficient in clothing and struggling to keep warm in the midst of the deepening cold of the approaching winter. They stumbled slowly westward in the center of a vast Continental Army column of over 12,000 men.

Since Germantown, the regiment had endured an excruciating two months of constant deployment and maneuvering. In early November, the Germans had been sent east to patrol the areas along the Delaware River. On November 21, in response to a potential incursion by Cornwallis into New Jersey, the regiment had, once again, been forced to cross the Delaware. They lingered in New Jersey for almost a week, until it became apparent that the British were not invading. On November 27, they received orders to return to Pennsylvania. Incredibly, the German Regiment completed its sixth crossing of the Delaware River just after dark on that day.

The movement of all of the supplies, wagons, carts, and artillery across the water had been an excruciatingly difficult task. To a man, the Germans prayed that they might never have to perform another river crossing. When the order finally came to return to the main army and fall in for the journey to their winter quarters, it was almost a relief.

One week later, as the men of the German Regiment climbed the trail toward the crest of Gulph Hill, they had high hopes for some much-needed quiet and rest. The area was heavily wooded and beautiful. There was good water. It was on high ground. The men of the Pennsylvania companies were all less than forty miles from their homes. It was almost a certainty that their family members and loved ones would be able to visit the camp. The tired soldiers held high hopes, indeed.

But none of them could foresee or even imagine the nakedness, suffering, privation, disease, starvation, and death that awaited them during that infamous winter encampment at the place known as Valley Forge.

PART IV

VALLEY FORGE

16

CHRISTMAS

Mid-Afternoon - December 25, 1777
Home of Nicklaus and Julianna Yeisley - Berks County, Pennsylvania

The wondrous smells of Christmas permeated the Yeisley cottage. The table was adorned with scrumptious German treats such as buttery almond cookies, potato dumplings, sauerkraut soup, apple-smoked pork, and spiced wine. A crackling fire in the large fireplace warmed the tiny space and filled the room with a cheerful glow. There was joy in this home, even though Nicklaus and Julianna's sons could not be there. Michael and George Yeisley were encamped in distant fields somewhere in Pennsylvania. Both of their boys were fighting for the independence of the United States of America.

The Yeisley family had been celebrating the birth of the Christ-child for many hours. They enjoyed all of their customary Christmas traditions. Their celebration culminated in a round of joyful Christmas carols from their German homeland. But, at long last, it was time for the music to end. The hour was growing late, and Magdalena Yeisley had to return her children to Northampton County before nightfall. *Opa* Nicklaus gave his mandolin a final strum as his wife, Julianna, sang the last note of a favorite, traditional Christmas song of old. Everyone in the house clapped and cheered.

"*Opa* Nicklaus! *Oma* Anna! Sing it again!" begged young Elizabeth. The other Yeisley youngsters joined in her plea.

The children of Michael and Magdalena Yeisley loved to hear their grandfather play his weathered mandolin. They equally enjoyed hearing their grandmother sing her timeless songs of Christmas. Each of the Yeisley children had heard the familiar yuletide hymns annually since their births. Though separated by decades and a vast ocean, these American-born children sensed in those songs a deep and abiding connection to their German roots and heritage.

Old Nicklaus Yeisley chuckled. "That is enough music for tonight, *Mein Mausebär*. Evening approaches, and it is time for you to return home. *Opa* Heinrich will be worried if you are not home before dark." He carefully placed the mandolin in its case and sealed the latches. "I will go and hitch the team." He rose and shuffled stiffly toward the door.

Magdalena patted Elizabeth's head. "*Opa* Nicklaus is right, my dear. It is, indeed, time for us to go. We have over an hour of travel to reach home. Dusk approaches, and the roads are very icy."

Julianna frowned from grandmotherly concern. "Are you certain that you cannot stay the night? We have plenty of room. The snow is so very deep. I simply cannot believe that you made the journey today in this frigid weather."

"We will be fine, *Oma* Anna. We have ample blankets to keep us warm. The snow is, indeed, deep on the roadway, but the horses had little trouble getting us here. Surely, today's warmer temperatures have brought some thawing."

Magdalena struggled to stand. She straddled her legs wide across the seat of the chair and pulled against the table in front of her. Rocking slightly, she found the perfect amount of momentum to propel her body upward and out of the chair. She swiftly grabbed the bottom of her green linen jacket and pulled it down over her greatly swollen belly.

"How much longer will it be, Magdalena?" Julianna inquired, concerned.

"About another month, I believe. I should deliver in late January."

"And Michael still does not know?"

"No, *Oma*. I have had no letters from him. I have written to him many times but have yet to receive a single response. I do not know where he is or if he is even alive." The rims of her eyes turned red as tears began to form.

Julianna reached out and squeezed the young mother's hand. "He is alive. I promise you that. I would know it if he were not." She smiled confidently. "And he is going to be so very happy about this baby. Perhaps this one will be a boy!"

Magdalena chuckled sarcastically. She pointed toward the floor full of girls. "That would be something of a miracle, would it not?"

"Well, no matter," Julianna declared. "He will be silly with joy, nonetheless."

"I hope so." Magdalena frowned slightly as she carried her teacup to the wash pan. She decided to change the subject. "*Oma*, I do wish that you would allow me to help you clean up this mess. My children have visited much disorder upon your home."

Julianna shook her head emphatically. "Nonsense! It is a treasure and a joy to have little ones filling this cottage with their voices and energy. If you are intent upon leaving, then you must go ahead and leave now. These dishes will wait until morning, anyway. Heaven knows, I shall need something to keep me occupied tomorrow." She pointed through the window at Nicklaus, who was outside tending the horses. "That wretched man will sit in his chair by that fire and sleep the entire day away!"

Magdalena laughed joyfully. "Thank you for everything, *Oma*." She hugged the kindly woman.

"You are most welcome, child. And I want you to take Heinrich his basket. I have prepared him some sauerkraut soup and fresh rye bread, with some *kletzenbrot* for dessert." Julianna walked quickly to the serving table and fetched a large basket shrouded beneath a linen cloth. "I do hope he feels better soon. He does not have a fever, does he?"

"*Danke, Oma* Anna. No, he has no fever. I am certain that he will be well in a few days. He has these horrible headaches from time to time. He has suffered from them throughout his life. The only thing that makes them better is reclining in the darkness and sleeping."

"Please give him our regards. I am so sorry that he could not celebrate the birth of our Lord with us."

"*Danke*. Happy Christmas."

Julianna hugged her daughter-in-law once more. "And a very happy Christmas to you, my dear."

Magdalena announced with authority, "Come, Yeisley children. To the chariot we go! We have many miles to travel."

The little ones whined and groaned with displeasure, but with Julianna's help, Magdalena managed to herd her brood of girls out the door and toward their awaiting wagon. Nicklaus already had the team hitched and ready to go. The girls said their final goodbyes and climbed aboard. Nicklaus helped the youngsters construct warm nests of blankets and quilts deep inside the soft, insulating hay that filled the wagon bed. The children nestled into their warm cocoons and readied themselves for the journey home.

Magdalena did not tarry. She had no desire, whatsoever, to travel the deserted county roads after dark. With most of the men of the region gone to war, the incidents of robbery and other crimes had increased rather dramatically throughout the more rural regions of Pennsylvania. Magdalena guided the rig confidently onto the highway and pointed her team of horses toward home.

Near Dusk
Upper Milford Township, Pennsylvania

THE YEISLEY GIRLS were almost there. Just another quarter-mile of snow-covered road was all that remained between them and their warm, inviting home. Magdalena was certainly ready to be there. The little ones had been no trouble throughout the journey. All but Elizabeth napped in the wagon bed. The oldest Yeisley daughter had actually been delightful company for her. The handsome little girl had remained seated on the bench beside her mother, conversing throughout the afternoon and asking curious questions.

Despite the excellent conversation and relatively easy travel, Magdalena was exhausted. Her body could simply withstand no more time in the bumpy wagon. Her back was aching horribly. Also, it seemed as if the baby inside her abdomen found great joy in jumping on her bladder. She was much in need of a visit to the privy.

As she guided the team around a curve in the road and emerged from the deep forest into open farmland, she spied a tall column of black smoke to the north. It emanated from just beyond the nearest hill. She experienced a pang of panic, as she realized that the smoke was coming from the direction of her home. She popped the reins, slapping them against the hips of the horses as an improvised whip. "Go, girls!" she urged them. "Go!" She prayed that there had not been a fire at the house. She instantly began to worry about her father.

As she neared the top of the hill, she spied a man standing in the roadway. Almost immediately, three more men appeared at the roadside. They were all soldiers of the local militia. The men were dressed in identical white hunting frocks. Knee-high buckskin gaiters and heavy leather boots protected their lower legs from the snow and slush. They wore an assortment of cocked and floppy hats. Each of them were armed with muskets and blades. Magdalena recognized one of the men. He was Captain Hans Braun, of the Northampton County Militia. As Magdalena approached, the captain raised his hand as a signal for her to stop.

He smiled grimly. "*Guten Abend, Frau* Yeisley. Happy Christmas."

"*Guten Abend, Herr* Braun. Why are you here? What has happened?" Magdalena's heart raced. She was in no mood for friendly greetings or pleasantries.

"There has been some trouble, I am afraid."

"Trouble?" she echoed nervously.

The captain nodded. He appeared to be choosing his words carefully.

"Are you aware that there has been an increase of crime throughout our county?"

She nodded. "Yes, I have heard. That is why we hurried home today, so that we might arrive before dark and avoid any highwaymen."

The captain bit his lip and stared, troubled, toward the ground at his feet. "It is most fortunate that you did not return home earlier."

Magdalena could feel her pulse pounding in her temples. "Why? What has happened?"

"Your home has been vandalized, I am afraid." He said nothing else.

"*Bitte, Herr* Braun, you are being so very vague. Tell me what is wrong! Where is my father?"

He stared, hollow-eyed, at the woman. "I am very sorry to report that your home and properties have been destroyed by fire." He paused. "And that *Herr* Mueller is dead."

"Dead?" she wailed in response. "Dead? How?" She stared numbly at the column of smoke. "Did he perish in the fire?"

The captain shook his head slowly. He walked closer to the wagon. "No, Magdalena." He glanced at Elizabeth and hesitated. "Your father was shot."

Her chest began to heave as a wave of sobs prepared to erupt from her spirit. "Shot? Why? Who would shoot my papa?"

"We think it was Tories ... Loyalists from Canada, perhaps. We have heard that there are bands of brigands roaming the countryside to our north and east. They have been robbing farms and taking supplies in the name of King George." He paused. "But murder is something altogether new."

Magdalena attempted to compose herself and avoid further upsetting Elizabeth. "And our home? Is it damaged severely?"

"It is a total loss, I am afraid. They burned everything. The bastards even burned your outhouse and smokehouse. They took all of the livestock and horses, of course."

"Our looms are gone, then?" she sobbed. "Our factorium is destroyed?"

"Yes, Magdalena. They are. I am so very sorry." He paused. "Do you have somewhere you can go? What will you do?"

She stared at the man through mournful, empty eyes. "No, *Herr* Braun. I have no place to go, and I do not know what we are going to do."

~

Dusk ... The Same Day
Winter Encampment – Valley Forge

THOUGH DARKNESS HAD FALLEN, the Continental encampment still glowed from its brilliant, white coat of thick snow. On the eastern end of the hilltop, in the area assigned to General Muhlenberg's Brigade, a shivering band of German Regiment soldiers huddled together for warmth deep inside their partially-constructed, makeshift shelter. The cramped, cave-like room reeked of smoke, filth, and the various odors of the human body. It was a cold, squalid existence. The men prayed that the snows would soon melt, so that that they might emerge from the putrid lair and complete construction of their winter cabin.

Upon their arrival at Valley Forge, the soldiers of the Continental Army had immediately begun to build over one thousand log homes, each roughly fourteen by sixteen-feet in dimension. With the ample timber available throughout the region, log structures were the most obvious choice for long-term shelters. Known as "huts," they were designed to house up to twelve enlisted men each.

The locations of the various huts and buildings for Washington's army had been carefully surveyed and plotted so that the makeshift "city" would have a semblance of military order and organization. The results of the engineers' and surveyors' planning were quite impressive. The encampment did, indeed, begin to resemble a city. The huts of the various brigades and regiments were arranged along streets and organized into blocks. There were fields for military drill and parades, kitchens, horse pens, quartermaster buildings, hospitals, and latrines.

With over 12,000 souls encamped at Valley Forge, it ranked in size with some of the larger cities on the continent. Indeed, its population was almost equal to that of Philadelphia. It was quite amazing to consider that one of the most densely populated cities in North American had "sprung up" overnight on a remote Pennsylvania hilltop.

Tragically, three days into the massive construction enterprise, the first significant snow of winter descended upon the region. A blizzard began just before dawn on December 23 and continued, unabated, for almost forty-eight hours. In the midst of the storm, the troops had to cease construction on their huts and weatherize whatever shelter they had already completed. The men scrambled to fashion temporary roofs and covers to somehow stave off the invasive winter cold and frozen precipitation.

On Christmas morning, throughout the fields and meadows of Valley Forge, the men of the Washington's army huddled inside their partially-constructed, damp, smoke-filled shelters. They were cold, hungry, and despondent. December 25, 1777, was not a very merry Christmas. Few people moved around the camp. Almost everyone remained inside, attempting to make the most of the meager warmth provided by their limited clothing, threadbare blankets, and tiny indoor campfires.

The men of Captain Weiser's company had a poor shelter, indeed. Their humble refuge from the cold and snow was a shallow, cave-like depression in the ground, surrounded by a waist-high log wall. Overhead, a haphazard layer of logs covered with cloth tarps, tree limbs, and grass comprised a lumpy, leaky rooftop. An ancient, discolored wool blanket served as the door to their shelter. It hung in a narrow opening in the log wall. Because of the low ceiling, the men had to crawl through the blanket-covered doorway in order to enter or leave the partially-completed hut.

Keeping warm inside the primitive shelter was quite difficult.

General Washington's construction plans required a stone fireplace inside each winter hut. However, without completed walls, there could be no fireplace. Weiser's men had not even begun that final phase of their building project. Instead, they dug a small fire pit in the distant corner of their underground room.

The men constantly nursed the tiny campfire inside its humble pit. They struggled moment by moment to keep the fire going, despite their limited supply of damp wood. The heat of the fire melted the snow overhead, bringing a constant drip of cold water through the roof. The ingenious soldiers positioned a large iron pot strategically below a couple of the more active drips in order to capture fresh drinking water. The smoke from their campfire vented through a small crack between two overhead logs. In reality, however, most of the smoke never left the shack. It remained inside, invading the soldiers' nostrils and stinging their eyes.

The twelve souls crammed into this unfinished hut were all that remained of the enlisted men of Captain Benjamin Weiser's company. The others were sick in the hospital, on furlough, or simply gone. Many had deserted, either during the journey to the encampment or shortly after. The ranks of the German Regiment had been decimated since their arrival at Valley Forge. Their numbers were dwindling rapidly. The winter encampment had only begun, yet their fortunes already appeared bleak.

Conrad Traywitz crawled across the cold, muddy floor and stuck his head outside for a much-needed breath of smoke-free air. Though the heavens remained shrouded in low, dark clouds, there was no more snow. Conrad drew his lungs full of the cold, fresh air and then ducked back inside the slightly warmer shelter. He announced as he crawled back toward his mates, "Well, the snow has stopped. Perhaps we can finish our hut tomorrow."

"It will be damned messy work, to be sure," Abraham groaned. "This field will be nothing but mud and mire once the melting starts and the men and horses begin to move about."

"Do you think we will earn the regiment's bounty?" mused Private

Henry Seyfert. "That extra twelve dollars, divided amongst us, would be helpful, indeed."

"Not likely," answered Private Eberhard Meyer through chattering teeth. "Captain Burchardt's company almost has their complete. They had their fireplace done and were already building bunks when the snow started. Surely, they will win the bounty for the first completed hut."

"Horse shite!" Abe exclaimed.

"'Tis true!" Eberhard vowed. "I saw it with my own eyes."

"How?" challenged Abe. "They have no more men than we."

"No. But they have two carpenters, a stone mason, and three lumbermen," replied the normally silent Private Philip Eackle.

Abraham grunted. "That explains it, then. We worthless fellows are nothing but a bunch of turnip farmers."

"And some of us are not even very good at that," quipped Conrad.

The men chuckled slightly, then fell silent. Each man shivered as the cold assaulted his bones. Deep in the darkness of the shelter, Private Peter Downy unleashed a thunderous fart. The sound and subsequent odor of deathly decay elicited a barrage of groans and curses.

"From which pit of hell does that come, Peter?" Abe Price demanded. "We have had only a mouthful of rice and a splash of vinegar in the past two days, and still your bowels manage to produce such foulness. It defies the laws of nature!"

Peter chuckled menacingly. "There are plenty more from whence that one came."

The men groaned with disgust. The sudden swaying of their blanket door, and an unexpected invasion of cold air from outside the shelter, interrupted their soldierly discussions of flatulence.

"Who is ready for Christmas dinner?" announced Michael Yeisley.

The men cheered and sat up in excitement. Michael crawled through the makeshift door and then closed the curtain behind him. He carried a small iron pot in his right hand.

"Is it stewed beef?" Conrad queried wishfully. "I am starved!"

Michael groaned. "How I wish! No, old friend. There is no beef to be had. It is the same as last night, I am afraid. Rice and vinegar."

The men groaned in disappointment.

"What? No plum pudding?" Abraham teased. "Don't they know it is Christmas Day?"

Michael chuckled at his friend's unshakable spirit and humor. "This is the only food available to the entire army ... for now, at least. And there is only enough for one cup per man. The vinegar is already mixed in."

"Where, in Heaven's Name, did they find rice in Pennsylvania?" Abe marveled.

"You know! I have been thinking exactly the same thing," Michael replied. "Cracked wheat, or even maize, would make so much more sense."

"Do you have coffee or tea?" Conrad inquired innocently.

"Where would you suppose that Michael Yeisley might find coffee or tea?" Abe scolded. "Do you think he should pull a brick of tea and a pot from his arse? I swear, Conrad Traywitz! You are an incomparable idiot."

"I was just asking," the chastised boy mumbled.

The men quickly fumbled through their haversacks and bags to locate their bowls and spoons. Michael expertly and efficiently dispensed identical amounts of sour rice into each soldier's chosen receptacle.

"Eat it slowly, boys," He urged. "Make it last. Lord knows when our next meal might come."

The men munched hungrily on the partially-cooked grain. Despite Michael's warning, they wolfed it down quickly. Such was their hunger and discomfort. Once done, they licked their bowls and spoons clean and returned them to their bags.

"Is there any news from the outside?" Eberhard inquired after the meal.

"Yes, there is." Michael paused dramatically. "Captain Weiser will not be returning."

The men exploded simultaneously, "What?"

"He has resigned his commission," Michael explained. "There has been a multitude of resignations amongst the officers. Many of those who have not resigned have returned to their homes, supposedly to recruit new soldiers for their companies or regiments. Most likely they are simply seeking to escape the winter encampment."

"Do you think Captain Weiser has turned coward on us?" Abe pondered.

Michael shook his head. "No, I believe his health is bad. You recall how ill he became after that final river crossing. I refuse to believe that anything other than sickness is his cause. But, whatever the case, I hold no ill will against him. He went home to recuperate, and likely is enjoying the comforts of his own hearth and bed."

"And his own wife," Abraham added jealously.

Michael nodded. "No doubt."

"So, what do we do now?" Conrad wondered out loud. "Who is in charge?"

"Jacob Cramer is in command of the company for now. Technically, we are considered a 'vacant' company because we have no captain. They may promote him. Or, they may not. Who can know what the army will do?"

"Lieutenant Cramer is a good lad," declared Private John Portner. "He will look out for us."

"I believe he will. Now, make room!" Michael demanded. He crawled into his regular spot between Abe and Eberhard. He snuggled deep into his nest of old blankets, scrap cloths, and grass.

A silence nearing contentment descended upon the hut as the men delighted in their semi-full bellies and the warmth provided by their shared body heat. They were each on the edge of sleep when Michael suddenly breathed deeply, then gagged and exclaimed, "What is that detestable smell?"

Their explosion of laughter echoed throughout the snow-blanketed encampment.

⁓

9:00 PM – Christmas Evening
Philadelphia

THE CITY WAS STRANGELY silent and undeniably beautiful beneath its thick coating of fresh winter snow. The recent heavy snows and frigid temperatures enticed most of the city's population to remain indoors near their warm stoves and fires. Nicklaus only hoped that it had kept the customary nightly British patrols inside, as well.

Nicklaus had never fancied himself a spy or an insurgent. But, being a prisoner in English-controlled Philadelphia had forced him to learn some new skills. He mastered his tradecraft quickly. As it turned out, Nicklaus was becoming a rather adept spy and smuggler, despite the fact that the British penalty for both activities was death. Of course, the Redcoats were not hesitant to dispense such justice. Already, almost a dozen men throughout Philadelphia, some guilty and some not so, had perished by military firing squad. Nicklaus did not desire to share their fate. So, he remained silent and hid himself carefully in the shadows.

The street lamps were not yet illuminated in the southern sector of the city. It was the perfect location for Nicklaus to meet his contact in the resistance. He desperately needed medicines, primarily elixir of paregoric. He required that particular drug to treat the rampant diarrhea on his ward. Some laudanum or other similar elixir of opium for pain would be a most welcomed bonus. Since the British would provide neither for the so-called "rebels," Nicklaus had to resort to doing business in the relatively new, but thriving, black market. That newly-established method of commerce had become somewhat synonymous with the rebel resistance movement. Though the suppliers of the illegally-obtained goods considered themselves Patriots, they still required payment, preferably in the form of silver or gold. And, as with all such illegal markets, their prices were significantly inflated and quite outrageous.

Nicklaus also hoped to glean some information from his contact regarding the situation outside the city. Not knowing what was occurring in the American prosecution of the war was torturing him. His mind burned with questions: *Where were George Washington and his army encamped? What was their condition? Was the army even intact? Had they won any victories? Were there any plans for prisoner exchange? How might he be reunited with his regiment?*

Nicklaus pondered his growing list of questions as he concealed himself behind a large, snow-covered wooden crate, just inside the entrance to a narrow alleyway. He was at the agreed-upon rendezvous point. He had been waiting for almost an hour to meet his supplier. The man was extremely late. Nicklaus was somewhat disturbed by the fact that the fellow, like most black marketeers, was also doing business with the British. He was beginning to wonder if the man could truly be trusted.

As the minutes dragged on, his level of stress increased. He feared that the entire arrangement was nothing but a trap. He could not risk waiting much longer. The lamplighter would be along within minutes, as would the next scheduled British patrol. If his contact did not arrive soon, Nicklaus would have to make his escape through the rear of the alley and somehow make his way back home.

He was just on the verge of departing when he heard a low two-tone whistle. He froze. He stared intently into the dark, empty lot across the street. A man's head appeared between two bushes. Nicklaus recognized the fellow's left-tilting Monmouth cap. It was his contact, Isaac Harmon. Nicklaus snapped his fingers three times ... the agreed-upon countersign. The fellow darted between the bushes and silently crossed the cobblestones. He dived behind the crate, joining Nicklaus.

Mr. Harmon shucked off his glove and extended his naked right hand. He nodded and grinned his customary toothy grin. He whispered, "Dr. Schell, I trust you are well."

"As well as a man can be in this horrid cold," Nicklaus retorted. "You're late."

"It could not be avoided. I encountered three patrols on my way here. I had to wait for quite some time for one of them to move away from me. One of the men in the patrol has the flux. He spent quite a while in the alleyway where I was hiding." Isaac shook his head and exhibited a look of disgust. "I did not know that a human being could shite so much and with such a foul presentation."

"The flux and other sicknesses of the bowels are becoming common in the city. I fear that it is going to get much worse. My hospital is badly afflicted. Which begs the question ... did you bring the paregoric for me?"

"I did, indeed." The man reached into the large leather satchel on his side and removed two green, onion-shaped bottles. Their stoppers were covered with a protective coating of wax.

"What about the laudanum?"

Mr. Harmon shook his head. "There is none to be found, Dr. Schell. But, now that the harbor forts have fallen, we are beginning to receive more supply ships from York City. I am expecting a shipment on Tuesday. My man in the English depot should be able to procure at least one case."

"We had an agreement!" Nicklaus hissed.

"And I intend to fulfill it, Dr. Schell. But, surely you know that I cannot produce opium out of thin air! When I get the product, you will get the product." He paused and held up the bottles. "Do you still want this elixir?"

"Of course." Nicklaus exhaled in disgust.

"Then I shall require payment."

Nicklaus reached inside the pocket of his coat and produced a small gold ring. He offered it to the smuggler.

Harmon eyed the ring skeptically. "This is not quite the volume of gold that I was expecting. You mentioned a brooch."

"Now you know how it feels to have unmet expectations," Nicklaus retorted. "I suppose that we will both return home a little disappointed tonight. That ring is a fair trade for the paregoric. When you deliver the laudanum, you will be reimbursed accordingly."

Harmon grabbed the ring from Nicklaus. He popped it into his mouth and bit down on the soft gold. He removed the ring and examined the marks left by his teeth. His low-pitch grunt revealed his satisfaction. Harmon handed Nicklaus the bottles. He carefully wrapped each one in a cloth and placed them inside his linen haversack. As he did so, he peppered the man with questions.

"Do you have the information that I requested? What of Washington's army? Where is the winter encampment?"

Harmon glanced both ways along the street, checking to make sure that they remained undiscovered. He nodded. "It took some doing, but I managed to find out a few things. The British seem intent upon keeping Washington's location a secret. I think they are worried that local citizens may make attempts to furnish supplies and relief for his army."

"Where are they?" Nicklaus demanded impatiently.

"Washington has about 10,000 men encamped twenty miles to the west. They are close to a small village along the Schuylkill called Valley Forge."

"Is Hartley's Regiment there?"

"I have no idea what regiments are there. I doubt that the British know, either. All I have for you is the location. They arrived there about a week ago. It appears that everyone is settling in for the winter."

Nicklaus was greatly disappointed. He wanted, more than anything, to locate Colonel Hartley and his regiment. But the limited information gleaned from his smuggler-friend would have to suffice.

"Same time, same place, Wednesday next?" Mr. Harmon suggested. "Perhaps I can have some more news for you then."

Nicklaus shook his head vigorously. "I need a rendezvous closer to the hospital. This is almost a mile from my home. Troops are crawling all over the city. It will take me two hours to make my way back tonight."

"Where, then?"

"There is an empty lot on Chestnut Street, three blocks north of the hospital."

Harmon nodded slowly. "I think I know the place. Beside the silversmith shop?"

"That is the one. There is an old shed in the rear of the lot that will provide a much more secretive meeting place. It is further from the British barracks and a much safer option for both of us."

"Very well, then. I will see you next week."

"Make sure you have my laudanum," Nicklaus warned.

"I will do my very best, Dr. Schell. If there is a problem, I will see that you get a message through our agreed-upon method."

Nicklaus nodded. "I will watch the Gazette."

The sound of shoes munching through snow echoed down the dark street. They heard voices ... British voices. An army patrol was coming! Isaac Harmon wasted no time at all. He departed without a farewell. He sprinted across the street and down the alleyway. Nicklaus watched him disappear into the darkness. He checked his elixir bottles to make sure they were wrapped and protected sufficiently. He was just about to make his own escape when he realized that it was too late. The British troops were already upon him.

"What's this?" exclaimed one of the Englishmen. "Sergeant, have a look! There are footprints in the snow!"

Nicklaus peeked from behind the corner of the crate. He counted four men. All were armed with muskets and dressed in heavy winter cloaks. It was a typical military patrol. The sergeant stepped forward and looked at the tracks in the snow.

"So?" he chided. "This is a by-God city, Private Fleming. There are thousands of people living hereabouts. Why should one be surprised to find footprints in the street?"

"But, Sergeant, these appear fresh."

"Oh! So, you are an expert tracker now, are you?" teased the sergeant. The other men of the patrol chuckled. "Your two months in the Colonies has made you into a real frontiersman, has it? Perhaps we should send you out to the Illinois Country to serve amongst the savages."

"I am merely informing you that there are some fresh prints in the street, and they are heading in an odd direction." He pointed toward the alley. "Perhaps we should investigate."

Nicklaus could feel his heart racing wildly. He was so very close to being discovered. He prayed fervently that the soldiers would continue on their way.

"Indeed. We should investigate," the sergeant declared. "We will pursue these mysterious footprints for a short distance. Perhaps, they will lead us to a warm brothel."

Again, the other two soldiers chuckled. One of them remarked, "If that's the case, then I say we check them out. I could use me a little bit of special warming of my members on this cold, snowy night."

"You mean, your 'member,' do you not?" quipped the other man.

All four soldiers howled with laughter.

"Let us go, then" the sergeant declared. "Perhaps Private Fleming is onto something. It is worth a look. There is certainly nothing else exciting occurring in Philadelphia tonight."

The four-man patrol turned and entered the alleyway where Mr. Harmon had made his escape. Nicklaus breathed a sigh of relief. He waited until the enemy soldiers had reached the far end of the alley before he made his move. He leapt from behind the crate and ran westward along the narrow thoroughfare. He was just about to turn the corner onto Poplar Street when he heard the shriek of a voice from far behind him.

"Halt! Identify yourself!"

Nicklaus lowered his head and willed himself to move faster. It was difficult to run on the slick snow. His leather-bottomed buckle shoes skidded and slipped in the ice. He felt perspiration erupt from his brow. It instantly soaked the fur felt of his cocked hat.

Suddenly, he heard the report of a musket, followed by a scorching burn on the left side of his neck. His silk neck sock ripped away from his flesh as a spray of bloody mist painted the snow in front of him. Nicklaus reached up instantly and placed his hand over the searing pain. A fine trickle of blood oozed from between his fingers. The injury did not feel deep. Nicklaus was convinced that it was only a superficial wound.

He continued running. Turning right, he sprinted into an empty lot between some two-story brick homes. There was a fence at the back of the lot. Spotting a tall stump to his left, he ran toward it.

Jumping onto the stump, he grabbed onto the top of the fence and vaulted over. His knees buckled slightly as he landed heavily on his frozen feet. After regaining his balance, he scanned left and right. The street was abandoned. The popular avenue had been heavily traveled during the previous day's hours of business. Knowing that his footprints would blend easily in the trampled, filthy snow, he turned to his right and ran toward home. Nicklaus disappeared into the darkness, leaving the frustrated, shouting soldiers far behind.

KATHARINA AND ELSPETH listened nervously to the commotion outside. The entire area seemed to be crawling with British troops. Both women peered through the apartment window, attempting to discern the cause of all the activity.

"Surely, they are not after Nicklaus," Elspeth wished out loud.

"Let us hope not," Katharina declared. She smiled at the young girl. "But, even if they are, they will not catch him. My boy is far too cunning for these daft soldiers."

"But, I thought I heard an explosion," Elspeth countered worriedly. "It sounded like a musket."

A faint knock sounded at the door. Both women jumped at the unexpected noise. It was a single tap, then a pause, followed by four rapid taps. It was their secret signal.

"He has returned!" Elspeth darted toward the entryway. She released the lock and threw open the door. She gasped when she saw Nicklaus, his blood-stained hand pressed against his neck.

"Oh, my God! Nicklaus! You are hurt!"

"No! He has been shot!" wailed Katharina.

"Calm down, ladies! And please be quiet! We do not want to alert the British," Nicklaus urged. He stepped through the door and then closed it quickly behind him. He patted his mother reassuringly on the back with his unoccupied hand. "'Tis only a scratch, *Mutter*. I am quite all right. The bleeding is superficial."

"I will be the judge of that," Katharina declared. "Sit!"

"What is that odd smell?" Elspeth demanded.

"It is oil of camphor ... part of the tincture of paregoric. Quick! Fetch another bottle. One of them must have cracked whilst I was running. We must not waste a single drop of the medicine."

While Katharina removed the ragged silk wrap from her son's neck, Elspeth ran to a cabinet in the kitchen and retrieved an empty wine bottle. Nicklaus handed her both bottles of the contraband elixir. She ascertained which one was broken and then performed a quick transfer to the new receptacle.

"He is right," Katharina declared, relieved. "It is a surface wound. It gouged the skin and muscle, but hit no blood vessels."

"That is what I told you, *Mutter*."

"Still," she replied, "It will make a frightful scar. And the wound may be difficult to conceal whilst we are on duty at the hospital."

"I do not plan on remaining at the hospital for much longer," Nicklaus declared resolutely.

"Whatever do you mean?" his mother demanded.

Nicklaus gazed into her eyes with a stare of conviction. "Washington's army is encamped for the winter only twenty miles to the west, near a place called Valley Forge. I plan on making my escape and rejoining my regiment."

"But, what of your patients?" his mother demanded. "Who will care for them?"

"The British will see to their care. They are not uncivilized."

A tear formed in Elspeth's eye. "And what about us? Will the British care for us, as well?"

Nicklaus reached out and cupped her beautiful face with his right hand. "*Nein, mein Liebling*. The army will be in dire need of nurses. I plan to take both of you with me."

17

FAMILY

January 4, 1778
Continental Encampment - Valley Forge

Michael despised overnight guard duty. He could discern little of value in the nightly enterprise. It was nothing more than six hours of mind-numbing darkness and boredom. And it was cold. Damned cold.

The knoll upon which the Muhlenberg Brigade's redoubt perched was one of the most exposed crests in the entire region. It provided an uninhibited view of the countryside and two of the major roads that approached the encampment, but the place was so very windswept, desolate, and cold. The stark absence of trees allowed the winds to howl, unabated, across the barren hilltop.

The landscape had not always been so devoid of vegetation. Indeed, the scenery had changed quite dramatically in the past two weeks. The entire area had once been carpeted in tall, thick timber. Now, however, after the rapid construction of over 1,000 log shelters for the army, there was not a tree to be found for almost three miles in any direction. In the purple-blue glow of the pre-dawn light, the

ocean of stumps and discarded limbs created an other-worldly, apoc-
alyptic landscape.

Besides the bone-chilling cold, the other hardship of standing
guard was the torture of solitude. Hours of inactivity and quiet left a
man with nothing to entertain himself other than his own thoughts
and memories. Michael's mind always transported him back home.
He retreated mentally to those happiest of days when he played bliss-
fully with his little girls. He remembered those cherished late nights
marked by pipes brimming with tobacco, competitive games of chess,
and deep conversations with his father-in-law, Heinrich. He lost
himself in the bliss of the intimacy that he once enjoyed with his
young, beautiful bride. Sometimes, the memories of Magdalena's
delicious taste, sweet scent, and warm touch were almost more than
he could bear.

Without doubt, the stark boredom of standing guard in the crude
fort was nothing short of agonizing. Ordinarily, nothing of signifi-
cance ever occurred. This particular night, however, had proven an
exception to the boredom rule. At long last, Michael would have an
interesting guard duty tale to share with his hut-mates.

Shortly after midnight, he had been horrified to detect the
thumping of footfalls on the roadway. Being almost certain that an
army was approaching, he sounded the alarm, rousing the men in the
nearest huts from their sleep. Three dozen drowsy soldiers deployed
immediately to the redoubt, pointing their muskets eastward and
manning the cannons.

Then, curiously, a lone woman appeared in the moonlight along
the muddy Ring Road, driving a herd of twenty noisy heifers toward
the encampment. Amazingly, the benevolent woman had guided the
animals all the way from the outskirts of Philadelphia. She simply
wanted to do her patriotic duty and help feed the army. The sleepy
soldiers welcomed her as a hero.

Michael immediately sent a runner to the quartermaster's headquarters and then allowed the intrepid woman to pass through the
gate. The officer in charge of the procurement of livestock, angry at
first for being awakened after midnight, became ecstatic at the news

of fresh meat in the camp. The stricken animals were delivered immediately to a temporary holding pen. A short time later, they were distributed amongst the brigades, butchered, and prepared. In all likelihood, the meat was already stewing in the regimental pots.

Twenty cows would not go very far amongst 12,000 men. But, mixed with ample water and thickened with flour, rice, or ground maize, the fatty beef would provide everyone in the camp with a much-needed portion of protein. Michael's mouth watered at the prospect of the coming noon-day meal.

Sadly, however, the night's excitement was finished. Cold and boredom had returned with a vengeance. Michael shivered as he pulled his thin, weathered wool blanket tighter beneath his chin. The lonely soldier sat, cross-legged, atop the wall of the easternmost redoubt on the outer perimeter of the Valley Forge encampment. From the neck down he enshrouded his entire body beneath his blanket, forming the curious appearance of a small, woolen tent.

Michael had been forced to craft a homemade garment to protect his cheeks and ears from the biting wind. He cut a strip of wool from the remnants of an old blanket and wrapped it around his head, binding it in a bulky knot beneath his chin. He secured his old, weathered cocked hat in place with a narrow leather thong. He even added an extra layer of protection to his hands by sewing a set of wool mittens, cut from the same tattered blanket that provided his ear wrap.

Despite all of his efforts at weatherizing, and the humble camp-fire that burned beside him, Michael was still freezing from the bitter cold. His threadbare linen hunting frock was not a suitable winter-weather garment. He longed for one of the wool coats worn by the men of the Connecticut and New York regiments. But, the notion of such a lovely, warm garment seemed nothing more than a fantasy for a humble member of the German Regiment.

As cold as Michael was, he realized that he was more adequately dressed than roughly half of the other men at Valley Forge. At least he owned a pair of stockings and some serviceable shoes. There were many who possessed neither. Indeed, there were a handful of poor souls in the camp who wore only a linen shirt and nothing more. They did not even have a set of breeches. Those pitiful men never left their huts and rarely left their bunks. Michael shuddered at the thought of suffering nakedness in the face of winter's numbing cold.

He stared sleepily down the deserted road in the direction of Philadelphia. There was no movement on the highway. It was too early for the local farmers to be out doing their daily business. No armies of soldiers clad in red tunics appeared. It seemed that the British were no more itching for a fight than were the Continentals. The battles were done for the season. Hopefully, it would be many months before combat resumed. Still, just in case, the soldiers of Washington's army had to occupy their redoubts and stand vigil over all of the approaches to Valley Forge.

"Anything to report?"

Michael jumped at the unexpected invasion of Conrad's voice into his world of thoughtful solitude. He angled his cold, stiff neck and observed his friend walking through the row of earth-filled gabions that lined the entryway into the fort.

Conrad grinned mischievously and pointed toward one of the cannons perched idly in front of its firing hole. He teased, "You did not use the artillery last night?"

Michael grinned back. "You *do* realize that I know shite about firing that thing. The contraption doesn't even have a frizzen."

Conrad chuckled and walked near to the place where Michael was sitting. He leaned comfortably against the chest-high wall and peered toward the east. Both men remained silent for a few moments.

"You are early," Michael declared. "I was not expecting you until later."

"I could not sleep. I was bored."

"Bored? Then, you have definitely come to the wrong place."

"Well, I had to do something in order to escape Peter's noxious bowels. Our hut smells worse than the First Virginia's latrine."

Michael laughed. "There is certainly plenty of fresh air on this barren hilltop!" He sighed, and then gently rubbed his aching jaw.

"Does your wound still trouble you?"

"The cold causes it to ache sometimes. Otherwise, I think little of it." He grinned mischievously and countered, "Does yours? How is your arse these days?"

"Still functioning. At least, I think it is. We have not eaten in so long, I cannot be certain."

Michael laughed. "That may change soon. Did you hear about the beef?"

"*Everyone* has heard about the beef. We received ten pounds at regiment just as I was leaving to come up here. The cooks are mad with joy."

"That is not very much," Michael observed, somewhat in disbelief.

"There are not many of us left in the regiment to feed," Conrad declared. "We were lucky to receive as much as we did."

Michael sighed. "Well, they certainly wasted no time skinning the poor critters."

"'Tis a fact."

Conrad leaned his musket against the wall and retrieved his clay pipe from the ties on his hat. He then removed the hat and took a small, cloth sack out of the liner. Michael immediately detected the unmistakable scent of fragrant tobacco. His eyes grew wide.

"Where did you get that?"

Conrad grinned. "Do you remember that old set of stag horns I found on patrol last week?"

"Barely."

Conrad placed a pinch of the tobacco into his pipe. "Well, in my spare time, I carved a spoon from the main beam. It turned out pretty nice. I traded it this morning to a sergeant from the 3rd Virginia ... a fellow by the name of William Mallory. It seems he needed a new spoon, and I needed a smoke. I received three ounces of dark Virginia leaf for that little spoon."

"That was a fine trade," Michael declared jealously.

Conrad nodded. "I thought so. As it turns out, Sergeant Mallory is in need of a pipe, as well. He broke his old one a few days ago. I have promised to carve him one from that same set of antlers. One of the forks turns perfectly off of the main beam. It will make a very nice pipe, indeed."

"You should be able to get a goodly amount of tobacco for such a valuable item."

"Oh, I plan to."

He reached toward Michael's fire and retrieved a small stick that was smoldering on one end. He inserted the glowing coal into the bowl of his pipe and drew deeply. After a few puffs, he offered the pipe to Michael.

"This should help warm you up just a bit."

Michael received the pipe with gratitude. He inserted the stem between his teeth and drew the warm, sweet smoke into his mouth. He allowed it to linger on his tongue for just a moment, then circulated the delicious, white cloud into the back of his throat and then slowly out through his nostrils. He savored the initial bitter bite of the leaf and the sweet, sugary taste that it left behind in his mouth. He enjoyed two more identical puffs and then handed the pipe back to its owner.

"I am grateful, Conrad. That was a pleasure, indeed."

"You are most welcome, old friend. But, let us keep it our little secret. If word gets out that I have found some tobacco, the fellows will pester me, for certain. We can enjoy a bowl up here in the redoubt, on occasion."

Michael nodded. "Agreed." He pondered. "I suppose I need to think of a skill that I might bring to this little industry of yours. The army seems uninterested in providing for us. We must better our own lots in this God-forsaken place."

Conrad declared confidently, "You are a smart fellow. You will think of something to create some income during our sojourn here."

There was a long period of silence as the men smoked and maintained watch over the road.

Conrad inhaled a deep, thoughtful breath. "Abe is very sick, you know."

"He will be fine. He just needs to rest and stay warm."

"I am not so certain, Michael. His fever is bad. And he has been uttering strange things. I believe he is outside his mind. He also began to vomit during the night. I had to fetch a piggin to place beside his bunk. Everything is quite the mess inside our hut this morning."

Michael shot a disturbed glance at Conrad. "He should be in a surgeon's care."

His friend shook his head. "I could not wish that upon old Abe. *No one* wants to go to the hospital. Most who go there do so simply to die. The ones who live come back naked. The men who are supposed to care for the sick steal their clothing, instead, and then sell it. And when the ill die, the same plunderers rob their bodies of anything that has value."

"These are desperate times," Michael declared. "Men will do anything in order to eat. Everyone needs food and clothing. Many need medicine."

Conrad nodded grimly. "What we need is a hospital here in our regimental area. There is some talk that General Washington has ordered the construction of small hospitals for each brigade."

"That seems sensible."

"But, we do not even have a surgeon in any of the regiments in Muhlenberg's Brigade. What good would a hospital be to us?" Conrad seemed most pessimistic.

"The army will find us a surgeon," Michael declared confidently.

"The army couldn't find a pair of whore's diddeys in a French brothel," Conrad retorted. "I can trade for tobacco to smoke but cannot find a mouthful of bread. It is one damnable, sorry set of circumstances." He exhaled in frustration. "We are fools to remain here."

"Are you thinking of deserting?" Michael demanded in disbelief.

"It would be lying to say that it had not crossed my mind."

"You have not always been so dour, Conrad. Only two weeks ago, you were filled with humor and hope. What has happened to the jolly lad that I once knew?"

"This place has changed me, I suppose. I am tired of being hungry. And I grow weary of watching my friends suffer." He paused.

"I now regret returning to the army with you. I should have remained dead. It seems that we are all dead men, anyway."

In the distance, they observed a farmer guiding his wagon from a side road onto the highway. The wagon appeared to be piled high with goods. The load was covered by a tan-colored cloth tarpaulin. The man pointed his rig toward the east and rode into the rising sun.

"Just look at that bastard! We are starving to death in this encampment, and there he goes, carting his jolly arse to Philadelphia to sell his goods to our enemies. If I had one of those Virginian's rifles, I might put a ball in his skull."

"Maybe you should trade for one," Michael teased.

"That would require an abundance of pipes. I will definitely need more antlers." Conrad grinned.

"Now, *there* is the Conrad Traywitz that I once knew." Michael withdrew his mitten-covered hand from beneath his protective blanket and patted his friend's shoulder. "Do not lose your hope, Conrad."

"I am trying, Michael. It just seems that hope is all we have left. And there is little of it to spare."

Near Schippach Township, Pennsylvania

IT WAS ALMOST DUSK. The temperature was dropping quickly. Magdalena had to find a place of refuge for her girls, and soon. The little ones could not endure the chill of a January night out of doors. And, to complicate matters, she was utterly lost. Though they had covered many miles and traveled well throughout the day, Magdalena was unsure if they were even headed in the right direction. She and her girls were negotiating unfamiliar roads. She could only hope that her limited sense of direction had not failed her.

"*Mutter*, I am cold," whined Mary.

Magdalena glanced at her little girl. The child lay buried, with only her face exposed, in the bed of the wagon beneath a mound of blankets and hay. Her tiny lips were almost purple, and her plump, dimpled chin quivered from the frigid air.

"I know, sweet baby. We are all very cold. Snuggle tightly amongst your sisters. We shall find a place to stay for the night very soon."

She wanted desperately to demonstrate certainty and assurance for her girls. But, as the light of day yielded to darkness, she found that her own confidence was waning. She was beginning to wonder if she had made a horrible mistake in traveling during the winter. There was not a town, or even a house, anywhere in sight. There were only dense, untouched forests, punctuated by the occasional dormant meadow. Truly, their prospects of locating lodging for the night were grim.

Magdalena Yeisley and her children were homeless and penniless. They had lost everything in the Tory attack. Once her father's remains were laid to rest, Magdalena had taken the only option available to her. She returned to the home of her mother and father-in-law, Nicklaus and Julianna Yeisley. But, after almost a week crammed into their tiny cottage, her pride would not allow her to remain another day. It was entirely too apparent that she and the five boisterous girls, despite how much their grandparents adored them, were a burdensome disruption in the older couple's lives. They were also consuming entirely too much of their hard-earned winter food storage.

So, Magdalena decided to depart and go in search of the army's winter encampment. She heard rumors that it was located a few miles to the west of Philadelphia. She hoped that she might be reunited with her husband there and find a place of service as a camp follower. Despite the objections of *Opa* Nicklaus and *Oma* Julianna, Magdalena packed their meager belongings into the family wagon and headed south. That was almost twelve hours ago. They had been traveling since daybreak. The girls were all cold, hungry, and exhausted. They needed to stop and rest for the night.

"*Mutter*, should I be watching for a good place to camp?" inquired Elizabeth, her oldest daughter.

"*Ja, mein Liebling*. I suppose so. We may have no other option."

She smiled reassuringly at the child. "We will have to practice our fire-making skills."

"I will keep watch, then. If we can start a fire, we will be fine, *Mutter*. We can sleep beneath the wagon." The little girl sounded supremely confident.

"*Ja*. We can do that." Her child's confidence was somewhat infectious.

They continued southward down the narrow roadway. About a quarter-hour later, Elizabeth spied a clearing beneath a stand of tall pine trees on the western side of the trail. There was a small pond, actually little more than a large puddle, toward the southern end of the opening within the trees.

"What of this place, *Mutter*? Will it suffice?"

"*Ja*. It will have to," her mother declared, surveying the spot. "There is ample water. Let us stop and make our camp here for the night."

She guided the team just off of the roadway and into the edge of the tiny clearing. Elizabeth vaulted from the wagon before Magdalena even reached a full stop. The energetic little girl ran toward the pond and leaned over to examine the water.

"It looks clear, *Mutter*!" she declared joyfully.

"We will still need to boil it, first. Come and help me with your sisters. I will get to work on a fire."

She noticed that Elizabeth was not obeying her direction. The child was walking, instead, toward the back of the clearing. She stared intently into the woods beyond.

"Elizabeth! What are you doing? I asked you to help me!"

The little girl ignored her and continued to peer toward the west.

"Elizabeth! Come here, child!"

Her daughter responded excitedly, "*Mutter*, there are wagon tracks back here! And I see a light deep in the woods! There must be a house!"

Magdalena could not see any light. She struggled to stand so that she might get a better look. She gripped the back of the wagon seat and pushed herself upward. Her swollen ankles and feet felt as if they might burst open. Once she was standing, she, too, saw it. There was just the faintest hint of light far to the west, somewhere beyond the trees. It appeared that the tiny wagon trail led in the direction of that distant light.

"Come, Elizabeth!" she commanded urgently. "Get back in the wagon. There is a house. We *must* go!"

FINALLY, the mysterious dwelling beyond the woods came into view. It was a rather large, two-story stone house. There were several stone outbuildings, as well. In a nearby pen there stood a half-dozen snorting, staring, curious horses. Inside the house several candles burned, illuminating the windows with their soft, yellow, dancing glow. Magdalena's heart pounded with anticipation. Surely, these people would allow them a place to stay until morning.

A man's unexpected, gruff voice invaded the quiet of the early evening. "Halt! Turn zat vagon around *und* be on your vay."

Magdalena pulled gently on the reins and coaxed the team of horses to stop. She did not move. She merely stared into the darkness toward the direction of the mysterious voice. She heard the dull click of a flintlock's hammer being pulled into the cocked position.

The thickly German voice growled, "Do not make me repeat myself!"

"*Bitte, der Herr.* I am a woman, traveling alone with small children. We merely seek shelter for the night."

"Zerr is no room for you here! Now, do as I have commanded. Turn zat rig around *und* leave. Now!"

"*Bitte!* Do not turn us away! My little girls are so very cold. The youngest is barely two years old. She may perish out here in the cold night." She began to weep.

"You should have thought about that before you began your travels. Your husband must be a fool, indeed, to allow you on zie road alone. Now, go back home!"

"But, sir ... I am traveling in search of my husband. He is with the

Continental Army, somewhere to the south. Our home was destroyed by Loyalists last month. We have nothing but our clothing and this team and wagon. We intend to join the camp followers and remain with the army. Please, sir. We are desperate for assistance."

Magdalena sensed a moment of hesitation. She dared to entertain the faintest glimmer of hope.

The guttural voice responded, "I am truly sorry about your circumstance, Madam. But, I have no room for you here."

Suddenly, a woman's shrill voice intervened in the confrontation.

"Herman Kleinschmidt! Are you sincerely going to turn zis poor child *und* her *Kinder* out into zie cold night? Put zat gun avay, you moron, before you harm yourself!"

An elderly woman wearing traditional German clothing stepped out of the darkness of the porch. She walked toward the wagon, her arms outstretched in the universal posture of welcome.

"Child, come down from zat vagon, immediately. *Und* bring your leetle ones inside. I shall see all of you varmed *und* fed."

Magdalena began to cry tears of joy and relief.

"Now, now! No need for all zie tears," the woman declared. "Just hop on down *und* let us get you into zie varm house."

"*Danke*, Madam," Magdalena declared, a lump of emotion in her throat.

"Call me Helga. I am Helga Kleinschmidt. Zie moron vith zie unloaded Jaeger gun is my husband, Herman. Vorry not. He vill do you no harm."

"I am Magdalena Yeisely. These are my daughters." She grabbed hold of the side rail and seat back and began her customary bodily contortions that were necessary in order for her to stand. Helga's eyes spread open wide when she saw the size of Magdalena's belly.

"Herman! Bring your useless self over here *und* help zis girl down! She is great vith child!"

Her husband shuffled from his place of concealment in the darkness and joined her by the wagon. He reached up and took Magdalena by the hand and then assisted her to the ground. Helga quickly began unloading the girls from the back of the wagon. She soon appeared around the corner of the rig, balancing one-year-old Eva on her left hip and guiding two-year-old Barbara by the hand.

"Come inside, ladies. I have a pot of lamb stew on zie stove *und* plenty of fresh rye bread." She paused and glared at her husband. "Herman, you shall take care of her team *und* vagon. *Und* vile you are doing so, I vant you to contemplate a suitable vay to apologize to zees leetle girls."

The old fellow stared, ashamed, as his feet.

"*Ja, Mutter.*"

"Do not stand idle! Be quick about it!"

As he turned toward the horses, again he groaned, "*Ja, Mutter.*"

Magdalena smiled, somewhat embarrassed. She was reasonably confident that the henpecked old fellow was quite accustomed to doing as he was told.

THE FIVE YEISLEY girls slept peacefully and soundly in front of the stone fireplace. They lay together on a fluffy pallet of blankets. The flickering firelight reflected off their shiny hair, casting an angelic glow about them. Elizabeth lay in the middle, flat on her back, with arms outstretched. The four younger girls were all snuggled against her, two on each side, enclosed within her protective arms. The dozing children were the picture of contentment.

Magdalena sipped her steaming hot tea and pondered their predicament. As she observed her children sleeping in a warm, safe environment, she offered a prayer of thanksgiving for the Kleinschmidts. Helga and Herman had been wonderful hosts, indeed. They graciously welcomed the Yeisleys into their home without question or condition. They doted fondly over her daughters and fed them all most generously. They prepared the pallets for sleeping and ample covers to keep them warm. The Kleinschmidt home was an oasis of generosity and peace in the midst of Magdalena's world of anguish, confusion, and loss.

Helga placed two more soft, crumbly butter cookies on Magdalena's dessert plate. "Eat some more, child. You must feed zat hungry baby inside you."

"*Danke.* But, I do not think I can eat another bite." Magdalena smiled gratefully and pushed the plate away.

"Very vell. But, you must take zem to your bedchamber. I remember zie hunger zat comes during zie night ven one is carrying a child."

"*Danke*, Helga. I will take them to my room. I do, indeed, get hungry at night."

"*Bitte*, my dear. You are most velcome. Now ... zie little ones are sleeping. You must tell us more about zis predicament of yours. You said zat your husband does not even know you are vith child?" Helga sat down across from Magdalena and rested her chin on her hands. Her eyes were filled with curiosity and question.

Magdalena inhaled deeply. She knew that this moment had to come. The Kleinschmidts had been both patient and understanding. They had wisely reserved their questions until the children slept. They certainly deserved an explanation of the circumstances that had brought Magdalena and her girls into their home and lives.

Once she began, the entire story poured out of her. She told them everything, beginning with Michael's respite at home after escaping from the enemy. She explained, tearfully, how their house had been invaded and destroyed on Christmas Day by Canadian Loyalists. She sobbed as she described her father's murder at the hands of the Tories. She calmed down, somewhat, as she recounted the past two weeks of homelessness and confusion endured by her little girls.

"So, now, you are planning to follow zie army?" Helga confirmed.

"*Ja.* I have no other choice really. My husband's family does not have the space for us in their tiny home or the supplies to sustain us all through the winter. We were more of a burden than they deserved to bear. It is our only option. I have heard that many women now follow the army. I assumed that I could do so, as well."

"*Ja.* But, I doubt zat many do so vith a half-dozen leetle ones," Herman interjected. "Most of zose vemmen are childless. *Und* I am told zat many are not attached, at all, to zie men of zie army. Zey are simply zere to provide ..." He paused and raised his eyebrows high. "Special services."

"*Und* how do you come to possess such knowledge, Herman Kleinschmidt?" his red-faced wife demanded.

His chin dropped in shame. "I have heard talk of it, Helga."

"Down at zat horrid pub, no doubt," she blurted. She stared, judgmentally, at Herman for a most uncomfortable period of time, and then returned her attention to Magdalena. "My husband is an idiot. But, he is right, my dear. Zie army is no place for leetle ones. I understand your need to find your husband *und* inform him of your situation *und* recent events. But, an army camp is no place for children. *Und* zat is particularly true of Valley Forge."

"Valley Forge?" Magdalena inquired, confused.

"Zat is zie small village nearest zie army camp," Herman explained. "It is about ten miles to our south on zie banks of zie Schuylkill."

"Then, I *am* headed in the right direction!" Magdalena responded, relieved.

Herman nodded. "*Ja*, you are. You do not have very far to travel. It is only a single day's ride from here. I have been considering a trip zere, myself."

"You have business at the encampment?" Magdalena inquired as she took another sip of her tea.

"*Nein*. Ve have no *business* there," Helga responded. "But ve do have a son in Vashington's Army. Ve have considered taking him some zings ... food, clothing, *und* elixirs. Ve have recently heard stories zat zie men are experiencing dire need."

"I was not aware that you had a son in the army."

Helga beamed with pride. "'Tis his own bedchamber zat you vill be sleeping in tonight. Ve long for him to return home *und* occupy it, himself. But, ve are most pleased zat you vill enjoy it in his stead." She reached toward her husband and took Herman's hand in her own. She eyed him proudly. "Our boy's name is Michael."

Magdalena gasped. "My husband's name is Michael!"

"Vell, zat is a vonderful coincidence, is it not?" Helga declared.

There was a glistening tear of joy in her eye. "Ve are most proud of our boy. He took part in zie victory at Trenton in '76 *und* has served faithfully since. Ve received a letter from him only zree days ago. He survived some horrible battles in zie defense of Philadelphia. He is now vintering in a horrible leetle cabin at Valley Forge."

"Is he in the Pennsylvania Line?" Magdalena inquired.

Herman shook his head. He announced proudly, "No. He is in Captain Daniel Burchardt's company in zie German Regiment."

Magdalena's heart skipped a beat. She stared, wide-eyed, at the kindly, elderly couple. Tears formed in both of her eyes and quickly escaped onto her cheeks.

"Vat is wrong, child?" Helga demanded.

"Nothing. Nothing is wrong." She wiped her tears with a linen napkin. "My Michael is also in the German Regiment. He is in Captain Weiser's company."

Helga's face erupted into a broad smile. "Zey are mates, then! Our Michael *und* your Michael surely know one another!"

"They must," Magdalena agreed.

The three of them were overwhelmed with joy. Suddenly, their connection became deeper that just their shared German heritage and culture. They were connected by a bond of patriotism and fraternity that only military families could understand. They were connected by the German Regiment.

Helga stared lovingly at her husband and smiled. He squeezed her hand firmly and nodded. She nodded back. Then, she gently reached across the table with her other hand and took hold of Magdalena's.

The older woman declared, "I have decided. My Herman vill deliver you to zie encampment tomorrow. He vill reunite you vith your husband. In zie meantime, your girls shall remain here vith me. Zie army camp is no place for them."

Magdalena objected, "But, I could never impose upon you in such a way."

"You have not imposed. I have offered. Your daughters are

velcome here for as long as zey need to stay. I do not care if it is for one veek or for zie entire duration of zie army's encampment."

Magdalena did not know what to say. Her heart was on the verge of bursting from joy. She had only met these people two hours ago, and yet she felt as if she had known them for a lifetime. Their bond was instantaneous and seemed deeper, even, than blood. It transcended understanding. Yet, it was real. It was profound. She could not explain it, but she trusted these people, even with the care of her daughters.

"I think that Elizabeth should go with me. She is almost eight years old and wise beyond her years. She has been quite the loyal helper throughout our times of trouble, especially during our journey. She would be very bitter and angry if I were to leave her behind."

Helga nodded slowly. "Zat may be vise. You vill need a helper, especially ven zie baby comes."

"That is what I was thinking. I have believed my time of delivery to still be several weeks away, but it feels as if it may come at any time."

"You have delivered five already," Helga grinned mischievously. "'Tis a vell-traveled pathvay for zie little one. You should birth vith ease."

"As well I know it. I thought that Elizabeth, my first, would never come. It felt as if she were going to tear me into halves. By the time I bore little Eva, my labor lasted no more than a half-hour. With this one, I am afraid to even sneeze, lest it should hop out on its own!"

The women chuckled joyfully. Herman's face flushed with embarrassment. He was not accustomed to being privy to such uncensored female conversations.

Helga squeezed Magdalena's hand. "Zen, ve are in agreement? Herman shall take you tomorrow?"

Magdalena smiled happily and nodded. "*Ja*. 'Tis a fine plan. Tomorrow, we go."

❧

Late Afternoon - January 5, 1778
Valley Forge

THE MEN inside the hut were in despair. They huddled around Abraham Price's bunk. His bed was on the lower level, immediately beside the fireplace. His mates placed him there after he became ill. They wanted him to glean as much warmth as possible from the meager fire that burned beneath the crude stone flue. Still, no matter how warm they kept him, his condition seemed to grow worse and worse. Abe was approaching death, and there seemed to be nothing that they could do to save him.

Michael struggled to maintain his composure. He patted Abraham's hand and asked, "Is there anything I can get you, old friend? Are you thirsty?"

Abe stared through hollow eyes at Michael and mumbled, "My mule is wearing shoes. Who put shoes on my mule?"

Michael reached up and touched Abe's forehead. It was searing hot and soaked with sweat. His face was a pale, strange, gray-green color. His eyes appeared to be withdrawn into their sockets. The poor man's lips were cracked and dry. His tongue was swollen and filled his entire mouth.

Michael replied softly, "I do not know what you are talking about, Abraham. What mule? You have never owned a mule."

"She is wearing three shoes. They are wooden shoes. Who put shoes on my mule? Are those my sister's shoes?"

Michael glanced sadly toward Conrad, who slowly and grimly shook his head.

"I told you, Michael. He is outside his mind. His spirit is already half-way into the beyond."

Michael ignored Conrad's spiritual observations. He demanded, "When did he drink last?"

"He has not been able to keep anything down since yesterday morning. We have tried to pour some water into him, but he keeps throwing it right back up. We attempted rum, with the same outcome. He simply cannot drink."

Michael rose to his feet. "I have to go and find help for him."

Conrad shook his head. "There's no help to be had, Michael."

"We must fetch a surgeon!"

"No surgeon is going to come here at supper time. Every single one of the doctors are over there in the officer's huts, enjoying a fine meal, whilst the remainder of us gnaw on camp biscuits and starve. The bastards!"

"We must do something," Michael growled.

"We can pray. It is all that is left." Conrad sounded defeated.

Michael walked to his own bunk and fetched his blanket and hat. "You can pray all you like. I am going to fetch a doctor whilst there is still some daylight."

"How will you compel someone to come?"

"I shall appeal to their humanity and their morals," Michael declared. "Surely, no doctor worth his salt will sit down to supper whilst a dying man lay only a few hundred yards away."

Conrad frowned pessimistically. "Well, good luck with that."

The door to the hut burst open. A breathless Eberhard Meyer marched swiftly into the room.

"Michael, you must come. Immediately!"

"Not now, Eberhard. I am just about to go in search of a doctor for Abe."

The young messenger shook his head vehemently. "Send Conrad for that. Anyone. But, *you* must come with *me*. *Now!*"

"Why? What is so urgent?" Michael was perplexed.

"You have visitors at the east entrance."

"Visitors? That is absurd. Eberhard, you are drunk!"

"No, Michael. I am not drunk. Colonel Weltner, himself, sent me to fetch you. He is with them now. They are at the gate nearest the redoubt."

"Who is it? Did you get a name?"

"I must not say, Michael." He grinned broadly. "But, trust me ... you will want to see them."

Michael stared at his friend with impatient disbelief. He turned to Conrad and pointed his finger in his face. "I am going to go and see what this is all about. You go and find a doctor." He moved his pointing finger in Abraham's direction. "If you fail, and then he dies, I intend to hold you responsible."

"But, Michael!"

He threw his hand up in Conrad's face. "No more words. Just get it done." He popped his hat onto his head and draped his blanket around his shoulders as a makeshift coat. "I will be back as soon as I can."

"YOU UNDERSTAND that I cannot allow you into our regimental area," Colonel Weltner explained. "Once you make your reunion with your husband, he will have to escort you and your daughter to the followers' encampment. It is approximately one mile to the west. *Herr* Kleinschmidt will need to deliver you there in his wagon. You cannot walk the distance in your condition."

Magdalena nodded. "Yes, sir. I understand fully. It is as I suspected."

"*Herr* Kleinschmidt, after you deliver *Frau* Yeisley to the ladies, I will see that you are reunited with your son. Later this evening, you are more than welcome to overnight with us in the officers' quarters. We have several vacancies in our captaincies, and there are ample bunks in their huts. I think you will find their quarters to be a bit cleaner and more comfortable than those of the enlisted men."

The older gentleman nodded gratefully. "*Danke, Herr* Colonel. I am most honored by your offer."

Little Elizabeth suddenly interrupted the adults with a shrill shriek of joy. She followed her happy scream with a single word. "Papa!" She took off running through the thick mud.

Michael and Eberhard had just appeared around the edge of the redoubt. When Michael saw his wife standing at the checkpoint and conversing with Colonel Weltner, he felt as if he might pass out. He was certain that his eyes were lying to him ... attempting to convince him of some manner of cruel hoax. Then, he saw his squealing little girl running toward him, arms outstretched. Michael sprinted toward the child and scooped her up in his arms. He showered her with kisses and almost crushed her with his hugs.

Elizabeth giggled. "Papa! You have sticky whiskers!" She rubbed her tender hands over his week-old stubble.

Michael cackled with delight. He kissed her again and again. Moments later, his wife was at his side. He gently returned Elizabeth to her feet as he stared at his wife. She looked different. Her face was a little rounder that it once was. Her cheeks had a delightful plumpness to them.

Magdalena observed his odd gaze. Smiling, she reached down and opened her long wool cloak, revealing her distended, pregnant belly. Michael's eyes grew wide with shock. He took hold of his wife and enveloped her within his arms. He buried his scratchy face into her smooth, lavender-scented neck. Silent tears dripped from the end of his nose and soaked her warm, tender skin.

Michael whispered, "Hello, Magdalena Yeisley. I see that you have brought me a little surprise."

She chuckled. "Hello, Michael Yeisley. Yes, we have much re-acquainting to do."

18

ESCAPE!

January 12, 1778
The Chatty Rooster Tavern – Near Philadelphia

Nicklaus and his contact in the American resistance huddled in a dark corner of the fetid, dimly-lit tavern. Though there were only a half-dozen other patrons in the establishment, the place still reeked of spilled ale, stale tobacco smoke, and human body odor. Nicklaus assumed that the unpleasant smells had become infused into the lumber and fixtures of the building over the decades. He attempted to ignore the foulness of the environment and focus, instead, upon his clandestine companion.

"If you are, indeed, a captive of the British, how can you be here unescorted?" Georg Jäger demanded quietly. "I was not aware that the King's soldiers allowed their prisoners to roam free throughout the streets of the city."

Nicklaus took a gulp of tepid ale from his chipped stoneware mug. "As a surgeon, I enjoy considerable privileges, *Herr* Jäger. I was, at one time, interred with other prisoners. It was during those early days immediately after my capture at Brandywine. However, since my captors brought me to Philadelphia and assigned me to the hospital, I have enjoyed a modicum of freedom. I am able to stay at my own home, and I come and go and enjoy commerce as I so choose. But, make no mistake, the British could place me under lock and key at any moment, if they so desired."

The farmer glared curiously at Nicklaus. "Why, then, would you desire to depart your current situation? Philadelphia is your home, is it not? You have your mother and fiancé to attend to you. The British treat you with respect. You appear finely clothed and well-fed. Sir, it defies reason that you should desire to leave Philadelphia and go to the army's winter encampment at Valley Forge."

"I have my duty, *Herr* Jäger."

Nicklaus' companion drained his glass of whiskey and then slammed the empty vessel forcefully onto the weathered pine table top. "Duty be damned! No one in their right mind wants to go to that God-forsaken place! Those poor fools are starving to death out there."

Alarmed by the sudden semi-drunken outburst, Nicklaus glanced nervously around the room. He hissed, "Sir, please restrain your voice! We could be discovered."

"Do not worry, Dr. Schell. You are amongst friends here."

"The British have ears everywhere," Nicklaus retorted.

"I can give assurance for these people. They are all on our side."

Nicklaus exhaled in frustration. "Perhaps. But, I would still prefer that our plans not be revealed to the entire country."

Mr. Jäger held up his glass so that the tavern wench might glimpse its empty state. The buxom young woman sauntered over and quickly remedied the fellow's predicament. He winked at the girl and made the extra effort to grab a healthy handful of her soft, plump backside as she walked away.

The bawdy girl giggled and then shouted over her shoulder, "That'll cost you extra, Georg!"

Jäger chuckled and licked his lips lustily as he watched the girl walk over to the next table. He finally turned his attention back to Nicklaus.

"You are correct, of course, Dr. Schell. I apologize for the untoward outburst. We must, indeed, be circumspect with regard to our intentions. Now, let us make certain of our arrangements."

Nicklaus nodded. "Yes. Let us do that." He was anxious to depart the unscrupulous tavern and return to his women-folk.

Jäger explained, "There is a farm about one mile to the east, along the Reading Highway. It is on the southern side of the road. That farm has a very large stone sawmill. There is none other like it in the area."

Nicklaus nodded. "Very well. That should be simple enough to find."

"The owner is a true Patriot. He also owes me a load of lumber."

"How does that help us?" Nicklaus queried.

"*Herr* Krause is a very clever fellow. He has designed a conceal-ment box that fits perfectly into a wagon bed. The end of the box that faces the rear has the appearance of stacked wood. You and your two friends will conceal yourselves inside the box. We will then stack lumber on both sides, as well as on the top, and then tie everything down with rope. It will have the appearance of an ordinary load of milled oak."

Nicklaus was somewhat impressed. "You have used this device before?"

"Twice. Both times, I removed the outer end of the box after the mission, and then returned it to him upon my next trip into the city. He merely re-mounts it on the end of a fresh smuggling box."

"Smuggling box, you say? For goods?"

"Yes. We have used this method to secretly move food, gunpow-der, and medicine to the encampment."

"Have you ever transported people in it?"

Georg took a swig of his whiskey and hesitated slightly. "This will be our first attempt with human cargo."

Nicklaus froze in fear. The plan seemed sound, but it was untested. He pleaded, "Is there no other option?"

Jäger shook his head. "Not if you plan to cross the Schuylkill and get past the Lobsterbacks. The King's army controls every bridge for ten miles. The river is high from the winter rains, therefore none of the fords are passable. I do not know of any other possible way for you to leave the city without proper British papers."

Nicklaus frowned. He still was not pleased with the notion of being pirated through a British checkpoint inside a wood box. He sighed. "When must we depart?"

"Dawn tomorrow. It is a full day's ride to the encampment. We will make our crossing before the daytime shift of guards comes on duty. The soldiers nearing the end of their shift will be weary and less interested in me or my cargo."

Nicklaus pondered the man's assessment. He drained his mug of ale, and then extended his hand toward the farmer. "Georg, I will see you at the sawmill one hour before dawn tomorrow."

Herr Jäger hesitated. "There is the matter of my payment, Dr. Schell."

"You will receive recompense when we are inside that box, and not a moment sooner."

The man nodded. "Fair enough." They shook hands. "I will be waiting for you at the mill. Please, do not tarry. We *must* be on the move before sunrise."

The Next Day
One Hour Before Daybreak - Outskirts of Western Philadelphia

"Do you see him?" Katharina whispered.

Elspeth shook her head subtly and continued to peer through a tiny knothole in the ancient door. "It is still so very dark. I can barely see anythin', a'tall."

Katharina yawned and then moaned. "Where can he be? It has been entirely too long!"

Elspeth sighed. "It has not been as long as you might think. Nicklaus merely wanted to check for traffic along the roadway. He will return soon. You must have faith."

Both women were exhausted. They were concealed safely inside a stone shed on the grounds of an abandoned farm. They had been awake throughout most of the night. It had taken several hours for the trio to sneak out of the city. They dodged three separate British patrols during their perilous journey. At first, the women were quite relieved when Nicklaus hid them away in the old shed. However, as they waited, the winter cold assaulted their bones. Katharina was beginning to lose feeling in her fingers. Elspeth's feet were growing numb.

Katharina declared, "We must move soon. Otherwise, we may freeze in here."

"It does feel as if the air has grown colder," Elspeth acknowledged.

The young woman gave a frightened squeal when the door suddenly swung inward toward her face. The rough, splintery lumber smacked her in the forehead, eliciting a dull thud. She tumbled backward and landed hard on the musty, earthen floor.

Nicklaus appeared in the open doorway. He grimaced when he saw his fiancé sprawled awkwardly on the ground and rubbing her head. He ducked inside the door and then closed it quickly behind him.

"Elspeth! What happened? Are you injured, *mein Liebling*?"

"No, I am quite all right. 'Tis nothin' hurt but my pride."

"But, whatever were you doing behind the door?" He reached down and helped the embarrassed lass to her feet.

Elspeth poked him angrily in the shoulder. "Lookin' for you, don' ya ken? Your mother'n I were beginnin' to think that you'd gone to Valley Forge without us! What took ya so long?"

"I had to make sure that the way was clear! There has already been much traffic on the road. Far more than I expected during the early morning. I had to locate a suitable place to cross the highway undetected. I think I have found it."

"Where, dear?" his mother pleaded. "Is it far?"

"No, it is not far. There is a small bridge that crosses a creek about a quarter-mile away. The creek bed is wooded, and there is a narrow footpath along the edge of the water. We can cross under the bridge undetected. But, we must make haste. The sun will rise soon."

"Then, let us not waste another moment," Katharina declared. She tossed her linen market wallet across her shoulder and grabbed her small leather bag.

Nicklaus grinned. "I did not know that you were such an adventurer, *Mutter*."

"I am not, boy. I am simply freezing to death. Now, let us go!"

ELSPETH STARED WIDE-EYED AT NICKLAUS. He was sitting in the wooden box in the middle of the wagon bed. She exclaimed, "Nicklaus! I canna' do it! It looks like a damned coffin!"

He reached out his hand reassuringly. "We will not be sealed inside, Elspeth. They will merely stack the wood on top. There are ample cracks for ventilation."

Herr Jäger added, "And you will not be inside for long, *Fraulein*. I would never make you endure the entire journey inside that box. Once we are well clear of the final checkpoint, I will stop and let you out. You will finish the journey in the open air." His voice became urgent. "*Bitte, Fraulein*. The guards will be changing soon."

Katharina urged the girl to action. She nudged Elspeth from behind. "'Twill be all right, my dear. Get inside. We must not tarry."

Elspeth climbed reluctantly onto the wagon bed. Katharina followed quickly behind her.

"We must lie on our sides," Nicklaus urged. "It will be a tight fit."

Elspeth moaned, "Jesus, Mary, and Joseph."

Nicklaus pulled her downward. She groaned as she lay on her side next to him. They faced one another. Elspeth appeared to be praying. Katharina lay down quickly behind her son. The mill workers immediately began to retrieve lumber to stack on top of them. Georg Jäger's face appeared over the back of the wagon.

"Dr. Schell, I must insist upon my payment."

Nicklaus reached inside the pocket of his weskit and produced a large, heavy gold brooch decorated with three sizable emeralds and a narrow line of tiny rubies. He thrust it in the direction of the smuggler. Jäger examined the piece and weighed it in his hand. He bit gently on the soft gold. He smiled.

"That will do quite nicely. *Bitte*, Dr. Schell."

"Just get on with it," Nicklaus barked.

Boards appeared overhead almost immediately. The box became dark as pitch inside. Elspeth shuddered each time a slab of lumber was deposited on top of the stack. Nicklaus held her close and whispered reassurances into her ear. Within minutes, the workers had deposited almost a foot of neatly-stacked boards on top of the concealed box. From the rear of the wagon, it appeared that the driver was hauling an ordinary load of wood.

The wagon creaked as the driver climbed onto the seat. The passengers could hear him releasing the brake and fumbling with the reins.

Jäger spoke in a rather normal tone of voice, "Can you hear me, Dr. Schell?" His voice was only slightly muffled.

"*Ja*. I can hear you very well."

"*Gut*. It is imperative that all of you remain silent and absolutely still during our time at the checkpoint. I will give you plenty of warning when we are approaching the soldiers. Do you understand?"

"*Ja. Ich verstehe.*"

Mr. Jäger wasted no more time. Within seconds, they were rolling down the western highway toward Valley Forge.

THE PAIN IN NICKLAUS' hip was almost unbearable. He wished that he had placed some type of padding between his hip bone and the rough wood. The bottom of the box seemed to magnify and direct the vibration of every tiny rock and bump directly into his pelvis and lower back. He prayed that they might be set free from the box very soon. His mother lay silently behind him, gripping onto the wool sleeve of his coat. The only sound that he had heard from her was one muffled groan when the wagon hit a particularly large hole in the highway. Elspeth's body was as rigid as the boards that encased her. She squeezed Nicklaus' hands in a death-like grip. She mumbled constantly. Nicklaus could not be sure, but he assumed that she was praying.

"We are approaching the bridge," Jäger announced in a very unemotional voice. "One-half mile further. The check point is on this side of the river. Remain silent."

The hidden passengers did not respond. They scarcely dared to breathe. All three of them knew that the next several minutes would be a matter of life or death. If Nicklaus were to be apprehended whilst attempting escape, he would be shot. It was that simple.

Minutes later, they felt the wagon slowing. They heard the driver issue a gentle plea to his horses to stop. The lumber shifted ever-so-slightly as the rig came to a complete halt. Elspeth gripped Nicklaus' arm tightly. He could hear her labored breathing and feel her strong pulse thumping in her wrists. He leaned toward her and kissed her gently on the forehead. All they could do now was listen ... and wait.

"*Guten Morgen,*" *Herr* Jäger declared.

A distinctly British voice demanded, "Papers, please."

Nicklaus heard the almost imperceptible sound of a piece of paper being unfolded. There was a brief time of silence.

"You are Georg Jäger?"

"*Ja.*"

"What has been the purpose of your travel into the city?"

"I delivered a wagon load of salt pork to your quartermaster department yesterday."

"Oh! Do you have your receipt?"

There was a moment of uncomfortable silence as Jäger rifled through his papers. Finally, he declared, "Ah! Here it is."

"Very well." More silence ensued. "Where is your home, Mr. Jäger?"

"Tredyffryn. It is a small village roughly twenty miles west of here."

"That is a long way to travel to deliver meat in the cold of winter."

"A journey created by simple economics. Your English pay is excellent, *Herr* Sergeant."

"Your home is in the vicinity of the rebel encampment, is it not?"

"*Ja*. It is only one mile north of my farm. I still have the stench of the horrible place in my nose."

The English soldier laughed. "Why do you not do commerce with them?"

"Why should I? Their horrid paper money has no value. Besides, they dare to make war against my Sovereign. I cannot do business with such dishonorable men."

"Of course," the soldier responded. He did not sound overly impressed or convinced.

Nicklaus listened to the crunch of the man's feet upon the rocks along the roadway. He was walking around the rear of the wagon. Elspeth uttered a slight, high-pitched whimper. Nicklaus quickly pressed his hand over her mouth.

"And what of this load of lumber? It seems most unusual for cargo. Do you not have wood available in your community?"

Several of the boards rattled above the hidden passengers. The soldier was shifting and moving some of the wood. Katharina reached across Nicklaus' back and grasped Elspeth by the hand. All three of the terrified passengers clung tightly to one another.

"Not of the same quality as that of Herr Krause. His is aged and dried properly and milled to perfection. I need the oak for my cabinetry shop. *Herr* Krause owed me one more load in exchange for several sheep that I traded to him back in November. He was supposed to bring it to me later this month, but I elected to save him the trip, since I was already here with an empty wagon. Fortunately for me, he included an extra fifty feet of boards for my effort." Jäger paused. "Are you familiar with Krause's work?"

"Indeed, I am. I have passed by his mill several times and visited his shop on two occasions. His sons produce some lovely furniture. Most surprising work for Colonials."

"It is the German craftsmanship, *Herr* Sergeant."

"Indeed. Well, everything appears in order," the British soldier declared.

"Everything is in order, *Herr* Sergeant."

"You are traveling at a most unseemly hour. The sun is barely up, and our daytime replacements have not even arrived. What is your rush?"

"I always travel in the early morning, *Herr* Sergeant. There is lighter traffic and less potential unpleasantness from some of the locals who hold to other political persuasions. Besides, there was a young tavern wench that I had to escape. She was sleeping in my bed, and I feared that she might desire some more of my manly attentions before the dawn. I could not risk returning home unprepared to do my husbandly duties this evening. *Frau* Jäger would be most disappointed."

The British sergeant laughed enthusiastically. Other men, presumably the other soldiers, laughed, as well.

"We certainly would not wish you to fall into the disfavor of an unsatisfied wife. Here is your documentation. All the best in your journeys, Mr. Jäger."

"*Danke, Herr* Sergeant."

"You are most welcome, sir."

Jäger clucked at his horses and urged them forward. The sound beneath the wagon changed as the wheels rumbled across the large beams of the bridge that traversed the Schuylkill River. Seconds later, they were across the river and back on the packed dirt and rock of the roadway. It was almost a half-hour before Jäger spoke.

"Dr. Schell, is everyone well?"

"I do not know. Mother, Elspeth ... are you quite all right?"

"I am fine," his mother answered. "I am simply ready to be out of this dungeon."

Elspeth mumbled, "I am well. Just frightened."

"We are well, *Herr* Jäger. How much longer until we can be released?"

"You and the ladies must hold on for another half-mile or so. I will be pulling onto a side road to unload the lumber. You will be free very soon."

~

Late Afternoon
Women's Encampment

"I AM SO grateful for your help, *Frau* Geyer. I do not think that Elizabeth and I could have survived without you. We would be starving in this horrid place, if not for your generosity."

"Nonsense, *Frau* Yeisley! You seem, to me, to be a most resourceful woman."

"Resourcefulness does not keep one fed these days, I am afraid. I did not think it possible that the women's encampment could have even less food than the soldiers. They are living on nothing more than crumbs, and we enjoy even less than they."

"We are the least of General Washington's priorities, I am afraid." Mrs. Geyer shook her head in disgust. "We are on our own. But, I rather think that we women-folk are more capable of fending for ourselves than are the men. Don't you?"

Magdalena chuckled. "I cannot argue with that. I love my husband. He is dear to me." She exhaled in frustration. "But the man is worthless around our house! Our girls could pull the roof down on top of us, and I do not think he would even look up from his news pamphlet!"

Magdalena frowned at the recollection of home. After all, she had no more home. That blessed house of her memories was reduced to a pile of scorched wood and ash.

Seeing the consternation on the younger woman's face, Mrs. Geyer attempted to move to another subject altogether. "Well, you have certainly been a wonderful helper for me here in the wash house. And that little girl of yours is a hard worker. She is wise beyond her years. Speaking of ... I wonder what is taking our children so long."

"I think they enjoy one another's company," Magdalena observed. "They should have all of the shirts and stockings hung out to dry very soon."

Magdalena plunged a filthy shirt deep into the steaming hot, soapy water. She then dragged it vigorously across the rough, hand-made washing board. She repeated the process and inspected the garment several more times before declaring it clean enough and tossing it into the rinse barrel. She stared mournfully at her soaked, shriveled hands.

"*Mein Gott*! My poor hands shall never be the same. This soap is consuming my skin!"

"It took two weeks for my hands to grow accustomed to the harsh soap and water," declared Mary Geyer. "But, I hope that you shall never get used to it. You should not even be here, in your condition. When do you expect to deliver that child?"

Magdalena shrugged. "One week. Ten days, perhaps. But, I can tell that it will be soon." She sat back and relaxed for a moment on her stool, arching her back in an attempt to relieve the stabbing pain in her buttocks and legs.

Once more, Mrs. Geyer shook her head in disgust. "Child, I will say it again ... you should not be here in this encampment. Something *must* be done!"

"Like you, I have nowhere else to go. My home has been destroyed in the war. All I have left is my husband, and he is in this encampment." She cut a quick glance at the older woman. "Why are you still here? I thought I heard you say that your husband has returned to your home."

"He has, indeed. My Peter received both a ball and a bayonet in the leg at Germantown. We are not certain that he will ever walk properly again. He is at home in York, under the care of his sister."

"But you remained?" Magdalena was confused.

"I had no choice. This laundry business is our only source of income. I have a husband to support, now."

"What about your son? John seems most capable of helping out."

"My John is a good boy. He did, indeed, remain here to help me. I do not know what I would do without him."

"Is he lame? Has he always walked with the limp?"

"Oh, no, dear! He, too, was wounded at Germantown. He took a ball in his right heel. He was a drummer for the 13th Pennsylvania," she declared proudly. "He and his father received their discharges a little over a week ago. Peter went home. John stayed."

"How long will you remain here?"

Mrs. Geyer shrugged. "Until the army moves in the spring, I suppose. Then I will have to choose between following them or returning home."

"You should definitely go home," Magdalena declared without hesitation. Her voice became quite forlorn. "I would, if I actually had a home." She sighed. "But, for now, Michael is my home. I must live out each day as it comes."

A deep voice spoke from the doorway, "Excuse me ladies, but I hear this is the best laundry house at Valley Forge."

Magdalena exclaimed, "Michael!" She jumped up from her stool and ran to her husband. He greeted her with a tender kiss.

He teased, "Is my wife sitting down on the job, *Frau* Geyer?"

The woman grinned. "At every possible opportunity, *Herr* Yeisley. I was just fussing at the child. If she is not careful, she is going to deliver that baby into my laundry tub. The customers will not be pleased."

Michael chuckled and then stared lovingly at his wife. He playfully tucked a stray wisp of dangling hair back beneath her mob cap. "That is why I have come, Magdalena. I have news."

"Oh? What news? Is Abraham better?"

"He is, indeed. We are not certain how, but he has made a recovery that the surgeons have declared to be nothing short of miraculous. He has been drinking very well and resumed taking food yesterday. His fever has also broken."

"So, he will live?" Magdalena confirmed.

"*Ja.* The surgeons say that he will live. But, we want to get him out of that hospital at Yellow Springs before he becomes ill again. We hope to have him back with the regiment in two or three days."

"How? He should not be back in that hut, Michael. From what I hear, your housing is full of vermin and disease."

Michael responded excitedly, "That is why I have come! Orders came down from General Washington today! We are tasked with constructing two new brigade hospitals in our area of the camp. One will be directly behind the German Regiment's huts."

"So?"

Michael beamed with pleasure. "So ... I believe that I have secured your assignment to our hospital."

"How?" Magdalena demanded. "And why would they make such an assignment for me?"

"It seems that the colonel is under the impression that you are a most qualified medical nurse." Again, he grinned proudly.

Magdalena placed both hands on her hips. "And how might Colonel Weltner have come upon such a notion?"

"I testified to the fact and Conrad confirmed it."

"Michael Yeisley! I have never been a nurse! I have never cared for wounded or sick men!"

"You cared for me after I was shot in the Jersey campaign," Michael retorted.

"But, you were already under a surgeon's care and fairly well healed when you reached home."

Michael's lip curved in a mischievous grin. "That is but an unimportant detail."

Magdalena shook her head. "I cannot believe that you have resorted to lies and artifice simply to better my lot in this encampment."

Mrs. Geyer, at long last, had to intervene. She slammed her bar of soap forcefully into her wash bucket. Water splashed onto her clothing, as well as onto the floor, in copious amounts. "Magdalena Yeisley, listen to yourself! You are being a childish fool! Do not place your pride above the needs of your daughter and unborn child. Your husband has provided a way for you to have warm housing and better food. You should cease your whining and go whence your husband tells you to go."

Magdalena bit her lip and stared at her mentor. Finally, she returned her gaze back to her husband.

Michael declared, "That is one wise woman." He hugged her close. "Can you hold out here for another couple of days?"

Magdalena sighed. "I will be fine." She withdrew from his embrace and stared into his eyes. "*Danke, Herr* Yeisley."

"*Bitte, Frau* Yeisley." He touched his finger gently to the end of her nose. "*Ich leibe dich, mein Schatz.*" He knelt down and whispered to her belly, "And I love *you*, my baby girl."

"How do you know it is a girl?" Magdalena demanded.

He smiled, quite amused. "Experience."

~

Early Evening
Washington's Headquarters – Valley Forge Encampment

GENERAL GEORGE WASHINGTON was relishing his quiet dinner in his headquarters at the Isaac Potts house. It was one of those rare evenings when he was able to dine alone and in peace. There were no other officers to entertain or endure. The house was completely silent. He rather enjoyed such infrequent moments of solitude.

Isaac Till, the husband of Hannah, the general's personal cook, quietly tapped on the door facing. "Gen'ral Washington, suh, please pahden my intrusion on yo dinnuh."

"Come in, Isaac. Yours is not an unpleasant interruption. It gives me the opportunity to declare my approval of your wife's fine meal this evening. Hannah has truly wrought a wonder for my table. The roast goose is extraordinary. And, though I have yet to taste one, the fried pies appear scrumptious. I cannot wait to devour every single one of them."

"Yassuh. I will tell her fo sho, suh. But, I brings a message from Colonel Hardy. He has a fella wiff him out in da kitchen. Da man wans ta see ya rat now. He claim he a surgeon in da army, done 'scaped from Philleedelpha."

"Oh? Did you catch the gentleman's name?"

"He say he name is Schell. He sound lak a German man. Dey picked him up at da wess gate, comin' through tha Valley Forge town wiff a fahmuh. He gots two womens wiff him."

"Indeed? How curious. The name does not sound familiar to me." He sighed, somewhat displeased by the sudden end to his private dinner. "Please, go ahead and bring these new arrivals to me."

"Yassuh." Isaac retrieved two empty dishes from the general's table and quickly departed the small office. The general sipped from a glass of port while he awaited the arrival of his unexpected guests.

Moments later, Nicklaus stepped into the doorway, escorted by two members of the commander's Life Guard. "General Washington, sir. Thank you for agreeing to grant me an audience."

The general rose slowly to his feet and placed his linen napkin in his empty plate. The man standing before him appeared vaguely familiar, but he could not seem to place him within his memory.

"Are we acquainted, young man?"

Nicklaus nodded. "Yes, of course, sir. I am Dr. Nicklaus Schell, a protégé of Dr. Benjamin Rush. I am surgeon to Colonel Hartley's Regiment."

A look of realization washed across the commander's face. "Yes! I remember you, now. You were the lad who was captured at Princeton and then made your escape."

"Yes, sir. We dined together once at Morristown."

"Indeed. My recollection has returned." He nodded to the guards. "You may go gentlemen. Dr. Schell is a faithful Patriot."

The guards snapped to attention, bowed to the general, and then exited the room.

General Washington stepped forward and shook hands with Nicklaus. "Did I hear Isaac correctly? You have escaped from the city? How did you become separated from your regiment? Why were you in Philadelphia?"

"I was captured in the evacuation of Brandywine. I had to remain with my patients at our improvised hospital in the tavern in Dilworthtown. The British took me into custody around dusk on the day of the battle."

The general nodded grimly. "That was a heartbreaking loss, indeed." He paused. "Did the enemy treat you well?"

"Yes, Your Excellency. They assigned me to work at the Pennsylvania Hospital. Ironically, that hospital is like a home to me. I worked there for several years before the war. For the past few weeks, I have been treating our army's wounded in British custody."

"But, you were compelled to make your escape."

Nicklaus smiled and nodded. "Yes, General. I felt duty-bound to rejoin my regiment."

Washington placed a proud hand on Nicklaus' shoulder. "Well done! Come, please, and sit! Drink with me! I want to hear the details of your story."

"Sir, I do not wish to impose, but may I introduce my travel companions?"

"Of course. I almost forgot. Isaac said that you were traveling with two women."

"They are not just any women, sir. I escaped Philadelphia with my mother and my fiancé."

"Oh?" The general appeared quite excited. "Please, do show them in. There are very few ladies of refinement in the camp. Most of the officers' wives have yet to come. I am still awaiting the arrival of my beloved Martha."

Nicklaus stepped to the door and motioned for the women to join him. They entered through the open doorway in a most solemn manner. Both women bowed and curtsied reverently before the general.

Nicklaus made the introductions. "Your Excellency, this is my mother, Katharina Schell, and my betrothed, Elspeth McClelland."

Katharina declared, "Please pardon our appearance, *Herr* General. We have been through quite an ordeal today and have had neither the time nor the opportunity to make ourselves presentable."

"Nonsense! You ladies are quite lovely, indeed." The general bowed graciously. "Welcome to my humble office and temporary home. I must declare, these stone walls have not entertained such beauty and grace since my arrival. Please, sit and rest yourselves."

He picked up a small bell and gave it a vigorous ring as his guests found a place at his table. The manservant, Isaac, appeared instantly at the doorway.

"Yassuh?"

"Isaac, please have Hannah send over something for my guests." He paused and glanced at Nicklaus and the ladies. "I assume that you are all hungry."

"Famished, sir," Nicklaus responded honestly. "We have not eaten since yesterday's supper."

The general nodded. "Very well. Isaac, please inform Hannah that we have three very weary and hungered guests. Tell her to send over whatever she has available to satisfy them, and quickly so."

"Yassuh!" The faithful servant darted toward the kitchen.

General Washington retrieved three stemmed glasses from a nearby bureau and poured a generous portion of port into each, offering it to his guests.

"Please, drink and enjoy. We shall have a hot, filling supper for you all very soon. Now ... tell me all about this audacious escape from Philadelphia."

For the next hour, the three of them captivated General Washington with their tale of conditions in the city and their subsequent escape from the British in a wagon box disguised as a load of lumber. The general was most impressed. He peppered them with questions throughout their account. In the midst of telling their story, they also enjoyed wonderful fellowship and a most delicious, satisfying meal.

Soon, however, the evening neared its end. Nicklaus could tell that the ladies were exhausted. It was time for them to bid their farewells and leave the general to his business.

Nicklaus declared, "Your Excellency, we must beg your leave. We are humbled by your generosity and graciousness. But, we also know that you have much work to do. We must say our goodbyes and go in search of housing for the night."

"Absolutely not!" Washington declared. "We have ample space in our upstairs quarters. There is an attic room that is quite warm and comfortable. The cots have fresh linens and blankets. You are welcome to stay there tonight."

Nicklaus was elated at the offer. "We are so very grateful, sir."

"Tomorrow, we shall send you to Colonel Laurens and have you assigned to one of our regiments. Just this day, I have issued orders for the construction of brigade-level hospitals throughout our encampment. Surgeons are a much-needed commodity. I have no doubt that we shall find a suitable place for you to serve."

"Begging your pardon, sir. But, I was hoping to rejoin Hartley's Regiment at the earliest possible juncture."

The general pondered. "Colonel Hartley is not in our encampment at this time. His regiment is guarding the Continental Congress in exile at York. I am not inclined to send you there. They have ample local physicians to see to their care. No, Dr. Schell. The needs are much direr here."

Nicklaus was disappointed, indeed. He had so fervently desired to return to his original command. General Washington sensed his consternation.

"Do not worry, Dr. Schell. Colonel Hartley will understand the circumstance. I will draft a correspondence tomorrow informing him of your gallant return to our ranks and your reassignment here." The general paused thoughtfully. "But, as for you ladies, I am somewhat in a bit of a quandary. Currently, we have no suitable quarters for ladies of status. It would be improper to send you to our women's camp. The residents there are ... shall we say ... from a different walk of life than yourselves."

"Perhaps you have labeled us improperly, General Washington," declared Elspeth. "I have never considered myself to be anythin' resemblin' a refined style of woman. I was raised by my parents to work and toil for a livin.' My life is filled with blood, bandages, and chamber pots."

"Both Elspeth and my mother are experienced nurses," Nicklaus explained. "If it suits the general, I would prefer that they be assigned to my duty station with me. We are quite accustomed to working together. They will be most helpful to me."

The general smiled warmly. "Indeed. And so, it shall be."

General Washington rose to his feet. The others followed suit.

"We are most grateful for your hospitality, *Herr* General," Katharina declared.

The commander walked around the table and took her by the hand. He lifted it toward his lips and, in a most gentlemanly manner, lightly kissed her on the knuckles. "This evening has been a most unexpected and splendid one for me, Mistress Schell. I hope that we may enjoy many more like it in the coming weeks and months. I shall have to invite all of you to return and dine with me once my beloved Martha arrives. I quite think that she will enjoy meeting you and hearing your amazing story first-hand."

He turned to Elspeth and kissed her hand, as well. "Miss McClelland, it has been a pleasure. Dr. Schell is a blessed man. Perhaps, if circumstances allow, we might even enjoy a wedding in our encampment with the coming of springtime. Would that not be a momentous occasion, indeed? And a first for our army!"

Elspeth blushed. "Perhaps, we shall, General Washington. I s'pose we must wait and see."

"Indeed. Very well, then. Isaac will see you to your room." He lifted the bell and rang it once again. The servant appeared almost instantaneously. "Rest well. We shall resolve the matters of your assignment and permanent housing tomorrow. Until your brigade hospital is complete, you are welcome to remain here in my guest room."

"Thank you, Your Excellency." Nicklaus beamed with pleasure.

"No. Thank you, Dr. Schell. Your patriotism and dedication to your country and duty are an inspiration to us all." He bowed slightly at the waist. "I bid you good night." He turned and swiftly exited the room.

Nicklaus glanced at Katharina and Elspeth. Both appeared quite weary and very overwhelmed. He smiled and declared, "Welcome to the Continental Army."

19

LIFE AND DEATH

Early Morning - January 16, 1778
Flying Camp Hospital – Muhlenberg's Brigade

Nicklaus surveyed his new hospital skeptically. He was not overly impressed, for it was a hospital in name only. Except for its size, the building bore an almost identical resemblance to all of the other huts that dotted the hilltops and ridges of Valley Forge. It was only slightly larger in its dimensions, and the ceiling was barely one foot higher. There was a single fireplace at one end of the hut and two small opposing windows to provide ventilation.

Nicklaus placed his hands on his hips and sighed. His hopes and expectations were somewhat crushed. Experience was beginning to teach him that the army never failed to disappoint, no matter the circumstance. The establishment of a Flying Camp Hospital to serve General Muhlenberg's Brigade was no exception. Nicklaus and his helpers had much work to do, indeed, before they could begin to house patients in such a primitive facility.

General Muhlenberg's reaction, however, was somewhat different. The brigade commander's smile could scarcely be contained. "Welcome to our Hospital of the Flying Camp, Dr. Schell! We are honored, indeed, to have a physician of your eminence assigned to our brigade."

"The honor is mine, General." Nicklaus continued to allow his eyes to wander around the newly-constructed cabin. He searched his mind for the right words to say. Finally, he declared, "Your men have worked most rapidly." He grimaced, fearful that his comment sounded more like a criticism than a compliment.

"They were highly motivated, Dr. Schell. My soldiers are quite thrilled to have a medical facility in our brigade area. They even constructed a new hut for the ladies. When we heard that your mother and your betrothed were assigned here with you, we immediately took upon ourselves the task of providing them with a suitable habitation."

Nicklaus nodded gratefully. He did not have to search for the right words to respond to such thoughtfulness. "That is most kind, General. Sincerely. I know that the ladies will be very comfortable and most pleased."

"It is the very least that we could do. Besides, as more of the wives arrive at the encampment in search of their husbands, we will likely need housing for them, as well. I am afraid that your ladies must expect some measure of company in the coming days. Indeed, there is one woman who will take up housing with them today. She is the wife of one of my German Regiment soldiers. I am told that she is an experienced nurse."

"A nurse, you say? General, that pleases me tremendously. It seems that I will have no shortage of helpers in this enterprise." Nicklaus felt his confidence increasing. He decided that he had to face the task confronting him with a positive attitude. "We shall endeavor to become the best hospital in the encampment, General Muhlenberg."

The officer smiled broadly. "Of that I have no doubt." He paused and watched the doctor as he studied his surroundings. He had been noting the young man's facial expressions. The general was no fool. He was a pastor by trade and well-versed in reading people. He recognized the displeasure and distress on Nicklaus' face. "Dr. Schell, I hope that you are not too disappointed in our efforts. I know that you are unaccustomed to practicing your medical arts under such primitive conditions."

Nicklaus smiled, embarrassed. "You forget, General ... I have amputated legs whilst operating on a tavern's bar." He nodded resolutely. "This building will do quite nicely. I will, however, need double this number of beds." He pointed to the nearest wall. "I would also like a row of cabinets over here for medicines and supplies. A desk and a work table would be most helpful."

The general beamed. "I like your attitude, Dr. Schell. I will send immediately for a work party. We have carpenters and tradesman aplenty in our brigade. We will have your beds and furniture constructed by the end of this day."

"We will need more straw and bedding, as well," Nicklaus added.

"We shall endeavor to meet all of your requests and needs, Doctor."

Katharina and Elspeth appeared in the open doorway.

The general exclaimed, "Ladies! Please come inside. I hope that you found your living quarters to be satisfactory."

"Quite so, General," Katharina responded. "It is a handsome cabin. The fireplace appears to draw a bit slowly, but that should get better with more frequent and hotter fires."

"And the ample pile of firewood is wonderful, indeed," added Elspeth. "Your men have been most generous toward us. We are truly thankful."

The general nodded proudly. "They were quite excited to learn that there were women-folk joining us in our brigade area. Your every wish shall be their command." He paused. "Well, then ... I have my duties to perform, as do you. I shall leave you to it. Please let me know if you experience any difficulties, whatsoever, with the quartermaster. Colonel Weltner will be your liaison in that department. He is quite capable. But, sometimes requests through official army channels require a general's touch." He grinned. "Or a general's forcefully-composed letter."

Nicklaus bowed slightly. "Thank you, sir."

Muhlenberg nodded respectfully to Katharina and Elspeth. "Ladies." He strode quickly toward the door and stepped out into the muddy field beyond.

The two women scanned the room. Katharine stared, wide-eyed, at Nicklaus.

"Well, *Mutter*, what think ye?"

"I think that it would be insanity to attempt surgery in such a place. Indeed, how can we care for critical patients in a facility with no supplies in stock or available?"

"The more critical patients are not within our mandate, *Mutter*. We will treat routine injuries and ordinary sicknesses. The men in this encampment are suffering from some relatively common maladies. There are ample cases of the camp itch, fever, and flux. Thankfully, there are scant few cases of the pox. General Washington's inoculation regimen has all but eliminated that. Our practice of medicine will be rudimentary and routine. We will evacuate, with all expediency, any cases that require more advanced treatment. They will go to the army's main hospital at Yellow Springs."

Katharina inhaled longingly as she continued to scan the room. "It certainly is not the Pennsylvania Hospital, is it?"

"Well ... it *is* a hospital *in* Pennsylvania," her son countered, smiling.

"We shall make it into a splendid little clinic. It will be the envy of the camp," Elspeth declared confidently. "'Twill require nothing more than honest effort and hard work."

"But, where do we start?" Nicklaus pondered.

"Elspeth and I shall start with the cots and bedding," Katharina declared. "You must be about your doctoring business."

Nicklaus frowned. "I suppose, then, that I must write my first letter of requisition to the quartermaster."

His mother nodded enthusiastically. "And quickly so."

∼

Mid-Afternoon

KATHARINA AND ELSPETH toiled throughout the day, cleaning their little hospital and making it ready for its first patient. Periodically, a small group of soldiers from one of the Virginia regiments appeared so that they might present yet another finished cot for the ward. From the manner in which they stared at the beautiful Elspeth, it became more and more clear that their intentions were not entirely altruistic. With each delivery, the men lingered in an effort to ogle the lovely young lass and, perhaps even, initiate a conversation with her. Katharina quickly grew tired of the constant interruptions and distractions.

"Elspeth, we are going to have to procure a ring to place on your finger. Or, perhaps, a large sign for you to wear that declares you as betrothed. I foresee entirely too many healthy men reporting here for sick call each day. Your beauty may elevate the army's malingering to an unacceptable level."

Elspeth giggled. "They mean no harm. They are simply nice young men, longin' for a word with a girl their own age."

Katharina's voice became somewhat harsh. "You are most naïve, Elspeth McClelland. You are a singularly beautiful woman in an encampment full of concupiscent men. It is imperative that you never wander through this camp alone. Ever. Do you understand me?"

"Yes, Mum."

"You must travel with myself or Nicklaus at all times. There are over 10,000 men in this horrid place. Any number of them may be inclined to steal your virtue." A knock on the door interrupted Katharina's admonitions. She stared, stormily, at Elspeth. "We shall speak more of this at a later time. Now, answer the door, dear."

Elspeth leaned her straw broom against the log wall and did as she was instructed. When she opened the door, she encountered a rather unkempt, dirty man accompanied by an extremely pregnant woman and a small girl.

"Hello. How may I help you?"

The man removed his tattered cocked hat respectfully. "*Guten Abend, Fraulein.* My name is Michael Yeisley. I am a soldier in the German Regiment. This is my wife, Magdalena, and our daughter, Elizabeth."

"I am afraid that the hospital is not yet ready to receive patients. Perhaps you could come back tomorrow?"

"Oh, we are not here as patients, *Fraulein*. My wife has been assigned to work at this hospital."

"Oh! You must be the woman that General Muhlenberg mentioned! I believe that we will be sharing quarters, as well." She smiled warmly. "But, I dinna know that you had a child with you."

Katharina cleared her throat in a most conspicuous manner. "Elspeth, don't leave the poor souls languishing out in the winter cold. Invite them inside."

Elspeth blushed. "Oh, yes! How rude of me! Please, do come in. Join us by the fire. We must get to know one another."

"*Danke, Fraulein*." Michael assisted his wife across the threshold into the cabin.

Katharina announced, "We have no chairs, but we may use two of the bunks to recline upon. If you could assist me, *Herr* Yeisley. Come, *Frau* Yeisley, and rest yourself."

Michael walked swiftly to the two bunks nearest the fire. He quickly and easily repositioned them closer to the warm flames. Everyone took a seat. There was a brief moment of uncomfortable silence. Michael stared, thoughtfully, at the older woman sitting across from him. She appeared somewhat familiar. He was almost certain that they had met before. However, he could not recall when or where their paths had crossed. The woman did not appear to indicate any measure of familiarity with Michael. She seemed more interested in his wife. Indeed, she gazed intently at Magdalena.

Katharina declared, "The general informed us that you are a most experienced nurse. However, he failed to mention your current condition." Displeasure was evident in her voice.

Magdalena stared, somewhat ashamed, at the packed earth floor. "Well, about that ... I am afraid that my husband was somewhat less than truthful in his testimony regarding my work experience. Unfortunately, I am not a nurse. He merely claimed that I was in order that I might have better quarters in closer proximity to his regiment."

"I see," Katharina mumbled. Her displeasure was increasing. "So, then, you have never cared for wounded or sick soldiers?"

"Only my husband," she confessed. "He was wounded in the campaign in the Jerseys. However, he was already much mended when he arrived back home."

"Indeed." Katharina seemed skeptical. She glanced at Elizabeth. "Is this your only child?"

"Heavens, no! We have five daughters. The other four are residing with friends whilst I am here at the camp."

"Goodness! You have five daughters?" Katharina exclaimed. Her expression brightened. "Then, you are more qualified for this job than you might think! A mother of five little ones is no stranger to nursing and care. Would you not agree, Elspeth?"

The young lass smiled and responded, "Indeed. She will do nicely, I'm a thinkin'." She eyed Magdalena's belly. "When will your bairn arrive?"

"Within the week. Honestly, I feel like I could go at any time."

"Well, then, you are most definitely in the right place. My son is the physician in this new hospital, and he is most experienced in the practice of midwifery. One might say that it is his specialty. He will be very pleased to take care of you and deliver your child."

The door burst open quite unexpectedly, startling the fireside conversationalists.

"*Mutter*, I have bad news and then some worse news. There is no beeswax or salve to be had. And the quartermaster does not even have a decent supply of ..." He cut off his words mid-sentence. "Pardon me! I did not know that we had company."

Michael recognized the voice immediately. He rose slowly to his feet and stared, disbelieving, at the man who had just entered the room. The fellow appeared slightly older and much thinner. But, there was no mistaking him. It was his old compatriot and friend, Dr. Nicklaus Schell. Nicklaus returned the stare, though at first, his face reflected no hint of recognition.

Michael stammered, "How ... I do not understand ... how can this be?"

The distinctive voice triggered Nicklaus' memories. His mind quickly replayed all of his many encounters with this fellow German. He could scarcely believe it. The skinny, filthy, whiskered soldier standing before him was Michael Yeisley.

Nicklaus dropped his meager load of medical supplies on the work table and strode toward his old friend. Michael met him halfway across the room, in the narrow aisle between the two rows of hospital cots. They embraced and celebrated their reunion with laughter and moans of joy.

"Michael! It is so good to see you!" Nicklaus paused and examined his friend. "Though, you do look a bit different. Perhaps a little soap and warm water, and a razor, might return you to a more recognizable state."

Michael ignored the teasing. He was too overwhelmed with joy. "I simply do not understand, Nicklaus. When I left you in Dilworthtown, the enemy was upon you. I thought you captured, for certain. Or dead, perhaps. I heard a volley of musket fire after we fled the town!"

"I was, indeed, captured. The British held me near Brandywine for about a week and then relocated me to Philadelphia. But, I eventually made my escape. I rejoined the army only a few days ago." Nicklaus placed a proud hand on Michael's shoulder. "'Tis good to see you, Michael. I should have known that you would be here in the army's encampment. Are you housed nearby?"

Michael pointed. "I'm in the third hut over the hill, on the pathway to the redoubt. If you came from the quartermaster's house, you passed by my front door."

"Indeed! Then, we are neighbors! I have been assigned to the hut with the company captains." Nicklaus nodded politely to Magdalena. "*Frau* Yeisley, it is truly wonderful to see you again."

She smiled. "'Tis a pleasure indeed, Dr. Schell."

The doctor's eyes widened when he noticed Magdalena's enlarged belly. "I see that our springtime sojourn in your home was quite ... fruitful."

She covered her mouth in embarrassment. "Yes, I suppose it was, at that."

Nicklaus walked over to Elizabeth and picked the little girl up in his arms. "And, how are you, *Fraulein* Elizabeth?"

"I am well, Dr. Schell." She gave him a vigorous hug and kissed him on the cheek.

Katharina was thoroughly confused. She blurted, "Nicklaus, you *know* these people?"

Nicklaus gently returned Elizabeth to the floor. "I do, indeed, *Mutter*. I stayed in their home after our escape from New Jersey. And you know *Herr* Yeisley, as well. He was, after all, your patient for several days a couple of winters ago."

She stared searchingly at Michael, attempting to place him. She probed her mind for the memory.

Nicklaus explained, "He was the fellow who fell from the wagon at the river crossing. He had quite a nasty bump on his head."

Her expression transformed from confusion to clarity. "Yes! Yes, I recall now! The weaver! And you had that handsome younger brother. What was his name?"

"George," Michael answered, grinning.

"George Yeisley!" she exclaimed. "Now, I remember. *Herr* Yeisley, I apologize that I did not recognize you before!"

"There is no need for apologies, *Frau* Schell. You seemed familiar to me when I first saw you, but I could not recall our earlier meeting." He grinned. "Of course, I was suffering from a blow to the head when I saw you last."

Everyone laughed.

Nicklaus turned, concerned, to his friend. "What are you doing here, Michael? Are you ill?"

"No. I am here because of Magdalena. She is nearing delivery. I wanted her out of that squalid women's camp, so I stretched the truth just a bit and managed to get her assigned here." He paused and mischievously cut his eyes toward his wife. "As your nurse."

"I see." Nicklaus nodded.

"I know that it was very selfish and wrong of me to do so, but I had to ..."

Nicklaus interrupted him. "Not another word, Michael. You made a wise decision. Of course, Magdalena is most welcome here. We look forward to her contribution to our little endeavor." He winked. "And we shall take most excellent care of her as the time of delivery approaches. Won't we, Elspeth?"

His fiancé smiled kindly. "Indeed, we shall."

Nicklaus clapped his hands together. "Well, then ... let us get to work. I have to sort through these supplies. Mother can help me with that. Elspeth, perhaps you could show Magdalena and Elizabeth to the ladies' quarters and help them get settled in?"

"'Twould be a pleasure," Elspeth replied.

Michael interrupted, "If I might ask one more thing before I go back to my regiment."

"Of course, Michael."

"One of my mates, Abraham Price, is in the hospital at Yellow Springs. You met him once. He was the fellow who was with me during the evacuation through Dilworthtown."

"Yes, I remember him vaguely."

"He has recently recovered from a fever, and is on the mend. We would like for him to return here as quickly as possible, whilst he still has his hunting frock and shoes on him. The poor lad cannot sleep at night for fear of being robbed of his clothing and belongings. Those large army hospitals are dangerous places to linger."

"You say he is recovering well?"

"Yes. His fever broke several days ago."

Nicklaus nodded approvingly. "I shall write the order immediately. You may deliver it to Yellow Springs yourself and then fetch him back to us this afternoon. He is to be our first patient."

"Thank you, Nicklaus." He grinned. "Now, I must warn you. Old Abe is an interesting sort of fellow. I hope that we will still be friends when his time here is done."

Nicklaus did not quite know how to interpret Michael's warning. He cut his eyes toward Magdalena, hoping for some clarification.

"He speaks the truth," she declared. "Abraham is an acquired taste. You will understand in a few days."

Mid-Morning
January 18, 1778

FOR OVER A WEEK, the people of southeastern Pennsylvania had enjoyed almost spring-like weather. Ample rain, along with endless mud and standing water, had accompanied the warm air. But overnight a weather front descended upon the region. The temperatures dropped dramatically. During the night, the numerous muddy puddles and ponds throughout Valley Forge froze over with a thin glaze of ice. When daylight came, the skies were sunny and clear, but the air was frigid. A stiff northerly wind pummeled the camp.

Thankfully, it was Sunday. The soldiers were not required to march or drill on the Sabbath. Instead, most remained inside their huts and huddled near their fires. As was becoming all too common, their only meal for the day would be camp biscuits ... flat wafers made from flour mixed with water, then toasted on top of rocks inside their fireplaces.

Despite the numbing cold outside, Muhlenberg's hospital was quite warm and serene. The fire burned brightly in the fireplace and the stones of the hearth radiated comforting heat. Most of the patients dozed happily. They enjoyed ample straw on their soft, cozy bunks. Each man also had a warm wool blanket to help capture his natural body heat.

Elspeth McClelland was the only staff member on duty this particular morning. Young Elizabeth Yeisley was her helper for the day. The eager, resourceful little girl was a delightful companion to Elspeth. Nicklaus and Katharina Schell were gone together to the quartermaster's house, as was usual, begging for supplies and rations for their patients. Magdalena Yeisley dozed, exhausted, in the bed nearest the fireplace. She had been experiencing intense pain in her lower back for the past two days. Dr. Schell believed that her delivery was imminent. Thus, he confined her to bedrest. She gladly obeyed his order.

Elspeth quietly hummed a happy tune as she swept the hospital floor. The simple task of sweeping was a welcome diversion from the unpleasantries associated with chamber pots. Thankfully, thus far on this particular morning, she had hot been required to attend to very many of those receptacles of foulness. There were currently only eleven patients in the little clinic. Well over half of the cots remained empty.

Truthfully, from a standpoint of philosophy, Elspeth thought it a bit ridiculous to be sweeping dirt. But, the building did seem more orderly when all of the pieces of scattered bedding straw were removed. And, to be sure, there was never a shortage of loose straw on the packed earth floor. Every time one of the men shifted his weight or rolled over in his bunk he expelled a fresh wave of the dusty plant remnants onto her carefully manicured floor. Keeping it orderly and swept was a never-ending task.

She whispered across the room, "Elizabeth, dear, can you fetch me the collectin' board?"

Elizabeth Yeisley grabbed the improvised dust pan from beside the nurse's table and scampered across the room. She knelt dutifully on the ground and held the board in place while Elspeth corralled the mound of straw scraps. Once all of the fibers were safely collected, Elizabeth carefully carried the refuse to the fireplace and deposited the pile into the fire. The flames burned high and hot with the addition of the fresh, dry fuel. Elspeth joined her by the fireside. Both of them leaned forward and warmed their hands near the dancing flames.

"Would you like some tea, Elizabeth?"

"*Ja, Fraulein* McClelland."

Elspeth grinned. "Go, then, and get the pot from our hut. And bring the entire bag of tea. There is no need for us to be selfish. We shall brew some for all the lads. They should be wakin' soon and will, no doubt, be much hungered. You and I can work together to cook 'em up a batch of biscuits to go with their tea."

Elizabeth grinned and then darted toward the door with childlike enthusiasm. Elspeth decided to take a brief moment to rest her feet. She placed a somewhat spindly ladder-back chair near the hearth and sat down to enjoy the fire. Her fleeting moment of peace was soon shattered by an all-too-common summons.

"*Fraulein* McClelland! I need you!"

Elspeth rolled her eyes in disgust. She was growing tired of the incessantly needy Abraham Price. The young man was no longer ill. He needed to be gone from the hospital. Lately, he had also become a bit too forward and familiar in his interactions with the pretty Scottish lass.

She responded quietly, "What is it, Private Price?"

"My bones are grinding against these boards. I need some more straw for my bed."

"We have no more straw, Private Price, as well you are aware. We expect more tomorrow mornin'."

"But, I do not think that my bones shall survive until tomorrow, *Fraulein!*"

"Oh, I have no doubt that they will, sir. I know for a fact that you will be gone from that bed by supper this very day."

"What do you mean?" Abraham demanded, wide-eyed.

Elspeth rose and marched to the nurse's table. She triumphantly held up a small piece of parchment. "I urged Dr. Schell to approve your return to duty, and he has consented. I have the order right here. As soon as the cap'n from your company comes to take roll this afternoon, you will be officially released."

"We have no captain in our company," he responded.

"Then, whenever your *lieutenant* comes. I doona care who is in charge of your bleedin' company. But, whoever it is, you shall be back in his charge before supper!"

Abe was mortified. He had grown quite accustomed to the better conditions and food afforded him in the hospital. He was certainly not anxious to return to his company hut.

"But, *Fraulein* McClelland, I still have pain in my ..."

The door exploded open, ushering in an invading wave of ice-cold air. Four grimy, poorly-clad soldiers burst into the room. They were carrying an unconscious woman by her arms and legs.

Elspeth gasped. "Who are you men? What have you done?"

"I'm Corporal Daniel Davis, of the Second Virginia, ma'am. We're all soldiers of that regiment."

"What is the meanin' of this intrusion? And who is this woman?" Elspeth demanded.

One of the soldiers answered, "Her name is Mary Riley. She is the wife of one of our mates. The woman is delivering, but something is wrong. No one can wake her."

Elspeth pointed toward the far end of the room. "Put her on the last bed, away from the others. And be quick about it!"

The men obeyed without question. They reverently deposited the woman on top of the blanketed bunk. They hovered near her.

Elspeth ordered, "Stand aside, men. Allow me to work."

The emotional men parted and allowed Elspeth access to the woman. She performed a quick examination.

"Why is she not awake?"

The corporal shrugged. "We don't know. She was in the women's camp. They said that the baby began to come quite some time ago. They sent for us when the difficulties began. She was already sleeping when we arrived. We've not been able to rouse her."

Little Elizabeth appeared in the midst of the confusion, carrying a large iron teapot and a linen bag filled with tea.

Elspeth barked, "Elizabeth! Leave those things by the fire and go find Dr. Schell, immediately! He is at the quartermaster's house, just beyond the gate. Tell him it is a matter of urgency."

"*Ja, Fraulein.*" The little girl dropped her teapot and sack by the fire and then quickly sprinted from the building.

Elspeth continued her examination. "Why did you bring her here?"

"Mrs. Geyer, the washerwoman, sent us. She said that she knew someone in this hospital. Anyway, we serve in Weedon's Brigade and are assigned sick call here. We figured it was as good a place as any."

A drowsy Magdalena Yeisley appeared over Elspeth's shoulder. "Did I hear you mention *Frau* Geyer? She is a dear friend of mine."

The soldier removed his hat respectfully. "Yes, ma'am. She said that this was the place where we ought to bring Mary. She don't trust them big hospitals one bit. But, she promised that you all was good folk."

"Why did you not bring her husband? Where is he? Is he drunk?" Elspeth scolded. "The man should be here with his wife."

"John is dead, Missy. He made the mistake of leaving the encampment last month. The lad was just scrounging for food, like half of the other scarecrows in this damned field. But, they court-martialed him for desertion and hanged him a week ago. Said they had to make an example of him. The bastards dropped his carcass in a hole right beneath the gallows and left him there to rot. Wouldn't let us bury him proper."

"How ghastly!" Magdalena wailed.

"Yes ma'am. That's a good word for it, sure 'nough. They left this poor little girl a widder woman. That son-of-a-bitch Washington wanted to drum her out of camp, too. But, the other women raised enough hell to compel him to leave her be. They been a feedin' her and carin' for her since then."

Elspeth protested, "I cannot imagine General Washington ordering such a thing!"

The corporal laughed sarcastically. "Oh, I know you fancy women-folk don't think old George's shite stinks. But, he's as cold-blooded as any of the rest of 'em. He doles out a hundred lashes of the whip before he eats his fine breakfast every mornin'. I'm sorry 'bout my language, Missy, but 'His Excellency' is a damned cold-blooded bastard. He killed John Riley without battin' an eye." The man nodded grimly at the unconscious girl. "Now, I reckon John's wife is dead, too."

Elspeth stared at him with determination. "Not if we can help it! Do not lose heart. The surgeon will be here soon."

The door swung open suddenly, pushed violently by the howling winter wind. It banged loudly against the log wall. Nicklaus and Katharina entered. The doctor slammed the door closed and walked swiftly toward the cluster of people at the end of the room. As he removed his cocked hat and scarf, he nodded to the soldiers gathered near the bed.

"Elizabeth met us on the roadway. What is wrong?"

"This girl is in labor. But, no one can wake her."

Nicklaus shucked off his wool topcoat. He began to spew orders. "Elizabeth, fetch my apron. Mother, I need my bag." He glanced at the soldiers. "You men may go. Return to your quarters."

The corporal began to protest, "But, sir ..."

"I have no time to argue. Please, leave my hospital. You are welcome to return later to inquire regarding your friend. You have served her well. Now, continue to do so with your obedience. Let us do our jobs."

The fellow nodded, defeated. "Yes, sir." He and his three mates departed reluctantly.

"Elspeth, we need boiling water and fresh linens. I intend to save this baby and this girl."

~

Early Evening

THOUGH THE FRIGID winds of winter howled outside, the hospital ward was pleasantly warm and quiet. The drama and trauma of the day were, at long last, done. Most of the patients were napping, as were Magdalena and Elizabeth. The exhausted mother and daughter snuggled together in the bunk nearest the fire.

Though Nicklaus and Elspeth had no appetites, they reluctantly forced themselves to eat. They needed to maintain their strength. Their supper was the same as everyone else's in the hospital that evening. They dined on a bland gruel comprised of ground maize boiled in water and flavored with a chunk of pork fat. They were

from Katharina. She obviously did not want to hear any philosophical explanation or encouragement. She stared silently at the log wall.

"Would you like to see your baby?" Katharina asked gently. "Would you like to hold her? I have her close by. I was waiting for you to awaken."

"No. I do not want to see her. Just throw her in the hole with my dead husband. At least they have one another." She wept. "I have no one else. Nothing else."

Katharina started to respond, but Nicklaus placed his hand on her shoulder. "Leave her alone, *Mutter*. Allow her to grieve. She needs neither our theology nor our assurances right now. She just needs to feel her pain. Allow her to experience this loss in her own way. Come, *Mutter*. *Bitte*. Eat your supper. You must be tired."

Katharina lingered by the morose woman's bed for just a moment longer.

"Come, *Mutter*. You need to eat. Elspeth will fix you a bowl of porridge."

His mother nodded reluctantly. Nicklaus took her by the hand and led her toward the fireplace.

Suddenly, little Elizabeth sat upright on the bed that she shared with her mother. She exclaimed, "*Mutter*, I am all wet!"

Magdalena groggily rubbed her fists in her eyes. "What did you say, dear?"

She giggled. "My petticoat is soaked! I think you wet the bed!"

Magdalena glanced down at her own petticoats. The layers of linen cloth were soaked with fluid. She peered frantically at Nicklaus and Katharina. "My water has broken! The baby! It comes!"

20

WHY WE FIGHT

January 19, 1778 - 4:00 AM
Five Miles Northeast of Valley Forge

T he cold was bone-chilling. Despite their improvised cloaks constructed from thick wool blankets, the Continental troops were freezing. Simple clothing was not enough to stave off winter's assault. The stiff January wind seemed to find its way through every crack and seam in their threadbare garments. The men needed shelter, and soon.

Conrad Traywitz whispered through chattering teeth, "Lieutenant, do you think this is the right house?"

The officer did not respond. He attempted to study his crude, hand-drawn map in the pale light of the gray, cloud-shrouded moon. He glanced, occasionally, toward the two-story stone farmhouse on the far side of the roadway.

Michael Yeisley was growing impatient. He pleaded, "Lieutenant, it is getting late. 'Twill be dawn soon."

The young fellow barked, "Give me a damned moment, Yeisley. I am endeavoring to get my bearings."

Michael glanced, eyebrows raised, at Abe Price. His recently hospitalized friend exhaled deeply from disgust and rolled his eyes in a most exaggerated fashion.

Abe groaned, "This has *got* to be the house, Lieutenant. We have not seen another like it. 'Tis just as the colonel described ... a two-story stone house with four windows and a gable."

"That sounds like half of the houses in Pennsylvania!" Cramer retorted. "We must be absolutely certain!"

Truth be told, Lieutenant Jacob Cramer was terrified and could scarcely think at all. It was his first time to command men outside the boundaries of the encampment. He wanted desperately to succeed in his mission and impress his superiors. But, most of all, he desired to get back to his warm hut alive and uninjured. It would be of added benefit if he could return all of the men under his charge to Valley Forge in a similar state.

Captain Weiser's vacant company, under the temporary command of the lieutenant, had been dispatched just before dark the previous evening on an armed foraging raid. Their target was a large Tory farm in the vicinity of the Pennypacker Mills. Colonel Weltner had ordered and authorized the twelve remaining soldiers of the company to raid the Loyalist farm and to, in his words, "... *relieve its owners of all confiscable livestock or foods stores.*"

There were ten well-armed German Regiment soldiers concealed inside the small thicket near the target house. The lieutenant left the two remaining troops with their wagons, which were hidden just off the road about a quarter-mile to the west. They were to remain at that location until the raid was over and then, upon receiving word from the lieutenant, proceed to the house for the loading of any potential booty.

Conditions at Valley Forge had become quite desperate. Foraging parties were beginning to roam the countryside in search of provisions. But, as far as Lieutenant Cramer knew, his was the first group tasked with an actual military raid on the property of a potential enemy. He did not want to foul things up. He wanted to perform his duty admirably. Command would not tolerate an errant raid upon a Whig farmer's home. There would be hell to pay if his company attacked the wrong house and stole goods from a Patriot farmer. That is why he was taking so long in making his decision to attack.

Abe groaned imperceptibly. He whispered to Michael, "I simply cannot believe my luck. I am fresh out of the hospital, and the next thing I know I am sent into the woods to freeze my bollocks off! I should be by our fire this night. What if I were to become ill again? Michael, I could relapse!"

Michael chuckled softly and shook his head. He huddled close beside his mates and waited. All of the men prayed that the lieutenant might hurry and make a decision, one way or the other. Anything would be better than sitting still in the darkness of a winter night and freezing to death. At long last, Lieutenant Cramer folded his paper and stuffed it inside the pocket of his cloak.

He declared, "I believe this *must* be the house."

Abe leaned toward Michael's ear and whispered, "Did I not just say that?"

Michael nodded and rolled his eyes.

"We will take them in their sleep." He pointed to three of the soldiers. "I will lead you three men in a breach through the front door. Private Yeisley will take Privates Price and Traywitz through the rear entrance. The remainder of you will keep watch and cover the windows. I do not want any shooting. I repeat ... you will not fire unless someone fires at you first. We are not here to wage war on the citizenry."

"We are simply here to steal their food," Abe added rather sarcastically.

"Exactly." The lieutenant nodded, completely ignoring Abe's futile attempt at humor. "And we can do so without bloodshed." He nodded to Michael. "Yeisley, you and your team go ahead and work your way around back of the house. Wait for my signal. I will give a shrill whistle when it is time to invade. Understood?"

Michael nodded nervously.

"Excellent. We depart immediately. Check your firelocks. Weapons on half-cock, only. I do not want any accidents. Godspeed, men. Let us go."

~

4:15 AM – Camp Hospital

IT HAD BEEN AN AGONIZINGLY long night. The baby had not yet arrived. No one in the hospital could sleep. Elspeth and little Elizabeth stood vigil near the fireplace, resting in a ladder-back chair. Elspeth cuddled the exhausted child as she sang a Scottish lullaby. Katharina busied herself by checking the other patients and attending to their needs. They, too, remained awake. Most were sitting up in their beds or reclining on their elbows, captivated by the tortured labor of the beautiful, young German woman.

Everyone in the hospital was eager to see the child born. They wanted the girl's pain to end. The only person who did not appear personally engaged in the birth drama was the despondent Mary Riley. The lonely woman lay in her bunk along the most distant wall of the hospital. She was on her left side, with her face against the wall. Her hands were clasped tightly over her ears. She wept softly.

"I do not understand!" Magdalena wailed through the searing pain. "It should not be this difficult! I have already borne five children! It should be out of me by now!"

Magdalena lay flat on her back, knees up in the air. A linen sheet covered the lower half of her body, providing a thin shroud of modesty. Nicklaus' head was beneath the sheet. His right hand probed deep inside her birth canal, searching for the cause of her prolonged labor. After several uncomfortable seconds, he withdrew his hand. There was blood on his fingertips. He thoughtfully wiped his hands on the small towel that was draped across his shoulder.

"What is wrong, Nicklaus?" his mother demanded, appearing at the foot of the bed.

The doctor moved his chair to the bedside near Magdalena's head. He sat down and inhaled a deep, thoughtful breath.

The laboring woman begged, "Dr. Schell, something is wrong. I can see it in your eyes. You must tell me."

Magdalena suddenly moaned and then wrapped both hands

around the bottom of her belly as another contraction squeezed her uterus into a rock-hard ball. She rolled over partially onto her left side in an effort to alleviate the painful torment. The intense contraction lasted for several agonizing seconds before finally relenting.

Nicklaus stared thoughtfully. He took a deep, resolute breath. "Magdalena, your baby has not turned."

"You mean, the head is up and not down." She wiped the sweat from her forehead with her left hand. "I suspected as much. My belly has appeared wider than usual and strangely-shaped for many days now."

"Yes. Normal birth is head-first, as you well know. Your body is ready for the birth. The canal is open. But, I can actually feel the baby's back inside the opening ... and the child is sideways, instead of up and down. I am certain that there must be a name for such a condition, but I must confess that I do not know it."

Magdalena nodded. "So, what can be done?"

Nicklaus subtly motioned to his mother, inviting her to join him near the bedside.

"Magdalena, your baby cannot be born in such a position."

"Whatever does that mean?" Magdalena wailed. "It has to come out!"

"It cannot. Your anatomy will not allow it. The baby would be crushed, and your own bones could be ripped apart." He paused. "There is already some blood. Something has torn inside you. Granted, it is not much blood. But, it could get worse."

Magdalena raised her head and made eye contact with Elspeth. She moved her eyes and head subtly toward the door. Elspeth received and understood her silent command. Clearly, Magdalena wanted her daughter out of the room. Elspeth began to rise from her chair.

"Come, Elizabeth. Your mother is resting now. We should go and do the same."

"But, I want to stay with *Mutter!*" the little girl whined.

Magdalena intervened sternly, "Do as *Fraulein* McClelland has commanded you, child! 'Tis not proper for a little one to be up at such an unholy hour. Go and get some sleep. I will send for you when the baby comes."

The child tarried and cried. *"Nein, Mutter!* I want you!"

Another contraction descended upon her abdomen. She gripped her belly with both hands. Her patience was gone. She screamed, "Go! Now, Elizabeth! Do not make me say it again!"

Elspeth bent down and scooped up the crying, protesting girl from the floor. Elizabeth wailed and reached, helplessly, toward her mother. The little girl was on the verge of hysterics. Elspeth lifted the wiggling, thrashing child across her shoulder and departed the hospital with all haste. Magdalena's contraction subsided just as the door closed behind them.

Once the pain had eased somewhat, Magdalena inquired in a weakened voice, "What can you do, Dr. Schell?"

He did not hesitate. "I must cut the baby out. There is no other option. It is called a Caesarian delivery. It is very risky, both for you and for the child."

"But, without it, we both die."

Nicklaus nodded. "Yes. Of that, I have no doubt."

"And you have done this surgery before?"

"Only once. And that was a very long time ago." He chose his words carefully. He did not want to tell her the complete truth about the circumstances of that procedure, or the fact that the delivering mother was already dead when he placed her under the knife. He pleaded, "Magdalena, there is nothing else that we can do. And we must not tarry. Each successive birth pang is pressing your baby, and you, toward a horrible, painful death."

She inhaled deeply. A tear inched its way down her temple. "Then you must cut it out of me, Nicklaus."

He turned quickly to his mother. "Send one of these men to find Michael."

Katharina nodded grimly.

⌇

4:30 AM – The Stone House Raid

MICHAEL AND CONRAD leaned against the cold stone of the outer wall of the home. Each man was on the opposite side of the back door. Abe knelt on the ground beside Michael.

"Have you checked the latch?" Conrad hissed.

Michael nodded. "It will open."

"That is good," Abe declared. "I would hate to have to attempt to break through this door."

"You and ten others like you could not accomplish such," Michael countered. "It would require a cannon to knock down this door."

"What is Jacob waiting for?" Abe whispered impatiently. "We had further to travel through the woods than he. And we have been here, beside this house, for a dreadfully long time."

"He is just being careful," Conrad responded quietly.

"Too careful," Abe hissed angrily.

Somewhere inside the house, a dog growled. Suddenly, the growl erupted into a mad bark. The barking grew louder and closer. It seemed that the family dog was on the other side of their door.

"Well, our secret is out now!" Abe whined.

A shrill whistle emanated from the front of the house. It was followed quickly by a shout and the loud thud of a door impacting against a wall.

"Let's go!" Michael shouted. He yanked the string, releasing the interior latch, and pressed inward on the heavy wood door.

Conrad was the first through the opening. He darted inside, musket at the ready across his chest. He was met, almost immediately, by a large, vicious hound. The animal leapt through the air and slammed, head first, into the lad. It sank its huge teeth into his left forearm. Conrad screamed in pain and fell backwards across the threshold and onto the damp earth outside. He instinctively pulled the trigger on his musket, setting off the weapon.

The sudden invasion of bright light into the pitch-black night temporarily blinded his mates. Michael could not see anything except a large, lingering ball of yellow-white light. He hovered just outside the doorway, waiting for his vision to return. Abraham stumbled past his two friends and resumed his invasion into the house. The sound of his footfalls against the wood flooring continued deeper into the dwelling.

"Michael, help me!" Conrad wailed.

The animal continued to bite into the boy's sleeve. He could feel its sharp teeth penetrating his skin and flesh. He released the expended musket from his immobilized hand and attempted to club the animal with the weapon, but it was too heavy. He could scarcely move it, much less gain enough momentum for a significant blow. Conrad felt a crunch as the dog's teeth crushed one of the smaller bones in his wrist. He screeched in pain.

Michael still could not see clearly, but he could somewhat discern the form of his friend writhing on the ground in combat with the hound. He cast his own musket aside and drew his knife. Reaching forward, he grabbed the stiff, bristly hair of the dog. Michael jumped on top of the animal and wrapped his left arm around its neck, reaching downward toward its chest. He grasped one of the dog's front legs and then shifted his weight toward the left. He rolled the animal off of Conrad, but the determined canine refused to let go of the boy's arm.

From inside the house there came the sounds of struggle and protest. A man shouted curses. A woman screamed. Glass broke. Children yelled and cried from fear. The raid upon the home continued without the assistance of Conrad and Michael.

The stricken soldier continued to scream for relief. The determined dog growled, writhed, and kicked its hind legs against Michael's efforts to restrain it. Michael wrapped his own legs around the large dog and then drew his knife high. He plunged the sharp blade over and over again into the dog's chest, puncturing its heart, lungs, and liver. The animal released Conrad's arm from the iron-like grip of its jaws. The growling stopped almost instantly and converted to a whimpering wail. The dog did not live long. Michael could feel warm blood pouring out of its wounds. The sticky fluid saturated his coat and hunting frock. He held the dog tightly until it gave a final, life-releasing shudder. Michael tossed the carcass to his right side and then rolled left onto his knees.

"Conrad, talk to me. How bad is it?"

"I do not know!" the boy yelled. "Something is broken, and there is so much blood."

Michael felt along the ground for his musket. He quickly retrieved it.

"Can you still walk, old friend?"

"*Ja*," Conrad responded. "I can walk."

Inside the home, the sounds of physical conflict seemed to have diminished. However, the shouting did not. The man and woman of the house continued their boisterous protestations.

Suddenly, there came the sound of flesh upon flesh. Lieutenant Cramer's voice rose above the others. "Sir! You will cease this damnable din, immediately!"

Conrad stood and cradled his shattered arm with his uninjured hand. "Did someone just get slapped?" he mused with great wonderment.

Michael chuckled lightly. "I do believe so!"

5:00 AM - Camp Hospital

THE STRESS WAS PALPABLE. All of the patients were sitting anxiously on the edges of their beds, waiting to see the outcome of the child-birth drama. Two of the healthier men, soldiers suffering only from the itch, were actually helping with the procedure. One fellow lay across Magdalena's legs, holding them in place. The other stood at the head of her bed, holding her by the wrists. It was the only way that Nicklaus could prevent her fighting against the cutting and the pain.

"Where is Michael?" she wailed. "I want my husband!"

"Calm down, child," Katharina pleaded. "We sent someone to

fetch him, but there is no one in his hut. They are looking for him now."

"I want Michael," she mumbled, her voice fading. "I have to see Michael."

Katharina turned her head away for just a moment. She did not want the tortured girl to see her cry. She raised her shoulder to her face and attempted to dry the unwanted tears.

Blood poured out of the gaping cut in Magdalena's flesh. Despite the considerable amount of laudanum and whiskey that she had consumed, the poor girl still groaned and thrashed from the searing agony of the deeply-cutting surgical blade. Nicklaus sliced skillfully through the skin and then quickly went to work cutting through the leathery muscle of the uterus. As he made the incision, his mind traveled back to that horrific ocean voyage. He remembered the violent seas and the sickness. In his mind's eye, he recalled the pale, lifeless girl who had miraculously delivered a living child down in the putrid hold of that ship of ruination and death.

That young girl had been a complete stranger. However, this woman was a personal friend. She was still alive. Nicklaus desired more than anything to keep her that way. Still, it seemed as if every force of nature was allied against him. He felt helpless and frustrated.

"Hold right here, *Mutter!*" Nicklaus shouted. "Right here! Right here! Right here, damn it!" He pointed, angrily, at the dangling flap of flesh that kept falling into his surgical field. "Hold that piece of tissue with your forceps! Do not let go of it again!"

"You need not scream at me and speak to me as if I were an ignorant child, Nicklaus," his mother responded calmly. "I am trying the very best that I can."

"I realize that, dear *Mutter*, but right now your best is falling short. There is no trying. There is only doing. This girl's life hangs in the balance!"

"Yes, Nicklaus. As well I know." Katharina refused to look at him. She maintained her focus on the incision and the portion of the operation that was in her charge. She was already upset and frustrated enough. She did not want to magnify her emotions with additional vitriol directed at her son.

"I cannot see!" Nicklaus wailed. He slapped his hands against his legs in petulant frustration.

"Control your tantrum!" his mother barked. "Think. Why is there so much blood?"

"I do not know, *Mutter*! Perhaps, I have cut a vein. I cannot tell. I do not know the female reproductive anatomy as well as I should, I suppose. My skills are lacking."

"I do not recall the other girl bleeding so much from her cut."

Nicklaus groaned as he reached inside the incision and felt for the child. "You forget, *Mutter*. That woman had no more blood left to lose. She had already bled out through the birth canal." He growled, once again, in frustration. "I can barely grasp the baby. It feels as if she is continuing to have the birth pangs. The muscle is so very resistant. Please, *Mutter*, pull that flap strongly!"

Katharina leaned back with all her might, stretching the upper fold of skin and uterine muscle. Nicklaus tugged on the baby, but could not coax it through the small opening."

"Damn it to hell! I cannot get the baby out of this tiny hole. I simply have to open her up more."

"Nicklaus, no!" his mother pleaded. "She has already bled so very much."

"I have no choice."

He sliced swiftly with his blade, opening the incision wider on both sides. Magdalena screamed softly. Her body gave a slight shudder and then went limp. Every muscle and sinew within her relaxed.

"The child has passed out," his mother announced.

Nicklaus ignored her. He reached inside her womb with both hands. More blood flowed from the opening. The dark, crimson-black fluid pooled on the bedcovers on both sides of her hips. It worked its way through the layers of cloth to form a steady drip onto the earthen floor below.

Quite suddenly, he tugged the baby free, feet first, through the incised uterine wall. Though covered with blood, the infant appeared normal. It was a healthy-looking girl. Nicklaus placed the child on her side on Magdalena's chest and then quickly tied off the cord. He skillfully cut the umbilical just a couple of inches away from the newborn's belly.

The infant was still not breathing. He grabbed the tiny girl by both feet with his left hand and flipped her upside-down. With his right hand he delivered three stinging swats on her tender buttocks. She emitted a high-pitched, hacking cough that spewed mucus and fluid from her throat. Instantly, she began to scream. Everyone inside the hospital cheered at the sound of the baby's cry.

Nicklaus smiled as he handed the infant to his mother. "Please clean her and wrap her. I will attend to Magdalena."

His mother nodded and smiled. She lovingly patted her son's cheek. "That was heroic, Nicklaus."

He shook his head grimly. "Only if we can save her mother."

~

Dawn – Stone House Raid

"JACOB, I told you this was the right house!" Abraham bragged as he added another fifty-pound sack of ground corn to the wagon. "This Tory bastard is flush with provisions!"

Lieutenant Cramer smiled as he added another mark to his makeshift manifest. It had been quite a haul, indeed. The German troops procured over five hundred pounds of flour, six hundred pounds of ground corn, and several stoneware crocks full of rendered lard. The smokehouse was brimming with pork bellies, hams, and dozens of rolls of sausage. And, to top everything off, they discovered six cows, a dozen hogs, four dozen hens, and two dozen sheep inside the various barns, outbuildings, and pens. They tied the livestock to the rear of their wagons with varying lengths of rope. They secured four cages full of chickens onto two hand carts that they happily liberated from the fellow's barn.

Conrad was seated on the wagon seat, watching the other men load their booty. His bloodied, injured arm was wrapped tightly and tied against his chest. He declared, "I do not think we can get anything else into this wagon."

"We?" Abraham mocked. "We? There is no 'we' about this endeavor, Conrad Traywitz!" He looked at Michael and shook his head in feigned disgust. "I swear, that boy will do almost anything to get out of his duties. First, he faked his own death. Now he sits happily on his arse, wounded in so-called hand-to-hand combat with a hound."

Michael smiled. It was all that he could do not to laugh out loud.

The owner of the property stood on the front doorstep of his house and fumed. "You men are without honor! You prance around here, exercising frivolity and insulting me! But, without these stores, my family will starve this winter!"

Lieutenant Cramer held up a stack of papers and waved them mockingly. "I daresay, based upon these receipts from the British quartermaster's office, that you have a considerable sum of guineas tucked away somewhere in this old house. 'Tis a pity that we could not find them. I quite think that you will be just fine. Anyhow, if times do get tough for you, you can always call upon General Howe and his comrades. It appears, based upon the evidence, that you are on most excellent terms."

Lieutenant Cramer turned his back disdainfully toward the Loyalist.

"I think that is everything, Lieutenant," Michael declared.

The officer nodded his approval. "Very well. Let us go. We have some hungry comrades who will be most happy to greet us."

"And whilst we are traveling, you can figure out how you are going to write up this mission for the colonel," Abe mused.

"Whatever do you mean?" the confused lieutenant queried.

Abe chided, "I want to know how you plan to describe the enemy soldier who was killed in action. Are you going to distinguish him by size or breed?"

The men laughed heartily as they climbed onto their heavily-loaded wagons. The drivers clucked at the horses, and they immediately began their trek back toward Valley Forge.

~

Mid-Morning – Camp Hospital

IT WAS OVER. Finally. Magdalena's eyes were barely open. Her face was so pale that she appeared to be almost blue in color. She cooed weakly to her baby girl who lay sleeping against her left breast. She did not have the strength to support the newborn's weight on her own, so Katharina had the child propped against her with wadded blankets and pillows. Elizabeth was sleeping soundly, snuggled against her mother's right side. Magdalena gently nudged her chin against the baby's warm head. She softly stroked Elizabeth's hair with her other hand.

Though the bedding and straw were fresh, a huge bloodstain remained on the floor below her bed. Magdalena had lost a catastrophic amount of blood during the procedure. Nicklaus closed and sewed her incision nicely, but it still leaked blood at a steady pace. He wondered that she still had any more blood to lose. Indeed, it seemed a miracle that she was still conscious.

Nicklaus stood, helplessly, at the foot of the bed. He held the quietly weeping Elspeth in his arms. Magdalena was dying. She, herself, knew it. Everyone knew it.

"Oh, my dear, she is a beautiful girl," Katharina declared with all sincerity. "Have you chosen a name for her?"

Magdalena smiled weakly. "I am almost out of girl names."

Katharina chuckled and smiled back. "Surely, you have one more."

She kissed her baby gently on top of her head. "My mother's name was Sarah. I have often thought that, were I to have another girl, I might name her Sarah."

"Oh, Magdalena! That is a lovely name, indeed. And absolutely perfect for this little one. Just look at her. The name fits."

"Then, Sarah it shall be." She looked down at the perfectly content, sleeping infant. "Did you hear that, my tiny angel? Your name is Sarah Yeisley."

The baby nuzzled happily against her chest. The spunky little one lifted her tiny fist to her mouth and began to smack loudly as she sucked on it.

Magdalena whispered, "You will tell Michael, won't you?"

"Tell him what, dear?"

"Tell him that her name is Sarah."

Katharina scoffed, "Do not be silly, child. You shall tell him yourself. He will be back from his patrol at any moment. The colonel said so."

A thin tear leaked from Magdalena's eye and tumbled down her temple. "No, *Frau* Schell, I shall not tell him. I will never see my husband or my other girls again. I feel myself going." She paused and inhaled a shallow breath. "But I am so glad that my Elizabeth is here. She has been such a blessing to me."

"Stop it, right now, young lady! 'Tis no need to be morbid. You are going to be just fine. You only need food and rest."

Magdalena turned her head very slowly toward the kindly woman. She smiled a very genuine smile of gratitude. "You are a poor liar, indeed, Katharina Schell." She breathed another shallow, raspy breath. "You and your son have been very good to us. We are grateful. But, Michael will need help. Please help him, *Frau* Schell." Her voice sounded weaker. Her breathing was becoming more and more shallow and labored. "He is a good man, but he does not know how to take care of our girls. Help him, *Frau* Schell. I do not want to worry."

Katharina reached out and took her by the hand. "Worry not, child. I will tell him everything. And Michael will be just fine. He is a good, strong man. Your babies are in good hands."

Magdalena nodded. She seemed satisfied ... peaceful. Once again, she softly stroked Elizabeth's hair. She leaned her nose toward Sarah's head and inhaled her scent. Then, she softly began to sing a familiar German lullaby entitled, *The Moon is Risen*. The melody was beautiful. The words transported many of the German-speaking people in the room back to the days of their childhood when their parents had sung the tune to them. Those lyrics carried them all back home ... back unto a time of quiet, and peace, and joy.

Magdalena's voice grew weaker and weaker with each passing word, until it became nothing more than a mumble. As she began the second verse, her voice failed altogether. A slight gurgle escaped her throat. Then, quietly and peacefully, she breathed no more. The room was completely still.

In the midst of the silence of death, Katharina Schell slowly and gently resumed singing the lullaby. She started at the beginning of the second verse. Nicklaus joined her. Then, some of the other soldiers, mostly men of the German Regiment, began singing, as well. By the end of the first line, over a dozen people, united by a common ancestry and culture, joined together in the solemn chorus. They sang,

> Wie ist die Welt so stille,
>> Und in der Dämmrung Hülle
>> So traulich und so hold!
>> Als eine stille Kammer,
>> Wo ihr des Tages Jammer
>> Verschlafen und vergessen sollt.

Again, the room fell silent. This time, no one else spoke or sang. Almost no one dared to breathe. The moment seemed eternal. It felt holy. It was Elspeth McClelland who finally broke the sacred silence of their makeshift cathedral.

"That was a most beautiful, haunting song, Nicklaus. What did that last verse say ... the one that you all sang together?"

Nicklaus hugged her close against his chest. "It is a child's song about bedtime. It tells of the moon rising. That verse says,

> How the world stands still
>> In twighlight's veil
>> So sweet and snug

As a still room
Where the day's misery
You will sleep away and forget."

"And now she sleeps … with no more misery," Elspeth declared. Nicklaus nodded. "Indeed. In this still room, her misery is done." She sighed. "I hope that we never forget this." "No, my dear. I do not think we can ever forget this." Slowly, reverently, the hospitalized soldiers each rose from their beds. They joined Katharina, Nicklaus, and Elspeth, forming a circle of heartbroken humanity around the beautiful young woman who lay dead, peacefully cradling her two sleeping daughters.

~

Mid-Afternoon

THE FORAGERS HAD JUST ARRIVED BACK at camp. They were so exhausted that they could not even enjoy the accolades being heaped upon them by their comrades. The weary men simply wanted to go to bed. They were famished, as well. However, fatigue trumped hunger. They elected to skip what would most certainly be a disappointing meal and go straight to their bunks. Conrad was the only exception. He reported to the hospital to have his wound treated by the surgeon. The others collapsed onto their straw-covered beds. They had been horizontal less than five minutes when the door to the hut burst open.

"Private Yeisley!" It was the somewhat gruff voice of Colonel Weltner.

Michael mumbled groggily, "Yes, sir."

"Get your arse out of that bed and report to the hospital! Immediately!"

"Which hospital?"

"The one where your newborn child awaits you."

Michael bolted out of the bed and stared toward the officer's silhouette. He could not make out any of his features because of the blinding sunlight that surrounded his form.

"Sincerely, sir?"

The colonel chuckled. "Yes, Michael. I received word this morning that your wife had gone into labor overnight. Surely, she has delivered by now."

Michael quickly donned his leather buckle-shoes and wool blanket coat and then darted through the door. He remembered half-way to the hospital that he had forgotten his hat. He didn't care. The hat would have to wait. He sprinted as fast as his exhausted legs would carry him toward the brigade hospital.

Finally, he arrived at the doorway that concealed his wife and newborn child. He flipped the latch and burst through the door, full of vigor and joy. But, once inside, a wall of sorrow slammed against his spirit.

Nicklaus and Elspeth hovered over Conrad near the fireplace as they tended to his wounded arm. Mrs. Schell was seated at a small table that served as the clinic's desk. About a dozen men reclined silently in the hospital's beds. To his right, in the distant corner, sat a young woman that he did not recognize. She was nursing a baby.

Something was very wrong inside that dark, gloomy hut. There was a dullness about it ... an overwhelming sadness that transcended the physical realm.

Nicklaus exclaimed, "Michael, are you injured? What has happened to you?"

Michael glanced at his hunting frock. It was stained with the blood of the hound that he had killed during the nighttime raid.

"I am fine. It is not my blood." He glanced excitedly around the room. "Where is Magdalena? Is she in the women's quarters?" He did not even wait for an answer. "I will go and see her there!"

He turned to leave, but Nicklaus shouted to him, "Michael, wait! Do not go. She is not there."

Michael was very confused. "Where is she, then? Did something happen? Did you send her to the hospital at Yellow Springs?"

Katharina responded quietly and carefully to his questioning.

"No, Michael. She is not at another hospital." She rose slowly from her desk. She walked toward Michael and reached out her hand to him. "Come. There is someone you need to meet."

Michael numbly received her hand. She led him to his right, toward the bed where the woman quietly nursed a tiny newborn.

"Michael, this is *Frau* Mary Riley. She lost her husband recently. And a child."

Michael nodded respectfully. "*Frau* Riley. I am very sorry for your loss." He turned to Katharina. "*Frau* Schell, I have no desire to be rude, but I do not understand why you have brought me to this woman."

"'Tis not the woman that I wanted you to see, Michael. I wanted you to meet this baby girl." She paused. Her lip quivered. "Son, this is your daughter ... Sarah."

Tears filled Michael's eyes. His chest began to heave. "Another girl. Magdalena knew that it was another girl." He looked helplessly to Katharina. His eyes pleaded for mercy. "I do not understand, *Frau* Schell. I want my Magdalena. Where is she?"

He felt a strong hand grip his shoulder. Nicklaus spoke softly. "I did everything that I could to save her, Michael. But, the damage from the birth was too great. Your Magdalena is gone."

The room began to spin. Michael's spirit felt as if it were departing his body. He mumbled, "This cannot be happening. God, help me. This cannot be happening." He composed himself as best he could. Suddenly, he remembered his other daughter. He blurted, "Where is Elizabeth?"

Katharina reassured him, "She is sleeping in our hut. The poor child had a very long night. You should know that she was with her mother when she went. Both of your girls were."

Michael's hands trembled. The muscles in his jaw pulsated. "Where is her body?"

"We kept her close by," Katharina promised. "I knew that you would want to see her one more time. We shall help you find a place for her to rest."

Huge tears erupted from Michael's eyes and overflowed onto his dirt and blood-stained cheeks. "Thank you."

"It will be our honor, Son." Katharina wrapped her arm around the man's shoulder and hugged him. "We are blessed, indeed, to have *Frau* Riley here with us. She has graciously agreed to serve as wet nurse."

"Would you like to hold your child?" inquired Mrs. Riley.

It was the first time that Michael had actually heard the strange woman's voice. He nodded almost imperceptibly. Mary withdrew baby Sarah from her breast. Her nipple popped free of the grip of the baby's lips and gums and spurted a tiny spray of milk onto her cheek. Little Sarah's face scrunched into an expression that was something between displeasure and satisfaction. She pulled her tiny fists to her cheeks and arched her back in a gigantic stretch. She yawned, and then her little eyes fluttered open. She smacked her lips and stared at her papa with bright, steely blue eyes.

Michael could not help but smile. Even though his heart was overwhelmed by sorrow and loss, still it felt equally filled with love and joy. He lifted the beautiful baby to his lips and kissed her gently on the cheek.

"Sarah was Magdalena's mother's name."

"That is what she told us," Nicklaus affirmed.

"It suits her, don't you think?" Katharina asked, smiling.

Michael smiled, as well. "*Ja.* It is perfect. She is perfect."

"She is, indeed," Nicklaus declared. He patted Michael fondly on the back.

Michael sniffed back his tears. "I should have been here, Nicklaus. I should have been here, not out in the countryside scrounging for provisions."

"You *were* here, old friend. You filled Magdalena's heart. Her final thoughts were of you."

"Indeed, they were," Katharina testified. "She begged us to be of help to you. She was much worried that you would have no idea how to raise this gaggle of girls on your own."

Michael chuckled, despite his tears. "Well, she was right. As always." He continued to stare into the captivating eyes of his newborn daughter. "What am I to do now, Nicklaus?"

"You will live, my friend. You will live, and love, and raise your family of little girls."

"It is a tremendous task," Michael declared. "I fear that I will fall short."

Nicklaus squeezed his friend's shoulder. "It is, indeed, a great task." He nodded toward the baby. "But, you are up to it. Michael, this is why we do what we do. This is why we toil and sacrifice. It is not just for country or for politics. It is not all about kings and congresses. It is for our loved ones and our children. It is for our future. *This* is why we fight."

EPILOGUE

Early Morning - March 7, 1778

Michael dropped the rear board into the locking slots on the back of the wagon. Mrs. Riley was nestled comfortably inside the wagon bed, surrounded by several soft mounds of insulating straw. Baby Sarah nursed hungrily at her breast. Elizabeth sat close by, ready to help if needed.

Katharina walked over to Michael and took him by the arm. "Do you have everything you need?"

He smiled. "We will be fine, *Frau* Schell. Apparently, we do not have far to travel. *Herr* Kleinschmidt has assured me that we are only a few hours from his home."

Katharina, in a most uncharacteristic display of public affection, raised up on her tip-toes and kissed the handsome young man on his cheek. "I know you must be aching to see all of your little girls."

"I am, indeed." He sighed. "I suppose that we should be on our way."

He gripped the wagon seat and nimbly pulled himself up to join Herman Kleinschmidt. The affable old farmer adjusted his position to accommodate his riding companion.

Nicklaus and Elspeth stepped closer to the wagon. The doctor reached up and offered Michael his hand. The friends shook and then held on to one another for just a moment more.

"Michael, I am so happy that General Muhlenberg finally granted your discharge."

"As am I. He was silent for so long that I was beginning to have doubts."

Nicklaus smiled mischievously. "I quite think that *Mutter* put the fear of God in the old preacher. She generally gets what she wants from the commander's office. He would never admit it, being a happily married man, but he is quite enamored with her."

Michael sighed. "Well, I certainly am glad that she got her way this particular time."

Nicklaus' eyebrows raised. "Do you have your discharge order?"

Michael reached into his pocket and pulled out a folded parchment. "Officially signed and sealed."

"Good. 'Twould be tragic for you to get arrested for desertion." He grinned. "Where will you go? What will you do?"

Michael shrugged. "I am not certain. For now, we will ride out the remainder of the winter with the Kleinschmidts. I have a couple of months to decide what comes next."

"Won't you return home?" Elspeth asked.

"I have no home to which we might return." He sighed and stared toward the south. "I have no home, no belongings, and no wife. I suppose we Yeisleys need to make a fresh start in a new place."

"Where?" Nicklaus inquired, curious.

"Oh, I do not know. Lately, I have been spending a lot of time with these boys from Virginia. They are an odd bunch, but they certainly do give their homeland a fine recommendation. Perhaps we shall go there."

Katharina asked, "If you relocate to Virginia, will *Frau* Riley go with you?"

Michael shrugged. "Until the baby is weaned. After that, she will have to make her own choices."

Nicklaus smiled. "Well, wherever you land, do not lose touch."

"I won't. I promise. I will send you a correspondence as soon as we are settled."

Nicklaus nodded approvingly. "I shall be waiting to hear from you. Goodbye, Michael."

"Goodbye, Nicklaus." Michael nodded to the women. "Ladies." He tapped Herman on the arm. "Let's go."

Herman snapped the reins and urged his horses to move. The wagon creaked and then lurched forward as the team headed eastward out of the encampment. Mary Riley and young Elizabeth smiled and waved as the wagon turned left and then disappeared behind a row of soldier's huts.

Dr. Nicklaus Schell stood in the middle of the roadway for a moment longer. He pondered how many times divine providence had brought Michael Yeisley into his life. He wondered if it would ever do so again.

He turned and smiled at his mother and his betrothed. "Well, ladies, we cannot stand here in the roadway all the long day. We have work to do." Nicklaus took both of them by the hand. They trudged through the thick mud toward the duties that awaited them in their humble little hospital.

THE REAL PATRIOTS

Michael Yeisley and Dr. Nicklaus Schell were men in my wife's family tree. They were both her 5th great-grandfathers in a distinctively German branch of her ancestral line. Both men were, indeed, Patriots of the American Revolution. They lived out their final days in the village of Shepherdstown, Virginia (now West Virginia), on a bluff overlooking the Potomac River. Their earthly remains rest in the cemetery of the Christ Reformed Church in that quaint little town. Their graves are roughly thirty feet from one another. I snapped this amazing photo of my wife during a visit there in 2017. She is pointing toward the locations of both graves.

Michael Yeisley's first wife, according to family tradition, was named Magdalena. Most likely, it was Maria Magdalena, or in English, Mary Magdalene. Her surname is unknown. Their date and location of marriage is unknown. The Mueller surname and the story line centered around her father and family were figments of my imagination. According to my best guess, she died around 1778, about the time of the appearance of their daughter, Sarah. Michael and Magdalena were the parents of either six or seven daughters, most of whom reached adulthood. They had no sons.

Curiously, local and family tradition holds that Michael was born around the year 1730. However, this early date of birth does not reconcile well with him having served as a private in the war. Furthermore, I have not been able to locate any documentary evidence to support such an early date of birth. It would seem odd, indeed, for a 46-year-old man to have enlisted as a private in the Continental Line. That was a rather advanced age for the time period.

Indeed, if, as genealogists claim, the historical figure named Nicklaus Yeisley was the progenitor of all of the Yeisleys of North America, this early date of birth seems irreconcilable. The Michael Yeisley of Shepherdstown would be too old to be a son of Nicklaus. He could be a brother, perhaps, but not a son. Ultimately, we do not know his exact date or place of birth.

After his first wife's death, Michael remarried at least once. We know that he wed a woman named Catherine Entler, the widow of Philip Entler, Jr., in Shepherdstown some time before December 19, 1796. I can find no evidence that the couple had any children together.

Michael Yeisley died after September 13, 1808, when his will was attested in Shepherdstown. He died a man of much means. He left an extensive estate and a great wealth of properties, buildings, and acreage to his widow and his many daughters and sons-in-law. These properties included his majestic stone house, which stands to this very day on German Street, the main thoroughfare in the village. My wife and I attempted to visit the house in the summer of 2018, but the new owners were not available. According to some knowledgeable locals, the interior structure remains virtually untouched, and looks much like an 18th Century home would have appeared. We took this beloved photo of my wife on the front porch of the home during our brief visit.

According to tradition, Michael Yeisley was a weaver and a businessman. He operated a shop out of this house. He was also a community leader in Shepherdstown and in his church. A local history book, *Prominent Men of Shepherdstown 1762-1962*, shows that his first record in the city was dated June 15, 1789. The book also credits him with obtaining a set of expensive bells from France in

1798, all of them rescued after the French Revolution, for placement in the bell tower of the Christ Reformed Church.

The book records that he had a headstone in the Christ Reformed Cemetery. Unfortunately, that stone has been lost to time. The only marker remaining on this prominent Patriot's grave was a bronze Daughters of the American Revolution plaque mounted on a concrete base. So, in 2018, my wife and I financed a new headstone and placed it there during our most recent research trip to Valley Forge. The stone includes the logos for both the Sons of the American Revolution and the Descendants of Washington's Army at Valley Forge. Though the 1730 date of birth is questionable, I went ahead and used it so that it would match with family tradition. I snapped this photo of the proud descendant on the day that we placed the stone in the graveyard.

In constructing my story, I used a later date of birth for Mr. Yeisley. It simply made more sense to me and provided a more dramatic introduction of the story through his birth at sea. I also wrote my story with the assumption that Michael was, indeed, a son of the original immigrant, Nicklaus Yeisley.

With regard to his military service, I used all available muster rolls, pay sheets, and record cards available through the National Archives. I placed him in his exact historical context, and chronicled the battles in which he participated, based upon those military documents.

I do not know if Mr. Yeisley was captured during the dramatic defection of Colonel Haussegger in New Jersey. He was listed as a deserter on the January, 1777, roll, along with several other soldiers. He then appears back on the rolls, without comment or question, in the month of March, 1777. I decided to write that fascinating historical event into my story, since it fits the timeline and documents so very well.

Likewise, the birth of a child and sudden disappearance of his wife, Magdalena, fit the Valley Forge narrative. Michael Yeisley was discharged, mysteriously, on March 7, 1778. There is no apparent reason for this discharge. He had not been listed as sick or unfit for duty on a single roll sheet. A dismissal for family hardship makes as much sense as anything. I felt that it provided a decent ending point for the book.

There is, however, a significant historical complication. It appears that there were two Michael Yeisleys on the continent during the American Revolution. This discovery could, in fact, cast some doubt upon the identity and military experience of the Michael Yeisley of Shepherdstown.

Our Michael Yeisley has been universally recognized as the Patriot who served in the German Regiment. Both the Daughters and the Sons of the American Revolution have scores of members who trace their ancestries back to this particular Patriot. His grave has been marked by both organizations. There has been little historical doubt that this was, indeed, the Michael Yeisley of the Continental Line.

However, I have discovered a record in the Pennsylvania Archives, dated 1822, that orders a pension of forty dollars for a "Michael Yeisly" of Union County. This was a full fourteen years after the death of Michael Yeisley in Shepherdstown. This discovery launched me into an investigation of a somewhat troubling mystery.

I further found during this investigation and search a testimony by the alternate "Michael Yeisly" within the pension records of a man named Conrad Traywitz/Trevits (the same fellow I included in my story). In this document, he claimed that they were mates who served together in the German Regiment! However, the Conrad Traywitz of the German Regiment was listed as dead on the January, 1777, company roll sheet. He never appears again on another military record. I did, in fact, "resurrect" him for my story. But, according to the documentation, this individual was dead. Interestingly, there was a well-known Pennsylvania fraktur artist by the name of Johann Conrad Trevitz. He, as it turns out, was the fellow who applied for the pension.

It appears that someone, somewhere, was lying. Either Conrad Traywitz deserted and/or faked his death in early 1777, or the fellow making the pension claim was *not* the actual Continental Line soldier.

Due to the lack of adequate records from the American Revolution, many of the early pension claims submitted to the government were somewhat questionable, if not dubious. Countless pensions were granted based upon the shakiest of evidence. Conversely, others that appeared incontrovertible were, in fact, denied. These Pennsylvania state pension claims may have been fabricated. But, then again, they may have been truthful.

We are left with only two options. Either the Michael Yeisley of Shepherdstown has been correctly identified as the Revolutionary War soldier or he has not. If that is the case, then the actual soldier was another fellow by the same name who dwelled in central Pennsylvania until his death in the early 1830's. Ultimately, we may never know.

Therefore, for the sake of storytelling, I have woven the two individuals into a single character. I used the family circle, history, and geography of the Michael Yeisley of Union County as the context for the Michael Yeisley of Shepherdstown. I pray that I have done justice to them both.

Dr. Nicklaus Schell, amazingly, left behind even fewer records than Mr. Yeisley. Family tradition shows his year of birth as 1746. I did manage to identify the ship that delivered him to Philadelphia and the actual date that it arrived. His name was listed on the manifest. I included these facts in my story. The *Betsey* was a well-documented ship. But, after his arrival, documentation becomes somewhat scarce.

It seems almost inconceivable, but the records of the Continental Line's medical service during the Revolution are sorely lacking. I have examined every possible document that I could locate and have discovered only three records in reference to Dr. Nicklaus Schell during the war.

The first is a listing of the Officers of the General Hospital North Department recorded in Albany, New York, and dated March 20, 1780. It lists one, "Nicholas Scull, Junior Surgeon," as being "on command – Pennsylvania."

The second record is in a volume entitled *History of Berks County, Pennsylvania: in the Revolution from 1774 to 1783*. It shows a payment to a "Dr. Nicholas Shell" for eighteen days as a surgeon in Col. Samuel Ely's Battalion of the Berks County Militia. That service was dated October 1-18, 1781.

The final and most definitive document is found in the pension records of a soldier named Jacob Hout. He gave testimony in 1813 that "Dr. Nicholas Shell," surgeon of Col. Hartley's Regiment, treated him after the battle at Germantown and certified him as unfit for service due to his wounds.

These three documents provide irrefutable evidence that Nicklaus Schell was, indeed, a surgeon in the Continental Army under Colonel Thomas Hartley. It makes sense, also, that he served in the local militia after the cessation of major hostilities in late 1781.

Dr. Schell arrived in Shepherdstown around 1785, when the town was still known by its original name of "Mecklenburg." In June of that year, he purchased the lot upon which he built his home. That home remains to this day. According to tradition, he married later in life. His wife's name was Rebecca, and she was listed in his will. His only child of record was a son, John, born in Shepherdstown in 1796.

Dr. Schell lived out his years as a respected surgeon and citizen in Shepherdstown. He died in 1804, shortly after the recording of his will. Interestingly, within that testament, he was quite adamant that his son attend German school so that he might master his father's native tongue.

Nicklaus Schell's stone remains in the Christ Reformed Church graveyard, but is no longer readable. The DAR has placed a plaque in front of the stone denoting his Revolutionary War service.

Interestingly, another ancient stone once stood beside his, but now appears to be lost. It was the headstone of one "Katharina Schel." In 1962, at the time of publication of the Shepherdstown history book, the writing on the stone was still visible. It recorded that she died in 1798 at the age of 85. This was Nicklaus' mother, who became such an important character in my story.

My wife's connection to both of these Patriots is found in two of their grandchildren. Around the year 1840, Isabella Schell, granddaughter of Nicklaus, married David Welshans, the grandson of Michael Yeisley. Mr. Welshans' mother was Sarah Yeisley, the infant born at the very end of my story at Valley Forge. She was, indeed, a very real person.

I included many historical characters throughout the book. I used the names of several actual soldiers from the German regiment. I also had a terrific time developing my own unique personality for and characterization of George Washington.

Elspeth McClelland was not one of those historical characters. She was another figment from my imagination. Dr. Schell had no wife by that name. But, I wanted to create a love interest that might bring another dimension of emotion and drama to my story. I fully intended to "kill her off" toward the end in order to close that fictional story line, but my wife shamed me into keeping her. In order to keep peace at home, I left her happy and healthy at the end of the book.

I sincerely hope that you enjoyed my story. It is yet another of my humble attempts to blend the truth of history with the wonder of fiction. I pray that I have done a decent job of honoring the memories of my wife's ancestors.

Until we meet again on a distant battlefield, or within the history of another unforgotten family of the American Revolution ... I bid you, farewell.

Geoff Baggett

ABOUT THE AUTHOR

Geoff Baggett is a Tennessee native and a small-town pastor in rural western Kentucky. Prior to his career in Christian ministry, he served in the U.S. Army Reserve, and also worked in clinical laboratory medicine. He holds degrees in the fields of chemistry, biology, counseling, and Christian theology. His hobbies include metal detecting, genealogy, Revolutionary War history, and writing.

Geoff is an active member of the Sons of the American Revolution. He has discovered over twenty Patriot ancestors within his own family tree from the states of Virginia, North and South Carolina, and Georgia. He is also an avid living historian, appearing regularly in period uniform in classrooms, reenactments, and other Revolutionary War commemorative events. He and his lovely wife, Kim, enjoy dressing in their period attire and operating their *"Colonial Book Shoppe"* tent at various Rev War and 18th Century events throughout the eastern United States.

Geoff and Kim live on a small, quiet piece of land in rural Trigg County, Kentucky, with their daughter, Katie, and grandson, Jackson.

THANK YOU FOR READING MY STORY!

PLEASE HELP ME MEET NEW READERS!

I hope that you enjoyed my work of fiction. It was a pleasure preparing and writing it for you. I am just a simple, "part-time" author, therefore I am sincerely grateful for every individual who chooses to read one of my books.

I would humbly ask that you help me spread the word about my growing library of Revolutionary War novels. It is very difficult for an independent writer to "break through" and find success in the overly-saturated American book market. But, you can help me in a number of ways!

1. **Tell your friends!** Word of mouth is always the best. Please recommend my books to the people in your circle of influence. Or, better yet, buy them a copy!
2. **Mention me and my books on Facebook.** This is just a "high tech" form of word of mouth. Be sure to "Like" my author page and tag me in any posts that you write. Simply search for my name, or "Cocked Hat Publishing," on Facebook.
3. **Write a review for me on Amazon.com and/or Goodreads.** Reviews are critical in today's marketing

environment. I am grateful for every review that I receive and review my titles daily in search of any new ones.

4. **Consider using my student books in your school curriculum.** Obviously, this is a plea to all you educators out there! I have been honored to have four schools choose my books for inclusion in their reading curricula. The potential for "crossover" between history and reading makes my short novels for kids an attractive addition to your educational arsenal. I have available a teaching supplement for my first book for kids, *Little Hornet.* Similar products are under development for my other children's titles (this is an ongoing project that my wife is pursuing). The completed resources are available as free PDF downloads on my web site. If you would be interested in a "class set" of a particular title for your school, please contact me directly. I make copies available for classrooms at production cost plus shipping.

5. **Book me for a presentation!** I have several fun, interactive, unique, engaging, and interesting Revolutionary War presentations available for groups or classes. I am a professional speaker and living historian. I will travel moderate distances if I can have the opportunity to connect to readers and sell some books! It is particularly helpful if I can arrange multiple audiences at one location over a period of a few days. Simply contact me through my web site, geoffbaggett.com, or through my Facebook author page to arrange an event.

6. **Finally ... Please follow me on Twitter and Instagram!**

Twitter - @GeoffBaggett Instagram - geoffbaggett

Thanks again for reading this product of my personal history and imagination! Please be on the lookout for my next novel in this series. I have not yet chosen the "hero" or the locale of my upcoming story. First, I actually plan to write the next book in the *Patriot Kids Series*, to be entitled, *Little Camp Follower.* I may also tackle another title in my *Kentucky Frontier Adventures* series before beginning the next "grown up" novel. But, I am confident that *Book 6* in the *Patriots of the American Revolution Series* will be in print before the end of 2020!

Huzzah!

Geoff Baggett

CPSIA information can be obtained
at www.ICGtesting.com
Printed in the USA
BVHW030302030820
585286BV00001BA/70

9 781946 896926